*and
Fish*

Adrienne Leslie

Additional Translations by Lee Hea Suk

Copyright © 2007 Adrienne Leslie

All rights reserved. Except as permitted under the U.S. Copyright Act of 1976, no part of this publication may be reproduced, distributed, or transmitted in any form or by any means, or stored in a database or retrieval system, without the prior written permission of the author.

This is a work of fiction. All of the characters, organizations and events portrayed in this novel are either products of the author's imagination or are used fictitiously.

ISBN: 1-4196-9192-9
ISBN-13: 9781419691928

2AJUMMA BOOKS
Visit www.amazon.com to order additional copies.

⌘ ⌘ ⌘

Praise For Bird And Fish

"I found the story to be very powerful, and (her) use of the little details-from Wendy Dale's interactions with the children at school to her tendency to wear her daughter's hoodies-really flesh out the narrative, lending it an authenticity …clearly (she's) familiar with both teaching and Korean culture and that comes through on the page."
—Katherine Nintzel- associate editor William Morrow an imprint of HarperCollins Publishers

"Finally an Asian-American tale without the usual Suzie Wong stereotypes. Leslie has woven two cultures into a fine silken chord."
—Christina Seid -author Saturdays In Chinatown

'… travel agents will have to keep up with the jump in tourism to New York and Seoul from readers of Leslie's extraordinary east-west love story.
—Emmanuel Tabones-Access2Korea

"What Pearl S. Buck did to teach Westerners about China, Adrienne Leslie has done for Korea, Koreans and Korean-Americans."
Incha Kim__New York City Community Board

Thanks to JY Park whose elegant movements inspired the physical embodiment of Huyn Jae Won

⌘ ⌘ ⌘

Acknowledgements

Only at their keyboards, are writers truly alone. The rest of their time is spent depending on serendipitous and generous friends and family members. Amazingly, I was granted many: Steve Brown whose two word mantra, 'Writers write.' placed me on the first steps of my journey, Dr. Aaron Gindea, healer and comedian, the staff of Community Cardiology, Helen Lee my translator, hand holder and treasured friend, Leslie Durand, Irene Zerboulis, Barbara Choit, Barbara Mogelof, Miriam Chabarek, Janet Huber, Shirley Gandharry, Lidiya and Michelline Winters who modeled the kind of women I wished to exalt, Dr. Robert Tepper, Edda Ramsdall and Susan Gomberg of CCFA, Linda Koteen of SHARE, Christina Seid, young enough to be my child, wise enough to be my mentor, my cousin and fellow redhead, Peg Mc Connell, my mother, brother and my spiritual guide and sister in my heart, Lyn Ujlaky all zealously supported my endeavors. Thanks to the Korean American community of New York, Misun Chang of Radio Korea, NYKAPA, Theresa Landis and the cyber fans of Koreandramas.net, NChristie and the members of CJK Runboard, as well as eagle-eyed Jim Fitzpatrick and the extraordinary Koreanwiz. I am humbled by your benevolence.

Conventionally in the Republic of Korea, students walk three steps behind their teacher so not to step on her shadow. There are no such traditions in the United States.

A portion of the author's profits from this edition are being donated to the Crohns and Colitis Foundation of America on Long Island.

⌘ ⌘ ⌘

To David, the father and the son

To Jim, the one and only

⌘ ⌘ ⌘

Episode 1: Korean Melodrama

In early September, New York's eastern end of Queens flaunts an uninterrupted nursery room blue sky with dot-dash clouds sweeping across the ceiling like children's pastel chalk rubbings. Just below, ancient sycamores posted along the sidewalks are topped in lush green leaves with only occasional edges of copper. But what really flirts with our senses are the gentle late summer breezes that nuzzle our hair before planting butterfly kisses on our cheeks. Remarkably, it is always on these golden days that the school year begins. In defiance of the enchanting weather, tension thickens the air inside the borough's public school buildings. The damp hovers like departed spirits in the hallways and stairwells stifling all entrants. Teachers, like mourners, paste on smiles hoping students won't notice their reluctance to relinquish the past two carefree months. At first-day meetings, administrators bunted into their wool-blend suits caution all staff members, "This will be a tough year." while tenured teachers nod to one another like conspirators acknowledging the warnings are the same as last year's and the years before.

Albert Einstein Middle School 347Q was built in 1955. The entrance boasts a 110-foot covered outdoor breezeway. This is welcoming only during September and June when visitors and staff can enjoy the momentary cooling zephyrs and shelter from the sun as they make their 30-second walk from the sidewalk to the lobby. Sadly, the greatest city in the modern world didn't hire an architect who knew that a New York school year is played out during its coldest weather. In November, this walkway will become a lidded icy tomb to all its hapless wayfarers, except the students—they'll have to use the side entrances. The grown-ups in charge would never allow 1,206 noisy students in their 2,412 dirty sneakers, Uggs, and Croc's ruining the look of their school.

This morning, the entrance has a clear view of Ms. Wendy Dale, running from her 2-door Sentra like the main character in Episode 1 of a Korean melodrama. The youngest red-head on staff is the Star of the Drama Department, Queen of the Lunchroom and unofficial President of the School Haters Club. Perfectly attired in New York City teachers' fashion; navy pinstripe suit with an ash pink sleeveless cowl neck shell, navy inch and a half heels and navy tights. All purchased on clearance with an extra 20 percent off. She's checked the time on her bangle watch from HSN and tossed her cell phone into her favorite Adrienne Vitadini, from TJ Maxx, navy leather bag. Ms. Dale's style is way too matchy-matchy for Manhattan, but in Queens she's haute couture.

'So why did I make my mammography appointment today?' the teacher asked herself as she balanced her handbag and Lord and Taylor shopping bag one to each of her arms. 'maybe to clump all this crappy stuff into one crappy ball. If I go to work, then the paint store, get my third nearly yearly mamo, make dinner, clean up, enter 132 names into my new roll book, shower, and take an Ambien, then tomorrow I get to do different crappy stuff. But it won't always be like this. Someday I'll die.' The teacher slowed her pace as she neared the school. "Remember; never let 'em see you cry. It's another school year so enter like an ancient Silla warrior, *Aja aja, fighting!*".

"Ms. Dale, Ms. Dale," The little Korean girl looked more like a doll in an Epcot Pavilion display than a student on the sidewalk. "Let me walk in the front entrance with you." She flashed her teacher an expensive orthodontic smile. "Sure, just follow my lead; Ms. Dale's going to tell a big lie." Wendy Dale said with a wink.

A willowy security guard with a latte complexion sat stoically at her post, but brightened when she recognized the teacher. "Ms. Dale, did you have a good summer?" the agent asked. She was two dress sizes smaller than Ms. Dale, but could still scare the mean out of the biggest ninth grader. The teacher was always happy to see Claire especially during a lunchroom scuffle.

"It was quiet. And I wasn't here!"

"That's good enough, Ms. Dale. How's your daughter, her," the guard placed her hand over her own abdomen. "...feel'n all right?"

"It was quiet too, Claire. That's good enough for us. Thanks for asking."

"You give her a kiss for me. Tell her to have a good school year."

Claire Jackson knew all about Jane's illness. She had known Ms. Dale before the teacher's child was taken ill. She was a bubbly happy woman who could be counted on to crack jokes with the regional superintendent, as well as the custodial crew. Now she carried her sorrow like she carried those two bags, fearing if she just tipped a little, it would all come crashing down.

The teacher cupped the girl's palm-sized shoulder with her hand.

"Ms. Claire, This young lady is going to help me wash my boards this morning. Mind if I bring her in early?"

"Just for you, Ms. Dale." Claire smiled then flashed a scowl at the pretty child.

"Don't think I don't know how you in here. Don't be tak'n advantage."

The student clung to her teacher's skirt as they walked directly to the drama room.

"The guard doesn't like me." The child's chocolate brown eyes studied Ms. Dale's face.

"Oh, sweetie, why do you say that?" asked the teacher knowing it would be an answer she'd already heard. "Because I'm Asian and she's black"

'Yep,' thought Ms. Dale, 'heard that before.'

"She's black?" Ms. Dale feigned shock. Then, just before the child could sort out her own reaction, added, "And you're not the future Miss Korea anymore? You'll represent all of Asia? *Whah!*"

The child hugged her teacher. Lesson understood and happily ended. Her thin arms wrapped around her mentor's waist. "I love you, Ms. Dale."

"I love you back, baby darling. You're my favorite kid. Now go find your friends and stay away from the front desk."

As the door shut behind the student, the teacher asked the empty room, "What's her name? Is she Hannah or is that her friend's name? Jackie, is it Jackie? But before an answer came to her, she was writing the date on the board asking herself other questions.

⌘ ⌘ ⌘

If teachers could go to their classrooms and teach in methods in which they felt comfortable and then reflected to see what worked for both them and their students, not one of them would ever leave teaching. In New York City the opposite is true. It's why most teachers ditch within five years. The Department's rules are; never put a teacher in her comfort zone, change the rules every school year and lower the educational bar so good teachers, extraordinary teachers and God-awful teachers all present information in the same lukewarm way.

Rather than fight this system Ms. Dale chose to hide in it. She transferred from teaching English where every lesson was taught in lock step and geared for the yearly state exams to Exploring Drama. At MS 347Q, Drama is in the general pool, which means it's given to short programmed seventh through ninth grade students as a fill-in and all sixth graders as an escape from their rigorous math and English classes. It was supposed to be a throw away course with grades that didn't 'count' into the report cards averages. Three years ago the principal, to ensure no visitors would observe Ms. Dale's unorthodox atmosphere, moved the class to an old "shop" room in the basement far from inquiring adults. A teacher would have to be crazy to put herself there.

However, Ms Dale's move enabled her to teach her way, a discovery method she invented years ago. She and her tutelages were left to their own creative devices in that room winning more state and national writing contests than other middle-schoolers, yet no Department of Education administrators asked for her pedagogical opinions. There were non-educators in Manhattan skyscrapers for those presumptions.

Along with the occasional salute to the Gershwin brothers and Dr. King, the teacher produced a Vaudeville inspired assembly program every year. This enabled the principal to show-case his students' talents to his regional superintendent and the parents to Cam-cord their precious offspring, while fellow teachers and students got to sit back and enjoy a show in lieu of math or science one morning each January. Administrators, children, parents, everyone was happy, except Ms. Dale. Luckily she never expected to find happiness at school.

The over-sized classroom was the only workspace in the school devoid of store-bought decorations. Within two weeks it would look like a thrift shop crowded with poems and pictures, Halloween scare-ems, scenes and skits all created by students. There were no rows of desks and chairs. Desks were pushed together to form six tables. Chairs circled the tables enabling her students to confer with each other or spread out their work. Ms. Dale counted out thirty-five 'The Play's The Thing!' Rights and Responsibilities sheets while puzzling over a favorite Oscar Wilde essay on school, 'What did he write?

'If I ran the schools, I would make them so wonderful that to punish a child, I would forbid him to go.'

It was something brilliant like that.' She noted.

But for now the room was quiet. Ms. Dale smiled at the empty chairs. She knew that by the end of first period the future occupants would be smitten with her. Girls and boys all would tell their mothers and fathers that their favorite teacher was Ms. Dale. It didn't endear Ms. Dale to her colleagues, but teachers aren't collegial anyway. That's why they picked careers that locked them away in rooms where no one was their equal.

The public address system's xylophone tones cut into her rambling daydreams. A voice culled from a deviated septum welcomed "teach-uz and stoodnts" back followed by, "Now, let's stand for the pledge."

Ms. Dale faced the yellowed $1.99 room flag and pledged along. No one at school knew her politics, her religion or her weight. Some noticed her stop short and pledge while on an errand in another classroom, but assumed it was a show for the kids. "I mean, who pledges anymore?" they'd ask each other.

Announcements were over. Chopin wafted throughout the building and the children played a kind of mob musical chairs getting to their seats before the Polonaise stopped. The sixth graders would be late. They were little strangers in a strange land and subject to getting lost. Ms. Dale stood smiling at the doorway.

"Come in. Come in. Ooh, I love those shoes—Nice back pack, handsome!" she fussed over each new entrant. "Take any seat, any seat you like."

The bolder kids couldn't contain their delight, "Any seat, yeah!" they said as they ran to unspoken for tables. Two Asian boys stayed alongside Ms. Dale. One was stout with a Beatle haircut and white Polo golf shirt. Like a munchkin attorney, he spoke up, "Teacher, this boy can only speak Korean. So, my homeroom teacher said I gotta stay with him 'cause I'm Korean too." Ms. Dale smiled. The "lawyer" hadn't yet noticed that about 70% of the class was Korean as well. 'Time to dazzle 'em!' she mused. She placed her right hand on the second boy's shoulder and said.

"*Ahm yung hah seh yo. Ms. Dale ehmnedah. Anjuh seh yo.*"

About seventy percent of the class looked up. The teacher was talking Korean! "What?!" She affected surprise, "You've never heard green-eyed *Seoul* before?"

Ms. Dale walked to the center of the room in her starring role.

"Good morning my darlings welcome to the best class you'll ever take. In this room you'll sit wherever you want the whole year unless you become a pain in the butt. Then I'll move you. She waited for the usual, "Did she say, butt?" rumblings to die down then waved a perfectly manicured hand gracefully in an arc.

"But look how you sat? What's so interesting about the way you picked your seats?" The children looked from table to table. Hands shot up. "What's your name, gorgeous?" "Mei-li Wu" whispered a double pony-tailed Chinese angel. "Nee Haw, Mei. How did you separate yourselves?"

"The girls are all sitting together and so are the boys. "
"Absolutely, Mei-Mei. You see in life we rely on our prejudices every day. Sitting with your own sex only…"

"Did she say, sex?" a brave boy asked his new classmate.
" won't make your table any better and it may not make you happier. Certainly, when we do projects in groups you'll want to be with hard workers and good students. You won't care if they're your gender or your color or even if they're the coolest kids in the school. You'll want to be with kids who've got your back. *Ah rhah suh?*"

All eyes were on the teacher who walked around the room in her one-woman play. She smelled good, smiled prettily and took no shit. Two boys she learned were Kang and Yu fought over a pencil. "*Yah Yah, hah ji mah!*" she shouted and then changed their seats. She picked up a bag of Tootsie Midgees and handed them out for correct answers and brave tries. She stopped for a moment mid-talk by confiding, "I usually don't like to share secrets the first day but you guys are terrific…." she trailed off heightening the drama. "Okay, I'll do it." She appeared serious. "One of you, close the door. The rest of you come meet me in that corner."

Attentively, they rose and followed their new teacher to the spot where the windows met the side wall. "Listen," she whispered. "In this school you're not allowed to bring candy to class". They nodded. Ms Dale looked all the way to the right and then slowly to the left as if seeking spies. "But in this room," another look around, "you can." Those who started to shout "Yes!" saw her eyes squinch and whispered their approval instead. All thirty-three children were smiling.

"But, there are rules. No sharing. I can't teach while M&M's are passed around. However, if I ask for some, you have to give me a little, just a little. I'm always on a diet. No leaving wrappers anywhere. I'm not talking about 'Fitty Cent'. I'm talking about paper. My parents didn't send me to college so I could clean up your litter, got that?" Thirty- three heads nodded as one.

"Oh, and the most important thing, if that door opens and a grown-up comes in, you must hide your gum. Stick it back here behind your last molar. She placed her index finger in the corner of her mouth and pulled back to show the exact spot. Sixty- six eyes like squirrels' caught in headlights couldn't stop staring at the teacher's lopsided grin. "Don't hide it here, she pointed behind her ear." Thirty-three giggles followed. "Not here," she pushed her hand into her armpit," Thirty-three snickers ensued. "And never, never …." her hand pointed behind her. Tethered pandemonium as thirty-three pre-teens squealed in delight. This *is* fun. Ms. Dale's expression instantly changed. A pretend frown stared down at all thirty-three. "Why are you all following me around? It's too hot. Go sit down."

The rest of the period was spent munching sweet mini Tootsies while filling out forms and going over rules and rubrics. All thirty-three were still basking in the teacher's glow when the music began again. She heard the "Aaws". She knew they didn't want to leave. That was her plan. She'd do the same thing three more times this week. Telling each group they were terrific. As the students exited, one well-scrubbed boy with blonde hair, fading tan and the stirrings of his first teacher-crush, lagged behind. "Ms. Dale, I'm Constantine Poulis."

Future senator.' she mused.

"Can you speak Greek too?" he asked politely.

"Sure, Gus, spanakopita, baklava, kourambeides."

His mother would cry if she saw how readily her son was changing his allegiances to his new teacher.

"Ms. Dale, that's just food."

"What else do I need to know?" she laughed. Her hand mussed his corn-silk hair. "I'll see you tomorrow. Oh, no wait, I'll see you at lunch. I'm the boss of the lunchroom." The boy she would affectionately call Gus for the rest of the term squeezed past the next awaiting class. He hadn't noticed his teacher saying the exact entry words to this new class that she had just said to his.

⌘ ⌘ ⌘

"Bathroom, bathroom, bathroom." Ms. Dale sprinted down the now empty hall. The teachers' lounge already held a cue of two adults awaiting relief. A painfully timid male music teacher had lined up behind a rotund history matriarch. Quick polite smiles sped across all three faces.

It's times like these that teachers question their career choices. New York City requires all its pedagogues to earn Masters' of Science or Arts degrees within the first five years of teaching. After that, they must earn another thirty credits beyond their graduate degrees to be at top salary levels.

A Big Apple business requiring under-graduate, graduate, and post-graduate work from its staff members would offer incredible perks, benefits and ambience. The restroom at such a workplace would never look like the space the three relief seekers stood in now. It would not expect both genders to use the same facility, with a system of door knocking and answering quickly to prevent unforgettable embarrassment. It would offer hot water as well as cold, white towels instead of prison brown, some form of soap and perhaps toilet tissue that didn't remind the user of graph paper as it brutally gripped one's genitalia or hemorrhoids. Teachers suffer from more urinary tract infections than any other career group. It comes from holding it in. If you're teaching, and nature calls, it better leave a call back number since you're not going anywhere till the bell rings.

Mr. Carlisle; Music, was pleasant enough but Ms. Casta; Western Civ. was a nasty bitch who filled her chalkboards with notes that enabled her to sit on her ever-spreading rear-end half the period while her charges copied them into their binders. Whenever Ms. Dale questioned her own abilities as a teacher, she reminded herself of Ms. Casta's methods and was instantly reassured. Right now she hoped their conversation would stay at smiles, eyebrow lifts and blowing air through their lips to show how hard it is for a teacher who has to pee. But it wasn't to be. Like all truly mean-spirited people, Ms. Casta could heat-seek the weak spot in everyone.

"My son is studying in France this semester. She announced to both teachers but meant for the thinner, prettier woman's ears. "He wasn't sure he wanted to leave his sister, but I told him, "You're young. You're healthy. Now's the time to enjoy yourself" "Am I right?"

Mr. Carlisle mumbled, "Sure." then quickly centered his eyes on the bathroom door sending telepathic messages to the early bird within. Ms. Dale carefully chose her reply; a counterfeit look of surprise, "I'm sorry, Ellen, I didn't hear you. I was just thinking that it's probably less crowded in the first floor lounge now. Have a good day, you two."

⌘ ⌘ ⌘

Ms. Dale returned to her room and locked the door. "Maybe it wasn't a 'my kids are better than your kid' slap. Maybe having a daughter with Crohn's disease makes me too sensitive." She opened the walk-in closet door. It was a remnant of the former woodworking shop storage area. "Too many nights in hospital rooms pushing two chairs together to sleep by Jane's bedside. Too many doctors writing too many prescriptions that made my Janie sicker have made me cynical." The teacher took a large Tupperware bowl down off the shelf and placed it on the closet floor. She reached down to take a handful of tissues from the Kleenex box already on the old linoleum.

"Maybe Ellen didn't mean anything by her "healthy" comment. The Hell, she didn't!" Wendy Dale, in a flash of movements that could only come with practice, pulled down her navy tights and ecru cotton panties, hiked up her skirt with her right hand and held onto the inside closet doorknob with her left. She urinated, wiped, hiked up her underwear, pressed down her skirt, closed the closet door, washed the bowl in the shop sink, placed the tissues in a baggy before tossing them in the trash, washed her hands, then sprayed a quick pulse of Bulgari on her wrist before slumping in her desk chair. The teacher was to begin writing her school's virtue-themed assembly program this prep period. She'd get to it soon, but for now she let the anger take her introspection from 'Fatso' Casta's stinging remark, to her mother's latest TIA, then on to her precious daughter's devastating illness. "I feel like Mrs. Job." She confided to her empty room.

Several years ago, lunch duty for New York City teachers was replaced with more cerebral activities. The unions argued, "Why pay teachers and administrators to baby-sit students during lunchtime, when for $10.00 an hour the city could hire school aides to watch the city's youth." It certainly pleased teachers. It pleased students even more because they knew the aides feared them. The school aides at many middle schools were forty-something former housewives who worked for the generous medical and dental benefits. They were not going to break up a fight or stop a drug buy for a twenty-hour a week job.

The middle school principals had to get creative. They took one full class from a willing teacher's program and replaced it with five periods of lunch coordination. The students had an authority figure to beat them back when visions of food fights danced in their heads and the school aides had an on-site supervisor. The process is called School Based Options. It means that a school may choose to use pedagogical staff in other ways, but only after a tedious antiquated union sanctioned vote. At M.S. 347, the principal was more daring. He created three lunch periods: grades six, seven and an eighth-ninth combination and formed a team of three aides, a security guard and a teacher lunch coordinator. Only in New York would five little ladies be responsible for the safety and well being of over 1200 school children.

Ms. Dale could barely tolerate the aides. They pretended not to see bullying, which in a school lunchroom is a daily occurrence. They never picked up litter left behind on lunch tables because it wasn't their job, yet watched Ms. Dale clean up daily. Worst of all, they exhibited real prejudices against those children who weren't in their own ethnic groups. The Indian aide would sneak sandwiches to Indian children then bark at the non-Indians who forgot their lunch money. The Columbian aide would make sure the Spanish speakers always had a school basketball for recess yet when non-Hispanic boys would demand court time she'd shoo them off. It's why Ms. Dale preferred Claire at her side. The two women made sure students neither went without lunch nor were prey to the schoolyard rowdies. The two of them would jump into any melee and shout down any ruffian, regardless of sex, race or national origin. They were the ebony and ivory equal justice league.

Other teachers may have coveted the lunchroom coordinator's position as a respite from marking tests and phoning overly concerned parents, but few could hack it. With no protection save a whistle and walkie-talkie, Ms. Dale sometimes had to extricate 200+ lb. ninth graders from kicking classmates. Some students when red-hot angry would throw things. Some bullied smaller children and some were just plain out of control. Even teachers who gave Ms. Dale a hard time about her easy program had to admit they didn't want her job. The school dean blessed her every day for lightening his load.

Adrienne Leslie

⌘ ⌘ ⌘

All five of Ms. Dale's senses were appalled as she scurried down the hall to the lunchroom. Her ears buzzed with the roar of a full grade of pre-teens and teens. They had just left the purgatory of their classrooms so now chose to communicate solely by shouting. Asian and white boys who couldn't find Harlem on a map of uptown Manhattan, yelled, "Yo Yo, brutha. Waz up?" to other non-blacks. Girls screeched and screamed syllables rather than words when greeting each other. A city subway station at its cacophonic best couldn't reach these decibels. But the sound was a kiss when compared to the odor. The smell like syrup clung to the insides of her nostrils. Acrid fried onions from the kitchen, choking bleach emanations rising off the tables, curdled breakfast milk forgotten in trashcans were stirred into a mélange of body odors from hundreds of not so clean children at their explosive hormonal peaks. The huge olive drab tiled walls with metal mesh wire window covers fenced in the children as if they were booked juvenile offenders. The long refectory tables with attached benches in faded institutional gray would have felt at home in a Dickensian workhouse. The school boasted an award winning art department yet there were no collages, watercolors or even stick drawings decorating these walls. 'Bon appetite kids!' the teacher mumbled as she hooked up the creaking sound system.

Ms. Dale ran her hand over a tabletop out of habit. "They're always sticky." She confided to the safety agent.

"Unfortunately, you never know the origin of the mucus you've just felt. When you try to guess, your stomach tightens up".

Claire laughed. "Is that why you don't eat down here, Ms. Dale?"
Wendy made a face usually seen on infants tasting peas for the first time.

"I'd have to Novocain my tongue before I'd subject my taste buds to this place, Claire. Besides, every time I've succumbed to hunger, and forced down a bit of Einstein tuna salad, I've spent the night slogging down Alka-seltzer to put out the flames."

The teacher looked towards the doors to see her closest school confident emerging through the seventh grade throng. "Libby, I'm over here." Wendy called out to her friend.

Elizabeth (Libby) Spring, sixth grade English/Social Studies was 16 years Ms. Dale's senior. Just biologically old enough to be her mother, she had auburn hair and green-gold eyes making the two teachers appear related. Once while visiting Jane at Mount Sinai Hospital, a nurse asked if she was Wendy's mom. Libby smiled genuinely, "I wish I were." Wendy was impressed with her graciousness.

"This is seventh, right? I don't know why you do this." Libby chided as she kissed the air near the left side of

Wendy's head. "I'm exhausted already. Good thing Adam's working late tonight. I stupidly defrosted a turkey breast without thinking about the roasting time. Tell me again how to make it."

Women who prepared dinner for their families were the last of a dying breed. It wasn't a blow to female rights but rather a shared passion for cooking and other feminine pursuits. On the rare quiet days when neither had serious matters on her plate their conversation would flow from chicken cutlets on sale at Waldbaum's and handbag closeouts at Filene's Basement to the durability of Esse's Fishnet Stockings nail polish.

"Carve out the breast halves to make two large filets. Marinate them in Italian dressing, chopped fresh garlic, a sprig of thyme and a splash of red wine or my mix of soy sauce, garlic and marmalade, 350' for about an hour. It depends on the size. Cut them like filet mignon. I make stock out of the bones and wings. I gave you that recipe. Didn't I?"

"Yes, 'Martha' you did but remind me." Libby grinned at her best school friend.

"I boil up the frame with carrots, celery, onion, garlic and dill for stock. After I strain it, I give the leftover meat to Fido with his kibble. You give Shadow table food don't you?" asked Wendy.

"Are you kidding? I cook more often for Shadow than these women prepare for their families!" answered Libby as she nodded to the school-aides talking amongst themselves while ignoring a tall boy kicking the Snapple machine.

"Hey handsome! Ms. Dale shouted to the six-footer, "Park your hiney. You're never getting that dollar back. Tell your mother to call the mayor." The boy, recognizing the voice of authority, turned toward his former teacher and bowed slightly. These students were returnees. They knew if they pissed off Ms. Dale, they'd be her cleaning crew for the rest of the week. She turned back to her friend, "Is everything all right?" Mrs. Spring smiled, "Yeah, I just thought we could chat. Are you going straight home today?" Wendy laughed, "If I had a life. No, I have to pick up paint for the hallway between the bedrooms. Tim finally gave in. We'll work on it over the weekends. I'll probably just pick up sample jars today, oh, and I have to go for my mammogram too. Would you believe I couldn't get an appointment during the summer? They were booked solid. You'd think they were giving away freebees." "Yeah, free black and blue marks." Libby joked then lectured like the former nurse she was, "Today's Tuesday, that's good. You never want to go on a Wednesday. With that new bullshit of them having four business days to call you, they'll find something on a Wednesday but won't call you till the following Monday and that tumor will keep growing. Wendy shook her head, "Don't say tumor. I've got to start. I'll see you tomorrow." They were busy women with families. They'd readily tell each other their darkest secrets at school but rarely met outside. It was the way they both wanted it.

Two Jennifers pronounced Jenny-purr in Korean-American English rushed towards their favorite teacher. "*Yah*, Look who's here; Jen One and Jen Squared." she greeted.

Two months of vacation led Ms. Dale to forget they were Miss Ahn and Miss Lee respectively. Their four arms wrapped around their teacher in absolute delight. "What did you watch this summer, Ms. Dale?" The girls and nearly all the student body knew their teacher was an avid Korean drama fan. Rather than hide her un-teacher like hobby, she used it to open communication lines with her students, besides they were her resources for all the gossip about the stars.

Ms. Dale twirled her shoulder length Scottish red hair and flicked a lock behind her right ear. She affected a Valley Girl accent and with a laugh said, " Oh my God, I spent…like the whole summer…like just watching!"

"Which ones? Which ones?" they asked in tandem.

"Well, at the beginning of vacation," Wendy Dale returned to her true voice, "I watched Mr. Goodbye. I hated her, hated the little boy, but loved him. Ooh, he's a cutie". "That's Ahn Jae Wook!" swooned Jennifer Ahn, "We're not related."

"Kuh deh?", Ms. Dale pretended regret. "I finally saw *Kim Sam Soon*. And you know girls, you were right. It is the best drama I've ever seen. All three females were giggling. The two Jens were jumping in place. Jen Squared confided, "I loved the scene on the mountain top, when he told her not to change her name." The Jens nodded in agreement. The teacher let her own tingle to escape, "Ladies, come on, the scene where he knocks down her ex boyfriend and kisses her in the men's room. That's my favorite scene ever." Wendy decided against revealing her impure thoughts for the drama's male lead. Anyway, she was pretty sure she was far too old for the handsome drama star even it was only daydreaming.

"Oh, I love Hyun Bin. "Me too" said the Jens. They had already broken up with Ahn Jae Wook in their imaginings.

"Ms. Dale, are you watching *Somunnan Chilgongju*?"

The teacher had to mentally translate. "Um, The Infamous Chill Sisters? I love that one too. I hope the young husband gets his act together. Doesn't it remind you of Fiddler On The Roof?

The girls smiled trying to please her.

"Because it's all daughters…." Her words trailed off. The conversation was over. Ms. Dale knew when not to take a second bow. "Girls, we've got to start lunch.

But we still have to talk about *Goong*. I'll meet you in the schoolyard. *Ahn juh say oh. bally, bally"*

Grade seven was well trained by Ms. Dale last year. Each student found his seat by perusing the cardboard class placards on the tables. Those who brought lunch from home ate immediately. School lunch students had to be called by class and not until the cafeteria was silent. Three whistle blows and everything stopped. In the wake of Columbine and 9/11, the teacher knew that in an emergency, their only hope was a setting quiet enough to hear her instructions.

To insure the students of her fairness, Ms. Dale broke the silence by greeting the grade in Chinese, Hebrew, Greek and Korean. She told them it was a Mr. Rogers day outside to which they added, "It's a beautiful day in the neighborhood." It was a shout-out they created last year. She threatened a stray talker with her famous diatribes,
"Hey, good-looking, over there, yes, you. You want to wear plastic gloves and clean up saliva-soaked bread off the floor this week? No? Then shut your pie hole."

It was as if she was an actress in two plays. In the early show, she was the fun Drama teacher, in the later performance, a prison guard coordinator. Both worked.

Seventh grade lunch ended and sixth grade lunch began. Those students who were in Ms. Dale's classes showed off to their friends by telling them about the tootsie rolls. Two children lost their lunches. One of them cried over it. Both were fed by the city. They were supposed to be billed for the soggy peanut butter and jelly sandwich, wilted salad and tepid milk, but Ms. Dale and the kitchen staff never reported these random acts of kindness. By the end of the week, this grade would be the best behaved. Sometime between May and June, the puberty fairy will wave her magic wand over them and they'll turn dopey and obnoxious. But, for now they are adorable.

The sixth graders exited and the eighth and ninth entered. By then the lunch team was tired and hungry. Unfortunately for them, the older kids were the ball breakers. They were louder and cockier than the lower grade students. They stole lunches and money from their friends, cell phones and games from the nerds and snacks from the kitchen. Ms. Dale would grab the worst offenders by the neck. It could easily get her fired and sued. But even the craziest kids took it as affection.

"Ant'ny, Ant'ny." she clucked in Brooklynese at Anthony Perez. "Give Son Ha her cell phone. My feet are killing me. I've been wearing these heels since six o'clock this morning, Ant'ny. This is not the day to piss me off." Big Anthony Perez was beginning this school year as he ended the last, with a ghetto whine, "I don't have it, Ms. Dale. I swear." Since every kid 'swore' none were believed. The teacher played it the way she knew how, with a lie as big as his. "Tragically for you, big man, I saw you.

Didn't you see me at the kitchen door? I was standing there watching you like a movie."

Ms. Dale looked straight into Big Anthony's dull eyes. He lowered his lids. "Bingo" she cheered to herself. She eased her grip on his neck and whispered, "Just give it to me. I'll give it to her and I'll say some kid found it." "Au-ight." he whimpered, handing her the purloined mobile. "You ain't call'n my father?" The teacher was just grateful there'd be no further discussions with the thief's and victim's parents after school. "What for?" she asked, "to tell him some kid found a cell phone? But, bother her again and death will be slow and painful. *Nah Ga!*" Even with the name Perez, he knew 'Get outta here!' when he heard it.

It was an exhausted teacher who removed a squashed fish stick from a table bench, wiped the greasy seat with a paper towel sheet she held for such occasions and then sat down next to and hugged a hysterical Yoon Son Ha. Even with the phone in her hand the girl couldn't stop crying. "My father would have killed me, Ms. Dale."

'What's with the scary fathers?' Ms. Dale's father was her childhood champion yet even she remembered crying, "Don't tell Daddy." to her mother after getting caught committing some long forgotten error in judgment.

⌘ ⌘ ⌘

Her daughter Jane, however, had her step-dad roped and tied. Tim O'Hanlon never corrected, reproached or censured his stepdaughter. Wendy chose to see his behavior as an echo of her own devotion to their child. Jane, although a fledgling to her intuitive feelings, knew the nice man was simply afraid of returning to the disharmonic family life of his childhood. Never giving him the title of Dad, Wendy's daughter considered the Big Irishman as the benevolent stranger who shared their space and board.

Before Jane became ill, Wendy was the house disciplinarian. Tim would come up with any excuse not to admonish the girl. After Jane was diagnosed and their days and nights were spent watching her grow paler and weaker, often too tired to get out of bed, Wendy chose to treat her 11 year old like a hand blown Christmas ornament. She lived in fear of losing her, something she didn't share with Tim. So Jane was never reprimanded again. Surprisingly, the kid turned out all right. Not flawless but, pretty darned good.

Lunch duty was over. Three children were absent this first day leaving 1203 middle school children fed, restroomed, recessed and sent back to their classes without a single hair on their heads harmed. Ms. Dale didn't expect an accolade. Like other New Yorkers she thought often of September 11th 2001, but as a teacher she had her own epilogue, "One million school children got home safely that terrible day and nobody said thank you." She returned to her room to eat a pre-packaged diet lunch and drink a warm Diet Pepsi in silence. Her friends often chided her, "You're such a good cook. Why do you eat that junk?" The teacher knew the answer, because everyone else in her life came first. She made her husband's favorite Catalina salad dressing from scratch, her daughter's favorite strawberry jam and even the dog's whole-wheat biscuits. Yet somehow eating defrosted fast food was good enough for her. The teacher shrugged her shoulders and sighed. She began working on the assembly program by sketching a backdrop of a giant scale of justice with one tray filled with bright red gemstones then wrote, "Far Above Rubies' recalling the bible proverb about a virtuous woman. 'Good title.'

The September sun had been toasting the city for eight hours when the children and staff left school. Like the rest of her female colleagues, Wendy Dale's day didn't end at three o'clock. They all had errands and chores. Many teachers, mostly her male counterparts had second jobs. If their school were just four blocks east, they'd be teaching in Great Neck where the average pedagogue's salary was ten to fifteen thousand more a year. It could have been a professional house painter running to Anycolor Paints instead of the weary Ms. Dale.

Wendy carefully laid her jacket on the passenger seat of her well-worn sedan. With just the cowl-necked shell and straight skirt, she almost looked sleek. The navy tights and heels belied her five feet three inch height but even the monochromatic lower half color scheme couldn't disguise the wearer's curvy pear shape. Wendy

Dale was a woman who had as many men look twice as she passed them as when she approached them, even at her age, whatever that was.

Parking on Northern Boulevard took nerves of steel and a handful of quarters so Wendy trolled for a spot on Glenwood and Broward streets. It couldn't be too far from the paint store. She might have to walk back with a gallon in each hand. The sun snuggled her bare arms like a cape as she step-swished, down the hill. Her daughter's symptoms had been in remission since her surgery last spring and Wendy was remembering how to walk like a woman again.

Anycolor Paints II had its grand opening in April. Its business model already tested with Anycolor I was brilliant. It had Korean owners in an ethnically mixed neighborhood, was on a well-known heavily trafficked roadway and most importantly, it sold paint. The Korean butcher next store, while enjoying a fairly brisk business never saw non-Korean customers or their wallets in his establishment.

Queens is home to more ethnic groups than anywhere else in the world. And every one of them, whether from Ecuador or East of Java, Thailand or New Castle on Tyme, would eventually need to paint a room. The owners were already scouting a location for Anycolor Paints III.

Wendy, noting the Korean translations on the new awning and storefront, decided to showcase her talents. Even in this multicultural stew pot, Koreans were surprised to hear a white lady speak their language. She straightened her shoulders, checked her watch and made an inauspicious entrance into the life of Hyun Jae Won.

"*Ah du see*," she took a step towards the lone man at the counter who didn't look up from his Korea Times.
"Samples *oh dee say oh?*" Ms. Dale made the universal sign for small jar by holding up her right hand so her thumb and index finger formed a backwards C.

The owner, his head still wrapped around the problems in Pyongyang, heard his home language but detected something not quite right. Had he thought about it, his first guess might have been that the customer was an US born Korean whose parents were remiss in her education. But Mr. Hyun had stopped pondering over things a while ago. He looked up from his paper to see an American woman standing near his Moorwood Wood Restorer section with a stupid smile on her face. "I speak English." He sniped in heavily accented Korean. The woman took ownership of the insult. "Was my Korean that bad?" She laughed like all Americans; out loud, he complained to himself, but at least this one had the decency to cover her mouth with her dainty hand. Had Mr. Hyun been born in Jamaica, Queens rather than Jamsil, Seoul, he would have rolled his eyes. Instead, he did the Korean equivalent and silently pointed to the sample jars of Benjamin Moore's latest colors to her right.

Wendy didn't follow his hand direction. A sweeping glance of the store's interior made her realize she had made a mistake. Every gallon can and sample jar, indeed every paint stirrer was labeled Benjamin Moore. An exceptionable product to be sure but Wendy had spent an hour at the Behr Paint web site yesterday choosing colors from their palette. She could turn and leave but that would mean this errand would have to be re-run tomorrow. 'Oh God, now I have to talk to Mr. Nasty again.'

"*Mee ahn hah dah.* I don't suppose you carry Behr paints too?" She tried to suck back the sentence but her naive question was already dancing in the space between them. Like other smart women, Wendy Dale didn't relish looking like a jerk.

Mr. Hyun contained his annoyance. "Is this the first time you're buying paint?" he thought he asked. It came out, Is thish dah pirst time you're buying painteh? Wendy was so angry, she wanted to counter-attack,

'*Shiro.* This is not the pirst time!', but discretion won over displeasure.

"*Shil smeedah.* I'll just look through your sample cards." Since, like most westerners, the rules of Korean bowing protocol were beyond her understanding, she nodded her head slightly in respect as if addressing parents at open school night.

Actually, she liked matching paint colors. It would take her to that same inspiring space her mother had denied her. She had become an obscure middle school Drama teacher instead of a nationally famous novelist thanks to her mother's 'good girls' mantra. "Good girls help their moms. They don't write books", Mrs. Dale pontificated to her daughter. "Writers are always sleeping around. Poets sleep around. Artists sleep around. Boys don't respect girls who sleep around."

An innocent poem Wendy dedicated to a neighborhood swain was torn up and tossed in the name of virtue. Wendy often joked to her friends that she became a teacher to protect her virginity. But the joke never made her laugh. As an adult, Wendy wondered what trauma her mother might have endured to make her so single minded but even if she knew, what would it change? She learned to be content writing assembly programs and choosing paint colors.

She had originally selected Behr's Feldspar 410C-2 for the hallway walls and ceiling with White Hydrangea W-B-420 on the crown molding. She was going to paint seven odd shaped picture frames she found at a yard sale Gallery Red 150F-6 and arrange them on the longest wall without their matting or pictures for a bold new look. The dark tired passageway between their family bedrooms had become a metaphor for the way they had spent the last three years. It was time for a fresh coat of paint.

Now she was abandoning the Feldspar for Benjamin Moore's Lemon Grass, divorcing White Hydrangea for Easter Lily and dumping Gallery Red for Louisiana Hot Sauce. She couldn't help feeling pleased with herself as she walked to the paint color distributor machine with her selections. Hyun Jae Won looked only at his task at hand as he began mixing her colors. The silence they shared ended when a Mexican handyman working on Broward entered the store in search of disposable roller tray liners. Wendy politely looked down at her watch while the men spoke. Her eyes widened as she noted the time. "Oh my God! I'll be late for my ma…my doctor's appointment. Would you just put them aside for me? I'll pay for them now but I have to go. I'm busy for a few days." Words kept tumbling from her mouth. "Friday, I'll be back Friday."

He couldn't believe his ears, *"Neh?"*

Weeks later he would recall that was the first time he had spoken Korean to an American.

Jae Won nearly ripped her American Express card from her hand as he mumbled angrily to himself. The handyman sensing trouble crouched down near the cans of Dap Plaster of Paris trying to look busy till the white lady left.

"We don't hold products here. We don't have the room". He tried speaking reasonably to her.

"I know and I'm terribly sorry. Friday, right after school." She called back to him. When the door shut and the lingering scent of her perfume was overcome by the smell of latex, the two men looked at each other in silence. It wasn't their vastly different cultures that prevented them from commiserating. Had the customer and proprietor been women, they would have balked and squawked about Wendy's behavior for at least 10 minutes.

Hyun Jae Won took the folded cash and the "Gracias" from the handyman and listened as the shop door closed. He finished mixing the red haired lady's paints and neatly stacked them under his counter. With a black marker, he wrote DALE across a receipt copy stapled with the sample strips onto the gallon can's wire handle. He would have, if only in the few minutes before the next customer, returned to his reading in peace except each time his eyes scanned two or three words, he found himself staring out the storefront window commemorating the back of that blue skirt.

Wendy Dale was already re-jacketed, in the driver's seat and heading east on Northern Boulevard. It had rarely happened before, but every once in awhile she'd spread herself too thin unable to complete all a day's errands. When she eventually recalled Hyun Jae Won, it was to frown at his surliness. Although, at the red light on Lakeville Road she thought he reminded her of that *quee up tah* drama star. What was his name, the one with the thick wavy hair? He wears it tied back too. Of course, Anycolor guy was much older. Her mean spirited remark made her snicker, "Yeah, much older, the way I'm much older than every Korean starlett in my dramas. Wake up, Wendy. You're mutton not lamb."

The waiting area at Community Radiological Associates and Affiliates could have been a Mondrian painting if Piet Mondrian had been born colorblind. The room was a labyrinth of straight lines and cross lines all in shades of gray and taupe. Men and woman, toddlers and octogenarians filled the seats and stood on the one line to announce their presence. Flabby disinterested receptionists accepted insurance cards, prescriptions and money all before bestowing the opportunity to be radiated. Wendy didn't like seeing children in the waiting room. It made her fearful for them. She knew first hand that children could be at their pediatrician and dentist's offices and be perfectly well but specialized medical office visits could predicate devastating news.

One receptionist who wouldn't make eye contact with Wendy gave her a mammography form to fill out before going in. The teacher sat in half of a Naugahide two-seater near a back wall, fearing a man or worse, a former student would sit beside her while she got personal with her paperwork. The form had a diagram of an anonymous pair of breasts. The circles that signified the nipples had numbers radiating from their centers indicating two clock faces. Below were more caveat reminders, "Did you wash the breast and underarm area thoroughly. Did you refrain from using cream, powder or antiperspirant?" Wendy hoped the scrub up before leaving school was good enough. She never wore antiperspirants or deodorizers anyway. Much to her pride, she rarely sweated and wasn't plagued by body odor. Besides, deodorants had their own cloying scents that a skewed her aesthetic senses when they interfered with her Bulgari. She drew a small circle at 10:00 o'clock on the left breast to show she had a fibro-adenoma there once when she was a young bride.

Seventeen years earlier Wendy Dale was painting her new home when she felt a pulling sensation under her bra band. She raised her arm to the bathroom mirror to see reflecting back at her, a dime-sized lump protruding from her skin. During the next three months, three doctors in succession told her not to worry. Each one instructed her to wait for her next period for it to disappear. It didn't. Finally a local surgeon who incorrectly guessed it was cat scratch fever said it had to come out. Wendy wasn't even sedated for the half hour procedure.

One morning, two weeks later, her first husband berated her for not learning the results of the biopsy then promptly left for work. That left Wendy alone to call for the diagnosis. She didn't understand why the receptionist had to put the doctor on the phone. She didn't comprehend when he said it was a fibro-adenoma tumor. She thought tumors meant cancer. But the doctor went on to explain that it was benign and wouldn't come back. His words reassured Wendy for many years. Still, it would have been easier for her if she could have confided her concerns to her mother that day. But her mother's signal was always loud and clear, "If it's bad news, you probably brought it on yourself." It not only led Wendy never to reveal her fears to her mother, it made her keep her own council with others, always with her first husband, often with Tim. It was a heavy crown to wear.

Wendy was the sixth patient to be called.

"Hi Dale. I'm Helen." It was such a common occurrence. People often reversed her names. Wendy was always amiable. "Dale's my last name. Don't worry. I'm used to that."

The technician smiled back while escorting her to the row of changing closets. She pointed to the folded hospital gown and began her memorized part. "Undress from the waist up. Put the gown on, opening in the front. You're not wearing any perfume, talc or anti-perspirant are you? After the first pictures, you're going to come back here but don't get dressed till I tell you. We often have to retake pictures. It just means the pictures were fuzzy. No need to worry. All righty? I'll call for you in a little while. Take your handbag with you when you leave here." Wendy removed her pink cowl shell and ecru underwire bra carefully hiding the brassiere under her top. In a moment she'd be handled like meat at a butcher's but for now propriety would be observed. She noticed a white 8 X 11 paper on the sidewall covered with circle stickers and tiny triangles attached by string. PLEASE LEAVE YOUR MARKERS HERE was written at the top. "As opposed to what?" contemplated Wendy "Using them for a book report cover?"

The louvered door opened and she was seated on yet another straight gray bench next to a stylish fiftyish woman with whom she exchanged smiles. "Mrs. Letsky." came a voice at a doorway. The woman stood, smiled a second time at Wendy and walked towards a cheery lab coated Haitian woman. "Mrs. Dale" called Wendy's technician.

The mammography room was as cold as Wendy had remembered it.

"You skipped last year?" asked the technician scanning Wendy's records. Jane was hospitalized that summer and everything else had to wait. The wait time lingered as Jane's chronic diarrhea and violent cramps became their family's sole event guide. Now even though Jane was in remission, Wendy stuttered as she explained why she had missed that summer's visit. For some reason she felt compelled to explain why she was remiss. It was a silly moment of pride. The technician placed a circle sticker on each of her now chilled and hardened nipples and covered her fibro-adenoma scar with the triangles-on-a-string. Questions about family history had Wendy reveal that not only had Grandma Dale died of breast cancer, but since her last visit, her maternal grandmother had too. "But," She was quick to add, "she was ninety two and her doctors said…." No one was listening. Wendy was being fed to the villainous metal breast monster with her right teat already in his grip.

Maybe if women didn't experience the pain of childbirth, they'd be more angered at the torment of mammography. It hurts. But, just as during the throes of labor they know in a little while they'll have a beautiful baby to hug, they're sure this pain will stop in a moment or two if they're just a bit more patient. So woman practice patience instead of voicing their opinions and no one has to create a more pleasant test. Wendy was shuttled back to her changing closet with orders not to re-dress. In a few minutes the door opened again and she was told that some of the pictures were indeed fuzzy and had to be retaken. This had also happened during her first mammography so Wendy was not afraid.

⌘ ⌘ ⌘

When Wendy's dog, old Fido III's legs could no longer hold up his tired blonde frame, Tim drove him to the veterinarian's office for that terrible final visit. Jane hid in her room. Wendy followed them to the car kissing the beloved Afghan hound mix on his snout whispering, "Mommy loves you. Mommy loves you, boy." The dog took his safety as a given and went willingly to his maker. This was the way Wendy accepted the fuzzy picture fib. She dressed, handed in her papers and shared goodbyes with the staff. Feeling free of the day's obligations, she even crammed in a stop at the dry-cleaners to pick up Tim's shirts.

FidoV was the first to greet her. Tim had let him out to the fenced-in yard when he arrived home with Jane. Jane, like all children with pets, adored Fido but she never fed, watered or cleaned up after him. She would however instruct others to do so. "Ma! Fido threw up in the dining room." was a familiar refrain. Now the ninety-five pound almost Doberman was turning in circles of joy at the sight of his mistress.

"Who's the best boy? Who does mommy love the best?" Ask any dog owner. Those two barks that followed Wendy's questions were really, "Me, mommy!"

As much as Wendy enjoyed dressing up, she happily shucked down to 'house clothes' as soon as she reached the bedroom. Clad in old brown sweat pants and last years' Football Team Korea cotton tee, she checked on her daughter's school supplies status, greeted her husband, washed her hands and whipped up savory oven fried chicken cutlets, golden roasted potatoes with rosemary, fresh broccoli-rabe sautéed with garlic and lemon and a tossed salad with homemade vinaigrette. "You don't have to be rich to eat really well." She liked to say.

Her colleague Libby insisted it was a kind of neurosis that led Wendy to keep a frozen stock of meats and poultry in her two freezers, pastas in every size and shape in her larder and an expensive well appointed bar in a home where no one imbibed.

Bird and Fish

By 7:15 her chores would be done, her clothing for tomorrow set out and her mauled body showered. She was more than ready to nestle in with Pure 19 and later The Infamous Chill Sisters, presently two of her favorite Korean dramas. In between shows, she tucked her daughter in. As she kissed the winsome child's pale forehead, Jane broke the tenderness of the moment. "Mom, you know the perfume you wear to work?"

"My Bulgari?" Wendy had no idea where the conversation would take them.

Jane coughed and continued, "It's nice and all but don't wear it any more. It reminds me of the hospital. I'd smell it every time you leaned over me like this."

Wendy smiled at her gift to the world. "It's history, baby darling. I'm tossing it right now."

Wendy softly shut her daughter's bedroom door, entered the bathroom and threw her rectangular spray bottle of Bulgari into the wastebasket. She pulled a sample bottle of Pleasures out of an Estee Lauder gift pack and placed it on her make-up shelf. Her movements were stiff but her thoughts flowed like a river. Three years ago when she traveled alone to Korea, she had a stopover in Alaska. It was late and she was tired. The airport offered a gift shop where she first sprayed her wrist with Bulgari. She loved its heady floral scent. During the next sixteen hours of her flight, she would breathe in its bouquet and fancy herself in Paradise. It became her signature scent till this very moment. Wendy couldn't cure Jane so she tossed away one of her own sweet memories in penance. At a little after 11:00, with Tim snorting and snoring in her ear, she'd take an Ambien and dream of Jane drowning while she tried to swim out to her in a roiling sea.

Episode 2: Nor Heaven nor Earth

Julius Caesar is not for girls. There are only two roles for women, Caesar's barren wife, Calphurnia who exits before the Ides of March are over and poor crazy Portia who cuts herself when depressed. But studies show that while boys will rarely read a story where the main character is a girl, generally, girls will read male dominated tales. Think Harry Potter. The sixth grade English/Social Studies curriculum includes the study of ancient Rome. Ms. Dale thought Julius Caesar was the perfect text for Drama. Her colleagues ridiculed her.

"Too hard. They're not gonna get it. Half of them barely speak English. They're going to understand Elizabethan?"

Ms. Dale listened to their objections then quickly ordered 250 copies. That was five years ago. She was never invited to submit a book order again. When several of the beloved paperbacks began to make unauthorized permanent home visits, Ms. Dale traveled to the bowels of the building's sub-basement to the old bookroom and discovered forty-three abused and torn copies. On the fly page of the top book was the familiar New York Board of Education Stamp: Name, Class, Date Received, Date

Returned and Condition. It showed that the last child to receive this Shakespearean treasure was ninth grader, James H. in 1971 who left the other columns blank.

"Jim" considered the teacher, "you must be nearly fifty now. Did we ever meet? Did we date?" She gathered up the school-worn sub-basement books knowing they'd be the last to be chosen. Kids, like Hollywood, only want what's perfect and pretty.

⌘ ⌘ ⌘

Friday morning arrived like scene one of Shakespeare's tragedy. The clear periwinkle sky above may even had mirrored the heavens over the Feast of Lupercal in 44 BC. The teacher was particularly selective in choosing today's attire.

Generally female teachers dress to impress other women, matching a brown sweater with brown slacks ending their half-hearted fashion statement with a too small brown and white scarf but, Ms. Dale dressed as one would use an exclamation point. Today she modeled an above the knee black on black embroidered a-line skirt with matching shrug-cut jacket covering a skimpy black lace paneled teddy. Black tights with blister inducing three-inch obsidian heels would help set the mood after dismissal. She dressed solely to humble one quite unsuspecting shop owner.

"Mr. Nasty will have to bow to me when I show up as promised." she gloated as she buttoned her jacket to

Bird and Fish

hide her lace-sheathed cleavage for the school day. She was dressing like an ex-girlfriend attending her first love's nuptials right down to the Maidenform push up bra. She hadn't time to question her motives. She was too busy gulping the last swallow of double-strength black coffee and shouting from the kitchen, "Janie, your pills are still on the counter! Don't call me at school later to tell me you're sick. Get in here!"

The slow cooker on the counter was already forcing a loin of pork, thyme and apples to give up their juices. Fido was curled up on the big bed waiting for their neighbor to come by at noon to give him quality time. Tim sat in logjam traffic on the Grand Central Parkway envisioning a Mets triumph as his Toyota crawled past the Shea Stadium East & West exit. Soon Jane and Wendy would join the family's daily motion by racing to the car that would take them to their schools. It was a simple domestic scene that plays out everywhere in the world. Wendy appreciated the serenity of suburban life but she couldn't help wonder what it would be like to have more.

By 8:15am, Ms. Dale and class 6A1 were on their way to the cafeteria. Two years ago, 'Big Mary' Schulmann, Einstein's head cook cornered Ms. Dale while in the throes of a Percocet high. She wiped her thick rough hands dry on the front of her food-spattered apron before taking a city banned cigarette out of her pocket and motioned to the teacher to follow her. Teachers are rarely asked to confer with kitchen staff on any level, but Big Mary took a liking to this lunch coordinator, mostly for not 'putt'n on airs' like the others. She led the teacher to a tiny locker room off the teachers' cafeteria. As soon as the door closed behind them, she lit up. The curls and wisps from her Newport co-mingled with the stench of ten thousand former smokes. Ms. Dale managed a friendly, "What's up?" while forcing down her nausea.

"Lookit, Claire told me your kid is real sick and you're running to the hospital every day after school to be with her."

Mary's Internet pills were causing her to slur her words but her concern touched Wendy. "So, what I'm saying is that there's a lot of leftover food from breakfast and lunch. By law, we gotta throw it out but you could always say you took it outta the garbage. Then it's OK. You're not really gonna get it from the garbage. I'll make up a nice package for you every day. This way you ain't cooking for you and your old man late at night. Wendy spontaneously took the huge woman's free hand and held it in her own. There were nearly one hundred people working at Albert Einstein and Wendy could count the number of those who were kind on Big Mary's bratwurst fingered mitt. The two women spent the rest of Wendy's prep time discussing their German roots, Mary's father's side and Wendy's mother's. Just before the passing music began, Wendy asked if there'd be enough breakfast leftovers for a class of thirty-three.

That's when she created Breakfast With Billy. She led her first period class to the kitchen each morning to select from the day's leftover cereals and milk, biscuits and eggs, reheated croissants and seasonal fruits. Her charges preferred it to the free breakfasts offered before school since there was no stigma of poverty attached. The children, on cue called out "Thank you, Ms. Mary" to the beaming though bleary-eyed cook and then, like a page out of Ludwig Bemelmans, <u>Madeline</u>, the children followed their teacher out in two straight lines.

"Boys on the inside. Girls on the outside protecting them. They're such delicate creatures!" the teacher teased. Back in their room, the chairs surrounded an old gym bench creating what Ms. Dale dubbed Story Corner. Her students were instructed earlier they had only five minutes to eat and talk with their friends. They could continue to eat throughout the lesson but not chat. Trays were not to be thrown out till class was over and then only in the blue can outside their room. Two <u>monitors</u> were selected; one to answer the phone the other to switch off two of the room's three light fixtures. 'Billy' Shakespeare's play was about to begin and Ms. Dale was setting the mood.

Even though they had till Monday, nearly all her students held up their books when asked to show they'd been covered. Ms. Dale held her copy in both her hands with the spine facing up. The iridescent flecks in her polished nails shimmered under the Department of Education's long ballast ceiling lamp as she held the front and back covers out like bat wings. "Shake your books like this." She said while shaking hers like a saltshaker. Thirty-three books shook. "Oh, oh look. Blood is dripping out!" She stared at the floor in such amazement that even the most unimaginative adult entering their room would have sworn the pages bled. The teacher became a weaver of dreams as she conjured up visions of murder and betrayal emerging from the imaginary viscous red pool. The spell was cast.

"What do you think they're wearing in this story?" she asked in her teacher voice. Little hands waved to her. She wouldn't remember all their names till next week. Her eyes found a tall freckled faced boy in a saffron polo.

"You, yellow shirt, your mother didn't really name you yellow shirt did she?"

Several children looked down to check their clothing.

"What's your name, kiddo?" she asked.

"Brian Edwards. Togas." he was enjoying his stardom.

"OK, Brian Edwards Togas, what were they wearing?"

Brian smiled till he blushed while other boys vied for the spotlight.

"Brian," she confided as if they were alone. "I had a student named Brian long before you were born. He's at Harvard now. He wants to be president someday. I named him Bri-Bri. Do you know he still likes to be

Bird and Fish

called Bri-Bri. You'll be my new Bri-Bri from now on. Is that OK with you?"

The new Bri-Bri nodded yes while his classmates begged for nicknames.

"You are right. They wore togas. But not everyone wore the same toga. We're all wearing shirts but everyone's is different." Thirty-two, one girl was absent; pairs of eyes scanned their neighbors' attire.

"What about uniforms?" Which Romans would wear uniforms?"

The enchanted children hadn't guessed this was a classic pre-reading activity. Find out what they know then learn what they need to know. In this case, they needed to know how Marullus and Flavius learned that the two commoners were a carpenter and cobbler. Scene i would take the whole period. The language was new to them and none of them knew what a cobbler was.

A Chopin Mazurka began. The children left the room reasonably clean for the next class. 6A2 would have to be appeased with the last of the Midgees, since the kitchen crew was now busily preparing for the lunch crowd. The jokes were the same as was the laughter. Julius Caesar conquered yet another world. This class boasted a round-faced comedian named Kenny Han who called out *"Hambok"* when asked what Romans wore. Wendy Dale laughed with the class. Her Jane would have done something like that. The class ended with only Ms. Dale knowing that Marullus and Flavius were doomed.

The teacher was cleaning two Midgee wrappers from the floor when the classroom phone rang. "Ms. Dale's room." She used that greeting so often occasionally she'd forget her surroundings and answer her home phone that way. "Ms. Dale, you have a doctor's office on the phone. Can you take it now?" Two words in an otherwise cheerful message made her heart pound. She answered, "Sure." but she was sure of nothing. 'Janie's in school. Her school would have called if she were sick. My mother? She's probably still sleeping'. The phone clicked twice. A woman's voice, sounding already bored at 10:10am, "Ms. Dale this is Chrissy from Community Radiological Associates and Affiliates. Your mammography shows calcifications that are suspicious. You'll need to come in. When are you available?"

A daydream covers a lot of ground as it meanders from thought to thought at its relaxed pace, but panic races through our heads like runaway trains. You try to make some sense of the flying images but the break-neck speed won't let you. The teacher tried to decode the words; calcify like in milk? Milk ducts? No, that's calcium. Think! Calcify like in hardening. Like chalk? Chrissy from the doctors' office repeated her last sentence. Wendy heard her own voice say, "Today. I can come now." Screw work. The receptionist had her hold for a time then came back offering a 3:30 appointment. "No problem." She assured the caller, but she could feel a terrible ache crawl from her groin to her belly signaling danger. The last time she felt that pain on her left side was the morning Jane shouted her awake with, "Mommy, there's blood in the toilet bowl." Now the pain wrapped around her waist again like a nightmare's serpent trying to cut off her air supply.

"Breathe, Wendy." She instructed herself then spent the rest of the school day performing the roll of teacher and lunch coordinator. She told no one at school. She hadn't even tried to reach Tim. When she called Lucille Dale at lunchtime it was her usual, "Hi, mom. How are you? I'm fine. Tim's fine. Janie's fine. Your granddog is fine too. OK, Mom, I have to go back to work. I'll call you tomorrow". She once joked to Libby that these were really 'Mom are you still alive?' calls. Besides what would any of them say? Wendy often played a mind game she called My Own Best Friend. In it she pretended she was a friend giving herself advice.

"It's probably nothing. Are you going to make yourself crazy all day? You'll see. You worried for no reason." That's what her best friend, would say. But the woman in the black embroidered suit wouldn't believe a word of it.

The '98 Sentra rode past Anycolor Paints ten minutes after dismissal. It wouldn't have caught the storeowner's eye anyway. He was in the midst of a sale with a local contractor whose spec McMansion on Handly Street was ready for decorating. The contractor expected a solid quarter million in profits and artist turned entrepreneur, Mr. Hyun wanted to relieve him of some of his net gains that afternoon. Jae was bored by the customer's color selections, Barely Beige and Super White. There'd be no ardor in this too large house. His gaze fixed on the pre-made mix under the counter. The red haired woman understood color. Let's hope she understands time as well. He shook off her memory while he led the contractor to the Purdy straight and flat brush display.

Paper jacketed Wendy met her new technician, a thin black woman with close-cropped hair. "Come here, baby." She beckoned as she fed Wendy into the machine. She even showed her Tuesday's original pictures on a light box. "See, they're like dandruff flakes." Wendy inspected the tiny white confetti on her x-ray. Nothing looked dangerous here. Maybe they'd let her off with a warning. Something like "Go on a low-fat diet till this clears up." But, after she dressed she was shuttled off to the radiologist's office. The doctor's diplomas and awards on her wall didn't excuse her from a terrible fashion sense in Wendy's opinion. She was all angles and lines like her waiting room. Her mousy brown hair was cut to look like Three Stooger, Moe Howard's. Her royal blue suit must have witnessed the doctor's sudden weight loss for now her slender shape was hidden in the oversized jacket.

"The amounts of calcifications are more than usual for a woman your age." She began. "They're also forming a swirl which is an indication of cancer. You'll have to have a Stereo tactic core needle biopsy. I do those here.

Bird and Fish

I'll send you back to the waiting area so you can make an appointment." Wendy no longer heard her. The rest came out like the trombone sounds the grown-ups made in Peanuts cartoons. "This woman is using the C word. My own mother doesn't say that word."

She remembered her fifteenth summer in Pine Tree Grove, New York. Lucille Dale invited a friend from a nearby town over for lunch. The two forty-year olds were gossiping when the neighbor asked about Lucille's mother-in-law. A frightened Wendy watched as her mother shook her head, no, then silently mouthed, "Cancer." And now this scrawny Dr. Whatever was using that word in front of her, about her. "Do you have any questions?" the radiologist asked. With her temples throbbing, her throat tightening and her knees shaking, Wendy Dale managed a quiet, "No. I don't know enough about this to ask questions, probably later." then she politely smiled and left the tiny office. Back in the waiting room, she was given a biopsy appointment and handed a booklet containing a hideous drawing of a woman lying prone on a table with her breast dangling from a hole. It looked like an S&M pornographic comic book. Wendy took four steps towards the doorway then turned back. She re-approached the row of fleshy dead-eyed receptionists and cancelled her brand new appointment, then she tossed the vulgar handout on a waiting room coffee table and left.

Wendy Dale was neither a vegan nor a tree-hugger. She didn't believe in acupuncture, acupressure, reiki or holistic approaches to anything. She was going to have this procedure but not at that place. She already associated it with bad news. Besides, Wendy couldn't even remember the radiologist's name just her full-of-herself remark, "I do those here." like she was hawking facials.

When she pulled into their driveway, Tim was picking the last of the Sweet 100's off a withering tomato plant. She walked directly to him in the garden. Her big Irishman, his eyes crinkling up for a smile noticed only her empty arms. "Hey, where's the paint?" he asked.

The words toppled from her lips like blocks kicked over in a playroom. She pointed and he nodded while the couple moved two folding chairs from the patio to the driveway away from Jane's bedroom window. This was becoming their secrets' ritual. It was where, for the past five years, they discussed how to tell Jane the new puppy, Fido IV, was dying. It was where they rehearsed explanations of Grandma's slurred speech and lazy left arm and weighed the benefits of telling Jane the seriousness of Crohn's disease. Now they sat knees to knees facing the likelihood of Wendy's cancer. In Shakespeare's tragedy, the gods took no pity on mighty Julius and Calphurnia. In Floral Oaks, Queens, the one true God tendered no mercies for the little lives of Wendy and Tim either. The two moved their chairs back in silence till Wendy, in a voice like eighth grader, Son Ha Yoon's urged, "Don't tell Janie."

Grown-ups stop looking forward to weekends at about the same stage they start dreading snowfalls. The two occasions become work demands when adults grow into homeowners. It was the same for Wendy. Saturday or Sunday, she still woke at five, stepped out of her silky rose pink pajamas and pulled on her velour bleached stained sweat suit. She tightened one of Jane's scrunchies around her hand-held ponytail forcing her russet red locks to the top of her head. The teacher looked like an advanced image of Pebbles Flintstone as she sat in her breakfast room making a memory out of a diet English muffin dripping with oleo and homemade lemon lime marmalade. After rinsing off her dish and knife, she would attack the bathtub with scrub brushes, bleach and scouring powder. She'd spray and wipe every mirror in the house then spray and polish every piece of furniture. Dusting this time of year was even more arduous since ceramic pumpkins, patchwork scarecrows and wooden skeletons crowded every available tabletop. She'd sweep the kitchen and parquet floors with a straw broom then make a return trip with a soft cloth. She deemed them clean enough only after going through the house with the Swiffer Wet Mop. Between stripping the bed linens from their beds and dropping off Jane at her Science project buddy's house, Wendy defrosted and prepared ground turkey for the workweek. She seasoned and palm-rolled meatballs to serve with catanisella lunga in a homemade end-of-summer marinara sauce, then mashed and patted onion soup mix, ketchup, Italian bread crumbs and egg into a turkey loaf that Jane would sneer at and Tim would gobble up. Wendy washed the ground turkey flesh and toasted bread remnants from her hands to vacuum the rugs and run a towel wash. Unwilling to revisit yesterday's conversation, she cleaned and tidied every room in their seven-room house. Tim, had a quick coffee then enjoyed a morning's lie-in in the freshly made bed sure that his wife worried needlessly. Wendy was equally sure Tim was wrong.

By late afternoon, she was done. Tim finished the sports section of The Daily News, poured a third cup of hazelnut-flavored coffee and thumped barefoot to the downstairs den. "I'm watching the Metsies", he proclaimed to his wife and dog. He wouldn't be seen upstairs again till Wendy shouted "Dinner" from the top of the steps at five. Usually this meant Wendy could chat with Koreanwiz or check out Koreandramas.net.

There are Drama Fan Runboards from the Big Apple to Hawaii filled with non-Korean netizens who like Wendy acquired a passion for *Hallyu*. The Korean Wave of entertainment had landed on U.S. shores. Five hundred years after the first Americans greeted Columbus, was now re-enacted by an Internet committee including Little League moms, college students and a plethora of young men both gay and straight applauding the new invaders' arrival. But, today Wendy re-wrote lesson plans, placed most of Jane's summer shorts and tees in the Worshipful Light of Brooklyn's Clothing Drive bag then cut and froze hands-full of sage, rosemary, thyme and chives from her garden. She filled a Hefty sandwich bag with thyme sprigs and marked it, 'For Libby'. Wendy had to keep working. She couldn't make any enquiries or appointments till Monday and time to think was unthinkable.

"Tim", she called from the top of the stairs, "What's that expression? 'Work shall make you free'?

"No", he answered without turning his face from the TV, "it's 'Work Will Make You Free'."

"What's that from, again?" she asked off-handedly.

"It's on the overhead sign at Dachau, the Nazi death camp." then to the screen he yelled, "Oh shit! Did you see him miss that?" Tim noticed his empty 'Spooktacular' coffee mug and added, "Red, could you make me another cuppa?" She padded downstairs and back up like a ghost. While stirring sugar into the Halloween cup, she muttered, "I'm so stressed, I'm quoting Hitler."

⌘ ⌘ ⌘

Jae Won might have preferred weekend cleaning to his self-imposed servitude. His cousin and partner, Yujin Kim was nearly ten years younger and should have gotten the less desired schedule. But, Yujin had two daughters and a formidable wife whom Jae Won tried to placate. The young wife liked to socialize with other young couples on the weekends, so Jae obliged. This was only half the reason.

Four years ago, after a lifetime of beating back her depression demons, Jae's wife Jung Son Choi began heeding them. Yujin caught an eighteen-hour flight to Incheon airport just to offer his support. When Jung Son threatened suicide, Yujin wired money to help with her care. When she made good her threats, Yujin convinced the widowed Jae Won to sell his apartment and invest in New York. The younger cousin was delighted to have his childhood idol as his partner and Jae Won was eager to leave his sorrowful past on the other side of the world.

While local hardware competitors were closed on Sundays, the mega-home supply chains were choked with long check-out lines made up of neighborhood contractors and handymen, leaving north-east Queens with an unserved market.

With one partner available weekends, Anycolor Paints could serve the community seven days a week. Americans loved to spend their weekend's spending money. With Jae Won and Yujin sharing the days, their customers could be obliged.

While Jae Won read the rules that shaped his life and accepted them, Yujin saw life's opportunities and coveted them. Yujin had a passion for Kareoke and Charm soju. His home boasted top of the line electronics including a 1080p plasma television, Blue-Ray player and Apple Power Book computer. Like magazine featured CEO's, he acquired a beautiful trophy although sometimes bossy wife.

Yujin found life in the US suited his personality. He was staying. He knew when his days finally ran out there'd be no mountain burial mound for this son of Chosun. His heirs could plant his tired ass out on Long Island.

Jae Won enjoyed his happy, daring cousin. His own parents were dour people who took tradition seriously. They were blessed with their only son late in their lives and assumed it was to fulfill their plebeian dreams. His teachers at Tae Myung Elementary School noticed the artistically talented boy immediately. They assured his parents he could be the next great Minhwa artist. The Hyun's were appalled. "Let someone else's son be a starving painter."

They reminded anyone who'd listen of Jae Won's *Dol*, his one-year birthday celebration when he selected the book.

As was the custom, their baby was dressed in a handmade Dolbok and traditional hood. He squirmed on his parent's couch in front of a low table that held a book symbolizing a scholarly life, money to predict riches, rice for a career in government, a sword to lead him in battle and thread signifying long life. "*Abdul*, pick the book." his mother called out when the baby's chubby hand ignored the scholar's symbol, so she dropped a brass tray of sweets on the polished floor. The startled baby blinked and changed his direction. By the time the rice cakes were packaged for the guests to take home, Hyun Jae Won's parents were content his fate was sealed.

He would be a respected teacher, husband and father in that order. No discussion. Actually, before his mother's 'accident', he was reaching for the thread.

The boy savored pigments the way great cooks taste food. A chef's palette decides his genius and Jae Won was no different. To him, basil, lemon grass and sage were colors he could discern and catalog. For young Jae Won there was nothing more pleasurable than mixing greens and whites to create celadon like the delicate pottery of his homeland. He'd play with combinations of yellows, grays and greens till tinctures of melon and feldspar sprung from his paper.

He was the best kite-maker in his grade. Even the older boys knew Hyun Jae Won made the coolest cloud busters. Color was his genderless best friend. At *Hong Eek* College it would become his mistress. Since he was resigned to a parent-selected bride, he didn't bother dating. His nights were spent in dizzying passion with his art.

To appease his parents, Jae Won painted solely for his own pleasure. He became one of three Art teachers at Kyung Gee Seoul High School and for a while hoped he might become mentor to an extraordinary student who would fatefully appear in his class. Instead, he spent his teaching career working with untalented passionless teenagers, depleting his days like widows knit, quietly waiting to die.

Bird and Fish

On Sunday morning, the ache in Wendy's belly awakened her. She rubbed her side as she tiptoed from the bathroom into her kitchen. The robust aroma of her just made coffee let her pretend everything was as it should be. She sat down with her cup, a stack of bills and checkbook to jockey numbers for nearly an hour. When she was through every account was paid in full and the book balanced. Even Jane's astronomical medical bills uncovered by their insurance were met on time. Back when Wendy stopped dreaming of literary stardom, she also stopped envisioning what perks that would bring. She had eased into a little life with old cars, unfashionable cell phones and clearance rack shopping at discount department stores.

Wendy woke her husband with a shoulder rub, showered then headed out to the supermarket on her weekly pilgrimage. By the time she returned, Jane was standing at the kitchen counter in her flannels sharing a handful of Cheerios with Fido. "Sit down and eat." Wendy scolded in her mommy voice.

"No, Mom. Remember, I have Crohn's Disease. I sit down after I eat." The girl waved her hand behind her bottom in a mock dispersion of odors. "Comedienne." Wendy chided as she placed two soymilk containers in the fridge. "What's for dinner?" her daughter asked even though she'd eat only a tablespoonful of protein and a fist-sized portion of starchy carbs at their evening meal.

"Roast chicken, couscous with almonds and apricots, and green salad with feta. I bought Mac's so, I'll make applesauce too."

"Mom," Jane put her arms around her mother's neck. "Could you make those round biscuits you made last week?" The pain in Wendy's side was nearing a fevered pitch. "Baby darling, I haven't sat down yet this weekend. How about *you* make Pillsbury crescent rolls?" Wendy felt guilty whenever she vetoed even the most insignificant request from her daughter. "Well, Ma if you're gonna slack off we'll have to trade you in for two twenty-two year olds." "Two twenty-one and a half year olds if you don't mind." came Wendy's swift reply.

Wendy finally brought in the Deli-counter filled grocery bag to Fido's delight. The scent of fresh sliced honey ham and chunks of blue and Parmesan cheeses were making the black and tan tail-wagger jubilant. Jane took a slice of ham and hand-fed the hound. That would be all the care she'd give him that day except for rubbing his ear with her toes while she gossiped on her cell. Wendy busied herself in their cramped New York kitchen. Cabinet doors opened and closed, shelves took on new residents and finally the empty bags were folded and stored for post-Fido yard duty later. She worried for her family. As wife and mother she was always slaying dragons for them at the castle gate. Would this latest monster cross the moat and turn her to ash.

Lifting himself from his lounger, Tim climbed the stairs to the well-stocked kitchen. "Janie, Can I watch the Jets today or am I chauffer guy?"

"Oh, I forgot," Jane responded, "Can Courtney eat with us today? I promise she'll go home by seven."

Before her husband could quickly green light the request, Wendy sighed.

"By 6:50 this evening I intend to be showered, in my nightie and watching 'Seoul 1945'. I think Kee Hee is going off with the ROK guy and I don't want to miss it."

Her daughter and husband's glances locked on each other. Soon all three were laughing. "Make fun of me." scolded Wendy. "Meanwhile, my drama addiction led me to a free trip to Korea, *Ah rhuh suh?*" In fact, she knew they were proud of her.

"Sunday dinner is at four sharp and Courtney is back at her house by 6:30." Tim took a plastic bag and his dog out to the yard. Wendy turned her thoughts and her gaze to her daughter. Jane was tall and willowy like her dad's parents. She had untamed honey blonde hair that flowed past her shoulders and Princess Di's soulful down turned eyes. Wendy's Jane was an honor student and trophy-winning swimmer. Sadly, now the same teachers who praised her as a wunderkind before her illness would shake their heads and whine, "Well you know, she's missed so much work." Her swim coach was still mulling over her permission to return. Before Jane's diagnosis, Wendy smugly judged other children by her daughter's success. They never matched up. But when Jane spent more of last December in Queens Hebrew

Hospital than school, Wendy felt as if it was the death of her perfect child. She hadn't stopped loving Jane, but she missed feeling cocky. It was why 'Fatso' Casta's remark still stung her. Three years ago Wendy could have answered back, "My daughter's planning a trip to Rangoon or Zanzibar or Mars." But now she wondered if Jane would ever plan a dream excursion with the shadow of a flare-up always lurking. Whatever the definition of flare-up was to others, Crohn's sufferers used the term to describe the severe lower right abdominal pain, fever, bloody diarrhea and even vomiting. In Jane's case, it had once included a fistula grown so large it impeded her ability to walk. Surgery as a stop-gap for her remission was their only option.

The house phone rang. Jane bolted from the kitchen toward the bedroom answering machine, "Mom, it's a lady from the Korea Times." Wendy salvoed back, "Just let the machine take it, I don't have time now." "Mom, she said they're running your DMZ article on Friday." Mother and daughter met in the still unpainted hallway to high-five. Wendy opened her bedroom's back window to tell Tim. Her husband tossed a felled lilac branch to Fido, stood with a half filled grocery bag in his hand and called back, "Good job, Red." It was a bit disappointing. She hoped he would have at least put down the bag of dog shit while praising his wife.

Late that night, while her family slept Wendy made a telephone to-do list for Monday. Call Dr. Goldberg the surgeon to make an appointment. Just in case.

Call Tri-County Radiologists, the ones who diagnosed Jane, for a biopsy appointment ASAP.

Don't forget after-school department meeting.

Paint store???

The weekend was over. The teacher, after downing an Ambien with a shot of Pathmark Diet Ginger Ale, squeezed herself into bed trying not to waken her wheezing dog or snoring husband. Perhaps if she had heeded the fourth commandment she would have been rested enough to sleep.

The first Fido was a wired-haired terrier bought by Wendy's parents when she was five. He had a pet shop dog's personality, content to eat, sleep, and poop. Still he allowed the kindergartner to hug and kiss him, making him well worth his exorbitant price. Wendy's mother would tolerate the dog only if her husband fed him daily and a professional groomed him monthly. Every first Tuesday, Greg the Groomer would fetch the squirming pooch, wash, trim, brush and cologne him then return him at dinnertime.

Fido I would dive under the kitchen table and hide for a full hour then, at the first opportunity, scoot out the back door to roll on the lawn retrieving his proper scent. For the first time, Wendy understood the premier Fido's dirt rub as she held the gift-sized bottle of Pleasures in her hand. This wasn't her scent. It was the first indignity of an undignified day. She tossed it into the wastebasket and left for work with only the slightest essence of her Korean made Charm Zone soap to say she was a woman.

⌘ ⌘ ⌘

Ms. Dale had just moved her time card over to the In side when she heard her supervisor call her name. It's probably the school setting that makes teachers quiver like students when summoned by their principals. She turned with a false smile on her lips wondering what she did wrong. "Good morning Mr. Rubinstein." Wendy knew the gaggle of teachers at the time clock was enjoying her imagined offence. "How can I help you?" her hand unintentionally rubbed her left side as she followed an Oleg Cassini outfitted Ira Rubinstein into his office. While the principal stood in tonsorial splendor; well-tailored gray pinstripe suit over a slate Calvin Klein shirt, lemon silk Nino Cerruti tie paired with a matching pocket handkerchief, his office was a jumble-sale of programs and state test information, textbook salesmen's freebies and family photos. Perhaps, his message was look at the man, not the title. Still, the teacher didn't get comfortable. She stood three steps from the doorway, her knock-off Coach handbag still on her shoulder. "How's the assembly going?" asked her boss.

"Tryouts start Wednesday." She knew her assembly wasn't the reason for this get-together and remained standing.

The principal took note of her body language and headed straight for the purpose of his meeting.

"All these parents leaving their kids off at the crack of dawn, I don't blame them. My wife and I both worked when our sons were small. It's tough. But now I've got the superintendent *hocking* me about safety issues. He wants a teacher out by the play yard at 6:50 every morning," The principal checked his watch. "It's only seven now. You'd only have to come ten minutes earlier than usual anyway." A second look at her blank expression and he quickly changed his tack. "It would mean that you'd clock out after your last lunch duty. On club days you'd have to come back at 3:45 for Drama. But during the rest of the week you'd be out of here at 1:10." Ms. Dale had to keep herself from whooping like a mating crane.

"Won't the union demand an SBO for this?"

Ira Rubinstein's brow furrowed. "I don't give a shit about your union. I'm well within my purview when it comes to school safety."

Wendy Dale had no reason to turn down his offer and the thought of time for a second job, errands or even a manicure at 1:30 on a school day was alluring.

"When do you need me to start?"

The principal's facial muscles relaxed. "Friday, I want the regional office off my back by Monday."

A grinning Wendy Dale exited. "Cutting out of school early, Whooeee. Things are looking up." She raced up to Libby's third floor homeroom to share her good news. "Hey, Ms. Lib, got some time to be jealous?" Her good-natured friend looked up from a mound of 6B1's journals.

"Why do we make them write their feelings? They're eleven years old. Who cares what they feel. They should be reading the classics to find out what really intelligent people feel, not purging themselves of puppy envy. No, I don't want to be jealous. So, what happened this weekend? One of your Korean leading men jump out of the TV and kiss you? By the way, nice outfit, the green goes good with your hair."

Wendy chuckled at her frazzled friend. "No Korean lovers I'm afraid but Ira just gave me AM Duty and I can leave at 1:10 every day!" The younger teacher was divulging the details, when her mentor broke in. "I hope this means you'll use your time wisely by shopping and getting mani-pedis. I know you Wen, you'll probably do volunteer work or worse, get another job." Libby watched her friend's expression change. "You *are* getting another job. I've had two careers too but I had the decency to have them at different times. For God's sake, why take another job?"

Wendy smiled at her dear friend who never bragged about her real-estate mogul husband or their showcase home in exclusive Munsey Park. Libby, owner of a summer home in the tony Hamptons as well, worked because she loved teaching. Wendy taught because she loved eating regularly.

"Just a little Christmas money, I'll stop before the first snowfall, really."

Ms. Dale's third period prep began with her comforting a whimpering Jeffrey Kirk. The eleven year old came to class with an uncovered copy of Julius Caesar. If the teacher had been informed that Jeffrey was a 'Nickelby, No Child Left Behind' from The Queens Park Housing Projects, she would have cryptically offered a free book cover as prize for any answer he would have given. His foster mom had five other children to tend so a Drama class book cover wasn't a priority. The sobbing boy wanted so much to please the new teacher who nicknamed him 'Preacher' after explaining his name meant 'church'. Wendy kept him after class, cut her gray paper shopping bag to size and covered his book. Money was scarce when Jane was little and a frugal Wendy learned to make book covers in every shape and size from grocery bags, gift-wrap and Daily News comic sections.

"See, no more naked Roman" she said then wrote out the boy's late pass. Preacher was still heading for stairwell C when Ms. Dale called Dr. Goldberg's office. "Dr. Goldberg retired years ago." Someone named Caroline explained. "I could get you an appointment with Dr. Gaspare. He's really good." Wendy made her appointment based on Caroline's testimonial knowing it had all the validity of Macy's cosmeticians pushing wrinkle cream. Procuring a next day core biopsy with Dr. Jeanne Ahn at Tri-County Radiologists followed. This was no easy feat. Next day medical test appointments are seldom available in America and never in New York. But, having already gone through every bitter medical ordeal imaginable with Jane, Wendy had learned a trick or two. Some offices save time slots for VIP's. It's not a distinction one wants to attain. It generally means that particular patient is very sick perhaps hospital-bound or doctor and patient are otherwise well acquainted. In a performance befitting her Drama position, Ms. Dale flattered and implored an unwitting receptionist into a recently cancelled four o'clock the next day. Wendy was a bit concerned when she failed to disclose taking daily aspirins and vitamins but she wanted this over with.

⌘ ⌘ ⌘

The next day after school, the teacher turned into a patient. She chose her own counsel as her guardian for the procedure. When a technician asked if she was accompanied, she lied "My husband's waiting in the car."

For the third time in two weeks she undressed from the waist up, hid her bra under her folded blouse, donned a paper gown and was pressed into yet another x-ray machine. While still in her radiology costume, she was walked to the procedure room. A nurse asked her to lie belly down on a table then guided her left breast down a bottomless hole. It seemed to Wendy that there were actually two holes with a speakeasy style sliding door to accommodate either breast. The nurse in the room busied herself in silence so Ms. Dale was left to her imaginings. Finally the need to communicate overwhelmed her. The body on the slab was going to talk just to prove she was more than a test.

"Is Dr. Ahn Korean?" Wendy asked. The nurse was startled. Was she expecting the lamb to go silently or was this an unusual patient question. "I don't know. I know she's oriental." New York City teachers work in the most politically correct environment outside of Washington D.C. Wendy was offended by the term since she was taught Easterners are Asian. Rugs are oriental. "Why do you want to know?" the nurse questioned.

"I speak a little Korean. Ahn is a Korean name but I guess she could be married to a Korean." The nurse whom Wendy would learn was Kathleen Iannuzi laughed, "Oh, no. Her husband's name is Schwartzberg. So I guess she is Korean." Even with her lips and cheek sticking to the paper tabletop, Wendy shared a giggle with Kathleen.

Then the doctor walked in. "Ms. Dale," she spoke as if reading off a prompter, "this procedure is useful for findings that we saw on your mammogram. They cannot be felt through the skin. They're called microcalcifications. In this specialized procedure I'll be using computerized mammogram equipment. I'll use a mammogram paddle to compress the breast, then very carefully pinpoint the suspicious area using mammography. The area will be numbed with a local anesthetic before I make a tiny cut and insert a special biopsy probe. The probe will take several small cores of tissue and leave a pinhead sized chip in place should you need surgery. This procedure is short; it'll probably take less than an hour. You can go home immediately afterward. Leave the bandage on your breast for 24 hours. Kathleen will instruct you about showering. How are you feeling?" Wendy was trying to picture the paddle.

"*Quen sha nah.*"

Dr. Ahn's lovely sable eyes widened. "Did you just say 'all right' in Korean?"

"She speaks Korean." Kathleen jumped in as if she and Wendy were old schoolmates. "Well, you probably speak better than me." smiled the doctor. My sisters and I were born here and it drives my parents crazy that we never use our language."

The teacher smiled back. Despite her surroundings, her only thought was, 'You mean 'better than I.' Just complete the sentence. See, better than I do, not *me* do.'

A bone-weary Wendy Dale drove south on Bell Boulevard to avoid passing Anycolor Paints on Northern. She knew if she drove by, she'd feel compelled to stop.

"The owner must think I'm a terrible person and he's right," sighed Wendy. She didn't have the strength to carry her fears let alone a bucket of paint, besides the pain in her side was kneading her innards like a mean masseuse. She hoped Tim heated up the turkey loaf but she doubted it. Later that evening, she'd sob with Pure 19's lonely farm girl but when the episode ended she'd wipe her dampened cheeks and imitate Tom Hanks in "A League of Their Own" by reciting, "There's no crying in real life. There's no crying in real life."

⌘ ⌘ ⌘

Just when we think our workweek will get stuck in Wednesday, gloriously it's Friday. The school year was two weeks old. Ms. Dale was dressed like an autumnal bouquet as she chatted with students in the play-yard. She paired a fall inspired paisley silk Ralf Lauren skirt with a teal tank under a bronze Kenneth Cole leather cropped jacket. She was hoping someone would ask about the jacket since she snatched it up for $74.00 at TJ Maxx last month. An eighth grade Korean boy shouted from the handball court, "Ms. Dale, d'ya catch Pure 19 last night?" and then sent a thumbs up gesture to her nod.

Tri-County Radiologists hadn't called last night and Tim was sure it was a good sign. Wendy allowed herself to share his optimism. She enjoyed the mild gust that made the treetops whisper. She drank in the cloud free aqua sky. Sunday she'd stop at Lord and Taylor's for a new perfume and a job application but today she'd just make a quick side trip to the paint store and be in her garden by 1:45. Just thinking about her new schedule made her grin like a thief.

6A1 was a bright class and therefore a joy to teach. They were up to Act II, scene ii in one week's time. The teacher couldn't recall any other class moving through Shakespeare so quickly even with reading assignments for homework. The students were finishing the last bits of their gratis egg and cheese bagel sandwiches when Ms. Dale began her lesson.

"Who's going to remind me what we read yesterday? Bear, are you feeling lucky?" Theodore Li newly knighted 'Bear' by his teacher wiped the crumbs from his mouth with his hand. "Yesterday we acted out the scene between Brutus and his wife, Por-tee-uh. We learned that Por-tee-uh was the daughter of a powerful guy so she wasn't afraid to speak her mind to Brutus." The teacher realized the boy must have forgotten Portia's name and hastily sounded it out from his book at breakfast. She didn't have to correct him. They'd soon read Portia's name again. So before his classmates could mock him, Ms. Dale lauded him. "Excellent. Who dares to add to Bear's brilliant statement? 'Amazin', do I see your little paw waving at me?" Ms. Dale had called every female student named Grace 'Amazin'' since she began teaching. "All right everybody, for our very own Amazin' Grace, just the first line." Instantly, thirty-three, children and one teacher broke into song. "Amazing grace how sweet the sound that saved a wretch like me. I once was lost but now I'm found. Was blind but now I see." Thirty-four voices sang out while thirty-four torsos swayed.

"OK, Amazin', you're on." The teacher moved the attention to the usually quiet Grace Lee.

"She's a cutter, Ms. Dale. She tells Brutus she wounded herself because he doesn't confide in her as a husband should." The teacher was jubilant. "Amazin', you're, well, amazing." The little girl would relive this shining occasion at every available moment throughout her day. The teacher moved on to Caesar and his wife. "Has anybody ever gone to a funeral on a rainy day?" Two hands rose. "It seems like the whole world is sad because that particular person died. Perhaps we feel that nature is crying too." Three heads nodded in agreement. "It doesn't always happen that way. Sometimes terrible things happen on lovely days. Who remembers 9-11?" Every child held up a hand. "Who can tell us the weather that day?" A tall girl wearing her mother's sparkly pink eye shadow answered, "It was nice out." Ms. Dale nodded in agreement. "It was beautiful like today. She looked out the window behind her, and then back at the children to disclose, "Maybe that's even sadder, when everyone else is enjoying the sunshine. Anyway," her voice gained volume. "This scene opens with Caesar still in his nightie talking about the weather." Then affecting an upper crust British accent, she recited, "Nor heaven nor earth have been at peace tonight. Who's going to be Caesar today?"

⌘ ⌘ ⌘

Ms. Dale was pleased with today's progress. The next class was just as rewarding and even lunch duty was surprisingly quiet for a Friday. At 1:20, the teacher parked her sedan on Broward just a short walk downhill to Anycolor Paints. She checked her make-up in her rear view mirror, hid her purse under the passenger seat, turned on her cell phone and exited her car. Tinny strains of the Loveholic drama theme song rang in her hand. Wendy pressed send and said hello. The caller was Dr. Ahn. Years ago the teacher had broken the medical phone call code. If a nurse calls with results, don't worry. If it's your doctor, start combing through your insurance policy.

"*Ahn yung hah shamika.*" Ms. Dale tried to sound pleasant.

"Ms. Dale, I've gotten your results back. There were cancer cells in the calcifications but don't worry they're in situ. Do you have a surgeon?" A voice hiding in her throat answered, "Yes, a Dr. Gaspare at Nassau North. Do you know him?"

The doctor's chipper patter remained constant. "Well, I know of him. He's good. Call him as soon as you can, OK? You must pick up your records from us and from the lab before your visit. That's important." Wendy took a breath then whispered, "Yes, thank you, bye-bye."

Bird and Fish

Wendy Dale shut off her phone, continued down the hill and entered the store. The owner was still at the cash register scanning his newspaper. For a moment he thought he detected the tang of his dead wife's soap but when he turned his gaze towards the doorway, it was the red-haired woman who faced him. She was finally back. "Missus Dale," Jae Won began then opted for icy silence. She could leave her packages all over Little Neck for all he cared, just not in his store.

"I'm so very sorry for burdening you." The woman's voice was barely audible. Now that he looked at her face, she seemed pale.

'Missus, don't get sick in here' he prayed.

She moved like a listing ship, "Do you think I could have some water?" An eerie pause heralded each of her words. "I just found out I have cancer." Wendy held up her cell phone as if in proof. Jae blinked at her. He assumed he misheard her. Wendy, in turn thought he didn't know the English word.

"*Ahme ya, ahme ya.* I need to sit down."

Jae Won surprised the teacher and himself by reaching for her left hand and rubbing the pillowy section under her thumb.

"Just look at me." He crooned to her. Try to breathe normally and keep looking at my eyes." Wendy obeyed and soon felt a calm spread through her like the first sip of just steeped tea. She gently removed her hand from his and straightened her shoulders.

"*Shil smeedah*. Really, I'm sorry to bother you. I'll just take my paints."

Mr. Hyun's original anger was replaced by pity for the injured bird before him. "I'll carry them to your car." He offered.

"I'm all right. I can't thank you enough. That was so kind of you. *Gom sah hah me dah.*" Wendy scooped up the gallon can with her right hand, the two quarts with her left and exited the store as if it was just another purchase. Through the shop windows Jae Won watched as she slowly made her way up Broward looking like the burdened farm girl in Julien Dupre's painting, A Milk Maid With Cows and Sheep.

⌘ ⌘ ⌘

Episode 3: Happy Cheosuk

A steady stream of customers getting ready for their weekend DIY projects kept Jae Won from reflecting on the Dale woman's problem. His cousin, Yujin had selected an odd schedule. Weekdays he'd open the store at 8:00am and work till 1:00. He'd leave it in Jae Won's capable hands till five then return for the evening hours. Jae chose not to ask about Yujin's unusual timetable. At 4:59, his cousin breezed in, talkative as ever unaware of Jae Won's failure to join in his comparison of former soccer stars Hwang Sun Hong and Hong Myung Bo.

"*Hyung,*" Yujin continued, "did you ever go to the *Bee moo jhang jee deh*, (DMZ) like on a junior high trip?"

Jae Won managed a smile. No one could change thought strands faster than his favorite relative.

"*Ah nee mee dah. Wheh?*" He spoke in Korean to prevent Yujin from abandoning their mother tongue completely.

"There's an article in today's paper by some local American teacher. There's some weird shit that goes on there. It's funny a white lady was there and we weren't. Where's the paper?" He reached for the Korea Times still folded at Jae's last reading on the counter. Yujin licked his thumb and turned to the middle section. "Here, read this. Unbelievable. Do you think she wrote this in *Han Gul* or some editor translated it?"

Hyun Jae Won didn't reach for his reading glasses. He had no interest in a Yankee viewpoint of his homeland and only intended to glance at the article long enough to be polite. The red-haired woman in the picture smiled back at him as she did the first time they met. Her name, Wendy Dale was written in English. The rest of her opinion piece was in Korean.

"*Noe ee yuh jah ah rho?*" Jae Won asked displaying an interest he had never revealed before.

"No, I don't know her. How would I know her?" Yujin tilted his head over his cousin's shoulder. "*E poo neh* but a little old for me. Do *you* know her?" The emphasized 'you', made Jae clear his throat, "kuhumph" and ended their conversation with, "I'm going to eat. I'll see you later." Jae folded the newspaper under his arm and headed for the door.

Two neighborhood matrons were returning several wallpaper books and corralled him at the entrance. "Mr. Hyun," the 70ish woman trilled, "this is my friend." The second white haired lady smiled.

"I told her how good you are with colors. Would you be able to help her too? There's just so much to look at. It gets very confusing."

Bird and Fish

Jae Won bowed slightly. "My cousin, Mr. Kim is very talented with wallpaper. He will help you today." Before they could entreat him to stay, his cousin flashed a movie star smile their way abetting Jae Won's escape. While the elderly grannies described their kitchens in great detail, Yujin wondered about his cousin's strange reaction to the photo and why he took the damn paper with him.

Hyun Jae Won had decided to walk to work earlier that afternoon and now with the September sunlight refusing to tone down its enthusiasm, he was grateful for the time with his thoughts. Along Northern Boulevard, the upright lines and orderly rings of *Han Gul* adorned every restaurant, nail salon, dry cleaners and jewelry store window. The pedestrians included enough Asian faces to allow the forty-six year old to pretend he was home. But the turn onto Marathon Parkway, although steep enough to equal any side street in Seoul, was a return to reality. The homes were traditional Northeast American fare; Tudors, hi-ranches, capes and an increasing number of McMansions. The latest models were so christened to describe the roseate or ochre stucco and brick turreted monsters that sucked the air and blocked the sun from their neighbors. Houses that expanded from fence line to fence line of the 100X40 plots often hid illegal apartments in this R1 zoned area.

The two schoolyards he passed were silent as the dinner hour was nearing. In Seoul the soft dirt play areas behind every school would be filled with students playing as hard as they studied till dusk muted the air. Here the cemented courts were empty. 'Where are America's children?' He'd have to ask his nieces when they returned from their ballet classes later.

His cousin had met and married Yoon-Yoo Son while they were students at St. John's University. The young couple was successful by all New York definitions; educated, hard working, high-earners, Lexus GX leasers and new homeowners. But even living as well as they did couldn't replace the young husband's family back home. Yujin convinced his lonely cousin to come live with them, which pleased Yoon Yoo as well. There would be someone to help guard the house, invest in their business and most importantly be a real Korean blood relative to their already too Americanized daughters.

A pair of joggers mumbled excuses as they hogged the sidewalk while passing Jae Won. He was surprised they said anything. He considered himself an indistinct vision: just under six feet with an Asian-slender build, brown sugar half moon eyes shaded by full dark brows. The bridge of his nose ended with flared nostrils making him appear Native American at first glance. If women found him tasty it was probably owed to his full tawny lips and long black hair that would fall to his collar if not tied back daily. Along with his college hi-jinks tattoo, his strong shoulders and steeled upper arms stayed hidden in oversized shirts.

He dressed like a J. Crew mannequin, white cotton shirt above khaki cotton slacks. The look he was going for was invisibility and had he worn a contemporary hairstyle he would have achieved it. This was light years away from Jae Won's university attire. At school his glossy raven hair flowed to his shoulders and his moustache was trimmed to barbed spikes. The art student's wardrobe consisted of fluid black and white silk garments creating a persona his friends called *'Iksookimai'* after the long thin striped fish with the triple set of catfish like barbells. After a night of post-exam celebrating, Jae Won talked a friend into becoming their own canvases. The drunken young men offered the tattoo artist their requests only to awaken the next morning with each other's design. Jae Won permanently sported a long tailed dragon.

Now the former *'Iksookimia'* was enjoying the summery green mighty pin oaks he passed on his journey home. How American they were, standing like giants in the soil squares lining the sidewalk. Bold and big they called all comers to task, as if shouting to the winter ahead, "We've been here two hundred years, and you think you can beat us?" They were a far cry from the ginkgoes that lined the avenues in Seoul. Those were lovingly tied down with wire on wooden slats to protect them from the spring's torrential rains. He had not seen delicate gingko trees in three years and had not painted them or anything else for five.

From two houses away he noted his Santa Fe was the only car in the driveway. Mr. Hyun sighed gratefully. While both he and Yujin's family respected each other's privacy, it would have been rude not to call on Yoon-Yoo and the girls to announce his return. Their absence let him freely enjoy his solitude. He lifted the empty paper-recycling can with his fingertips and led it back to its shed at the head of the driveway. Then as all returning homeowners, Jae-Won eyed a quick inventory of his property before reaching for his keys.

Last year, with the help of a builder Yujin knew from church, the cousins tore down a derelict two-bedroom cape they purchased and built a high ranch. From the outside, a visitor would be impressed by the center herringboned patterned brick walk that led to circular steps topped by double oak doors with beveled glass windows. Two large bay windows flanked the entry while the second floor boasted a set of three identical cathedral windows. The exterior of the lower floor was brick washed in Brandy Creme the second story Chocolate Sundae shingled. A single carved brass mailbox to the right of the entrance displayed the hyphenated house numbers. The side door was far enough up the driveway that passersby didn't realize this lovely Queens manse with its marigold lined walkway was yet another illegal two family house.

The side door opened to a four foot by four foot eastern style mudroom complete with its owner's slippers on the top step of his living room. Jae-Won padded across the tiled foyer between his living room and blinding white kitchen and dining area. His cousin's wife had designed the new apartment with Jae's future family in mind. She considered a kitchen prep island and the latest appliances a deal maker, should he meet a woman. When Jae-Won requested a simple studio basement apartment in their new home, the husband and wife gasped simultaneously.

"A basement apartment is for a man with no plans." chided Yujin.

It was easier to go along and by the year's end, Jae was grateful for the open spaces. A semi-enclosed spiral stairway linked the two apartments to each other and the basement. Downstairs was Yujin's electronic chapel. The shared space boasted an acoustic guitar and keyboard, two computers, the washer and dryer and an IDOLpro karaoke machine newly arrived from Korea. While the family and cousin had equal rights to the underground room, Jae preferred to wash his clothing by hand when feasible and sent to the Chinese laundry when not. On the few occasions he joined his cousins for a karaoke evening, it was enjoyable, even fun at times but fun, like treacle is only appreciated in small portions.

Yoon-Yoo placed his mail on the steps between the apartments daily. Jae walked there now to retrieve a letter from an elderly aunt in Jamsil and his cell phone statement. He turned to the kitchen sink, filled an electric teakettle and took a ramen container from the cabinet. In his bedroom, he returned his hand weights to their shelf, changed into a tee shirt and sweatpants then as quietly as before returned to his kitchen. He liquefied the ramen with the boiled water and took the soup and two chopsticks downstairs.

Jae Won sat in front of his nieces' computer. He already was a man with a plan. He knew if he used the house computer, Yoon Yoo or Yujin were sure to notice. He folded back the paper lid over his ramen and balanced the bowl on his lap while typing 'Julien Dupre A Milk Maid With Cows and Sheep.' in the Google rectangle. When the painting appeared in miniature, Jae slurped down the salty noodles, studying the woman in the scarlet kerchief. Even in this grainy reproduction, Jae Won could see the milkmaid looked nothing like Wendy Dale. The girl in the painting was younger with a peasant's square chin. While he couldn't be sure, she appeared to be a brunette. The two women were fair complexioned but given that they shared European roots it was a minor distinction. There was something stronger connecting them. Jae Won drank the last of the soup stock, put the bowl under his chair and wiped his mouth with his hand. The newspaper photo of Wendy Dale still lay on his kitchen counter. He didn't need it. He moved his head towards the screen. It was right there. They were both weary yet still formidable. There was no frailty in their stalwart expressions just the tiniest allusion to trampled dreams. When the viewer turned away, that bloody but unbowed essence lingered in his memory.

Yujin had installed Paint Shop Pro 7+ for the girls one evening and their older daughter, Seromie invited the family to see her artwork. The 11 year old filled the screen with drawings of Mini Valley characters to impress her younger sister. Jae-Won regretted not paying more attention to her methods as he started with 500X500 pixels and then flood- filled the background with red, orange and yellow gradient to create a sunburst. He opened the lights filter dialogue box and later after several failed attempts added the scan of the milkmaid. The girl balancing the tin bucket contraption stood alone in the dark with the setting sun at her back. Jae Won became a magician as he presto-chango'd her headscarf into sumptuous buckwheat honey waves. Her dark eyes lightened to peridot. The maiden's white peasant blouse, jerkin and cerulean skirt were replaced with a teal tank under a short bronze jacket and autumnal shaded skirt. He pressed print and the first artistic creation by Hyun Jae Won in five years chug-chugged into a tray. 'It was hardly art, just a toy played with for fun.' He told himself as he left the site. Nearly two hours had passed since he sat down at the keyboard.

Yujin's daughters, Seromie and seven year old Ahromie arrived home. Still in their ballet leotards and tights, they called their intentions of visiting their cousin while thumping downstairs. With surprising stealth, Jae-Won slipped off his chair, poked the remote till the television opened on a KBS show, dropped himself on the black leather sofa and hid the just dried picture in his pocket. The girls seemed oblivious to their cousin's unusual location till Seromie asked, "*Kunapojee*, do you watch Pure 19 too? Even the lunch teacher at my school watches it."

Korean dramas famous for their poignant, music-swollen flashbacks couldn't compete with the day's replay in Wendy's head. When Tim arrived home at four she paced till he drove Jane to a schoolmate's birthday sleepover. Finally they sat at the breakfast room table where Wendy laid out her poisonous day between them. She spoke like a misanthrope's caricature of women, giving the minutest details but reciting events out of sequence. Tim took a paper napkin from its "BOO!" holder and wiped the perspiration from his forehead. "What are you saying about the guy at the paint store?" he tried not to sound impatient.

"I was so embarrassed. I told him I had cancer." Wendy shook her head. "He must think I'm a lunatic."

Tim wanted to shake the answers from her. "What does that have to do with anything? Stick to what's important. What exactly did the doctor say?"

His wife reiterated the phone conversation. Tim took a moment to sort out her story. "All right, 'in situ' means in place. It hasn't spread. That's good. She didn't say you had breast cancer." He was trying desperately to make this a bump in the life road but Wendy wasn't allowing it. She wanted to hit him, right on his head, right where the napkin daubed. Why wasn't he comforting her? Why did this feel like the Goddamn Inquisition? "I have to get the paint out of the trunk." She rose from her chair.

"I'll get the paint," he said calmly.

"I'm going on line to look up microcalcifications." she announced while massaging her side.

"That's a good idea." he answered as if he were talking to one of his learning impaired students.

"Would you take me to the surgeon on Wednesday. I did everything else alone. I need you to come with me." she commanded."

"It's kinda early in the school year to take a day."

His wife's eyelids lowered producing a frightening Lady Macbeth stare.

"I'll take you." he assured her then walked to the kitchen, took his keys from the drawer and headed for the Sentra's trunk. Wendy went into Jane's room where their family computer had been left on. She typed in microcalcifications and the first twenty links popped up. She clicked on a medical help-line she'd never heard of and discovered a Q&A. She didn't know which was more alarming the desperate tone of the questions or the chilling vocabulary: 'This can lead to lumpectomies or mastectomies.' 'Could I have high grade comedonecrosis?' 'Did your doctor mention Ductal Carcinoma In Situ?'

After a torturous perusal, she was convinced she had DCIS, stage 0 cancer. More reading brought her to 'Only one in a thousand calcification biopsies are cancerous.' "So I'm the one in a thousand." She mused. "If I was going to beat the odds, I'd rather it was in the lottery." Wendy heard the garage door open assuming Tim was storing the paint cans. Her head, so filled with terrifying images couldn't calculate that several minutes had passed and the door still hadn't come back down.

'I can't read any more of this.' She left the help line and visited CJK Runboard, a California Korean drama website scanning each spoiler to learn which episode would show Farm Girl and Ice Man kissing to calm herself down.

Tim O'Hanlon was a bear of a man. Tall and muscular, he looked more like a stevedore than a special education teacher. The all-female staff in his department cheered when he was selected to teach the Separate Instructional Environment students. They were the system's most violent and he was picked out of a pool of six solely by his size and gender. With frost blonde hair and Irish blue eyes he still turned heads at forty-five but he stopped looking back a dozen years ago when he met Wendy Dale. That fall the reading course he needed to complete his Queens College Master's Degree wasn't available. His academic counselor suggested he take it at C.W. Post College on Long Island. Tim entered that first class in Tillis Hall to find several worn-out teachers trying to gobble up graduate school in order to fatten their paychecks. He sat behind a middle school teacher who couldn't be ignored. She took the lecture on Bloom's taxonomy and played with its applications till the professor was impressed. The whole time she and the professor spoke, Tim couldn't get the image of garnets out of his head.

A girl he dated had shown him garnet earrings once in the hope it would stir him to gift giving. She even added that they were his January birthstone as if this Celtic lad would care. But one look at the jewel red curls cradling Wendy's pale face made him envision a garnet studded crown on her queenly head. Tim O'Hanlon would never open a conversation with a woman and to his credit, in the past there was no need but this woman only nodded when he stood up and flashed his best smile during their break. Tim returned with two cups of coffee, light with sugar and machine flavored holding one out to her.

"Oh my goodness." She replied showing a gleaming smile. "I can't thank you enough but I'm terribly sorry. I'm pregnant. No coffee for a while. Sit here by me." She pulled a folding chair a foot closer. "I'll breathe in that aroma while you enjoy the taste." Like an old fashioned record skipping, Tim's mind played "I don't care." over and over. 'I don't care' as he eyed her gold wedding band. 'I don't care.' when she patted her belly at her word, pregnant. 'I don't care. I don't care.'

It would have emboldened Tim even more that day if he had known Wendy was already in the planning stages of a marital separation. Living with the bully her mother touted as a good catch had run its course. If she never met another man it would be fine.

Six years later, Tim and Wendy married. After re-mortgaging, Wendy surprised her new husband by keeping the deed in her name only, making him merely a tenant in their little Cape Cod. Tim was grateful. With a bank balance of only two digits, he was hardly in a position to become a homeowner in Floral Oaks. At New York prices, the new husband felt Lou Gherig's speech was written for him. He could enjoy a backyard and a front lawn with never a thought of finance.

After work, they'd race home to their new cozy life. Even Mrs. Dale warmed to Tim after observing his gentleness skills with her only grandchild. Wendy was sure betting on the Irishman had paid off. But like a loan shark, happiness demands payment. Just when you think your basket is full, it comes to collect.

Jane awoke one morning with dozens of canker sores in her mouth. The couple examined her teeth, gums and lips, checked her forehead for fever and made an appointment with their dentist for Saturday. By Friday the painful ulcers were gone and the appointment cancelled. A month later, Jane was plagued with unrelenting diarrhea. Wendy fed her bananas and steamed rice. Two weeks later their pediatrician suggested a colonoscopy and Wendy made the appointment. The flux stopped as quickly as it arrived and the family planned a Disneyworld winter break vacation.

Then Jane stopped eating because her tummy hurt.

Then there was an inconclusive MRI scan and three more tests.

Finally, an overworked emergency room intern at Queens Hebrew Hospital who faced the distraught mother in the wee hours before dawn said, "I'm sorry. She has Crohn's disease." Wendy wanted to hug the weary physician, for months she feared it was cancer.

But the Crohn's gangster wanted his vig. Jane swallowed sixteen pills a day just to feel 'not so bad'. When the pills stopped offering any relief, Wendy called Long Island's chapter of the Crohn's and Colitis Foundation. Like super heroes, CCFA fought for the shattered family offering recommendations, self-help workshops and ever-present shoulders to lean on. After Jane's surgery and remission, Tim's tough guy strut returned. Life for their family trinity should have been returning to its rightful place. Except now he was standing in a darkened garage crammed in with a forgotten pile of lounge chair pads and stored automotive supplies, bicycles and Christmas decorations unable to let go of the paint cans from his grip. The big man finally released them to the cement floor.

As much as he liked his stepdaughter, when she was ill he feared mostly for Wendy. His wife's ocean green eyes muddied, her cheeks paled and her weight fluctuated wildly as she binged or starved as a coping mechanism for Jane's illness.

Tim had enjoyed being on his own since high school graduation but he dreaded a return to a life without Wendy. Without notice, he balled his hand into a mallet and unmercifully pounded the stack of chair pads. Whap, whap, whap, a full minute went by. "You are not going to leave me, Red. You are not going to leave me." The pounding became a drum accompaniment for his words till Fido, tired of the squirrel mocking him from the neighbor's yard entered the garage to check on his master.

Wendy was already in bed when Tim and their hound returned. He judged her early Korean show was over by the timer light on the VCR. It was gearing up for the ten o'clock drama. For the first time since their story began, Wendy pretended to be asleep. The big Irishman in keeping with his own cultural bugaboos pretended along.

When she heard Tim's steps on the den stairs, Wendy sat up. She knew he would fall asleep in his 'Archie Bunker' chair and not return to their room for hours. Wendy didn't take sleeping aids on the weekends. It was her feeble stab at healthy living. She quietly marked homework papers, "Design the Set for Brutus' Backyard in 100 Words" in the blue-gray television light. At 2:20, the pencil dropped from her hand onto the polished wood floor as she slipped into her four-hour night's sleep that the rest of us would label napping.

Less than five miles away, a sweat soaked Hyun Jae-Won woke from a nightmare. His dream took him back to

Palgongsan, a mountain area he hiked and painted as a young man. The opal twilight was collapsing into darkness but he needed to visit the *Gunwi Triad Buddha Grotto.* He had stumbled but rather than fall, a pale hand reached out to grip his elbow and right his stance. He turned to thank the stranger but instead faced his dead wife. Her dripping wet hair fell like hematite sleet from her head. Each icy lock was replaced by an auburn one springing from her scalp like growing seedlings. Her skin was as white as her hemp *hambok.* Jae Won tried to run back down the path but the bottoms of his feet began to burn. Roots as thick as ginseng grew from his calloused soles, anchoring him into the *Taebaek* trail. His own moans awakened him. Jae sat up waiting for his normal breathing pattern to return. Regaining calm, he entered his kitchen to drink water from his kettle spout. Yesterday's Korea Times was still on the counter. Once again he looked at the smiling woman's photo.

"Wendy Dale, who are you and why are you haunting me like a *Gweeshin?*"

Sunday morning found Wendy humming and flipping chocolate chip pancakes at her stove. Her pity party had ended thanks to a triumphant return to the Floral Oaks swim team by non-other than Miss Jane Dale Pierce. Yesterday, Janie beat the Speedos off the Glen Bay girls. Her effusive coach downed his crow fairly easily after Jane led his team to victory. The day got even better when Jane's friend Courtney let slip in the car that a certain seventh grader named David was 'Jonesing' after her daughter.

Years ago Libby told Wendy that mothers are only as happy as their children and today Jane and Wendy were happy. And if that weren't enough, the house was clean, the homework graded, a Lord and Taylor job application was on her bureau topped by a circular ringed bottle of Insolence her luscious new fragrance from the house of Guerlain. One spritz in the busy store made her feel like a movie star on a comeback. She stepped away from the stove, put her nose to her wrist and breathed in her new scent. "Uhmmm." "Jane, Tim, breakfast."

That afternoon Jane, Courtney and another friend, Caitlin were chattering and giggling in the girl's room. Tim was cheering on his beloved Mets while Fido, barred from the preteen domain, lay sleeping under the dining room table. Wendy took the ingredients she bought at the local Korean market and began to make an Americanized kimchi. She sliced, salted, rinsed and drained a head of Napa cabbage. The passionate cook made a marinade of rice vinegar, sugar and hot chili paste. To that she added grated ginger, garlic and scallions. She poured the mélange over the cabbage mixing it lightly with a plastic gloved hand. Wendy scooped the mixture into a new plastic container and placed it on the bottom shelf of the refrigerator far from questioning eyes. A voice in her head asked why she hid the kimchi but it wasn't answered.

The cabbage dish certainly wasn't traditional but it was tasty and she was eager to show the Anycolor owner her appreciation. Wendy had already written and sealed by hand her thank you note:

"Two thumbs up for your quick thinking! Thank you so much for your care and compassion. Very truly yours, Wendy Dale" and under that in childlike *Han gul,* "*Gom sah hah me dah.*"

Tortured souls are always grateful for Mondays. They welcome the time restraints on their morbid thoughts. The teacher luxuriated in the bustle of a busy day; early morning duty, teaching, assembly rehearsal, lunch duty. All had to be performed under the scrutinous eyes of children. 6A1 and 6A2 clamored for their returned homework assignments like street children begging GI's for Hershey bars. The badly kept secret was that Ms. Dale inflated their grades. She would add up grade averages and then sprinkle extra points on top like sugar. "After all," she thought, "Drama grades don't count so, why not have a number a child can point to with pride?" At the start of her third period prep, the teacher sat alone in the still classroom, taking inventory of the colorful student generated samples that already covered all three bulletin boards. In a few minutes the student-actors from the assembly's Tiger's Whisker segment would bound into the room for rehearsal. Last year she had rewritten the Korean folk tale into play format and was eager to see how it played. Her hand had just reached for her desk drawer when angry shouting blasting down the hall reached her open door. Teachers share a professional courtesy when it comes to discipline. If a colleague raises her voice to a student, so be it, as long as the raised voice isn't partnered with "stupid", or "idiot" or worse. The chancellor's regulations regarding verbal abuse specifically mention language that tends to belittle or subject students to ridicule. Easy for him to say, he's never been threatened or called a "cunt" by a teenager twice his size.

The shouting grew even louder and was teamed with slamming doors. Wendy recognized the teacher's voice, Ms. Foster, ninth grade Western Civ. The woman was fifty-four with thirty years of teaching experience and graying hair in a single long braid down her back. The eternal bridesmaid gave into the crankiness from her lowering estrogen levels making her the school curmudgeon. "Where do you think you're going?" Slam. "I'm calling the dean. Let him deal with you. Get in here!" Slam. Foster's screeching and the whoosh-bang of the door bounced from tile to tile along the hallway. Ms. Dale stood listening. "You mother fucker, bitch, I tol' you not to play me. Why you always playing me?" It was RayShawn Wilson, a morbidly obese, bronze skinned senior whom Ms. Dale taught three years earlier. No matter what was occurring now, Ms. Dale knew him as a sweet natured child who apologized when reminded to take the pick out of his hair and thanked her when he repaid forgotten lunch money. She took a step towards her doorway planning to intercept him but the hulking boy showed amazing speed for his girth and was already at the hall's double doors. There

Bird and Fish

were two rapid thunderclaps followed by a sound like spring hailstones on a driveway. RayShawn had beaten the netted glass door insets with his fists. A spider web pattern of broken shards was mostly trapped in the octagonal netting. Some pieces managed to escape and lay glittering at RayShawn's size twelve Nike's. Ms. Dale raced to the boy's side. She held his wrist keeping his cut hand away from both of them and walked him, her hand on his immense back, into her classroom. She rinsed his knuckles at the sink and wrapped his fist with a fresh paper towel. The pair sat on the Story Corner bench together as easily as they did when he was her sixth grader.

"Now, I'm gonna get suspended 'cause of her. You watch, Ms. Dale. That nasty bitch gonna suspend me." Tears flooded his eyes making it hard to see his former teacher's intentions.

"Listen to me RayRay, in a minute the dean is going to storm in here followed by the security guard. Whatever trouble you're already in is going to get much worse. Right now I don't give a rat's rear end what went on between you and Foster but destroying school property is a big deal. You just keep crying and let me do the talking. When I'm finished, you'll repeat exactly what I said. Are you getting this, RayRay?"

Even after the 2006 Amish schoolhouse debacle, an M.S.347Q teacher's only outside recourse when faced with threatening situations or unruly students is to use the classroom telephone to inform the school's main office. A secretary will then use her desk walkie-talkie to alert the dean. Luckily for RayShawn, the whiny Ms. Foster and the nasty school secretary had an ongoing feud over the teacher's missing time card. So when the secretary coolly informed Dean Hemmings he was wanted yet again by Ms. Foster in the basement, he felt no urgency to abandon the serial cell phone abuser he was chewing out in the third floor hallway. Claire Jackson, while making her first floor rounds also heard the call and ran down the nearest stairway. The twisted glass and wire window greeted her first. As she pushed open the adjoining door, she heard Ms. Dale's instructions to RayShawn Wilson and sussed out a fair estimate of the occurrence. RayShawn wasn't exactly a choirboy but, like Wendy Dale, Claire saw goodness in the child often missed by other staff members.

Wendy was glad to see Claire enter first. It would be her report that decided RayShawn's fate. "What happened?" Claire asked.

"Some crap. RayRay cover your ears. I may have to use cuss words. He got into it with Foster and she called his mom even though he made up the work. He says, when the white or Asian kids hand in late work, she lets it go. I don't know."

Claire watched as Ms. Dale's left hand pressed a circle pattern into her side. "You get hurt?" RayShawn joined his teacher in a resounding, "No." The security agent looked down at the seated student. "You a damn fool boy." As if on cue, Scott Hemmings entered the classroom followed by eight boisterous Drama students ready for practice. He turned back to his followers and asked them to wait outside. "What's going on?" The portly defender of order asked. Ms. Dale placed her hand gently on RayShawn's shoulder in protection.

"RayShawn and Ms. Foster were discussing his late assignment. He got so upset when she told him she had already called his mom, he thought he was going to throw-up. He ran out of the room but, when he got to the swinging door, you know how those doors always stick Scott, it wouldn't open. He panicked and pushed it too hard,..."

The teacher paused to give RayShawn time to take it all in.

"...on the glass part. Thank God he wasn't hurt."

'And my mother didn't want me to be a writer.' mused Wendy as she continued her tale.

"I've got to rehearse with my kids. I'll take them to the auditorium and stop by the custodian's office to take care of the glass. Are you feeling better, RayRay?" The now composed boy nodded his affirmation. She turned, grabbed her script and exited. Claire Jackson locked her eyes on RayShawn. "That's the whole story, right?" She looked back innocently at the suspicious glower of the dean. "You don't have to write this up, Mr. Hemmings.

I'll just give you a copy of the one I gotta send my supervisor." Scott Hemmings rubbed his hand over his stubbly chin. He was attempting another beard to distract eyes from his balding pate. This wasn't the first time he chose bullshit over truth in the name of peace. It certainly wouldn't be the last. "Thanks Claire. I'll take RayShawn to the nurse to look at his hand. We'll call his mom from there. Do me a favor. Just tell Miss Foster to stop by my office when she gets a chance. No hurry. Come on, son." The classroom snatched back its silence. It would remain empty till last period when the 'room-share' French teacher would cover Wendy's board with idiomatic expressions ignoring his students tearing apart 6A1's Drama projects on the back table.

⌘ ⌘ ⌘

Once years before her troubles, a perky Wendy Dale sat opposite her principal at an assembly program meeting. The planning was going well when in a gesture of camaraderie; a jovial Ira Rubinstein shared a bit of unwrapped school gossip with his favorite sixth grade teacher. "Ira," she giggled, "everybody already knows that." The principal was astounded. "Really? How can that be? I just found out this morning." Wendy tapped the side of her nose with her index finger. "There are no secrets at 347." There still weren't any. By the time the eighth/ninth grades lunch period arrived every student regaled Ms. Dale's good deed. The usual bad boys roughhoused less. The shrieking girls seemed more demure and even the thievery was abated. But while the students cheered Ms. Dale as their ombudsman, many of her colleagues considered her a traitor. The best part of leaving early meant she didn't have to defend her actions in the teachers' lounge.

Early that morning with the same care she had put into her apparel selection, she cut the half-price tags off a new cocoa and aqua silk scarf that would serve as a *bolgagi*, the Korean wrapping scarf and tied the corners around the kimchi's plastic container and thank you card. Wendy nestled the package between Jane's after-practice water bottles in the Nissan's trunk cooler. Later she stood on Marathon Parkway bending into the car's cluttered trunk gently removing her prized package. The teacher placed the scarf wrapped container on the seat beside her as gently as she buckled in a younger Janie. She folded her olive and gold pinstripe peplum jacket over the passenger's seat, scanned her olive tights and olive ribbon and leather heels for runs or scuffs and drove northeast to Broward Street for a new parking spot. The department store application lay on the back seat giving Wendy her excuse to be a tad over-dressed. After she turned off the engine, she reapplied her lip-gloss and sprayed a quick shot of Insolence on her décolleté. Wendy covered her silk and lurex scoop necked sweater with her suit jacket, cuddled her gift and stepped onto the curb like a golden magi in the fiery breaths of September's sunlight.

⌘ ⌘ ⌘

We've seen it in soap operas often enough, the winsome but wearied leading man stands alone on the sidewalk looking out on a jaded world while the love of his life quietly passes behind him. Only this time it was real. Jae Won had just left his shop with Sujeong Lee. The wealthy newlywed had parked her Capri blue Mercedes-Benz SUV directly in front of the store at the bus stop to pick up two dozen double rolls of faux bookshelf wallpaper. She spoke in Korean explaining to the obliging storeowner that this would be a surprise for her husband. She was creating a study for him in their new home. Mr. Hyun busied himself by smiling back and carefully placing the heavy tubes onto her car's backseat and floor. His smile trapped his opinion. *Ah keh shee*, this paper is *mot seng kyut dah. Ah rhuh chee?* Ugly.'

Neither the bottom half of the bending man nor the Korean speaking young woman standing at the luxury car held significance for Wendy. She entered the empty store and walked to the counter at the back. The teacher respectfully called out, "*Sun jang nim* then posed facing the backroom door in silence. Jae Won re-entered his store. A beguiling scent of early spring irises and mountain violets jarred him till he followed it to the once again smiling Missus Dale. He smiled too. This time his sealed lips held back the words, 'If you were my woman, I'd have you wear that perfume all the time.'

"I came to thank you for the other day." She used her parent conference voice, respectful yet authoritative. She didn't want his pity. She needn't have worried. Two decades of quashed emotions began bubbling up inside him and not one of them was pity.

"*Quen sha na?*" Jae Won placed himself behind his counter to appear relaxed.

"I'm fine, really. It's just a bit of bother. I just heard, you know, that word and got thrown. Really, I'm fine. I wanted to give you this to show my appreciation." She placed the package near his elbow.

"It's a very American version of kimchi. We like everything instantly. No fermenting in jars over the winter for us."

He couldn't get his mouth to stop smiling. "Did you like the *ongi* when you were in Korea?" Jae Won wasn't sure that was a proper sentence.

"Did I tell you I went to Korea?" Wendy asked.

"*Ah nee*. I read your article in the newspaper. Your Korean is very good." At first she didn't understand then she placed her hand demurely over her mouth and laughed. "I wrote that in English. Someone else translated it. My Korean is very poor."

Jae Won finally lowered his gaze; "I think your pronunciation sounds really good." Wendy reached across the counter and teacher-patted his arm sending shock waves from her palm to his rock hard bicep and back. She pretended not to notice.

"*Sun jang nim*, my father could imitate any language in the world. When I was little we would have long rambling conversations where he would sound French, German, Chinese, Indian and I would have to answer mimicking his sound first and then changing accents. I grew up believing all daddies and daughters played that game. So when you hear me speak Korean..." the teacher looked furtively around the store as she did in her classroom the first day of school. "I'll tell you a secret, *bi mil*, I probably only know a dozen phrases but I say them very well. You're not to tell my students." She linked her pinky finger with his, put on a serious expression and said, "*Yak soak?*" Jae Won was as delighted as her sixth graders. "*Yak soak.*" he repeated.

"I'm off to get a job. Thank you again." She turned to leave.

"Aren't you a teacher?" he asked.

"Yes." she replied, "But this is New York. Everybody hates teachers. Whenever we ask for a raise, somebody in Manhattan shouts, 'You don't work summers!' and we're turned down or have our hours extended. I've got a little girl and Christmas is coming. I'm offering my services for two hours a day, some evenings and weekends if I must." Wendy had only taken a step when the storeowner's thoughts escaped into words.

"We need someone here to read our paperwork and make sure the English is good." The teacher turned back to the storeowner.

"Really? I'm a licensed English teacher. Should I bring in my resume?" Jae Won was swimming in uncharted waters but he couldn't stop talking.

"It would have to be cash. We're not reading resumes. The job is yours if you want it. This is our quiet time of the day, so you'll be able to concentrate." He stuttered through the last sentence. "When can you start?"

The teacher tried not to wince thinking of her Wednesday appointment. "I can start Thursday, one thirty to three thirty, if that's all right?"

The question of salary was never broached.

Two of the gardeners who worked at the corner house on Broward stood outside Anycolor Paints' door. The taller man needed window caulking for his whistling bedroom windows and asked his friend how much money he could borrow. Their Spanish banter brought Wendy and Jae Won back to the world.

"That's fine. You can park behind the store. We have a lot."

"Thanks but I'll leave that for customers. I guess I should know your name." Wendy was tempted to hold out her hand for a business-like shake but opted not to.

"*Yeh, yeh*. Hyun, Jae Won, my name is Jae Won. My American friends call me Jay." They were plausible lies.

The only person who would call him Jay stood in front of him and as of that afternoon, he had no American friends. She walked towards the men entering the store then tossed her hair as she looked back.

"I know I don't look like a good cook but I am. Try the kimchi. I'll see you Thursday. *Chal ees suh.*"

"*Jhal ga.*" He answered as if they were colleagues at Kyung Gee Seoul High School.

Ten years earlier when the numbers of Korean students began to swell the ranks of Einstein's student body, Ms. Dale was invited to attend a New York Korean-American Parent Association dinner. After a convivial evening of singing, dancing and music the likes of which the European-American educators had never witnessed before, Wendy had been the lucky recipient of an orchid plant door prize. Two days later one of her grant proposals had won her an all expense paid workshop weekend at Chicago's National Louis University to present her literacy model. When the NY-KAPA president called to congratulate her, Wendy had voiced her surprise of being so blessed twice in one week. "But of course it would happen." the president admonished. "Koreans believe good luck brings good luck."

By the time she had reached her car, the jubilation of their affable exchange was raised to even greater heights by her firm belief that the ease in which she landed this job would bring more good fortune.

'Wednesday is going to be child's play. I've done this before. I hate it when people call themselves cancer survivors. A survivor is someone barely breathing on the side of a road. Me, I'm going to be The Cancer Slayer.'

Inside the store, Jae Won was wrapping up the sale at breakneck speed. The customer handed the owner seven dollars in crumpled singles and assorted coins. He was still thirty cents short for the four tubes he needed. Jae Won waved the air with the back of his hand signaling he'd forgive the loss. He was desperate for a quiet place to sort out his thoughts which were now crammed confusingly together like the mess in a kitchen junk drawer.

He had to compartmentalize the events that just unfolded. He had arranged to keep her close but to what end? He wasn't sure how he would inform Yujin. He didn't dare think of Yoon Yoo Son's reaction. Of course he would pay Wendy Dale out of his own money but how many days could he keep up the charade of old business correspondence passing for something important even if he emptied every file cabinet drawer in both stores? For most of his life, he had been a healthy functioning man with desires he could tame yet nothing about his feelings was familiar. He blamed her. Why was she so casual? How could her hand caress his arm while her lips spoke offhandedly of a childhood memory? He unwrapped the kimchi container and burped the top's corner. The native aromas of garlic and cabbage chased each other to his nose. The replay of her last words "I know I don't look like a good cook." made him inhale the air around him back to his mouth in a traditional Korean gesture. 'I know one thing for sure. A woman who says that knows she is beautiful.'

⌘ ⌘ ⌘

If all the lies children told their parents and parents their children were written down, the pages would surely reach to Pluto and back again. The morning of Wendy's pre-surgery consultation, Tim and Wendy had contrived a professional development meeting they both had to attend in the city. Jane enjoyed the relaxed atmosphere at the table. Even though Fido received the lion's share of her egg and toast breakfast, it was pleasant to be served. Wendy had even laid out her school uniform on her bed. Her mother often doted on her, so nothing about this morning's activities seemed ominous. Tim even offered to pick up Courtney for school as well if Mrs. Dunbar could get her daughter ready on time.

Later, as if a celestial stage manager called out, "Cue the rain." the sky's cotton candy clouds turned gray as New York snow. The first dying leaves flew like birds, under and over the treetops on invisible gusts. Even the plastic light-up Halloween bats on Wendy and Tim's front windows awakened and rap-tapped on the glass. The couple drove to Manhasset, Long Island's up-scale community made up of beautiful homes, high-end shops and a dose of hospitals and physician's offices. The multi-surgeons' waiting room kept the secrets of its occupants. The man whose colon had to be removed sat across from the teenager with the unbecoming mole. It made for a calm atmosphere. Some patients were there for minor surgery and their relaxed moods elevated the ones of those less fortunate. Wendy handed over her pictures and lab reports only to be given another packet of forms and HIPA warnings. Tim read the latest Thomas Harris book with the concentration of a Talmudic scholar, as if his own life wasn't scary enough.

Wendy's name was called and a smiling Scandinavian blonde nurse guided her to an examination room. The teacher once again undressed steeling herself for the groping by the next stranger. Dr. William Gaspare was pleasant. The exam was quick. The nurse stayed in the room for the doctor's protection. Wendy wasn't offended. She was a new patient with no recommendations who could have been a crazy lady about to cry, 'rape'.

When she was told to dress and wait in the consultation room, she asked that her husband be informed. Tim was waiting for her when she entered. Dr. Gaspare blandly explained the imminent surgery.

"It's an out-patient procedure. The surgery itself takes about a half hour. The most important aspect is that we get clean margins. That means there are no leftover cancer cells after surgery. If there are, we have to go back and do the procedure again." Wendy shivered and sideglanced at Tim who was nodding like a bobble head doll.

"What the Hell is he agreeing with?" she wondered. Then she remembered how he repeated, "Uh huh, I see. Good." to Janie's doctors while they delivered their horrific soliloquies. This was Tim's coping mechanism. 'Lord,' Wendy asked in silence. 'Why did you send this man to me if all I can offer him are fears and sorrow?' Dr. Gaspare cleared his throat. Some women opt for mastectomies to insure it doesn't return. That's certainly an option. I recommend the removal of the cancerous cells followed by radiation. Wendy blinked twice. She was tracking her brain's shut down. Right now she couldn't define any of his vocabulary.

"Radiation, is that when you get sick and your hair falls out?"

Tim and the doctor said, "No."

The doctor continued.

"Radiation is a treatment you have every day for five weeks. It makes you very tired but not sick. What you have is not that rare. About one in two hundred and fifty women are diagnosed yearly."

'So much for the veracity of the Internet.' "Is this DCIS?" she asked.

"We'll know more, after the surgery." was his non-committal reply. Her little list of questions stayed folded in her jeans' pocket.

"Our daughter just had surgery last spring. She has Crohn's disease." Wendy interjected as if he would gush, 'Oh, in that case forget about all this. You've been through enough.' Instead Dr. Gaspare smiled and stood before saying, "Your daughter's surgery was a lot more difficult than this. You'll see."

In the car, while the wipers kept time with her pulsating side pain, Wendy heard Tim ask, "Did you really not know what radiation therapy means?" She stared ahead envying the rain crying down the windshield. "I knew two weeks ago. I just can't process everything. I had to make sure of only one thing." Tim stopped at the red light on Northern Boulevard and Lakeville Road. He rested his hand on her knee. "What's the one thing?" Wendy's leg muscles tightened. "That the treatment was something I could hide from Janie."

The Queens School for Gifted Children adhered to their strict dress code. Both girls and boys dressed in khaki slacks and navy cotton golf shirts with the school logo, 'Mens sana in corpore sano' above their hearts. Jane entered the house like the gusts outside. In her bedroom her uniform flew from her body and onto the Burberry plaid carpet in a pile at her bare feet. For a moment she could glimpse the foot long scar that began under her navel and traveled to her hipbone in her wall mirror. With the poise of a beauty pageant contestant she averted her eyes and pulled her wayward curls through a scrunchy at the top of her head. The pre-teen tossed on a worn XXL Big Apple Anime Fest tee shirt and plowed through her homework. The beckoning emanations from her mother's baked ziti led her to shout above the ipod earphones and closed door, "Is dinner ready? I'm starving."

Janie sat between her mother and stepfather chattering on about her English assignment. We have to write what we think the school motto means. You know, "A healthy mind in a healthy body" only I don't have a healthy body but I don't want to 'share' my Crohn's story at school." Tim dropped a forkful of pasta into Fido's bowl near his chair. Through daily practice, the dog managed to retrieve it without disturbing any of the kibble surrounding it. "You don't have to tell anybody anything. Why don't you approach it from the standpoint that a person should respect his body by not doing drugs or smoking and value his mind by reading and studying." Jane pulled at a bit of bread crust. "Yeah, that's what I was thinking. Wendy left her daydream to join in. "Why not look up Juvenal. He wrote it. Look in Satire X. See what he has to say. I'm sure it's translated on the Internet. Everything else is." Tim and Jane turned to the woman at their table. "How did you know that?" Tim asked.

"I'm a teacher. We're supposed to know everything."

The family laughed.

"How'd it go for you guys today? Was it boring?" asked Jane.

"It's always boring." Tim answered quickly.

Bird and Fish

Wendy poked at her salad. "They change teaching methods every few years yet your generation comprehends no better than grandma's. For thousands of years teachers used the Socratic Method and their students learned. Believe me nobody offered anything new today." So add another page to the parent lies making their way back from Pluto.

That evening, Pure 19 went on at 7:06. Iceman's mother slapped Gukhwa, the farm girl across her face with a crack that startled her American fans. The poor teenager crawled back to her rooftop room sobbing to the strains of the melodic theme song. Opposite Gukhwa sat Wendy Dale, upright in her bed weeping. Her tears dropped from her jaw line making uneven aureoles on her nightgown. The farm girl wasn't the only one to get slapped today. Wendy wiped her face with her fingertips. She turned on the table lamp and walked to her closet. The time relegated to thoughts of pre-surgery, surgery and post surgery were over. Perhaps it was more than chance that led her to an all black ensemble of a narrow leather skirt and silk shirt. Perhaps it was her mood sticking in its two cents worth.

Our personal schemas often separate us from each other. While Wendy deemed her outfit funereal, tomorrow Jay would see elegant black. For a thousand years, his ancestors wore white during mourning. The silk, leather, silk, leather of her blouse, skirt, hose and shoes would hold no sad connotations but rather delight him in appreciation of her application of textures.

⌘ ⌘ ⌘

While their daughters slept, Yujin and Yoon Yoo whispered to each other in bed. Usually the couple spoke in a coded English-subsidized Korean to exclude their children. Tonight they spoke in English in the remote chance they'd be heard by their cousin two floors below.

"I think he found someone." His wife whispered.

Yujin was tempted to turn on the table lamp to fanfare the startling news,

"*Moh*? Because I also think he's been acting strange since Friday."

"Didn't you tell me something about an article in the newspaper that made him snap at you?"

"That was nothing."

"What if I told you the same newspaper was on his kitchen counter when he left for the store this morning. Don't look at me like that. I just peeked for a second. There's something else. There was a sort of computer picture of the same woman folded next to the newspaper."

"The American woman?" Yujin leaned over his wife and turned on the light. "*Gom bah hess sum nee dah*. When he left the store, he took an old fashioned Korean wrapped package out of the mini fridge. Why would the American woman give him that? Maybe he was bringing it to her."

"She can write in Han gul. She wrote that she was in Korea. Maybe she made him lunch. You know if you look at people like that, your eyes pop out. Anyway it only took me a minute to read that little article."

Yujin rubbed his pointer finger across his left eyebrow. "When I got to the store, he told me he hired a part time worker to help him with his English. I didn't tell you because he said he was paying for it himself. Jae Won with an American woman, oh my God."

"*I goo*" his wife repeated in Korean. "with red hair."

⌘ ⌘ ⌘

The insults to Ms. Dale's injury began early on Thursday when the payroll secretary took her doctor's note from her hands and smirked, "It's good ya have a note 'cause he..." her pale rabbit eyes rolled till her irises pointed to the principal's door. "doesn't like it when teachers take off so early in the school year." Wendy knew by lunchtime every secretary, school aide and kitchen worker would know she had been to a surgeon. By three o'clock, the news would reach the teachers and security staff, which meant she had to tell Libby and Claire before noon.

A gaggle of Korean girls cornered her in the play yard. "What dramas are you watching, Ms. Dale?" The teacher looked at each adorable face. Their ginger beige complexions were smooth and clear. Their hair like fine silk cords hung neatly to their shoulders. The girls were speaking in English and Korean so quickly they rivaled the chirping sparrows in the red oak trees overhead. Their laughter was infectious. Ms. Dale joined in with her synopsis of the popular royal family drama, Goong. "Why do you like that one so much?" asked a seventh grader.

"I think we often lock away the best part of ourselves. I guess Goong reminds me that there's a prince or princess with just the right key. He'll come and unlock the door inside me setting my real soul free." The girls hushed themselves till the bravest of them offered, "You should write a story like that, Ms. Dale, like you write your plays for us."

While the other girls agreed, Chopin's Polinaise cut in.

"*Cham gon mon.* Wait. Remember do your best today. *Ahn myung.*" The teacher waved. A little girl with buttonhole eyes remained at her side while hundreds of students talked and walked themselves into the building.

"I didn't try out for the dance part of the assembly but I take ballet. Can I audition just for you?" She wasn't one of Ms. Dale's students. The teacher correctly assumed the child felt comfortable making the request since she viewed Wendy as her lunch teacher.

"Of course, sweetie. Meet me third period in the Drama room."

Suddenly, the white throated sparrows run-wayed off the treetops, circled above them and headed southward.

Bird and Fish

The teacher and student tilted their heads towards the brilliant aquamarine sky while shielding their eyes with their hands.

"I have a painting of birds like those in my room. My cousin was an artist. He made it for me when I was born."

"*Chung mal?*" You're lucky. There are no artists in my family." Wendy's hand gently moved a narrow sheath of wayward hair from the girl's face to behind her ear. "I'll see you later.

Once during a late April storm, a baby bird roosting in the front yard's Japanese cherry tree had fallen to the ground. Wendy watched from the safety of her kitchen as a half dozen birds flew round and round the traumatized nestling while 'tu-weeping' and tweeting songs of encouragement. After a few minutes, Wendy put on her raincoat and hat and braved the rain. She scooped up the bird, climbed the tree to the nest and guided the little fellow in.

Most of the people she knew would offer consolation and reassurance but in the end who would scoop her up and guide her?

⌘ ⌘ ⌘

Wendy Dale sat perched on an unpadded stool behind the counter of Anycolor Paints II. She was greeted like the peasant's daughter in Rumpelstilskin. Not with straw to spin into gold but rather a pile of bills of lading, business proposals and agreements from which she was to glean grammar and syntax errors. It was hardly a formidable task. She had often graded and edited scores of test papers in a single sitting. Her new boss placed a small orange juice container near her work and chivalrously took her purse from the floor and placed it on a bottom shelf. Most of his time was spent with customers and restocking shelves. She couldn't help notice he seemed too quiet and worried he had changed his mind. Perhaps this was her last day here as well as her first. Actually, Jae Won was so flustered when she appeared at 1:20 in her narrow leather skirt, he rethought every word he might say to her then opted to forego them all.

He had planned to use the back restroom ten minutes before her scheduled arrival time so not to ring out the sound of his urine hitting the bowl while she was in earshot. Her early appearance curtailed his schedule making him even more uncomfortable since he envisioned their two hours filled with him stuttering nervously and breaking wind.

After two hours, Wendy finally found an error she deemed noteworthy. "Jay, there are two different dates on this proposal. Which one is correct?" He knew he should stay at the mini-blind display and ask her to read the discrepancy out loud but he followed her voice and beckoning wild iris scent to be near her. Jae Won leaned over her shoulder as Wendy pointed to the error. The store was quiet yet neither heard Yujin Kim stepping in from the backroom. It rattled Jae Won enough that he failed to question Yujin's startling change of habit. With the charm and confidence of a Korean superstar, Yujin walked directly to the conferencing couple. He offered Wendy an American handshake, which she readily took and matched his strength. "Ah, our new English tutor, welcome. You're the famous teacher, Wendy Dale. I'm Jae Won's cousin and partner, Yujin Kim. Wendy quickly stepped off the stool and stood. She wasn't sure what he meant by 'English tutor' but she was schooled to respect her supervisors. Besides he was the prettiest Korean man she had ever seen off screen.

Not even after the rigorous labor of re-damning a flood zone during his stint in the ROK army made Jae Won as drained as he felt now. "Wendy," he began. "I forgot that Mr. Kim and I have to meet early today. It's time to go anyway. I will see you tomorrow, OK?" Wendy was glad to hear she still had the job. "Absolutely, Jay. It was good to meet you, Mr. Kim." She reached down to fetch her oversized black handbag from under the counter. Unlike his cousin, Yujin felt obligated to enjoy the bending skirt and its owner. He melodically added, "Please call me Yujin like Jay does." then in a childish stage whisper, mouthed, "*Ung dengee.*"

Wendy smiled politely and exited quickly. Once past the corner windows she told the air around her, "Nice going, Mr. Kim. Did you really think a middle school teacher in this neighborhood wouldn't know the Korean word for 'rear end'?

The shop's door re-opened bringing the Handly Street contractor inside. Before he spoke, he noticed the owners staring out the side window at a red-haired cutie in a tight skirt. He joined them in silent appreciation. After a purchase of two more Purdy's, he left.

As soon as the cousins were alone, Yujin, in a falsetto voice teased, "Absolutely, Jay." It was worth cutting short his afternoon gallivanting for this moment.

"*Ha ji mah*, Stop!" Jae Won's admonishment was swift and angry. Yujin quickly withdrew his intrusion.

Wendy sat in her car without turning the engine key. A terrible sadness filled every breathable space of the Sentra's interior. She had plucked the most obscure worry from her mind and pondered it. She longed to express one simple reflection and couldn't think of a single person she could tell. Finally she took her cell phone from her bag and tapped key 7. "Hi, Libby. I just finished working at the paint store. The owner... he's the loveliest man." she told the electronic voice. She pressed 'end' and listened to her own voice mail. Another unfamiliar female introduced herself as Alexandra from Nassau North Hospital. Would she please call back at extension 1155 to make her pre-op appointment. Dutifully, Wendy obeyed. She was instructed to go to the ambulatory pavilion for pre-procedure testing at no more than five days before her surgery. Dr. Gaspare's office had scheduled her procedure for Wednesday, October 4th.

The teacher checked the UFT calendar she kept in her purse. She had already written 'Korean Thanksgiving' in the date's little square. "Happy Choesuk. Happy crappy Choesuk." she sighed and turned on the car's engine.

⌘ ⌘ ⌘

Episode 4: Papa's Thousand Voices

Yujin Kim was a superb juggler. The 'wife' ball stayed highest in the air at all times, circled by his daughters, cousin, in-laws, business and occasional girlfriends. Every day of his life he could depend on his cousin to love and value him and yet he pulled an adolescent prank that surely would be destructive to their kinship. In the store, Yujin bowed sincerely to his cousin's glare, offered, *"Mee ahn hah dah"* and left the way he came. He drove south on Little Neck Parkway barely aware that he had to be back at Anycolor II in less than two hours. Stopping at home was the obvious choice. Yoon Yoo would scold him affectionately, and then ask for details as if he were describing a sumptuous business dinner. He'd have to recount everything the teacher said and what she wore. The second part was easy. His wife would then remind him of his schedule and perhaps after a cool drink or a quick conjugal visitation, he'd be returned to his commerce a happier man. Instead, he lit a Marlboro, turned west on to Horace Harding Boulevard heading for the eastern end of Flushing and the foolishness of a dead end dalliance.

The four-family apartment building was middle class and tidy compared to the tightly packed tumbledown architecture of downtown Flushing but still a far cry from bucolic Floral Oaks. He parked the company's Entourage in nearly the same place he had driven from earlier while in a lustier mood and took two bottles of Charm soju from his trunk cooler. He was buzzed in at the stainless steel lobby door and opted as always to use the stairs to the second floor apartment. He repeated these motions nearly three times a week down from an earlier five, yet he had no keys. Yoon Yoo would smell a key like a prized hunting dog on the trail. He pressed the doorbell aware that just last spring the woman inside would have been waiting at the door after his lobby buzz-in. Yujin pressed the doorbell till its owner opened the door. Mary Oh was petite even by Asian standards and while attractive, was no match for Yoon Yoo's soft features and soulful eyes.

"Ohpah, did you forget something?"

It wasn't lost on him that she didn't invite him inside.

"I forgot another round." he quipped and held up the two familiar green bottles.

"Did something happen? Did you get caught?"

This was becoming another embarrassment.

"No, no. I have to see an associate nearby and I'm too early." Clearly, it was the wrong response.

"Ohpah," Mary no longer melted at the vision of this tall handsome man with dyed golden highlights in his hair and toothpaste ad smile. "I have to go to work. Go to a diner for coffee if you have to kill time. I'll see you Monday. OK? Monday." In respect for the better times, she waited for him to have the last word.

"I may not get here Monday. I have a meeting. I'll see."

She was finally able to shut the door. Yujin wasn't disappointed or surprised. Love affairs always end the opposite way they begin. Light a sparkler. Get blinded by the stars shooting from its core like silver hummingbirds. When the fire bottoms out, you're left staring at a cold blackened remnant that can be seen all too clearly. He sat on the top step of the stairwell taking two swigs from one of the bottles reliving the afternoon. He couldn't even remember why he had planned the backfired joke. The same Jae Won who gave no response while he apologized and bowed his head, was a God to him when they were children. The older cousin ran faster, swam stronger and could make toys out of scraps of paper. Once, the year he turned five, his father and uncle had gone fishing and brought home a giant Snakehead. The grownups laughed as the women cleaned and gutted the fish for stew. Yujin placed himself in a corner of the kitchen and began crying at the thought of cannibalizing the eight-pounder. Jae Won was the only one to notice. The older boy led his baby cousin to his room where within minutes he recreated the fish on paper restoring it to its former majesty forever.

Hyun Jae Won was always a filial son and later a doting husband to a sick barren wife. Yujin took another swig and grimaced. Yoon Yoo was prettier than ever, capable, a devoted mother and loving partner. So why couldn't he stay faithful? He tapped the emptying bottle lightly on the banister support, "*Com beh*" he toasted. "In one afternoon I betrayed two people I love. Oh God, and I was rude to Jae Won's friend. She's probably good for him." He got to his feet and back to his car. He would have to face his cousin again today but first a quick stop to Anycolor Paints I to startle his manager, Yoon Yoo's younger brother.

"The best part about wearing a school uniform" Wendy Dale often told her daughter, "is when you need a really hot outfit, we have the money and time to shop." Wendy delighted in sharing her consumer savvy with her daughter and while Jane's taste ran more to Seattle grunge than her mom's Queens' chic, she still loved recreational shopping with her mother. Unfortunately, Jae Won Hyun's self imposed work uniform of khakis and cotton twills left him feeling out of synch next to the fashionable Missus Dale. He stood staring into his closet for the first time since college only this time what he faced seemed like another man's clothes. Yujin's childish actions yesterday still stung otherwise he would have gone upstairs and borrowed something more stylish. He would have to buy more eclectic garb so his new employee wouldn't see him as a boring businessman in his boring business. Finally he located a black on black silk dress shirt which he paired with black wool pants. The feel of silk on his still well developed biceps let him erase the last two-dozen years temporarily.

Wendy's Ambien wore off at 4:30 that morning, giving her ample time to select her day's apparel but the looming images of her surgery proved exhausting. She didn't have the gusto to change handbags. Yesterday's black Via Spiga would decide today's outfit. She chose simple black trousers with a starched white cotton blouse. She'd supplement the subdued selections with onyx button earrings and the faux Bulgari onyx and gold necklace she purchased in *Itaewan*. If she could see into Jae Won's bedroom this morning the English teacher would no doubt be reminded of O'Henry's Christmas story since both she and her new employer had just dressed like each other.

The store's lull had begun earlier than usual giving Jae Won time for the bathroom and time to spare. He sat at the counter reading the newspaper but found himself going over the same sentences till be grew bored. He sharpened the pencils he left for her and then selected one to doodle on the edging of a neighborhood flyer. He was sketching a carp twisting itself into a semi-circle as if morphing into the right half of a Yin and Yang symbol when she returned to him. "Well, Mr. Snow, here I am." she announced as she walked to her assigned seat and placed her bag on its shelf. He had no idea what she was saying.

"It's from a famous American musical called Carousel." she told his quizzical expression. "A woman sings about the day the man she loves will marry her. So what do you think this expression means?"

Jae Won wanted to be right. "I have arrived?"

She waved her pointer finger at him and winked. "Excellent. It means I am here."

If you need your trousers hemmed get a tailor. If you want your shrimp butterflied, ask your fishmonger but to have something explained so that you finally understand, you need a teacher. Jae Won would have happily sat next to her and had her explain the mysteries of the universe forever but instead he brought her an orange juice and began shakily, "Yesterday...my cousin." She stopped him immediately, "You just said it all. It was yesterday, in the past and he's your cousin. We don't pick our relatives so we're not responsible. Actually, he was pretty funny in a junior high way." Her eyes sparkled as she granted him another smile. Wendy reached for the lone pencil resting near the creased Stylish Nails flyer. Jae Won's carp seemed to wriggle off the page. "You're a Minhwa artist?" The astonished man allowed himself a lingering look at her face. "I was." he confided to her. Wendy took his hands in hers as if preparing to play a child's game. She turned them over and back again before letting go.

"They don't look broken to me. Were you struck blind? *Suh jah nim*, you *are* an artist. It's charming. My father and his friends used cornmeal dough for bait when they fished for carp. I think my mother pickled the carp and served it cold. I don't eat fish so I can't recall. Do you fish?"

"Not for awhile. When I was a boy, I fished with my father and uncle. Sometimes Yujin went with us."

"My father loved fishing so much. After he died, I envisioned him seated on a celestial lakeside rock, his cornmeal bait in the water, just waiting for the rest of his family to arrive. It was our dog, Fido II who would soon join him. I'd picture him running to my dad who would turn, arms out to greet him. Later when my daughter was a kindergartner I wanted to write a children's story about my father's heavenly fishing hole, but." She shrugged.

"*Ahjummah*," He took hold of Wendy's hands flustering her. "They don't look broken to me. Were you stuck blind? You can still write your story."

"You are very funny and you draw beautiful fish. If you're not careful, I'll start calling you that funny fish man."

They quickly dropped hands when a sixtyish matron with shiny brown lipstick on her otherwise unadorned face entered the store. "Oh," she said as she perused the shelves. "You don't carry Dutch Boy, huh." Before Jae Won could answer, the woman turned and left. Wendy laughed into her right hand. "*Sun jah nim*, are you going to give her a job too?"

It was three o'clock when an exiting customer in the doorway said, "Excuse me" to a bouquet holding Yujin Kim. Like the heroes in Wendy's dramas he strode up the aisle till he neared her. She looked up from her work and stood.

"Missus Dale. I am an idiot. Please accept my apologies for my rudeness."

The younger cousin bowed his head slightly and held out the pink and purple flowers wrapped Korean style in pink floral netting.

"Please call me Wendy like Jay does." She grinned wickedly. "Thank you."

The cousins spoke in Korean. Wendy strung together the words she knew but still couldn't guess the topic. Jae Won looked at the store clock and asked her to return on Monday. She filed the papers in their folders as Jae Won instructed earlier, thanked the men for her juice and bouquet, nodded her head slightly and left. Yujin and Jae Won watched her exit like an audience hoping for an encore. Softly, Yujin said, "*Hyung*, She's a good looking woman.

"*Uh.*" Jae Won agreed.

"She seems like a nice lady."

"*Neh.*"

"She's married."

"*Ah rha yo.*"

The door opened letting in their next customer and the beginning of autumn's sharper air.

⌘ ⌘ ⌘

Years ago on the Phil Donahue show, Phil was chatting with an audience member who was extolling the wisdom of her divorce. "Come on." He needled the woman. "Don't you miss him a little, like at Christmas?" "Sure I miss him at Christmas till I remember how much we fought over where to put the damn tree." Likewise, Saturday morning brought the Dale-O'Hanlon-Pierce family to the entry level of visiting Gramma at the little house near the pines. As appealing to outsiders as that bucolic image may seem the Floral Oaks clan knew the day would probably bring bickering and regrets. Even Fido made a mad run to the back fence to protest the inevitability of being nipped again by one of Gram's geese. They drove north on the Throg's Neck Bridge just as the sun's beams began jostling Long Island's western-most border awake. Wendy looked out onto the East River. It was easy to see why she had felt so at home in Seoul. It was nearly the same landscape of skyscrapers, water and bridges. Was Seoul, New York City East or was New York City, Seoul West?

For two solid hours that ticked by like four and a half, they sat squished among the packages of vegetable casseroles, coleslaw, jumbo sized Charmin and a twelve pack of Bounty in Tim's aging Camry. The heat off their massive hound pacing in place next to Jane fogged the windows. Wendy's attempts to sip coffee from her cup coincided with Tim slamming his brake pedal till her jeans were patterned in mocha splotches. The pain in her side had snaked down her left thigh forcing her to choke down a halved Vicodin while spilling a bit more of her drink. The pain soon subsided but the medication left her nauseous.

"How come we're bringing Gramma flowers?" Jane unplugged one of her earphones to hear her mother's answer. Wendy closed her eyes. 'I took the damn flowers because I didn't know the culturally correct way to turn them down. I should have left them. That jerk really upset Jay.'

"I got them as a gift yesterday."

Her husband assumed they were an offering to Lucille to soften the report of Wendy's diagnosis and jumped in to help. "One of mom's Korean students must want an 'A'. But, Janie, we know mom wouldn't put pink flowers in our Halloween themed house. They would clash with the décor. Haha."

Tim looked forward to visiting his mother-in-law. The air in Pine Tree Cove was crisp and invigorating. He enjoyed the attention of being the lone male in this three generational female line as well the assurance of becoming lord of the manor upon Lucille's demise. He never fully understood why Red's mother irked her. Tim's own mother died long after he wished she would. He and his sister Megan never formed an alliance against Nancy O'Hanlon's daily insults or nightly beatings. At sixteen, Megan ran off to California leaving her brother to absorb her share as well. Five years later when Tim graduated from Flushing High School, he fled to a basement apartment in Kew Gardens, took courses at Queens College and illegally tended bar along Bell Boulevard at night. Lucille Dale could be stubborn even argumentative but she never raised her hand to her daughter and she worshipped her granddaughter. Tim thought Wendy was too sensitive.

The older woman stood on her top floor deck barking orders like an unhappy landlord, all the residual effects of her last stroke seemingly gone. Her bare heels scrunched down the backs of her dollar store black sneakers. Her navy sweat pants were faded and stained. She covered a threadbare tee shirt with the zippered sweatshirt Tim had left after their last visit. Lucille's auburn hair had turned to gray while she was still in her thirties. This morning she had covered her thinning drab curls with the mint and white cashmere cloche Wendy had given her last Christmas.

"Tim, grab a couple of logs before you settle in and bring Fido right in after he does his business. There's a brazen skunk roaming around. Where's my Janie? Janie, before you run down to the Parker girls', come and give

Gramma a kiss. I haven't seen you in so long. Wendy, did you bring the Charmin? Last time you brought that single ply."

She shook her head in remembrance.

In the past, Tim and Wendy would look back at each other and hold their gaze to say 'In twenty five years, will we be like this?' This morning, Wendy turned away quickly. She was no longer sure she still had twenty-five years.

In less than ten minutes, Jane was jogging down Lake Road still wiping her grandmother's saliva from her face. The crumpled ten-dollar bill that was pressed into her hand as if the matriarch was dealing cocaine was now in her jeans pocket. Maybe she and her summer friends would walk into town. Tim changed light bulbs in the dining room fixture while Wendy put away her mother's groceries and prepared lunch. Lucille Dale returned to her plaid loveseat and CNN. She beckoned Fido who needed no invitation to rest his head on her lap. Tim turned to his mother-in-law before leaving for the barn. "Lucille, d'yu still have that green tandem bike. I'd like to take a look at it."

"Where's it going to? I can't ride it anymore. I'm all alone here. Your wife knows what it's like. She was a widow once."

"Mom," Wendy's Vicodin wooze was ebbing. "I wasn't really a widow. I was separated when Grant died."

"I hope you don't tell anybody that. People think they're liberal, but they'll look at you differently. Lucille pulled the cloche from her head as if just remembering she was inside and pointed like a hitchhiker at her son-in-law. They'll look at him differently too."

Tim watched his wife raise her eyebrows and pull back her lips. It was his exit signal.

Wendy brought her mother a light sweet coffee while she held on to her own straight up black in her other hand Their mannerisms were different, their tastes worlds apart. Their philosophies and politics shared no common ground but the DNA that created those generous green eyes tied the women forever.

Lucille caught Fido looking up at her and met him with kissing sounds. "You're so handsome. Yes you are." Taking that as an invitation he hauled his barrel belly and slender legs onto the small couch nestling in.

"I never liked dogs but this one, he's something else. Who would believe it? Before your father died, I was a fancy lady living in Bayside Hills. I thought Dad was crazy when he bought this place now I just want to stay here in my nightgown all day. I think the strokes did this. You know strokes can cause all kinds of damage."

"Maybe, ask your doctor." Wendy always stopped short of offering her mother sympathy. It helped her maintain her anger of not receiving any. "Mom, remember when

I was in my twenties, I had a bump under my arm" she didn't dare use any words that would upset the senior Mrs. Dale. "Well, I went for my mammography and they said it came back but now it's little particles." The story was losing more and more of its authenticity with each word.

Lucille snapped to an upright stance. "It's not serious is it?

"No, not really. It's a pre-cancer, but it's got to come out like last time." She opted to omit the details. Her mother wouldn't see her till Thanksgiving this year so why bother. Besides, the elder woman could slip and tell Janie.

"There's nothing like that in my family. My mother was past 90 when she had that lump, remember? Even the doctors said that doesn't count. Where the hell did you get this from? You don't take care of yourself. Make sure you call me after they…after. Wendy, my closets are all messy again. Could you put them like yours. You know with the pants on one side and the tops on the other and the colors matching. Since the last stroke I have no patience to pick out clothes anymore."

And just like that her daughter's cancer was dismissed.

Wendy straightened her mother's closet, set the table for lunch and tossed a salad with dried cranberries and walnuts. She had planned to go through her parents' Broadway show LP collection but her Vicodin nausea was subsiding allowing her side-ache to return. "Mom, I'm going down to the lake for a bit. I'll come back with Tim."

"What about Janie? Why'd you bring her here if she's just going to play with the neighbor's kids all day?"

She chose silence as her response as she walked across the damp front lawn and followed Lake Road to a row of pines. The trees hid the lake from out-for-a-drive vacationers. It was the same trip she made with her father countless times though she had only fished with him once or twice. She preferred writing poems about the lake or the surrounding mountains. He didn't mind. Neither father nor daughter was quiet as a rule but here, they respected nature's cathedral. They fished and wrote as if in prayer. The teacher found a moss free boulder chunk to rest on and looked out across the tea green water. 'Dad, if you're anywhere, it's probably here. I know you're not watching over me because the past three years have been hell. I have some kind of cancer but I'm not asking for favors. If I thought you could pull any strings, I'd have you cure Janie.'

A fish the color of lake water broke through the stillness and dove back.

'Is this where you and your friend Herby caught that giant carp. Maybe that was the Walkill. I can't remember. Anyway, I met a man who drew a fish just like that one. He reminds me of you. Not his looks. He's not a fair Scotsman like you. He's Korean."

Wendy picked up a gray and white stone to rub between her fingers.

"Remember how you grew that weird goatee till mom made you shave it. She told you nobody wore beards like that anymore. Well, this man has a Japanese shogun's ponytail. So I guess he doesn't have a wife to make him cut it off."

She stood and walked to the water's edge to toss the stone in. The last time she was lakeside she wore shorts and a tank top. Now the mountains hid the lower autumn sun. The once flourishing birch trees nearly stripped of their golden leaves left branches looking like bony fingers clawing at the dingy bed-sheet sky. She rubbed her hands together and blew her steamy breath into the cup shape they formed.

"Not to worry Dad. I'm not planning to become the thrice-married Ms. Dale. It's a good thing I kept your name huh, cuts down on paperwork. I miss you, Daddy. I'm almost as old as you were when you died. Guess I should stop calling you daddy." Then as if he was behind her packing away his tackle and reel, she looked back at the chipped boulder and said, "Au revoir, mon pere, ahn yung, shalom." and walked to the barn.

⌘ ⌘ ⌘

Fridays are generally the most dangerous days in a school lunchroom. They are second only to foul-weather Fridays when students are confined to the cafeteria for the whole period. But this seasoned coordinator knew that trouble could find its way to the lunchroom even on a sunny Monday like this. It was why Ms. Dale in a calf length taupe suede skirt and high-heeled boots sprinted like an Olympic athlete before the first chorus of "Fight, fight, fight" was over. A beet-faced Anthony Perez roared that Michael Lohan was a faggot and deserved a beating. Actually, a ninth grade girl, Anthony's secret obsession, showed Michael her smile and that set the stage.

Counting the two custodial staff men and Mr. Kent, the bar-belled toned kitchen worker, Anthony was still the biggest person in the lunchroom. He weighed in at a little less than a Sumo wrestler with a shaved head and the beginnings of Andy Rooney's eyebrows. Attributes not lost on lanky Michael who was flailing his arms and legs like an upside down pill bug on his overturned food tray on the floor while Anthony attempted to break his nose with his sweat soaked forehead. The school aides scurried as far away from the storm's eye as possible. They busied themselves by blowing their whistles at every honor roll student who was eating quietly to remind them to stay seated while Wendy raced from the lunch line to the fracas. She was neither gentle nor polite as she pushed her way through the gathering crowd blowing her ear-piercing whistle to startle the clamorous onlookers. It was already too loud for Anthony to hear her as she stood above the tangled male mess.

On her first day at Middle School 347, her union chapter leader informed Ms. Dale that she was never to touch a student during a fight. If she were injured, the department would not pay her medical costs because her job description was to inform security, period. Then with a wink he told her if she did get hurt, she'd get free medical and time off by reporting she was in the vicinity of the violence and a student accidentally fell back on her. It was the silliest and most indecent nonsense ever offered to her. She wasn't about to tell the parents of a hospitalized Michael Lohan that she was waiting for security while the bridge of their son's nose was bashed into his brain. She fell to her knees on the greasy floor, made her right hand a vise around two thirds of Anthony's monster neck and clenched his shoulder with her left. She leaned as close to his face as she could stomach, "Ant'ny" she shouted for all to hear and then whispered "I'm going to put it all over Myspace that you have a hard-on for Michael. He was going to come out and you panicked. You don't believe me? Keep fighting. We'll see. Oh, let me add this. If there's a run in these new pantyhose, I'm going to punk you out anyway." The teacher ended her speech by blowing the whistle in his ear.

The same ninth grade girls who helped instigate the fight now helped their teacher up complimenting her bravery. Wendy looked around the refectory. Claire was in the play yard. Even if she could have reached her on their finicky walkie-talkies, it wouldn't have been soon enough to help Michael. Two aides who were skulking out of harm's way a minute ago offered to escort the boys to the dean's office. "What a good idea. Thanks." The teacher answered without a smile. The good thing about sarcasm is if those two witches filed a complaint about the way she addressed them it wouldn't look like an insult on paper. She was also well aware that they would dawdle till the period was over, leaving her the sole guardian of the remaining two hundred teens.

Wendy checked her skirt for stains.

'You never know where the day will take you. This one had started out so well.' The little ballerina practiced in the auditorium last period and the teacher knew she'd be a showstopper. 'Where's that piece of paper with her name on it? I think her name's Salome. That would be funny to have a dancer named...' Ms. Dale caught a glimpse of her left hand. It was swelling, taking on purple hues and sporting a dangling broken nail. 'I'll kill him!'

⌘ ⌘ ⌘

Wendy, her cheeks flushed from running, opened the store's front door and called to Jae Won.

"*San jah nim*, I'll be back in five minutes. I'm just going across the street. Do you need anything, a soda?" Jae Won stepped out from behind the Color Your Imagination display he was showing a customer.

"*Oh tuh kay?* What's wrong?" he corrected himself for their patron.

"I broke a nail. I just need it filed down and re-polished. That's my salon across the street." Her right arm arched gracefully as her hand pointed to the Stylish Nail Shop and then she was gone with just a cool wild iris breeze to say she was there. Jae Won tried to sympathize with the customer's tale of bumpy dinette walls but he was cataloging the joy of having her back, the pleasure of learning another piece of her life was nearby and the wonder at her completely feminine reaction to a torn nail.

She returned quickly as promised hugging two cans of Pepsi, one diet the other regular and two paper cups. "Which one?" she asked placing them on the counter. This was easier than having to tell him she hated orange juice. Her injured hand looked like a scarlet wing next to her white wrist and arm. "What happened?" Terrible thoughts visited him but he kept his voice calm.

"Most people think teaching is all talking and writing. Sometimes we have to break up fights. I'm just glad I didn't ruin my skirt. Suede is not a good choice for school."

"You shouldn't be called when the bad children have fights. Where are the men in your school?"

Wendy wasn't sure if he was serious. He certainly wasn't politically correct.

"Ah jhuh sheh, What century are you from?"

He was weary of their small talk and a bit afraid she used it to keep him away.

"You told me you had cancer and you never spoke of it again yet she tell me about torn nails and ruined clothes."

The sun surely rose in the west that morning because for the very first time Wendy Dale was speechless. She tried to fill the silence by pouring a drink but her left hand throbbed too much to grip the diet Pepsi well enough to remove its tab. She handed the can to Jae Won. "Please." He pushed the ring up and down then poured half the contents into a cup preparing to apologize when she spoke again.

"Jay, why would I burden you with tales of surgery on Wednesday and radiation treatments and God only knows what else after that. This is not the first time I've hidden in the temporal world. My daughter is a very sick little girl. She's better since her bowel resection but I freeze in fear every time she sounds tired or seems pale. It's far easier to concern myself with pretty clothes and manicures." She took a sip to prevent herself from saying more. The bubbles from her cup leaped to her nose. Wendy took a paper towel from the counter shelf and daubed the residue.

"I didn't mean to upset you. A mother with a sick child has the right to cry." He wished he could speak comfortably in Korean to her.

"I'm not crying. When Janie was younger I told her everything in the big wide world came second to her. She was my number one, but I couldn't cry when she got sick. I was busy making phone calls to hospitals that specialized in gastroentorology and searching on line for Crohn's disease information. Weeping was a luxury I hadn't the time for. Now I'd be ashamed to shed tears for myself." She forced herself to leave his gaze by looking at her puffed hand. "You know when I let myself cry?" She didn't wait for an answer.

"When I watch Korean dramas. War Of The Roses, that was great for crying. She dies. Damo, that's an historical drama. They all die. I prefer the love stories. There's a lot of scolding and crying but very little …kissing, very cathartic. Do you watch dramas?"

It was Jae Won's turn to be silent. Everyone in Korea watched dramas. He remembered a nightly news anchorman once reminded the viewers to set their VCR's for the last episode of the popular, *Nae Ireumeun Kim Sam Soon*.

"Sometimes." He answered coolly.

Wendy tilted her head like a canary hearing a song then smiled broadly.

"*San jah nim,* you're becoming very westernized. That was a macho American answer." His pointer finger curled on his top lip while he joined her in laughter. Wendy seemed unconcerned that the store held just the two of them. He was grateful she hadn't noticed the front door sign was turned to CLOSED.

"No work for me?" she looked at the empty counter.

"Not today. I need to practice my English. Could we just talk?"

The teacher wasn't surprised by his request. She had often supplemented her income by tutoring Korean adults in English. It certainly would be more interesting than penciling in spelling corrections on three-year-old correspondence.

"Of course." she answered. "I'll tell you what puzzles me. People who study Korean art from the late Chosun era don't usually sell house paint. Who are you really, Mr. Hyun an escapee from the North?"

Jae Won retrieved another stool from the back room and placed it facing hers near the wire cage where the spray paints were displayed under the Adults Only sign. He sat down and poured the rest of the Diet Pepsi into her cup.

"I was an artist. While I was a university student, there was a revival of Minhwa art. The simplicity of its lines, the muted earth-tones in its landscapes or vibrant reds in its symbolic themes reached into my heart. It reminded me I was Korean. Following the Minhwa artists made me proud to be among the people who made delicate celadon porcelain and pungent kimchi and took a destroyed city and created a new Seoul."

She made no move to end his monologue. The story of his life like Aladdin's genie would soon be revealed. "My parents were very conservative." He continued. "That's the right word, I think. They wished me to be a teacher and so after college and the army, I taught high school art. I married but my wife agreed with my parents that teaching was more suitable. After she died, Yujin convinced me to come here." He had wound down like a clockwork toy. His eyes began to fill with tears making the half-moons glisten. He should have turned his face from hers but instead said, "She didn't die. She killed herself. The signs were all there but I didn't pay attention. Those last years were so hard. I just wanted peace."

Wendy took another paper towel sheet off the roll. "When my Janie was diagnosed with Crohn's, I asked the doctor if the fertility pills I took to become pregnant caused it. He practically rolled his eyes at me when he said, 'Of course not.'

Because I felt so powerless, I thought taking the blame would help. Should I roll my eyes at you? Of course you couldn't stop your wife's suicide anymore than you could stop her illness if it was ulcers in her intestines. You've been swimming in your own guilt too long. *Kah*, go in the back and mourn your wife's death." She pressed the second towel in his hand and walked to the front door. "I'll re-open the store. We'll probably sell more paint if the customers come inside, right funny fish man?" When she turned back the stools were empty. Jae Won stood alone at the tiny bathroom sink sobbing quietly into the towel. He was a grown man yet he wished he could hide at the faucet till she'd gone. She surely wouldn't have any interest in him now. He washed his face and hands. The melodic strains of Korean pop music reached his ears. "Jay, could I please play this CD? It's the soundtrack from Goong. I'll keep it low."

It was all the invitation he needed.

"*Uh*. Yujin's collection is in that box below. You can borrow anything you want."

He was returning the second stool to the back when she put her hand on his arm making him cough to hide his pleasure.

"I assume you just want to work on your pronunciation. Your vocabulary is better than most of my colleagues."

He didn't know what to make of her words. Was she trying to put him at ease after a too personal moment or was she dismissing him?

"Yo," called out one of the two black men who just entered the store. "you know that stuff? It's like a powder. You put it in the paint so the bathroom don't get all moldy." Jae Won helped the customer while Wendy straightened the counter. The younger of the two patrons peeked around the end cap to better glimpse Wendy. "Ms. Dale? Is that you? You used to be my English teacher. Remember me, Malik?" The teacher raised her head to reveal a beatific glow.

"Malik, Oh my goodness. I couldn't have recognized you. You're so tall and even more handsome. Mr. Hyun, this young man was one of my favorite students. How are you? Everyone at home well?"

Malik Thorne beamed as if blessed. He hurriedly introduced Wendy to his friend. The teacher told the other young man he must be wonderful as well to be Malik's friend. The men left after their purchase with smiles, final hugs and promises to return. After the door closed behind them, Jae Won looked at the drama teacher. "You didn't remember him at all did you?"

"What gave me away? I didn't use details?"

Jae Won shook his head, "*Neh*. You forgot I was also a teacher. We only remember the very best and the very worst. You're a good woman, Wendy Dale."

"*Go ma wha moy yo*, Fish man."

Ever-present patrons shortened the next conversations between them. Wendy was delighted to match buttercup yellow gingham wallpaper with a barnyard wainscoting for a woman whose toddler slept peacefully in his stroller. Jae Won shared a joke with two Korean businessmen who were trying to barter paint for lighting fixtures. The store was theirs again only as she was leaving.

"When can you work again?"

"Probably not till Friday."

"Isn't your surgery on Wednesday? You think you can work on Friday? *A cham*, How about this? Come to work on Sunday. Do you work Sundays?"

"I'm a mommy, I always work. Oh, you mean because it's Sunday. Yes. I'll work on Sunday."

"Wendy, do you know this? It's good to say before your surgery." He bent his elbow and made a fist. "Fighting!"

"Fighting!"

Wendy last experienced ambulatory surgery twenty years ago. As traumatic as it must have been, she couldn't recall any of its details. The pre-op exam yesterday was new to her. She sat alone in a large atrium with sufferers of every imaginable ailment till she was called to a closet of an examination room. Her A positive blood was drawn. She was weighed and measured. Two foreign born physician's assistants stood at opposite sides of her as she sat in a flowered hospital gown on their examination table. They introduced themselves by firing questions at her as if she were a murder suspect. The senior PA sounded Indian. Wendy could easily distinguish her accent and understood her questions but the younger assistant's words were undecipherable even to Wendy's practiced ear. Mr. Dale's daughter was attempting to recall the sounds of Turkish and Portuguese to help her categorize this woman when the older white-coated women began questioning again. "When was your last period? What medications do you take? How much Zocor? We have to know the dosage." Wendy took her pillbox from her handbag and relinquished it to her captors. The Indian woman took charge by dictating the medication's names to her underling. "Simvastatin 40MG." Wendy heard 'Simba dahtin' and became alarmed. The same woman then pronounced the name of Wendy's beta-blocker medication, "See beta." Her partner seemed confused and stopped writing. She attempted to repeat the Indian woman's word, "T-beta? Oh, C- Beta" and began filling in the space with a C. Wendy pictured tomorrow's eleven o'clock news feature, 'Are our hospital staff's poor English skills killing your loved ones? Stay tuned.'

Wendy decided to use her teacher-voice, "Excuse me, I take Zebeta for my arrhythmia. I sometimes get rapid heartbeats. I have to take it every night. It's Zebeta like in zebra. Zed." The snakes in her gut twisted together like a caduceus. Wendy made no motion to massage her side. If her two jailers suspected ill health, they would reschedule her surgery and she'd never get this over with.

Bird and Fish

They released her with a list of caveats. 'No eating after seven. No medications except Zocor in the morning. No aspirin. "When did you last take vitamin E?" The PA looked directly into Wendy's eyes as if to 'catch' her. "Oh, I haven't taken my vitamins for weeks." she lied. They told her to dress. She was exhausted but she was sure there'd be a sleepless night ahead. "May I take an Ambien tonight?" The Indian woman frowned. "If you really can't sleep." The teacher wanted to snap, "Why else would I take it?' but she longed for the safety of her home and chose to mumble "Thank you." to the women before dressing and leaving.

At that evening's dinner table, lies were passed from parent to child along with the garlic smashed potatoes and bacon-feta stuffed chicken. Tim and Wendy had concocted an infected pimple on mom's arm that had to be lanced the next morning. Jane took their story as gospel. They promised to be home when Mrs. Dunbar dropped her off the next day. Jane raised and lowered her shoulders, "No biggie."

Festooned with jack-o-lanterns and silk fall bowers, the breakfast room was at its October coziest. Jane picked out the bacon pieces from her plate and passed them under the table to a grateful Fido. She reached for the corn bread muffin on her mother's plate. "I have my blood test Saturday. Swimming's at ten. Could we go for pancakes in between?"

Wendy rapped her daughter's hand. "Next time ask. We'll go to the pancake house right from Dr. Tapman's.

This way you'll have more than an hour to digest that gunk."

Jane kept facing her mother while her left hand crawled up to Tim's plate and stole his half eaten muffin. "Tim, after practice, could you drop my friends and me at the Mall?" After her surgery, Jane began addressing Tim by name. Before then she went to great lengths to avoid giving him a title. She would just begin her sentences as if she had already said, 'Tim'. The couple pretended not to notice. During one of their secret driveway talks, they decided to let her find her own way of addressing him.

"Don't worry, I'm chauffer guy. Red, you haven't slept-in in a dog's age. Why don't you rest this Sunday?" He dropped another golden corn studded treat on his stepdaughter's plate.

⌘ ⌘ ⌘

Wendy snatched the muffin back and returned it to Tim. "I'm tutoring this Sunday." It wasn't really a lie.

A month before her fortieth birthday, Wendy Dale shocked her husband by suggesting they videotape themselves making love. Tim's voice went up an octave when he asked her why she made this extraordinary offer. His wife, wrapped in white terrycloth was standing in front of her closet door's full-length mirror. She had just returned to their bedroom after showering. Her wet hair hung heavy to her shoulders. She let the towel wrap drop to her feet and studied her image. 'Still smooth and taut. What isn't alabaster white is rose petal pink.'

"Because we're never going to look any better than we do now." Wendy climbed up on the bed and molded herself to her husband's side.

"When we're old, we can watch it and remember our youthful passion."

Tim often recalled his decision with regret. "I think," he kissed the top of her head. "that after we're old, we'll die and Jane will find the tape. The pictures of our youthful passionate asses will keep her on a shrink's couch for the rest of her life."

Wendy emerged from her surgery eve shower, dried herself off, ring-tossed her silk nightie over her head and pulled her arms through. She was careful not to catch her reflection even as hazy as it was in the steamed mirror.

'Shame on you, Wendy Dale. Your daughter has a twelve-inch frankfurter scar across her belly and she doesn't complain. *Ahjummah*, you're forty-three years old. In ten years your breasts will point to your belly button anyway.' Her private pep talk wasn't working. Instead of worrying how ugly her scar would be she realized how little it would matter in a few years. She was growing older and in America that meant becoming invisible.

Wendy threw on her sweatsuit, stepped into her flip-flops and met Fido at the side door. The two cantered to the

Adrienne Leslie

vegetable garden in the early darkness. The evening news told everyone it was the warmest autumn on record and she was happy to stand above her sage and chives without feeling chilled. The rosemary branches were covered in their piney needles. She gently grasped a bunch and let its oils coat her hand. It had the same wintry scent of evergreens but it always reminded her of spring, perhaps because she served roast lamb with yogurt, rosemary and garlic, Tim's favorite dish, every Easter Sunday. 'What would their lives be like this Easter?' She inhaled the pine tree essence one more time before taking her dog back inside.

Choesuk in New York was a watered down version. The children attended school, the adults worked. But Yoon Yoo still took her girls to her parents' home the weekend before the holiday to prepare *song pyun*, the traditional sticky rice balls eaten on Choesuk. She and her daughters joined her mother in making the rice cakes. It always cheered her to hear her mother tell the girls, "If you make pretty *song pyun*, you will have pretty daughters." The girls followed with, "Did mommy make pretty rice cakes?" and her mother always answered, "Your mommy made the prettiest." Yujin joined Yoon Yoo in this Korean-American tradition when they were dating. He would talk and drink with her father while the women cooked. After their girls were born, he came less often. Somehow it grew into another of her sole responsibilities. Her mother had warned her that he was too handsome. She closed her eyes and pictured her husband. The image in front of her was of the young lothario who followed her to class and hid in the back row in St. John's University's

Bent Hall just to be with her. Why was she making herself crazy? Even her friends told her how lucky she was. Her reverie was broken by her oldest daughter dancing for *helmonee*. The eleven year old looked like a jewelry box ballerina twirling around the kitchen.

Two days later Yoon Yoo was still preparing for the holiday. A floor below her, Jae Won was sketching bamboo stalks in one of Ahromie's forgotten water color pads when he heard Yoon Yoo and her daughters hastily moving furniture. The younger girl, probably tired and cranky began to fuss. Jae chuckled as Ahromie's crying was cut short with the crack sound of Yoon Yoo's hand on her daughter's bottom. His stomach bubbled in anticipation of tomorrow's feast; rice cakes filled with honey-sweetened peas, chestnuts, and best of all sesame seeds. Upstairs, Yoon Yoo was carefully arranging the *song pyun* between handfuls of washed pine needles in the giant steamer she used for entertaining. The house soon boasted the fragrance of a pine forest, inspiring Jae Won to draw a woodland landscape. Soon a mountain lake surrounded by pines greeted him from the page. He nearly convinced himself it was in homage to artist Shin Yun Bok when he added a male figure sitting among the rocks fishing.

⌘ ⌘ ⌘

The blended East and West of a New York *Cheosuk* benefited the cousins. While Jae Won chose to wear the customary *cheogori* and *pahji*, a slate blue jacket with ties replacing buttons and loose fitting pants, Yujin was comfortable in his Hugo Boss suit. As the eldest sons of the household, they presided over the ceremony at Yoon Yoo's elegantly prepared ancestral table early in the morning. The men bowed and knelt in front of the burning incense and half peeled Asian pears before offering their departed loved ones food and drinks. After the girls returned from school, they and their mother changed into their billowy *hamboks* to the delight of *harambojee* and *helmonim*. As in the preceding years, Yujin extended an invitation to Jae Won to join them at his in-laws. As always the elder cousin declined thankful for the peace and remaining rice cakes. He was traditional enough to find this new custom of spending the holiday at Yoon Yoo's parents' home disconcerting. Even though he had profoundly broken tradition this morning by telling his dead wife this was the last memorial he would share with her. 'It was, like they say on the American talk shows, time to move on.'

⌘ ⌘ ⌘

Wendy and Tim had just walked from their car to the NNH Ambulatory Surgery Pavilion when her cell phone rang. She could hear the familiar sounds of a classroom before Libby's hello. "Listen, I have to make this quick I told the kids I was calling Mr.Rubinstein. Just get through today and I'll treat you to a manicure when it's over. OK? I'm plugging for you. Oh, a couple of your Korean kids were looking for you this morning. Is it a holiday? They brought you nice food gifts. Hold on. Get in your seat please! Gotta go." Wendy wasn't sure if she managed to say thank you.

Chosuk celebrations seemed conspicuously absent here. The waiting area was the same place she marked papers yesterday but this morning after her name was called, she and Tim were sent to hospital room that was new to her. The same questions she was asked the day before were asked again. Blood was drawn again. She was wearing a hospital gown again. She spoke only when spoken to again. Tim was allowed to stay until they called her to x-ray. They promised to call him back after surgery. Everyone but Tim was wearing a paper hat. They all looked like candy factory workers with Tim as the company president. Wendy watched her husband's clear blue eyes scanning her face. Life offered no pregnant pauses for profound speeches. There was only enough time for sound bite thoughts. 'Thanks for finding me that day. Thanks for accepting my Janie. If I don't wake up, will you marry a harridan who'll hurt my little girl?' She returned her husband's smile.

"Time for pictures." a paper-hatted nurse chirped to the teacher. Wendy and her husband kissed goodbye as if they were siblings making their surroundings more important than the past they shared as a couple. Wendy Dale in plastic coated socks padded behind the woman with the chart. She was taken to an x-ray/ultra-sound room where two Indian women greeted her with replays of the same questions. The x-ray process seemed longer. The tighter the machine hugged her the higher she stood on her toes. The woman Wendy guessed was the radiologist told her a thin wire would be inserted to guide the surgeon. The English teacher pictured a hair's strand headed somewhere near her underarm and tried taking Lamaze breaths to keep calm. To her shock, while the other woman held on to Wendy's shoulders, the radiologist drove a thin wire spike into the side of Wendy's left breast and tapped it in with what appeared to be a hammer. The teacher's knees twitched then jiggled then vibrated out of her control. She needed to vomit. She wanted to lie down. The pain in her side was exploding like July fourth fireworks.

'Don't say anything. Don't say anything. They'll only have to do this again.' But the little voice inside her found an opening through her lips. "I'm sorry, I don't feel well." The women stepped back as if Wendy controlled them all along. One went to the wall phone and called for Dr. Feinstein. The other woman asked Wendy to sit on the cot behind them. "Your anesthesiologist is on his way." The phone woman said.

'Oh shit.' A chilling sweat could be felt under her nose and above her breasts, under her arms and behind her knees. 'Anesthesiologists don't know how to talk to awake people. I've just made it worse.'

Dr. Feinstein arrived just as Wendy lied down on the cot. He was young and cheerful, just what the patient ordered. "Hey you, what's up?" he asked while rubbing her socked foot. "I think I just felt nervous." she apologized.

"Lucky you, I've got stuff for nervous. I'll send it in to you. Ready to go now?"

"Sure." she answered him and to herself noted, 'Wendy Barrie Dale, you always were a pushover for a friendly smile.'

Bird and Fish

She and Tim were home by lunchtime although neither was hungry. Tim took her prescription for Percocet and walked to the local drugstore. His Viking good looks and Irish good manners had the pharmacist eat her first proclamation that all orders have a wait time of two hours to "Stay right here, I can fill this for you now." He sported a big manly smirk all the way back down Union Turnpike. Tim brought Wendy a leaf-patterned glass of water and one pill. She took only a half. It was enough to make her bedroom walls melt as if heated, a snowy white carp to appear in her hands and the Fox News reporter to speak in Korean. 'No wonder people take this stuff.' She fell asleep with Fido curled like a coil resting his head on her hip bone.

⌘ ⌘ ⌘

When Tim finally made his break from his mother, he visited his namesake uncle in the Bronx for a loan. Uncle Timothy was happy to help his nephew and godson get away from that banshee his poor dead brother married. Three years later the kindly gentleman of the aulde sod was diagnosed with liver cancer. Tim rode the subway from Main Street to Bainbridge Avenue weekly to check on his benefactor. On one of his last visits, he apologized for repaying only two of the ten thousand he had borrowed.

The wizened face smiled at his brother's son. "Tim, lad, when you've got a touch of the cancer, you've got to wipe the slates clean. You're no longer beholden to me."

The Celtic son spent the following years studying, working and drinking. A six-pack for breakfast was followed by uncounted shots of Johnny Walker throughout the day. The occasional blackouts scared him but not enough to go on the wagon till he met Red. The top of her head barely met his shoulder but she didn't flinch when she waved her teacher finger at him.

"I didn't leave a tyrant to marry a drunk. Stay sober or go."

He chose sobriety. He even quit smoking. He missed his vices like the longings for a first love but till this day, he had kept his word. Tim took one of the Percocet tablets from the bottle and went downstairs to the den. Like a sleepwalker, he opened the bar's cabinet doors, found a Christmas gift bottle of Grey Goose and poured himself two fingers worth. He saved the last swig to swallow the pill down. "I'm sorry, Red." he said aloud affecting his uncle's brogue, "This touch of cancer wipes my promise slate clean." Until his stepdaughter came home, he sat in self-imposed exile in his lounge chair while Channel 46 recapped the war in Iraq.

"Mom, you awake?" The juxtaposition to ill mother and well daughter was preferable to Wendy.

"I'm almost awake. Where's Tim?"

"I think he's sleeping in the den. Don't worry I let Fido out. What's for dinner?"

"I made the barbequed drumsticks you like and macaroni and cheese on Sunday. They're ready to be reheated. Do you have much homework?"

"Not really. Mom, can I see your scar?"

"Absolutely not. Will you put the trays in the oven for me? Just put them on 350 for an hour. I'll set the table in a little while."

Thursday's sky looked like angels ran amok with white finger paint. Swirls and glops of clouds decorated the moody gray canopy. Just below, the trees were Bollywood dancers swaying and waving scarves of maize, gold and orange. Wendy watched the autumn morning unfold from her breakfast room windows. The sports bra under her nightgown was her only reminder of what had happened yesterday. She squinted to try to jog her memory: voices asked her three times to confirm which side her surgery would be on. Dr. Gaspare spoke to her after the surgery but she couldn't recall what he said. There was a print-out with post surgery rules for the week. It was probably on her dresser. She remembered she was instructed to wear a bra to bed. She pulled away her silk nightie and bra strap with her thumb. A quick peek showed a surprisingly small bandage.

The phone call to her mother last night left her drained. She was needlessly tormented by all the lies she thought she'd have to tell. Lucille, before Wendy could begin, burst in with, "Well, that's over. When are you coming back? I've got all this corn and squash that you'll need for Thanksgiving. You can't let them go bad." Wendy was a grown-up with a child of her own yet it still hurt when an ear of corn had precedent over her. Earlier this morning Libby called but instead of consoling her friend she scolded her when she learned Wendy served dinner the night before.

"What's the matter with you? They can't help out once in a while? You just had surgery, for God's sake." Wendy's Percocet half was wearing off. 'No wonder I prefer dramas. Real people are too hard.'

Had Tim offered to stay home today she would have assured him she was fine and asked if he minded a dinner of reheated turkey noodle soup and sesame rolls she had prepared and froze last week. But he hadn't. Instead he supplied a cheek kiss before leaving never doubting dinner would be on time that evening. Courtney used her cell phone to tell Jane they were outside waiting. Jane gulped down her English muffin half and raced to Mrs. Dunbar's car leaving Wendy alone at the kitchen counter, pouring her third coffee of the day. She looked at her hands. She was graced with long delicate fingers topped with tapered square filed nails. They were feminine hands, a source of pride for her. Now they mocked her.

'Hey lady with the nice manicure, think you're perfect? You have cancer.' She concentrated on her injured hand. At least that was returning to its former self, but rather than recalling the cafeteria incident, her thoughts ran to Jay. A tickle went from her nape to her shoulders when she revisited the day he took her hands in his. Her coffee sloshed as her mug gaveled the counter. Wendy dashed from the kitchen as if escaping a ghost. She made Jane's bed and sat down at the computer. 'I'll just chat awhile with the fans at Koreandramas. Someone must know if Jinjin from A Woman's Choice returns to her first love.' But the teacher's fingers disobeyed and tapped the Microsoft Word icon instead. The blank page was ready for a staring match but Wendy typed in *Papa's Thousand Voices* and began the story of a girl who lived not so long ago and not so far away with a father who gave her an extraordinary gift. She'd save it in My Computer like so many other bits and pieces of stories. It was past one when Fido stirred from his morning nap.

"Hey, sweet boy, do you want to go out with mommy?"

They ran in circles on the back lawn till Wendy's body reminded her to rest. She sat on one of the driveway folding chairs noticing a trio of forgotten tomato cages resting near the garage door The teacher was lifting the door with her 'good' arm ready to store the cages when she saw the Anycolor Paints' stickers on the cans beneath the lounge cushions. She repeated the phone number over and over as she completed her chore and returned to her kitchen to dial from the house phone. Thankfully, she heard Jae Won's voice.

"*Yuh bho seh yo, Nah yuh* It's me, Wendy."

"*Whah*, Wendy, your Korean is so good. I thought you were a Korean customer."

"Jay, do you want me there at 1:30 on Sunday? And also, should I dress as usual or would it be all right to wear jeans?"

"Yeh yeh, come at the usual time. Jeans are OK. *Quen sha nah?*"

"I'm fine. I'll see you Sunday." 'Please God, no dead air, no dead air.' "Bye."

"Bye."

Four miles apart Wendy and Jay sat down shaking as if together they'd witnessed the sky on fire.

Global warming and insomnia; let others denigrate these gift horses. Wendy Dale appreciated them. New York City usually offered biting cold temperatures that left blackened hills of permafrost snowdrifts on each city corner. The chill that aimed for her fingers, nose and toes at Thanksgiving would stay in her bones till she hung an "Erin Go Bragh" banner on the drama room door. Not this year. The second Sunday in October felt more like July with near 80 temperatures. What gave the season away were the fall colors poured onto the treetops like paints from Mr. Hyun's store.

She had awaked a little after three but rather than curse the darkness, she considered it a hidden day to complete her weekend chores. She marinated chicken parts, oven baked breaded cutlets and par boiled sausages. The teacher checked her daughter's homework then completed grading 7B1 and 7B2's "The Tonight Show, Vaudeville and Far Above Rubies: What are the ties that bind" assignments. She pumped up a package of sugar cookie mix with flavorings, cut the rolled dough into ghost shapes then baked and iced them for an after dinner treat. Fido poached a cooling cookie while Wendy mixed warmed marmalade and maple syrup into a glass bowl for the French toast she had prepared for breakfast. The day's first meal that took a half hour to prepare was devoured in less than twenty minutes.

By noon, Janie and friends would be at Colleen's for the ninety-ninth showing of The Devil Wears Prada. Tim's babysitter would be the playoffs. This left Wendy, already awake for nine hours, to shower and dress with the tired good feeling of a marathoner finishing the race.

Sunday's relaxed parking meter rules enabled Wendy to park just steps away from Anycolor's entrance, in time to see Jae Won pulling down the metal security doors over the storefront. "Did something happen?" she asked as she stepped onto the curb.

"We're closing at one on Sundays now. Didn't you hear Yujin and I talking about it?"

'Maybe, but I don't know how to say close or Sunday in Korean.' "Where are we going?"

"I thought we could practice in the diner at the corner but could we please go to my house first. I forgot something."

Wendy hadn't dated in a dozen years but a line was still a line. "Mr. Hyun, even in America women don't just *go* to men's homes."

"*Doh, doh, doh,*, you can wait outside. Do you want to follow in your car? Should we walk? It's a beautiful day."

'Perfect. All the neighborhood students can watch Ms. Dale in tight jeans with a samurai at her side' "I'll follow you."

For the second time that day she drove past her school but soon they pulled up in front of a lovely new home with the kind of bay windows Wendy longed for. Jae Won walked back to her car. "Do you want to come in with me? There's something I'd like to show you. I promise we'll come right out. Yujin and his family will be back from church any minute. You're safe."

'You're safe. Sounds like something a rapist murderer would say. I must be crazy.' Wendy trailed him to the side entrance mudroom. She knew the house was newly designed since Western homes didn't have the step up feature for changing shoes. She removed hers to get a better look at the obscenely large white kitchen.

"It's very minimalist." She was searching for the kindest word.

"I didn't design it."

"Oh, then truthfully, it looks like a hospital operating room.

"My cousin's wife Yoon Yoo picked everything out."

"Like I was saying, clean tasteful styling."

As if orchestrated by Yoon Yoo, they sat opposite each other at the kitchen island swapping histories and joking. Jae Won would have gladly stopped time. The woman of his dreams, albeit a nightmare, was sharing his counter space. A black tight-knit sweater covering her crossed arms over her bodice showed off her titian hair. The glimmering soft pink of her lips was repeated on her neatly trimmed nails. "Your lipstick matches your nail polish." He regretted the personal comment even before it was completed. Wendy Dale combed her hair behind her ears using her fingertips and chuckled, "Do you think that's by accident?"

Jae Won removed a watercolor of a fisherman netting his carp at a mountain lake from the under-counter drawer. "I wanted to show you this."

"Jay, this is so beautiful. It's like the lake my father fished. I would walk right along that edge." Her finger moved above the sharp thin black lines of the path. This is even better than Tanwon's work."

"*Yeh?* I *was* thinking of Kim Hong-do. *Whah.* You used his other name. You're very smart."

The silence that followed embarrassed them. Wendy stood up putting her handbag strap on her shoulder.

"Let's go to Cob's Diner near the store. I brought some ESL workbooks we can use."

"Wendy, I forgot this." He handed her a vertical envelope that held a stack of twenty dollar bills she didn't dare count. As she put on her shoes, her gaze swept the living room and kitchen.

"There's nothing alive here. No dog. No plants. You need something that breathes and isn't white. Fishman, you should buy a goldfish. Aren't goldfish carp?

"*Uh.*"

"Two Carp together symbolize something in Asian art. I can't remember what that is. Can you?"

"*Ahn nee.*" But he absolutely remembered. He just couldn't tell her. Not yet.

They stood close together on the side steps while he locked the door. Yujin's showy Lexus made a left into the driveway and faced them. Like a buck and doe frozen in the car's pathway, they stood still to meet the moment head on.

The back passenger door opened first with Seromie racing towards them while the rest of the family unbuckled.

"Mommy, this is my lunch teacher. Ms. Dale, I can show you my cousin's bird painting now."

⌘ ⌘ ⌘

Episode 5: Gom Bah Gom Bah

The summer of her Korean trip, along with packing an appropriate wardrobe, Wendy armed herself by researching appropriate behavior rules. She had no intentions of causing America any embarrassment. One of her Korean colleagues instructed her not to blow her nose while eating, never leave her chopsticks standing straight in her leftover rice and refrain from writing a person's name in red. The instructions weren't helpful. She wouldn't blow her nose at her own dinner table let alone in Seoul. She already knew the proper use of chopsticks and it wasn't likely she'd pack a red pen for her trip. She chose to use western good manners and hope for the best.

As Jae Won's family approached her she felt as she did before her trip.

"What is the least embarrassing way to get back to my car? She was committed to Seromie's request. Crushing the child's ego wasn't an option. Yujin took over as official greeter.

"*Yobo*, this is Misses Dale. *Sun seng nim*, this is my wife, Yoon Yoo Son. The women sized up each other with practiced eyes. Each knew the cost and store origin of every garment the other wore. Each acknowledged the other was attractive. Yoon Yoo invited Jae Won and Wendy to their apartment for lunch. Ahromie reminded her parents she had to use the bathroom moving all six people closer to the front door. Wendy turned to Seromie, "If it's all right with your parents, I'll look at cousin Jay's painting. But then I have to fetch my own little girl at her friend's. *Ah rhuh so?*" With practiced dexterity, she turned to the girl's parents, "Your daughter is the pride of our assembly program. I'm so lucky she has offered to dance for us. Thank you for giving our school such a wonderful student." Jae Won looked at his cousins. All but littlest Ahromie who hopped from foot to foot on the top step were beaming.

Seromie's lilac and blush bedroom was immaculate. The bed could have passed a military inspection even with its Little Mermaid II quilt and sham. Wendy couldn't help but compare it to Jane's. Her daughter's daring teenage posters taped to her Burberry beige walls were upstaged by her red and black bed linens that were only occasionally arranged properly. Janie was eagerly racing towards her teen years. Seromie was comfortable in childhood. 'Who's to say what's better.'

The bird and blossom watercolor was above the white ash headboard next to the child's Sunday school cardboard crucifix. Ms. Dale and Seromie held hands as the teacher leaned over the bedside to examine the painting.

"It's as beautiful as I imagined and you were right about the birds. They're two little white-throated sparrows just like the ones we watched that morning. Look how your cousin daubed blues and greens on the brown rock. Why do you think he did that?"

"So that it would look wet?"

"That's what I think too. Were you born in the spring?"

"Well, my Korean birthday is in May."

"That's why there are so many pink crocuses. Take very good care of this. One day you'll give it to your own child."

Jae Won stood at the girl's dresser watching. For a few moments he could pretend they were his wife and child although the likelihood of Wendy producing a child with Seromie's ebon hair and eyes was unrealistic. Had he turned toward the bedroom door, he would have noticed his cousins' scrutiny. Husband and wife each noting it was Jae Won's first smile since coming to share their home. From the girls' bathroom, Ahromie called for her mother, breaking the spell.

Seromie and Wendy turned to face the girl's family. All eyes were locked on the teacher and child. The teacher knew her Jane would have said something smarmy to switch off the awkwardness. Seromie offered to tend to her sister. There was a flurry of Korean conversation.

The two couples left for the game room with only Wendy silent. She hadn't bothered trying to translate. She was plotting her exit. She felt as guilty as a house burglar caught in the act. These were lovely people and she was a liar and a cheat. They guided Wendy to a sleek leather couch. At her left was a huge Karaoke screen. Yujin selected a remote control from a side table and the monitor came to life. Swirling colors and tinny repetitious chords announced themselves like one of Janie's games on pause. Jae Won spoke in English first. "In two weeks there's a Korean Festival in Flushing Meadow Park." He paused summoning up the best words to convince her. Wendy watched as Yoon Yoo left the room as stealthily as a family cat. "Our stores will have a booth there and we'll all be going." Wendy looked back at him, waiting. Yujin couldn't believe his cousin's timidity. He quickly cut in with, "We'd like you to sing." The teacher would recount this scene four times to friends and family in the next twenty-four hours embellishing it with, "In that nano-second I was praying 'sing' was a Korean word I didn't know."

"Sing?" She envisioned herself rising to say, 'I'm Wendy like in Barrie's Peter Pan. You must think I'm Louis Carroll's Alice since we've just entered Wonderland. Yujin continued as his wife reappeared with a tray filled with peeled Asian pear slices sporting cellophane topped toothpicks. "Sing?" Wendy repeated.

"Oh Missus Dale," Yoon Yoo purred like every Korean mommy who came asking for a grade change. "You'd be perfect. Everyone knows you in the Korean community."

"I can carry a tune, but I'm not a singer." Wendy considered that perhaps they had contracted some sort of family madness.

"Jae Won will sing with you. It's a couple's contest. We'll pick out something now and you can practice here after school. Yujin will have to change his schedule for a little while."

'Tough lady' observed Wendy. 'She's not letting me go.' There was also something odd in the way Yoon Yoo spoke of changing her husband's schedule.

The teacher acquiesced, "Sure. When is this, two Sundays from now? I'll sing the Three Bear's song from the Korean 'Full House'" Then like applause driven Drama teachers everywhere, she stood, gestured, sang the Korean children's song and took a long bow, her red hair cascaded in front of them like an autumn leaf shower.

When she raised herself up, she placed her right hand flat across her sweater's vee neck to modestly hold the material to her skin. It was a traditional Korean woman's movement that met the approval of her audience on the couch. After their applause, they resumed their three-way conversation in Korean. Yujin brought out a Korean catalog filled with lists and numbers. Yoon Yoo and Jae Won shook their heads at every suggested item. The IDOLpro came to life. Dancers, rainy nights and high divers kept the beat as *Han gul* appeared at the screen's edge. Wendy had never seen a Karaoke machine except on her dramas. Those scenes began with heart aching break-ups, solo drinking at tent bars then tear stained faces singing in front of Karaoke screens like this one. Some of the melodies were ballads she had heard before. 'I'm not singing a mushy serenade with Fishman in front of an audience that's probably made up of my former students and their parents. Manhattan's a big city. Queens is a patchwork of small towns.' Steamrolling into her thoughts came the chug ba ba bah, chug ba ba bah of a locomotive and a bouncy inviting tune. Her hosts seemed pleased. "You'll do this one." Yoon Yoo commanded.

'Not so bad." thought Wendy. 'At least it's not a love song.'

It was nearly 3:30 when she and Jay stood at her car. She tried to place her pay envelope in his hand. "This will be too much. I didn't work today."

"You did in a way. We picked out a song." He took the envelope only to keep it from tumbling to the street. "It's a good advertisement to the stores."

"*For* the stores."

Jae Won chuckled. She was his tutor after all.

With an ease he never possessed as a young man, he managed to sweep his thumb across the top of her index finger while handing back the envelope. A soft breeze rattled the last coppery leaves of a dying sycamore branch, dropping one to the top of Jay's tie-back. Wendy reached for the leaf helping it fall to the ground.

'I shouldn't have done that, not a mere few miles from my home and under the two noses pressing the glass of the third cathedral window. I should never have done that. I can't believe I'm saying this but…'

"When are we rehearsing? I'm afraid I have a department meeting tomorrow and an appointment on Wednesday."

"I'm going to Manhattan for art supplies tomorrow, so we'll meet on Tuesday, Thursday and Sunday again. OK?

"Where are we practicing on Tuesday and Thursday? Was Yoon Yoo serious?"

"She was serious." Jay tried not to make any facial gestures that would be noticed by his cousins behind the vertical blinds. "But my cousin is still a Korean man. He wouldn't want us to see her control him. We'll meet at the store. I have the CD."

For the first time since she began her Zebeta regimen, Wendy's heart began to race. She wasn't about to begin her breathing exercises in front of Jay or his relatives.

"Oh, I'm running late." He couldn't help but notice her breathlessness.

With a wave she was gone. He'd never imagine she pulled in front of the brick three story Mc Mansion on Culligan Street just out of sight. She sat quietly at the wheel breathing in four counts through her nose, holding it for seven counts then out through her mouth for seven more. Wendy repeated the pattern twice more till her heart's electric circuit righted itself bringing the familiar cold sweat on her neck. 'What's going on here?' she asked her image in the rear view mirror. 'Nothing. I'm not doing anything wrong. Oh, my mother would see right through that one.'

The three eleven year olds chattering in her car produced the noise of a rainy day cafeteria duty. They talked primarily of the movie's fashionable costumes, which they coveted but Wendy was shocked by their blasé discussion of the two male roles.

"I still like Adrian Grenier, the Entourage guy she lived with."

"No, the blonde guy was cuter except when he was in the towel, ew."

That was enough for the Wendy to hear. "What was the rating?" she interrogated.

Courtney failed to read her friend Jane's frantic hand and eye signals to stay quiet. "PG13, Ms. Dale"

"They let you buy this film?"

"They always let us."

"Surely not R rated ones?"

"No, not R."

Wendy rubbed her hands over her eyes at the stop sign on Mark Lane. There she could recall the softly hued little girl's room with the gold sprayed cross and delicately painted sparrows.

By Monday morning's second period class, Caesar was deader than shoulder pads and 6A2 was preparing versions of Marc Antony's Friends, Romans, Countrymen speech in his honor. To save auditorium rehearsal time, Wendy pressed the whole class into the Far Above Rubies assembly program with promises that they'd be catapulted into stardom during their portion, The Virtue of Loyalty. The sixth graders rushed through her doorway pulling white and not so white sheets from their book bags. For this period, as the last, the teacher would show them how to create ancient Roman costumes with sheets, ladies' brooches, flip flops and gold-sprayed plastic ivy vines. But before the class became a free for all with students running around chairs after stealing each other's sandals, Ms. Dale gathered them about her, some sitting on the floor some the tables to have them recapitulate Brutus' fatal error. Eric Son nicknamed Sonnyboy by his teacher was already antsy. His mother's donated flowered pin was sharp. He was inches from his best friend's soft spot when his teacher called the children together. The boy tapped his sneaker heels on the floor showing his impatience. Ms. Dale's celadon suit made a soft swish sound as she crouched down beside him.

"*Ahdul*, you stick that into anybody and I'll show you how fast I can get your mother to visit me in this very room."

"I wasn't really going to do it. Ms. Dale, *Ahdul* means my son. I'm not your son."

The teacher tsk-tsked, "*I goo*. What a perfect time for a Latin lesson. In Loco Parentis. That's what I am to you the whole school day. Your personal homework tonight is to look that up and hand in a paragraph on its significance. *Ah rhah Chee?*"

"*Ah rhah suh.*"

"Till the last waltz of the day, I'll worry about you like you're my son."

She stood as gracefully as she could muster given that the pain in her side was making macramé knots with her intestines. "So what was Brutus' big mistake?" she asked the quieted room. Brittany Kim, fastest hand raiser in the class was picked. "Quickdraw, tell everybody." Ms. Dale instructed.

"He let Antony speak. No wait. He let him speak last."

"Quickdraw, let me shake your hand. You're a baby genius. Antony turned out to be a better speaker and much craftier than Brutus and his buddies thought. He knew audiences could just take in so much. It's better to be the last speaker than the first. Some of you may want to run for school office this spring. Remember that."

"Ms. Dale" a hand waved at her.

"Yes, Scoobydoo." She could no longer recall the boy's given name.

"What if you think you're last but another kid ends up after you."

"Well," the teacher's eyes opened wide in an imaginary sweep for grownup spies in the room. "When no one's looking, kick him into the orchestra pit."

Why do comics work in nightclubs when it's so much easier to get a laugh from pre-teens. Two boys high fived and one little girl held her belly guffawing while Gary Senot's laughter felled him from his table perch. The teacher's mouth went dry. "What's Gary doing?" she called out to his tablemates. "Nothing Ms. Dale. He's fooling around." She felt like a child's clay stick being twisted in two. She bent over the boy and immediately rose up again.

"Listen to me. Just like we're at a fire drill I want everybody to get up silently and exit through the front door. Leave your things. Go as quietly as you can into the hallway. Her hand grabbed the shoulder of her class monitor, "Rabbit, go straight to the dean. If he's not in his office go to Ms. Sakai's. Say Ms. Dale's class is unattended in the hallway. Just like a drill. Good man." Wendy called the nurse's office from the classroom phone. "Hey, Rita it's Wendy, Basement Room 4. I've got a little boy in Grand Mal. He's starting to come down but I don't like his color. He's turning blue."

She squatted down next to the child till the room filled with grown-ups. The dean arrived first to lead the class away after Wendy instructed three students who were the least likely to gawk, to enter quietly and collect all 6A2's belongings. The school nurse rushed in next followed by the assistant principal, Claire Jackson, two shaved headed EMS workers who commended Wendy's response and finally a shaking Mrs. Senot.

Claire stayed a few moments longer than the rest to check on her friend. Wendy talked about poor Fido IV, their shepherd mix puppy with idiopathic epilepsy. The memories of the violent seizures he had in his short life visited her like Scrooge's ghosts. She never imagined it would make her the day's celebrity. The women checked the room for forgotten supplies and found a book bag under a chair.

"This is some Chinese kid's bag. Look, it got Chinese stickers and writ'n all over it." Wendy had heard this before by other staff members. They called everything Asian, Chinese.

"That's Korean, Claire. It says I love you."

Wendy Dale, you tell'n me you read Korean now?"

"No, well I can recognize 'Kim' easily enough. It looks like a little package with a seven and a one and a little box underneath. One of the girls taught me how to write I love you. See," she swept her finger under the letters. "*Sah rang heh.*"

Wendy had already tossed her unheated frozen diet lunch in the room's trashcan and thrown back a Vicodin half with her diet Pepsi when Libby entered breathing noisily from her three floor run downstairs.

"Well, someone's had a busy day." The elder teacher said between gasps.

"Every day's a busy day. I have a Drama Team meeting this afternoon I'm not looking forward to."

Libby took an ancient copy of Big Book of Maps from the shelf behind them pretending to fasten it to Wendy's shoulders. "Wear this so when Nick Shutter stabs you in the back, you'll have some protection."

"I always wondered why he goes after me. I'm not the one in charge of the musical; I'm not the one with the 10,000-dollar budget. What's his problem?"

"Just off the top of my head, the kids love you. They think he's creepy. With a questionable money trough, he scares up rehashed 1960's shows. With no money, you put on original productions that also serve as learning tools. Remember when he first came and you oh so nicely shared ideas with him. What did he do?"

"Libby, I can't dwell on that."

"Come on, what did that skinny little sissy boy do? Don't give me any 'walk a mile in his shoes' bull. I'm not a prejudiced person. I can honestly say I'd hate Nick even if he was straight."

Wendy pressed her palm deep into her side hoping to push back the ache. "I can handle Nick. Whenever he goes after me, I just make penis references. He's very sensitive to that. I happened to hear him on his cell last year chatting with someone named Roland. I've got leverage for a while."

Wendy shook her head while dismissing a growing thought.

"Lib, I don't know how much longer I can take being a teacher. When I'm in a classroom, I'm fine but when I have to deal with the administration's new mumbo-jumbo and test after test after test. There's no other way to say it. I'm starting to hate this place. Not the kids, just everything else."

The door opened slowly. 6A2's Hannah Kim stood under the lintel with her hand still holding the Board of Education's pewter doorknob.

"Ms. Dale, I think I left my book bag. Hi, Mrs. Spring."

She wasn't one of Libby's students so Wendy's favorite mentor smiled at the child and asked her colleague, "Who is this beautiful young lady, Ms. Dale?"

"Why that's the famous Hanna-Banana. She's playing a flute solo in our assembly program this January. She's amazing." The teacher lifted the bag from the floor holding it up for Hannah to see.

"Mrs. Spring and I wrote all over your binder and ate your lunch. Tell mommy the *bimbimbap* was delicious."

Hannah's eyes looked like little smiles when she giggled into her palm. "Ms. Dale, I know you're fooling. She made me chicken today." She thanked her teacher, bowed her head slightly and left as quietly as she arrived.

"Not the kids."

"Just everything else. Libby agreed.

As the afternoon's drama meeting began, Wendy regretted her agreement to meet Libby at Stylish Nails on Thursday after rehearsal with Jay. She was turning her days into marathons again. 'What's the definition of crazy' she asked herself 'When you keep doing the same things over and over again but expect different results. That's why I agree to things I don't want to do and then regret them, I'm crazy.' She heard her name and looked up. Mr. Shutter, his Queens College protégé by his side, began his appeal. If he was dressed to impress, the fashion conscience Ms. Dale failed to be enthused. Tall with a dancer's slender body, dyed blonde spiked hair and a tiny pearl nose ring he refused to give up for school. Mr. Shutter had a passion for semi buttoned Hawaiian shirts over black Brooklyn tees and young male student teachers. He was five years older than Wendy, had ten more years in the system with not so much as a thank you letter in his file. Her awards stuck in his throat like fish bones.

"I was just saying that in order for "Wildcat" to go on, Wendy's program has to be moved to the spring."

Wendy waited for her principal's response. Ira Rubinstein respected her work but he wasn't about to be the only regional principal without a school musical. He wished she had taken the lead drama position three years ago. She turned him down and this hack wormed his way in. 'Sorry Wendy, I know your daughter was sick but I needed you then. So be it.'

"We invest a lot of money in our show. Most of our funding is from the budget and my Principal's Choice money but a lot comes from the PTA so we need it to be a blockbuster. Wendy, can you make this concession?"

The teacher smiled to keep Nick Shutter from enjoying his victory.

'Springtime, when our students are studying for state mandated tests, springtime when my little troopers are bug-eyed tired from too many months of rehearsing, springtime when our school trips begin with whole grades out of the building and in the Planetarium. Is there a real reason this jerk and I can't equitably share the auditorium. I hate doing this to my cast and crew but I just don't have any fight spirit to spare. I have to concentrate on Janie's recovery and mine. I might not even be here this spring. Hell, I've barely had the time to speak more than a few sentences to my husband all week.' Her throbbing head began keeping time with the beat of her angry gut. 'But mostly I'd like to rise like a phoenix from this table, hover till I've left bird poop on their heads and fly out that window. Too bad it's covered in prison metal wires.'

"It'll be fine. If Mr. Shutter is unable to perform, if he thinks his production isn't firm enough yet, "Rubies" will shoot for the spring."

Fido met Wendy at the kitchen door with his favorite rope toy in his mouth. The barrel-chested mixed breed dropped his treasure at her stocking feet and stood towering over her with his front paws on her shoulders. "Oh so many kisses!" she spoke quickly to clamp her eyes and lips shut avoiding his pre-moistened tongue. "Come have a treat." She beckoned while hand feeding the hound homemade bacon flavored snacks.

"What's that smell? Like alcohol? Tim, are you in the basement? What's that smell?" Her husband called back from the storage area, "I'm cleaning tools with this new stuff. Smells like a country-boy's still. I'm getting buzzed on the fumes. Let me finish up. This really reeks. I'll shower down here. Throw a towel down, Red."

"Who's getting Janie from swim practice?"

"Would you mind, Red. This cleaner really gave me a headache."

'No problem and then I can stick a broom up my bum so I can sweep as I walk around the house as well' *"Tess soy o."*

"What? Tessy will go?"

'This would be a funny story to tell. I answered my Irish husband in Korean but whom would I tell? Not Jay.'

"It's fine, it's fine."

Tim came up from his shower to find his wife chopping the end-of-summer cucumbers. "They're a little bitter. I'll make them sweet and sour style just for us. Janie can't eat these." He came up behind her only meaning to buss the top of her head but turned her from the cutting board and kissed her deeply as he hadn't for weeks. Wendy noticed that she could barely hold her own wrists as her arms circled her husband's yearly expanding waist. When the entwining ended, she teased him. "Missed me, huh? Nice touch brushing your teeth, very gallant. Moments later when they made love, it was like parents everywhere; quickly, between chores and picking up the kids.

"Do you want to split a diet Pepsi with me before I leave for the Y?" Wendy had just washed and redressed. That sat elbow-to-elbow skirting any discussion of the monster that now lived with them.

Tim began. "I took a look in that paint company envelope. That was some payoff you got from tutoring. Is that the family who asked you to sing?"

"How much was it?" Wendy regretted her words. This was way out of character for the wife who methodically balanced their checkbook like an anal accountant.

"A lot. I didn't count it. They must have given you a bonus. I told everyone at my school that they asked you to sing. You should have seen their faces when I told them you said yes. You remember Kevin Logan, Math? He said anybody could sing but what if they asked her to juggle? He doesn't know you, huh, Red? I said my wife would have picked up three oranges and practiced all night."

At midnight, Wendy pounded her pillow for the last time and tiptoed into the kitchen. She wasn't sure of the tune but she could memorize the song's beginning by memorizing the phonics sheet she created at Jay's house. Jay and his family told her the song's name was the first line. By the light over the stove, she snapped her fingers and sing-songed, Bee neh ree nun ho nam som. 'Is *Bee neh* right? Or is it bimil like secret? No. It must be Bi like the Korean word for rain or Rain the actor from "Full House." Maybe this is a children's song, "Bah ba ba bah,

Bah ba ba bah. The little train rode in the rain. Dah dah dah."

⌘ ⌘ ⌘

As Jae Won knew he would, Yujin made his way downstairs to beg a favor. Would Jae convince Yoon Yoo that he must stay at the store with Missus Dale during the week? With a wink Yujin assured him he'd keep the family away on Sunday afternoon then shrugged as if to say, 'I am what I am.' and returned upstairs. Jae Won continued mixing a perfect viridian for the grass surrounding the farmer in the bamboo hat watercolor with his new brushes and paper. 'If we were home or this was two decades ago, Yujin would have told her himself.' He sucked the kitchen's air back to his mouth and continued his art.

⌘ ⌘ ⌘

The teacher's red dress captivated him when she entered the store pushed by the frenzied autumn winds outside.

"This weather is crazy. It was a beach day on Sunday. Now, brrr. I didn't dress appropriately at all."

"*Chai?*"

"Tea would be perfect. Thank you. I couldn't remember the tune, but I think I've memorized the top part. What does Gomp bah Gomp bah mean?"

"I forgot." Then he tapped the heel of his palm on his temple as if imitating Homer Simpson.

"You don't remember what it means?"

Jae Won held his flat abdomen with his forearms to keep from laughing too hard. Wendy joined him with the hesitant laughter we use when we're not sure what's so funny.

"*Gom bah hess im nee dah* means I forgot."

They laughed till the wind blew in three middle-aged Korean businessmen in matching golf jackets who cleared their throats in disapproval.

The CD player began and stopped with the store's trade. One of the singing duo quickly hit its pause button the moment a gust announced another customer. Like children, they used wooden paint stirrers for their pretend microphones and giggled at each other's mistakes.

"I will now respect any singer who memorizes a foreign language song. It's very difficult to remember random sounds. Do you know the word mnemonic?"

Jay shook his head no.

"It means things that help us remember. If I say 'bird', I can picture a canary or even an eagle to connect the word with the image of a bird. If I must memorize 'ird', I have no picture to help me remember."

"You don't know what this song is about?" Jay tried to get her to look at him but she held her gaze to study the lyrics sheet as if it would hold the answer. The last line, 'Tang she nul sah rang heh soy oh' suddenly revealed itself as if highlighted.

'Oh shit. It is a love song.' She looked up to hear his translation.

"It's about a man remembering the last time he saw his love. The train makes something in his memory, you know, flash. Gom bah Gom bah, I forgot for a second but now I remember. At the end he tells her...."

"*Ah rha oh.*"

The shop door opened for two Catholic schoolboys in their uniforms.

"Do you sell spray paint?"

"Not to you." the teacher jumped in. "Boys, you know better than to ask. Go home and finish that science project." They left questioning each other on how she knew they had biology assignments due. Wendy rubbed her arms with her hands. Her thin clingy wrap-around was better suited for last week.

"Are you cold?"

"No, I'm fine, really." But he watched her gaze leave the moment and go to her own thoughts. It wasn't about weather. The red with black piping von Furstenberg dress was one of her favorites, not only for its mark down at the outlet but the way it strategically hugged her body. Unfortunately, her under wire bra that was crucial to the look felt thorny near the site of her scar. 'If I had any sense, I'd go home. Maybe I should mention Thursday first.'

"Jay, Are you sure we're rehearsing here on Thursday?"

"*Wheh?*"

"Seromie's mother called me at school today. Don't look so shocked. It's an accepted practice at my school. To the secretaries it was just a parent call to her child's teacher. I, on the other hand was a bit taken back. She told me to meet you at the house after today because it'll be much better to rehearse with the Karaoke machine. She also said Yujin would be here at one so I wouldn't have to wait outside for you. Is this the plan?"

Jae Won shook his head and tapped his right fist lightly on his chest. "*Uh.*"

"Are we in the middle of something?"

"What do you think?"

"I think you tie up a dog when you're worried he'll run away."

The phone rang startling the gossipers. The caller needed information on Roman roll-up shades. Jae Won thought of buying his cousin-in-law a present for affording a place with Wendy free of interruptions.

⌘ ⌘ ⌘

Luckily, Jane didn't suffer from her mother's insomnia, enabling Wendy to work in her daughter's room after the eleven year old drifted off that evening. Jane liked it cold, which meant opened windows chilling Wendy's fingers as she worked at the computer. She studied the original draft of Papa's Thousand Voices and immediately deleted it all. She typed like a machine spitting out three new titles and four different openings till she settled on these:

A Thousand Voices by Wendy Dale

The king proclaimed that August 12th would be Thousand Gifts' Day in honor of his daughter, Princess

'Princess what? I don't want to make Jane the princess. I want her to be the daughter of the fisherman, the star. I guess I could Google baby girls' names. God, I've taught hundreds of little girls what's a good royal name? Seromie? Then the King would have to be an emperor and Jane couldn't be Jane. Jenny-purr. Good. That will be this author's private joke.'

in honor of his daughter, Princess Jenny-purr's birthday.

She pulled her arms through one of Jane's hoodies and typed till she had the beginning three pages of her very first book.

Hyun Jae Won was not as wide-eyed as he sat at his kitchen island. He was downright sleepy but needed more time to scrutinize his latest watercolor. He slid his reading glasses to the top of his head and held the painting at arm's-length for a new perspective. Behind the tiger he had painted a terracotta stone wall trimmed in black. The artist's striped beast rested nobly on his bent back legs while his head turned uncomfortably back to face a magpie. A westerner might see the tiger as fierce with his unyielding glare, reddened cheeks and white saber teeth but Jae Won was depicting an ancient eastern symbol of power. The bird stared across fearlessly, her mouth opened to bring good news. He lived in the States long enough to know when Americans chose words they paid far less attention to their implications than Koreans. But he couldn't help replaying her turn of phrase earlier that afternoon. "Are *we* in the middle of something?"

"We. We." He pushed his palm against the island top and spun his stool seat into a circle. "Whee."

Queens-Nassau Radiation Therapy was across the street from New York Radiation Therapy and across the hall from Community Radiological Associates and Affiliates. What the staff and doctors wouldn't confide to clients unless asked was that they were all owned by the same company. Patients who thought long and hard over their medical choices were getting very little to choose. Wendy signed papers while crunching on two butterscotch candies when a technician plunked down a cerulean blue mesh face mask alongside the counter's candy dish. Laced through two of its wires was a tag marked Peterson. Wendy couldn't swallow the candy remnants that now felt like glass shards in her mouth.

'Somebody named Peterson has a brain tumor. This is for his treatment. The brain tumor mask and I are sharing this terrible place.'

A tall ruddy-faced Irish nurse called her name and led her to a row of dressing stalls. Wendy disregarded all the woman's instructions till she heard "Your gown should be opening in the front." It was the only information she found useful. When she stepped outside in her thin cotton wrap, the sight of a similarly dressed male patient startled her. The twenty something dark haired man sat crossed legged casually reading a magazine. The teacher silently took the seat furthest from him clutching her wrap front closed.

Her little gown offered no warmth in the chilly examination room. The Irish nurse seemed oblivious to Wendy's one-word answers. Marybeth Flanagan had seen every possible cancer patient reaction. Some cried, some got nasty, some put on a brave face. 'This little lass just lost a bit of her spirit. Ach, see she's smil'n. She'll be fine.' If Marybeth had said this aloud, Wendy would have inventoried "She'll be foin." for

A Thousand Voices. But the nurse filled out forms, ignoring Wendy except to say. "Dr. Plotkin will be here in a minute."

After her new physician's examination, Wendy sat up for their one on one talk. She couldn't help but like Aaron Plotkin. He was like the mother-approved boys she dated in high school, soft-spoken, polite and friendly. His wife was a teacher so they talked of the job. He told her he was originally a surgeon but after his first stroke, he changed to radiology.

'That's why I like him. He's been a patient too.' Wendy tried to catalog the endless facts and statistics he mentioned but it was hopeless. She managed to capture that the treatment would take five and a half weeks. It would happen Mondays through Fridays at half hour sessions. The area would feel and look like a sunburn. She would feel tired. Radiation's effects are cumulative and might extend past the treatment for a few weeks Then came the final caveat, the one that had patients searching for an exit sign. Dr. Plotkin paused, looked her square in the eyes and cleared his throat. "There's an increased risk of primary lung carcinoma. It's rare, only one in a thousand but I have to inform you before you make your decision."

Wendy felt surrounded by feedback hum. It hurt her ears. She would have liked to shake her head like dogs sometimes do, back and forth, back and forth but the good doctor was waiting for her to speak.

"One in a thousand is rare? Not to me. I work in a building with over 1300 human beings but I'm the only one with this." She pointed to her left breast but quickly returned her hand to her lap. Wendy sighed, 'What's the difference? Let's just get this over with.'

"When can I start?"

Marybeth said the scheduling office would call with Wendy's appointment dates. She wouldn't be allowed to shave under her left arm for a while. She needed to buy and wear soft sports bras and must use a scent free soap. But before any of this would be relevant, she had to go for a simulation to mark the exact spot for her radiation. That would be done at their Stuart Avenue office. Marybeth could tell the woman was educated, so didn't bother with simple definitions. The nurse may have considered herself a reaction expert but she misjudged Wendy's. The teacher nodded her affirmation, took all her new forms and pamphlets and thanked the nurse without the slightest idea what her medical future had in store.

Wendy often envied those Teachers' Lounge women who lived their lives as helpless aging girls. They couldn't cook, hadn't the strength for grocery shopping, and hired cleaning 'ladies' because they had bad backs, allergies or carpal tunnel. Their husbands bought them expensive gifts and their children accomplished lists of chores daily. No one ever took care of Wendy Dale. She always beat them to it. Not today. The house chores could wait.

The car found a spot on Glenwood off Northern. Wendy walked north arching her back every few steps to ease her aching side. When she reached the boulevard, she turned right. Three stores down was TANKS A LOT the local aquarium and pet fish store. She had never been in aquatic pet store before. She had never owned a live fish but she knew she had half of her Anycolor Paints cash in her handbag giving her enough money to spend.

Happily the owner was absent with the only worker a shy pimply chinned teenage boy to greet her. The last thing she needed was a sales pitch.

"I'd like two goldfish, pretty ones. I'll need a bowl and rocks, food and instructions. Did I forget anything?"

"I wouldn't recommend a bowl. They don't live long in bowls. Goldfish need a lot of surface air. You'll need a tank and a filter."

'Even this is becoming a pain.' Wendy cryptically squeezed her waist while making her decisions.

"How about this? I'll get a really big bowl to last a few weeks. Then I'll buy the tank. If getting fish turns out to be a bad idea, I'll return them to you. I don't want my money back. Just resell them to good homes."

The high-schooler snorted so not to laugh. He showed her to the tanks of fish on display. They waved in front of her like medieval pennants in the wind; beautiful, shimmering, golden, and orange.

'Ooh, there's even a black one. No wonder people keep them.'

The teacher left the store with a wide mouth clear bowl, three pages of instructions, a bag of stones, underwater greenery, a thermometer, Tetrafin fish food and a plastic bag containing one velvety black Moor and a big eyed Telescope with red-gold flowing fins.

"Mom, this is so cool. Is it for your students?" Jane made it so easy. Her husband and daughter hushed themselves as they watched Wendy set up the goldfishes' new home. Even Fido poked his nose through the onlookers for a moment before he grew bored. Wendy was their family's expert even though her only prior goldfish experience was walking by the tanks at PetSmart on her way to buy Fido's toys.

"How'd it go today? Tim asked his wife as they lay shoulder to shoulder bathed in the television's blue-gray light.

"Horribly." Wendy was trying to erase the day with the Korean spy drama that played out in front of her. "What did the oncologist say?"

"What oncologist?"

"Didn't you go to the oncologist today?"

"No, I went to the radiologist, but thanks for remembering I had an appointment." The sarcasm was not lost on him.

"It doesn't mean anything. I made a mistake. Just remember you're not in this alone." Her husband stifled a yawn then tried to slip his arm under her nape. Wendy turned to face him.

"I know you think of this as some kind of glitch but to me it's more stones in my load. Sick mother, sick child, sick me. In the whole world, who would trade with me? Nobody." She took an Ambien from her night table and downed it with a half glass of water. Tim understood her signal. He slid his arm back and turned from her. He was snoring in less than a minute. Wendy unsuccessfully tried to follow the new drama but was drawn to the fishbowl to the left of the TV. Earlier she had cautiously placed it out of Fido's reach in case the hound got curious in the middle of the night. Before the pill took her, the teacher watched the fish swim relays in their new pond.

⌘ ⌘ ⌘

She was late. It was only five minutes but he was afraid she reconsidered coming to his home. He had never paced in wait for anyone before. His gut tightened while his fingers fidgeted with each other. He winced at the prospect of a life filled with moments on edge like this. She was now six minutes late. Jae Won left his slippers on his top step then slid his toes and thrust his heels into his shoes. He'd wait outside where the air was fresh. Jae Won paced the length of his house stopping once to greet an elderly neighbor out walking his dog. After his second lap he saw her worn out sedan pull up in front of his walkway. 'Why am I standing in the street? What realistic excuse can I give her?' He was rescued by her apologies as soon as she exited her car.

"*Mi ahn hah dah*. I'm a bit late but I wanted to bring something to your cousins for their hospitality so I picked up Asian pears and candy corn for the girls. Wendy took a breath. "Fishman, I need you to have a very American reaction to what I'm about to do. I'm well aware that one should never buy living things for others but, well anyway, if you don't want this, please say so. No hard feelings. I can just take it back. I can even bring it to school, really."

'What is she saying?'

Then she leaned over forcing her forest green skirt to rise a few inches and brought out a fishbowl with two surprised goldfish. Jae Won took the bowl from her hands.

"*Whah*. This is for me? *Co mah woi yo.*" He would have been happy to accept a nest of vipers. The woman who had him nervously pacing like a caged tiger had just brought him a present.

Bird and Fish

Jay dutifully took the food upstairs to his cousins' kitchen counter. When he reached the bottom step he knew she was right. The fish and bowl did enliven the kitchen. His eyes could readily dismiss the surrounding whites for the dancing gold and black in the room's center.

"What are you going to name them?" Wendy asked, happy her gift was accepted.

"You name them."

"No, that's too personal. I wouldn't let anybody name my dogs. I named them all Fido. It means faithful in Latin. Not just because dogs are loyal to their owners but also it's my pledge to them; good dogs and bad ones, healthy or sick. I'll care for them till their time on earth is done."

Jae Won wondered if the woman who chose her clothing the way he mixed colors could care for him till his time was done.

"How about *Uh-ri?*"

"*Uri*, oh, Korean for you and me. I like that. I'll be the gold one. She matches my Scottish red hair. Your hair… Jay, even your clothes today, match the black Moor's."

"Are you Scottish?"

"Like so many Americans, I'm a mixed breed. My father's family was originally from Scotland. That's how I got the name Dale. When he died I promised myself I would honor him by keeping his name, even after I married. That's not very common for American women."

"It's very Korean."

"I know. It seems like everything in my life led me to Korea. There's enough Oprah, Martha and Rachel on TV to pick from but I watch Korean dramas. There are over a hundred ethnic groups represented in the city's student population but I teach mostly Korean children. NYKAPA, the Korean parent association only sent school administrators to Korea, but then they sent me. *Uri*, we're singing a Korean song at a festival. Fate wants me on this path. I just don't know why."

Jae Won suctioned air back into his mouth and tentatively asked about her marriage.

"Your daughter, she has your husband's name?"

"She has her father's last name. I was married before."

She watched his smile flatline and hastened to add, "I was a widow." His continence immediately softened.

Wendy conjured up her mother's last warning to her, 'Dammit, Lucille you were right.'

Jae Won feigned fascination with the goldfish playmates while directing his words to her.

"You are married now?"

"I am married now."

As if waiting in the wings, Yoon Yoo Son came down the stairs smiling. After a polite nod, she addressed Wendy.

"*Sun seng nim.* Thank you so much for the pears and candy. I just came in and saw them with your note. We have to practice. *Kunapogee,* would you please get everything ready downstairs. Misses Dale and I will prepare the pears."

Wendy returned Yoon Yoo's stony smile as Jae Won made his exit.

'Sister, I know you heard everything. You didn't seem surprised by this fishbowl because you've been listening since Jay dropped off the fruit. I don't know a damn thing about football or combat but I'm pretty sure the best defense is offense.'

"*Seromie eommah,* I'm happy to help you but why are you pushing Jay to spend so much time with me?"

"*Sun seng nim,* this singing contest is sponsored by KoreanRadio. It's very good advertising." Wendy reached for the younger woman's hands, placed one inside each of hers and held on while she spoke as an older sister. "*Yoonashee,* What I meant to say is why do you need us to keep your husband at the store?"

Yoon Yoo Son's slender body folded like a kindergartener's paper fan landing her on the kitchen stool. Her delicate fingers pressed hard over her mouth to keep from sobbing aloud. Her tears soon reached her hand and were joined by the watery syrup from her nose.

"Mrs. Son, I'm sorry." Wendy reached for the tissue pack in her handbag but remembered all those dramas where heartbroken women used only their hands to wipe their faces. She dropped the tissues back inside then walked behind the whimpering Yoon Yoo to serve her a glass of tap water. Wendy stood at the woman's shaking shoulders and rubbed her back as she had done with Jane in too many hospital rooms.

"So, Bae Yong Joon's cheating on you?"

It was an old teaching technique. One hysterical child can't be the teacher's only job in a classroom of 33 so Wendy would say something silly to get the crier to laugh. After class was a better time to deal with problems. It worked in this setting too. Yoon Yoo smirked, "Bae Yong Joon, you're right. How do you know who he is?"

"I know if I was ever in a snowstorm, I'd like to be rescued by him."

Bird and Fish

Yoon Yoo laughed at the teacher's allusion to the famous Korean star's breakout drama, Winter Sonata. Wendy walked around the counter to face her.

"What are you going to do?"

"Nothing. Please *sun seng nim*, don't say anything."

Wendy reached over the counter top and gently patted the younger woman's arm. "But why are you pushing your cousin to be with me? I'm married. I have a family. Surely you don't want to hurt someone else's family."

"Right now, I only care about mine." A fully composed Yoon Yoo rose and turned towards the sink. Wendy blinked two or three times before she was calm enough to head downstairs. 'Peel your own fruit, *ma-nyeo!*'

⌘ ⌘ ⌘

Black men talk politics in their barbershops, a practice begun at the end of the American Civil War. White men have argued teams and stats in their sports' bars from the last half of the twentieth century while Korean men have been singing their troubles away in Karaoke rooms since the popular phenomenon traveled east from Kobe, Japan in the 1970's. But to learn the soul of a woman, any woman, be a fly on the wall at her nail salon. In northeastern Queens, where nail shops are overwhelmingly Asian owned, a client can let slip the grief from her heart to her nailist without fear of condemnation mostly because of the language barrier. The history of the manicure goes back five thousand years to ancient China, yet this age-old custom of patrons purging their souls while manicurists gently massage and rejuvenate their fingers and hands is still regarded as frivolous by men. Wendy often referred to her weekly ritual as the 'cheapest dope on earth.' Once each week, for eleven dollars, four of that her over-zealous tip, she could spend an hour listening to the feathery xiao and guzheng music, have her hands and neck gently manipulated and practice basic Chinese greetings with her manicurist. Occasionally she brought her daughter along to treat the pre-teener but lately Jane preferred going to their neighborhood's salon with her friends. This actually better suited the teacher. Wendy preferred the quiet atmosphere. She didn't come to rehash her troubles; she came to pretend she hadn't any.

Wendy and Jae Won drove in tandem back to their first meeting place. She parked on Broward and dashed across busy Northern Boulevard to meet Libby at Stylish Nails. Jae Won parked in the store's lot then unlocked the back door to relieve his cousin from work. He entered the store in time to watch Yujin escort a local builder reeking of Budweiser out the front entrance.

"Quen sha nah ay o?"

Yujin turned towards his cousin. "*Uh*, oh him? No problem. He must have gotten paid and remembered he promised to Spackle something at home. I'll get the

Lysol spray." As he walked closer to Jae Won, he affected a throat clearing, "My wife was home?" he garbled.

"Neh."

"She say anything?"

"I don't know. I don't involve myself when women talk." The anger in his belly heated.

"You didn't notice anything?"

"*Tess soy oh, tess soy oh.* Everything was fine. You want to know what I had to do? I hid in the basement when they talked.

Yujin couldn't suppress his laughter. "*Mee ahn hah dah.* I'll stay here another hour and then I'll go straight home. *Ah rhah suh?*

"Just grow up. You have a family."

"So does *she*." Yujin was emboldened by his own caustic remark. The younger cousin lived as an American for half his life enabling him to let slip traditional respect for his elders. His personal revolution ended as quickly as it began when put his arm around Jae Won's shoulders and apologized in English. "I'm sorry. Come on, lighten up. I thought I saw Wendy run across the street. Is she coming back?"

Jae Won shook his head side to side, not to answer his cousin's question but questioning Yujin's behavior.

"She's meeting her friend across the street."

Libby had already picked out a deep red polish and seated herself while a sweet-faced woman the clients called Cindy removed the final bits of last week's coating. The manicurist's birth name, Chen Chi was one the customers couldn't remember. The three seated women raised their heads when Wendy stepped through the salon's door. "Hi, Wendy." they greeted in unison. "Nee Haw Mah everybody. Were you waiting long? What color is that?" Libby and her manicurist laughed. "I just told Cindy what happened last week. One of my ninth grade girls liked my polish and asked me what it's called. There was no way I was going to say 'After Sex' to this kid, so I looked her square in the eye and said, I don't remember!" She eyeballed her friend's pale hands and polish. "It's October. Why don't you get something darker?"

The younger teacher answered by stepping to the rack of 20 red-brown shades and after two preliminary selections settled on Well Red. Libby continued talking, "Don't forget this is my treat for being a brave girl."

"I wasn't all that brave." She turned to her manicurist. "Susie, I remembered 'Tway pi.'"

"Oh, Wendy, your Chinese is so good."

"I'm trying. Did you watch "Surrender" this week?"

"You know Liu Ye very famous." Susie usually tried not to use English words with r sounds but felt more confident around Wendy. Libby felt like an outsider.

"Are you two gonna talk Korean dramas?"

Susie answered first. "No, this is Chinese drama. Wendy loves this one, right?"

"I do. It's about a street thug and an innocent college student, two people who have no right to be in love. That's why it's called, 'Surrender to the Naïve Girl'."

"Libby shook her head. "You're one of a kind, Ms. Dale."

By now the woman were speaking rapid fire to each other while looking down at their hands. They accomplished this awkward stance with ease soon lowering their voices to maintain the peacefulness of the space. Wendy nodded her head to the paint store across the street. "That's the store."

"You mean that's the guy."

"Wait till I tell you what happened today."

"Tell me right now."

Wendy, without too much embellishment, recanted the tale of the goldfish, Mrs. Son and Jay's probable cowering in the basement.

"It's comical, she hid on the stairway listening to Jay then he hid listening to her. It was like being in a drama."

Libby let her perusal leave the emery board making dust of her fingernail tip. She looked at 'the naïve girl' beside her.

"His cousin is a player. Is it a family trait? How far are you going to take this?"

"There's nothing to take. There's nothing going on, really."

"When your mother was in that stroke rehab place and you had to drive there every day to pick up her dirty underwear and bring her candy, you looked washed out all the time. When Janie was so sick, well, you looked like shit, pardon me for saying so. Now you've got this major cross to bear, don't shake your head. This is every woman's nightmare, yet right this moment you look, dare I say it? You're glowing."

Wendy blushed in hues of scarlet that put the nail polish rack to shame. "You're right. I should stop this nonsense before, well before anything."

"You misunderstand me." Libby wagged her freshly polished index finger.

"Cindy, don't cut them today just push 'em back, yes, like that. Thanks." "Wendy, you're not my daughter so I may be off base but, if befriending this guy can get you through the big C, maybe you should go for it.

"But you're a mother and wife. Could you betray your sons or your husband?"

"You haven't betrayed anyone. You've just teamed up with someone who can see you through this. Cancer kills more than healthy cells. It's not always a *person's* fault when a marriage dies, but honestly, if I was diagnosed with cancer, I'd put my guys' needs on hold till I was well. I don't mean to confuse you but there are two sides to this coin. So, if you don't mind, when I'm dry, I'm going to tap into my good-man bad-man radar, cross the street and buy me a paint brush."

The women turned to each other, made gibbon noises and clasped hands causing their nailists to cluck and gently return the friends' hands to their towel covered armrests.

The nail dryers, as was often the practice in salons, were strategically placed at the shop windows, affording the pampered women a view of Northern Boulevard's fast paced traffic and Anycolor Paints' II front entrance. Wendy's pulse raced as she watched her friend dash through the crosswalk in her Jimmy Choo patent and metal heels. For a moment she was Wendy Dale, high school student, showing off her first crush.

Jae Won and Yujin also watched. From the front windows they could make out the outline of the two red haired women in the salon across the street. When the elder woman headed towards their store, they each busied themselves. Libby hadn't been a highschooler in many years. She was a no-nonsense person who could keep her demeanor pleasant and unobtrusive. She purchased a one-inch paintbrush she would later use to baste meats. She remained deadpan when handing money to the younger man and smiled fleetingly at the older one. She was back at the salon giving her approval in ten minutes.

Inside Anycolor, Yujin spoke first. "*Hyung*, you should be flattered. Misses Dale's friend just checked you out." Jae Won affected a 'so what' stance but he felt like breaking into a shaman's nature dance. The woman's smile told him he was approved. More amazing; Yujin wasn't. After his cousin left for home, Jae Won placed a CD on the Bose tray and danced to the tune Wendy called "the Gom Bah Gom Bah song." till a customer opened the door.

Wendy arrived home in time to hear Dr. Tapman's nurse's voice recording on the house phone. 'Good. It's just a nurse.' She raced to learn Janie's blood test results.

"Oh, you're there, Mrs. Dale. Dr. Tapman would like to speak to you. Hold please."

Wendy couldn't remember where her husband and daughter were. She let Fido out when she arrived leaving her alone at her bedside in the silent house.

"Mrs. Dale, hi. Don't worry but Jane's liver enzyme levels are a bit high. It might be from the Azasan but it could just be the foods she's been eating. I'd like to test her in two weeks. Tell her to watch her fats. Mrs. Dale, I don't want you to worry. It's probably nothing"

The teacher crumpled till she was seated on her bed much like the folding motion of Yoon Yoo Son's body earlier, but unlike the cool headed Mrs. Son, Wendy had no other family she could sacrifice.

⌘ ⌘ ⌘

Episode 6: Lydia The Tattooed Lady

Yujin was capable of keeping some of his promises. On Sunday, the high ranch remained free of him and his family while Wendy and Jay sang, ate and tapped the fishbowl. Had his cousins arrived at this very minute, they would have listened like nosy neighbors on the stairway.

"Why don't you want to do it?"

"I'm too shy."

"You are never shy."

"That's not entirely true. Please don't ask me again."

"You'd look beautiful. Just do it."

"When I was in Korea, a Californian posed in one for a picture. It wasn't beautiful. She looked like a big fat blonde in a hambok.

"You're not fat. You're not blonde."

"I'm not Korean. I have a closet filled with clothes that still have the tags hanging from their sleeves. You won't be embarrassed." Wendy stood her ground. Not her usual stance. She wore a hambok for a school assembly once and had the audience clapping and on their feet when she announced, "I've been a bride but this is the prettiest dress I've ever worn. She was tougher, more self-assured and knew her audience, but that was then. Eleven and twelve year olds were easily impressed. Ms. Dale, wearing somebody's mom's hambok at school, was instantly catapulted to rock star prominence. This was different. There might be hundreds of strangers there. Some of them were bound to feel like she was having fun at their expense. 'More importantly, this lovely gentle man thinks I'm still pretty. With all the beautiful Korean woman in this neighborhood, slender and regal, he chose me. I'm not going to disappoint him by looking like I'm on my way to a Halloween party. Unlike Barrie's Wendy, I don't miss my mother and I want to stay in his Neverland a little while longer.

Jae Won hadn't asked a woman to wear anything particular before. Now he knew why. She could easily turn him down. He was worried of his status in their relationship but the red haired woman seemed nonplussed by their conversation. Was hers a usual woman's reaction or a usual American's reaction? It didn't matter. He wasn't concerned about how she would dress for the contest. Everything she wore was meticulously planned with a total tableau in mind. Even today, she sat relaxed in wool camel trousers with a camel sweater that flowed off her shoulders flaring slightly at mid-thigh. She managed to procure a wide beaded belt with flecks of crimson, sage and burnt umber. He had seen this sequence of colors used on a screen in the Seoul Museum of History. An ancient craftsman used them to embroider the ten longevity symbols. He didn't need her to dress up like a Korean bride doll. His cousins had suggested it. He didn't blame them for asking. He'd been following the instructions of others all his life.

"Did you visit the Seoul Museum of History when you were in Korea?"

"I may have. I visited several museums. Does it have a depiction of a burial mound in it?"

Jay chuckled, "Now I'm embarrassed. I don't remember. I visited to look at their examples of Minhwa. Did you learn about Minhwa at a museum?"

"No. As part of the visit, I stayed with a sponsoring school family for three days. The mother was much younger than her husband. She and I were the same age and got along very well. Her name is Mi Young Yi. They even had a dog, Eagle."

"Eagle?"

"The father loved to play golf so they named their dog after two strokes below par. I have a picture of the whole family at home. I'll bring it to you. They thought it was so funny that Eagle followed me everywhere and even slept in my room at night. Maybe he sensed I was Fido's mom. Wendy's eyes crinkled as she affected a naughty grin. "Maybe he just felt safe that I wouldn't eat him."

"Wendy, dog soup is…."

The teacher covered her ears, *"Shiro, shiro.* I don't want to know. Anyway, Mr. Kim owns art galleries in Insa-dong and Seoul. Their home was beautifully decorated to showcase his Minhwa collection. I think he's pretty famous." Jae Won couldn't believe what he heard. He'd have to thank Buddha tonight. This woman half way around the world knew Kim Dong Kook.

The artist, in one nimble move leaned across the counter and held her face in his hands. "I've only seen his collections in magazines. Some of his pieces are loaned to museums. When I was young I fantasized, fantasized right? … that I'd be discovered by Kim Dong Kook the way other teenagers dream of becoming film stars. Which collection pieces do you remember? What did he tell you?"

Wendy assured herself he was just enthusiastic but her better judgment led her hands to cover his and remove them from her jaw line even though his pinky fingers on her neck changed her pulse beat to a drum solo.

"The colors inspired me. After I returned home that summer, I repainted my breakfast room to match the muted fall tones of the pictures. I remember the workers and peasants were like children's book illustrations and I envisioned writing a story for my students based on those depictions."

"Why didn't you write the story?"

"Why didn't you bring your work to his gallery?"

"I spent my life doing just what I was told."

"*Nah du.*"

⌘ ⌘ ⌘

When the teacher arrived home she changed into one of Jane's discarded hooded sweatshirts and a pair of washed out jeans before pulling the last of the vegetable plants from the garden. The hoodie became a private sauna as she tugged and dug up shriveling scotch bonnet stems but she kept her neck covered sure the places his fingertips touched would radiate like scarlet letters revealing her broken promises.

⌘ ⌘ ⌘

Third period found Ms. Dale seated next to Miss Ariel Pride, a first year drama teacher who while pleasant wasn't quick enough to fully impress Wendy. The student announcers had just begun the first act when Ariel laughed as if just getting their joke, "That's pretty funny, when that little boy says, 'Is boring a virtue? Cause if it is this assembly is very virtuous' is so cute. Who wrote this?" Wendy tried not to mock the slow-witted teacher.

"I wrote it."

"That's right, Ms. Dale, I forgot, you wrote it! Why don't you package this and sell it. Teachers would love to have a book of pre-made assembly programs. That's what I'd do."

'The kid's not so dumb after all.' "Maybe, someday. How's the He-Lion skit working out?"

"There's a problem. The parts were given out but I've got two Special Ed kids who insist they're good enough to be in the play. Ms. Dale, they can't act. They can't even read. They show up at my rehearsals and harass the other kids.

"You should have told me right away." The senior teacher choked down a quarter Vicodin with the saliva mustered up by her purloined butterscotch candy. The unforgiving wooden auditorium seats seemed to twist and push her tailbone painfully into her side. She stood, microphone to her lips. "Where's The Tiger's Whisker cast? Sajjan, what's the problem?"

The seventh grader was a foot shorter than his fellow announcer but his voice projected as if he was a giant.

"Ms. Dale, what is ah da se-o? I don't know how to say it 'cause I don't know what it means. I don't speak Korean."

"OK Sandman, just watch me. The line is yada yada, yada, the virtue of patience. Come watch this folktale from the land of the morning calm, *Ah rhul suh?* then give a thumbs up to the audience and repeat, *Ah rhul suh!* It means, OK? OK! You try it now." The kohl eyed little master repeated her inflections.

"Sandman, that was perfect. Where are you from?"

"Me? Ms. Dale, I'm a Punjabi boy."

"Only in Queens can you find a Scottish-German lady teaching Korean to a Punjabi boy, *Ah rhul suh?*"

"*Ah rhul suh!*"

The play began again. Wendy turned to the twenty-two year old teacher beside her. "Don't get in the habit of using the label, Special Ed. They're tortured enough by their schoolmates. Come down to lunch some time. You'll see them huddled together away from all the other children. Besides if it falls on the wrong ears, you'll get chewed out. I have a doctor's appointment today but I'll be back in time to speak to them. Who are they?"

"Taequanna Roberts and Omar Washington."

The teacher smiled. This wouldn't be a problem. She knew them, more importantly they knew her.

Northern Boulevard was so named to mark its run along the north shore of Long Island. The route starts at the Fifty Ninth Street Bridge, corridor to Manhattan and ends in Calverton, one of Suffolk County's more verdant communities boasting farms, the Naval Weapons Industrial Reserve Airport and like all ends of the line, a cemetery. The roadway wove through Wendy's life as well. When a teenager, she walked to its Bayside bus stop to ride into Flushing's hub catching the 7 train to the world's greatest city. She often drove to college using this route to save her from the relentless traffic on the expressway. The boulevard was home to her favorite shopping haunts and most feared hospitals. Seasons throughout Jane's childhood were marked by daytrips to the U-Pick farms for strawberries in early summer and pumpkins in the fall. Her daydream was shaken by the now familiar ache in her side. The last memory she conjured was of a five year old Janie who held handfuls of strawberries near her ears and called out, "Now I have hair like mommy's." Illness had stolen so much from them. She couldn't recall a good belly laugh at home in years. All carefree joy stayed locked in the past. 'The last time I had a good laugh was at Jay's. When he told me what *Gom bah* meant but life's neither a department store nor pyramid. I can't exchange my family's happiness for mine or build happiness atop their misery. Can I? No answer came to her even as she drove past Anycolor II Paints on her way to a medical procedure that would mark her for life.

The Stuart Radiologists and Associates offices offered a parking lot. Wendy stepped out of the Sentra to be greeted by October winds flexing their muscles. She wrapped her scarf twice around her neck and closed the middle button of her chesterfield. The teacher was diligent last night and placed her insurance card and all necessary forms in the same compartment of her Franco Sarto handbag. Had she been a bit more diligent she might have included researching exactly what was going to happen to her inside the gray brick building.

Once again she sat in a thin cotton wrap in a row of uncomfortable flowered chairs. This time flanked by a tall young black man with his very pregnant wife and an elderly woman who knitted to pass the wait time. Wendy looked at the thirtyish father-to-be in the blue wrap and wondered why he was there. He looked fine. Wendy eavesdropped on the couple's conversation but it held no clues. She decided to concentrate on the silver haired woman's knitting instead, chastising herself for attempting to compromise their privacy.

When her name was called, she followed a baby-faced young woman to an icy room with a giant beige doughnut shaped machine at its center. Wendy stopped for a moment in the doorway.

'I don't want that top part covering my face. If it covers my face, I'll crawl right out of there. I should have taken a half of a Xanax. My mother always pumps herself full of tranquilizers before her tests. I can't take Xanax. I have to drive. And who's this girl? She doesn't look much older than my ninth graders. How much faith do I have in her expertise?'

As if reading her mind, the young woman told Wendy that the table would only move her through the X-ray image tube up to her chin while the rotating gantry circled. Wendy began to tremble slightly from the room's tomb-like cold air and her own fears. Before the teacher lie down, she glimpsed several faces in a window overlooking her and the scan. There were two men on the other side and she was half naked.

'It's comical really. When I gave birth to Jane, I didn't care who was watching. The guy with the mop down the hall could have stopped by for a flash. Now I'm ashamed. This must be how sexually assaulted women feel when a hospital staffer whips out the rape kit.'

Laser lights coordinated lines on her chest and underarm. The young woman approached her with a hypodermic needle and first made a hair's width dot under her arm. She waited until the laser's markings realigned and repeated the process between Wendy's breasts. The technician looked back at her handiwork and added a bit more dye for good measure. The second go around left the teacher with a flat blue spot that would forever be the focal point above every ball gown, bathing suit or brassiere she wore.

"This is the same dye as tattoos. It won't wash off."

'What was she talking about? Did anyone tell me this before? Maybe someone did. Could I have really blocked this out? I've got to get up. My side hurts. I have to take something.'

Bird and Fish

"Wendy, are you all right?" The teacher paused before answering. She wasn't comfortable with someone so young calling her by her first name.

"I guess I'll have to change my name to Lydia, the tattooed lady."

The young woman's lips barely turned upward.

'She doesn't know who the Marx brothers are. Maybe she is a ninth grader.' "Thank you. Which is the way back to the dressing rooms?"

⌘ ⌘ ⌘

The teacher's two-inch heels clicked-stepped down the hall heralding her return to school. Drama Room 2 held eight student actors and three scenery painters as well as the harried Miss Pride and her hecklers.

"Who's the King? I'm the King!" belted out Jasmine Brown as He-Lion. In respect, the children stepped out of character and turned their attention to the senior teacher. Wendy waved the back of her hand to the players signaling them to continue. She revered this African-American folk tale. Its origins began in Africa's oral tradition with griots teaching village children the virtues of bravery and humility. It stowed away on the slave ships and was reborn in the American south adding rabbits, possums and bears to the African lion's kingdom. She rewrote the story as she did Tiger's Whisker for her students to perform. It was a labor of love. Her reward was watching the shyest actor dressed as a big round sun step across the stage while the boldest milked her Slave #1 part by shouting, "He-lion was thinking and thinking. By the time he finished, the sun had warmed the w-h-o-l-e world." She applauded their rehearsal then applauded their director, Miss Pride.

"It's really jelling. Bravo! Omar, Taequanna, meet me in the hallway for a minute." The teens dressed in matching 44' waisted fat jeans and XXXL Sean John tee shirts put down a toy rifle prop they were trying to dismantle and followed meekly behind the stern-faced teacher. Ms. Dale folded her arms in front of her signaling her displeasure. She faced the boy knowing he would buckle sooner than his friend. "Omar, I'll talk to you first then I'll get Tae's opinion." Taequanna jumped in before her partner in crime could answer, "That lady's a racist, Ms. Dale."

"Now you see, this is why you didn't get a part. You don't take direction. One of you get me a chair my feet are growing blisters in these shoes. She sat in a chair and began her lesson with the two heirs of ancient griots seated cross-legged in front of her. Neither student met their teacher's gaze.

"Why can't I play for the Knicks?"

The ninth graders looked at each other in confusion.

"Why can't I play for the Knicks? I love basketball and I want to play."

Taequanna answered quickly, "You a woman and you too short." Then after a snicker, "You too old too."

"Everything you said is true but why won't they let me play?"

Omar took his shot, "Cause everybody on that team is better than you."

"Why can't I sing with Beyonce?"

Taequanna called out, "I get it. Don't matter just cause you want somethin'. You can't always get it."

The teacher gently held the girl's chin upward with her hand. There are things you're the best at. Tae, you're in Chorus. You sing much better than I ever will. Omar, you're the pride of our basketball team. Those kids in there, this is where they shine. It may be the only thing they're good at. Don't try to take it. It's theirs alone. But there is something we can do. Three slaves tell the story. Right now they face the audience. I think it would look better if let's say Omar was on stage raking and Tae, you were peeling apples. When the first slave begins the story, you'll stop your chores and pretend to listen. Do you think that would be more realistic?"

The teenagers nodded their approval.

"Understand me, they're non-speaking parts. You're Slave #3 and you're #4. One more thing, Is Jasmine black, is

Rasheed? Didn't Miss Pride give them parts? Just give her a chance. Please put the chair back for me. I'll talk to your teacher."

As Wendy re-entered the Drama room she nodded to a substitute teacher listening in her classroom doorway. Tomorrow, Ms. Dale wouldn't remember the woman's face. That was unfortunate because tomorrow she would hate her.

Wendy day-dreamed of collapsing on her side of the big bed at home as she said goodbye to Claire at the front desk. Mrs. Ok, seven months pregnant and waddling out the office doorway to the lobby called out, "Ms. Dale."

What is it about pregnant woman that pleases us? Maybe it reminds us of spring's renewal. Outside the trees were shedding their orange bonnets leaving their spiny branches to diagram the sky. But here in the quiet lobby, the soft-spoken Korean teacher was in bloom.

"*Ahnyung hah seh oh. Quen sha nah?*" greeted Wendy.

"I'm fine, a little tired. I see you're still watching dramas." The bubble-bellied woman finally reached Wendy's side.

"I'm up to eight now. Insomnia has its perks. I watch my tapes while my family sleeps. I have a question. I've seen a commercial on HTV where they say, *Oh suh hah say yo.* Is that a different way to say hello?"

"*Oh suh hah seh yo* means welcome."

"*Co mah woi oh, ahjummah.* That makes sense. It's an ad for a hotel chain. Let's walk out together.

"Were you working with your assembly students? That makes the day so long."

"*Neh.* What were you doing?"

"I had a department meeting."

"I'd rather rehearse with the kids."

"*Nah du.*" The younger teacher laughed.

Wendy joined her, "I know what that means, me too!"

"I heard you had surgery. Are you feeling better?"

"I'm fine, thanks."

"Sea weed soup really strengthens you. Have you had any?"

"The same soup you're supposed to eat on your birthday or after giving birth?"

"That's right. You know so much Korean culture. Now I know why the kids love you. One of them asked me if you were Korean. I'm serious."

Wendy preferred dark chocolate to soup but her colleague's description enticed her. Sitting behind the Nissan's steering wheel, her thoughts wouldn't let go of their hot comforting soup images. She had homemade split pea and ham soup in plastic containers in the basement freezer but was in the mood for something Korean. She headed for Flushing's New Seoul restaurant.

While the Korean restaurants she knew looked different from each other they shared the same smell. It wasn't a food aroma. It was the lingering trace of fuel used for the table-top barbeque centers that always reminded her of her meals in Seoul. She was the only non-Korean in the half filled restaurant but that was usual. Bagelries, pizza parlors and Chinese restaurants fed New Yorkers breakfast, lunch and dinner but Korean cuisine was still waiting for its big break.

"*Oh so hah seh yo.*" beckoned the hostess, leading Wendy to chide herself for not making the connection earlier. She placed her take out order and waited patiently while glancing at the patrons and their side dishes.

Yujin Kim, at a table near the kitchen sat smiling across at his partner as if it was their first date. The pair barely spoke. Wendy noted the handsome man had already downed two glasses of soju since he entered her line of vision.

'Is that Jay's cousin and his wife? Maybe it's their anniversary. I shouldn't interrupt them. Still, if she turns around and sees me, I'd seem rude. Wendy's brain hadn't signaled her legs to walk yet when the woman with Yujin turned to signal a waiter, *"Yo gee oh."* The profile wasn't Yoon Yoo Son's. Neither was the voice. The teacher's green eyes widened till she looked like a color version of Max Fleischer's Betty Boop. She frantically sought a place to hide as if she was the one caught inflagrante. She stole a seat at a booth nearest the front door and held her trembling hands together till a waiter arrived with her order.

She wouldn't leave her parking space on 150th Street till she felt calm enough to drive. 'I will never think another mean thought about Yoon Yoo Son again. What was the name of that Judith Viorst book Janie and I read together? "Alexander and the Terrible Horrible No Good Very Bad Day". Well, this is Wendy's and I've got a big blue freckle to remind me of it forever.'

⌘ ⌘ ⌘

A sky the color of Grandma Dales's moonstone ring brought torrential rains the next morning. Ms. Dale had to ask the administrator on duty for permission to bring the students into the steamy auditorium rather than have them wait outside in the deluge. If the administrator couldn't be located the children would stand in the rain thus confirming the teacher's soured opinion of the city's education system. Of course Wendy could have brought the children in on her own but if any child fell or was hurt in a scuffle, she'd be left swinging with "No one gave you permission to make that decision." reverberating in her ears. She and Claire barked at and cajoled about nine hundred students to their seats when Wendy saw Edgar Armon approaching. The well-tailored Social Studies teacher looked so much like Barack Obama he was often teased by his colleagues about his political aspirations. He was the topic of every teachers' lounge in 1995 when he wore a pro O.J. pin during the infamous trial.

"Hi Edgar, are you looking for a student? I'll get them quieted." She began to put her ear-piercing orange boat whistle to her lips.

"Actually, I'm here to see you. I was told, I don't know if it's true, that you're making black kids play slaves in your play."

Three years ago, a happier Wendy would have called the accusation preposterous, explained the situation and ended her dissertation with additional snappy patter. While Jane was bedridden, the teacher would have lowered her head and apologized for being insensitive with a meager defense of the assembly program. Now was the wrong time to pick on Ms. Dale. Claire took charge of the auditorium as Wendy led the tall man behind a worn stage curtain.

"Listen and listen good, you hypocrite. I have never, never treated any of my students like they were second class citizens. The play He-Lion has a vibrant African and African- American history that will enrich the minds of all the students at our assembly. I won't apologize for using the word slave since I'd use it freely in a play about Moses. Don't you dare hint that I'm a racist. And I in turn, Mr. Armon won't tell anyone what a God damn phony you are!"

"Wendy, I'm just acting on what a substitute teacher heard in the hallway yesterday." Like all bullies when faced down, he was already retreating.

"A sub?!" I've been at this school twenty years. You're a Social Studies teacher. What have you done for our black kids? Do you produce a Jazz salute to Dr. King every winter? I do. Did you start the Einstein Double Dutch Jump Rope Teams with the bused kids from South Queens, I did. Did you create the Do Something For Others Assembly program for Black History Month? No? That's right I did!"

"You're the Drama teacher. I teach…."

Wendy wanted to punch him. Every so often the very feminine Ms. Dale wished for a man's upper body strength, like right this minute.

"Doesn't your Social Studies colleague, Mrs. Silverberg do a Holocaust Memorial Day every year? How come she doesn't wait for a drama teacher to do it?"

"You have to admit, you're a lot closer to the Korean kids." It was a weak retort.

"You're right and they've even taught me Korean but not enough because right now I wish I knew the Korean word for asshole.

She pounded her already tight Chinese Laundry pumps on the stage side steps till she reached Claire. Her cheeks were flushed and her heart raced furiously but she felt surprisingly good. 'I haven't stood up for myself in… ever.'

"Claire would you please see if Mrs. Durango's sub is in the building today and let me know where I can find her. Not now, when you're free."

The security guard nodded and walked to the back of the auditorium pretending to quiet three bad-boy eighth graders but actually lay in wait for Mr. Armon. As he sheepishly passed Wendy and neared Ms. Jackson, the guard momentarily stopped him with her hand. With the same disdain in her voice she used for RayShawn's violent outburst she repeated, "You a damn fool."

Later that morning, Claire entered Ms. Dale's Drama room to report that the substitute teacher wasn't in. It no longer mattered, Wendy's ire had long since dissipated.

"The sub must have thought she was doing a good deed, best to let it go."

The teacher invited the safety agent to share a room temperature diet Pepsi. Claire declined by pulling her clamped lips back and down while shaking her head. She strategically placed herself on a student chair that could not be seen through the room's windowed

Bird and Fish

door. Agents on patrol are not permitted to sit unless given desk duty. Wendy poured half the drink into a chipped Teachers Are A+ mug then sat across from Claire.

"I guess I should have called them farm workers instead of slaves. I'm sorry if I offended anyone."

Claire Jackson slumped down into her chair and folded her arms in front of her. Her plum hair extentions were pulled back revealing a pretty freckled face. Except for her navy trousers and matching uniform jacket she looked like an upperclassman.

"My great, great, great grandparents were slaves. That means somthin. They was kidnapped and survived. They was beaten and survived. And when they was worked to death, their kids survived. For them, I survive. Please don't tell me I'm the last in a line of farm hands. I'm a descendant of African slaves." The agent stood up to the crackling emanations of her walkie-talkie. She leaned over enough to take the mug from Wendy's hand and took a sip. She squeezed her eyes shut as the lukewarm soda sloshed over her taste buds.

"Ms. Dale, you the only white lady ever have me over for a meal. You educated. You gonna let that no account, Lord don't let me use that word, change who you are?"

"Do you think I favor the Korean kids?"

Claire laughed out loud till the peals reached the walls of the room and made their way back. "Yes ma'am, I do. But they ain't the only teachers' pets in this building."

Wendy stood and massaged her side while thanking her friend.

"Ms. Jackson, can you tell me why you never became a teacher?"

"Cause the only kids I like is mines! See y'all later."

Ms. Dale cancelled her solo singers' rehearsal period that morning to allow her time to call for her radiation schedule. She preferred her treatments at 1:30pm weekdays. She'd have to change her work schedule with Jay to 2:15 to 4:15 but that would probably be all right and it would allow her ample time to get dinner ready and spare her family additional disruption. She dialed and was soon speaking to a perky young voice named Heather. Without a pause, Heather informed Ms. Dale that her appointments were at 9:30am Mondays through Fridays.

"I work. I can't possibly come at 9:30. What do your other patients do?"

"They take off work." Heather was losing her cheerfulness as well as her patience.

The teacher mumbled that she'd call back. She had to think in a quiet place. The door re-opened for an animated Mrs. Spring who waved her arms and clucked her tongue at the rumor of Armon's indictment. Wendy allowed her thoughts to drift to a safe harbor. Libby, paid up member of AARP still out-dressed all her colleagues at school. Wendy couldn't guess how much her friend's turquoise and brown leather suit cost. The price of those matching turquoise Choo's was probably her week's salary.

"How do you wear those? I tried them on once at the Off 5th outlet. They pinched all my toes together."

Libby was happy to redirect their conversation to something pleasant. "Firstly, I have lovely narrow feet my dear. More importantly I've had a bunionectomy so I can get my tootsies in these." Libby noted the cell phone still in Wendy's hand. "Were you on the phone?"

Wendy repeated her conversation with the unmovable medical secretary.

"Where did you say you were going for your zappings?"

"Queens-Nassau Radiation Therapy."

"On Northern, 270-00? Give me the phone." The elder teacher snatched the phone from Wendy and hit redial. "What time do you want to go?"

"Are you going to fight with them?" Wendy had enough battles for the day.

"No darling, Adam and I own that building." She held up her index finger to hush her friend, "This is Elizabeth Spring from Ad-Lib Realties. I need to speak to Aaron Plotkin."

In less than ten minutes Wendy had a new schedule of 1:30 weekday afternoon appointments. The younger woman threw her arms around her smiling friend. The women stood for a moment with their cheeks touching and their hands patting each other's backs. They sat on student chairs swapping salmon recipes but Libby soon tired of maple glazes and potato crusted fillets and asked about Jae Won. Wendy answered by letting her thoughts spin out.

"I'm afraid he's becoming too important to me." When Tim and I first married, I couldn't wait to get home each day. I'd pick up Janie from her after-school program and race home to make dinner for us. I had a tiny two-bedroom house, a rickety old car and had never been further than Disneyworld yet I still felt like the whole world envied me. Even after my mother's strokes, I thought, well these kinds of things happen to aging parents. But when Janie became ill, our house wasn't my haven anymore. When I sat on my side of the bed, I could watch her door and the bathroom door. I'd keep sentry by counting each of her bathroom visits. I'd time how long she was in there. The sound of her moaning made the trunk of my body feel squeezed in a vise. My chest burned. The muscles in my arms ached. Some days I felt nauseous and hardly ate. Others, I binged on Mounds bars. Pill bottles and doctors' appointment cards seemed to be piling up everywhere pushing me out of my nest. Now this. Every time the phone rings I jump because I'm sure the caller will bring another calamity into my house." A half-minute had passed. Wendy didn't realize she had stopped speaking. Libby called her name and added, "Are you saying home doesn't feel like home anymore?"

"No. I'm saying he feels like home. I'm home when I'm with him."

⌘ ⌘ ⌘

A cloudburst targeted Wendy as she shut her car door and ran to Jae Won's steps. The ginger highlights in her hair glistened like crushed copper foil from its rainwater baptism. Jay opened the door holding a fresh towel that gave away his posting at the living room window as he waited for her.

"*Ohpah*, I got in a fight at school today." She slipped off her dampened pumps and rubbed her stockinged toes.

"Did you win?" He asked as he handed her the towel. Wendy tipped her head down and wrapped her hair with it as if exiting a shower stall. "*Krumyo!*" she boasted.

He longed to untwist the towel and dry her hair, something he had only seen in Korean films but offered her tea instead.

"No thanks. You never have chocolate chip cookies to go with it" she said as she opened her huge patchwork handbag to retrieve a small photo holder. "Here are the Kim family's pictures. I put them inside an old pocket album this morning to keep them dry. Don't mind the other shots." They sat next to each other on his living room couch while she patted her hair and underscored what he viewed.

"That's Mi Young and Dong Kook outside the Folk Museum. See her Burberry plaid slacks? She was so cool."

"Did you call him Dong Kook?" Jae Won was visibly taken aback. Kim Dong Kook was 65 years old.

"No, I never addressed him directly. I was afraid of making a mistake. Mostly we smiled at one another. He enjoyed showing me his collection and teaching me a little about it. I learned that Min means folk and hawa means painting. I thought he'd be better matched with a male teacher. He seemed to view women in a simplistic way. The only time I won his approval was at breakfast one morning. He placed Eagle on his lap and fed him bacon from the table. Mi-Young was terribly embarrassed till I showed them a snapshot of Fido licking the side of a plate at my table at home."

Wendy turned the page.

"That one is with their daughters, *Nan-Young* and *Geun-Young*. The middle school twins smiled back at Jay.

"We still e-mail each other. Hopefully the girls will come and stay with me on one of their vacations. Mr. Kim called me last year when he was in Manhattan. I had planned a dinner party for him but Janie was taken to the hospital that afternoon."

"Wendy, do you remember this big painting behind them?" Jae Won's artist's eye, led him to the bridal transport piece.

"That was a cover for a wedding cart. That's why the flowers are so vibrant. Can you make out the fan? It has the wedding date on it. This one looks like your work. The original painting was next to the poster but that picture didn't come out"

A single exhibition poster filled the center of the photo. The artist's name, Kim Man Hee was printed boldly to the left of three speckled fish rolling in an ocean's eddy.

"*Uh*, my government has proclaimed Kim a cultural asset." I have a copy of this poster. It's still packed in one of my trunks."

The setting sun beyond the fish tail was reminiscent of the fading sunset he put behind his first rendering of the woman who sat cross-legged at his side on his couch.

Wendy, like most woman had selective hearing. She stopped listening after, "my government."

"You're not an American?"

"*Ah nee. Wheh?*"

"I just thought you were or would be soon." She was unfashionably patriotic. 'Surely anyone who came here would long to stay, would choose America.' "I guess it's hard." she sighed trying to be unbiased, "America is not like your mother who loves you the moment she holds you in her arms. She's more like your mother-in-law. If you prove yourself over and over again, she'll let you feel at home."

He didn't wish to ruffle her feathers, so he chose his answer as carefully as his old *Helmonim* sorted soybeans for fermenting.

"Wendy, America is a wonderful country. I just don't know if it can be my country." He inadvertently turned to the back of the leatherette holder. A picture of a fair-haired strongman type was quickly flipped over to reveal a toddler with pink ribbons in her honey curls and her mother's eyes. "Is this your daughter?"

"She was three. She's Seromie's age now. Wendy couldn't contrive how to take back the album. Jay asking questions about Tim's pictures would dampen the afternoon more than the storm outside. Jay turned one more page. Wendy, happier than he had ever seen her, was dancing in the snow with a daughter who was forever Ahromie's age.

"That was before she was sick." It was a perfect segway to retrieve the photos. "We haven't taken family pictures in a long time."

"What if a student told you that after he got sick, his mother wouldn't take his picture?"

"You're right. I should capture her at this age too. Oh, Fishman, that's why I like being with you." The teacher turned the plastic coated pages back to Man Hee Kim's poster, "You swim so well in the big wide sea and I'm afraid of the waves."

To touch her hair and skin, he pretended to move a non-existent dampened curl from her forehead with his fingertips. Wendy's head and neck stiffened. Her cheeks reddened. In retrieval, Jae Won pointed at the poster photo in her book. "I see the sun and sky, ocean and fish. No Hyun Jae Won. He must be on the shore afraid as well."

The electricity between them was punctuated by an actual crack of thunder leading the pair to the basement and countless renditions of "Bi neh ree nun ho nam som." At 3:30, the sky had cried its last for the day and allowed the couple to linger at Wendy's Sentra. She had let slip spying Yujin and friend to his cousin in a burst of female solidarity with Yoon Yoo. Jae Won showed no surprise.

"Didn't you say you liked to fish?" asked Wendy.

"*Uh*."

"You're his older cousin. Take him fishing. I think you can still catch bass upstate. Remind him that anyone of his wife's friends could have walked into that restaurant. What if Yoon Yoo decided to treat the girls to a snack." She stopped when she caught his expression. It was the way her father looked at her when she talked passionately but too quickly. She began writing and drawing map lines on a notebook page she ripped from a student's folder on the passenger seat. "This is my father's fishing spot. It's easy to get to, only two hours. My mother's house is up the road. Here's the address. Her key is under the red pot on the deck. Don't worry; she'll be gone after this weekend. My cousin Diane takes her till Easter but they spend the holidays at my place." Wendy, shamed by her cousin's generosity added, "Diane's retired."

Jay took the paper from her hand, folded it into eighths and slipped it into his billfold. The owners of nearly three paint distributorships had little time for all day fishing excursions.

"I'll see you Thursday. Can you come Saturday for one last rehearsal?"

"I've begged my daughter to go shopping with me after her swim practice. If I cancel, she probably won't have time for me till she's a bride."

"When do you start your treatments?"

His question was more intimate than his fingertips on her neck and face.

'He's still interested in me but only because he can't see my scar and blue tattoo.' "Monday, so we better win that contest. It will be the only fun I'm going to have in a long time."

"Wendy, after the contest, we'll go back to meeting at the store during the week. Yujin has to feel, um, how do you say?"

"Do you mean he has to feel it was his decision?"

"Neh."

"Next time, remind me to teach you the term, enabler."

⌘ ⌘ ⌘

"The baker's daughter, apple cheeked and plump as a muffin top stood at her father's side counting his thousand gifts to honor Princess Jenny-purr. The chocolate chip cookie pile stood taller than a wedding cake boasting selections of dark chocolate without nuts, milk chocolate with chopped pecans and white chocolate chippers with diced dried cherries. There were bite sized ones and some the size of Frisbees. The chubby girl licked her lips. "When do we start the pies, Papa?" her words nearly drowned out by her tummy rumblings."

Wendy leaned back in her daughter's computer chair and reread the pages she had written. It was nearly three and still she couldn't sleep. Maybe changing my Ambien to only three nights wasn't a good idea. She stretched her arms up toward the ceiling and wiggled her fingers. A sharp pain in the hollow of her left armpit reminded her where she really was. Not in the storybook land of A Thousand Voices, not in the picture of Janie and she singing and dancing to "Knees Up Mother Brown" in the snow and certainly not on a off-white velour couch breathing in the man-scent of Jae Won Hyun. Instead she had a mother who was more antagonizing than loving, a husband who retreated to his basement recliner nightly, a daughter awaiting another frightening blood test and her own appointment with an oncologist tomorrow. She tapped the save icon and returned to her bedroom to watch As The River Flows.

'Oh Jong-Tae' her fingers pushed her teardrops towards her hairline. 'I think you're going to lose your first love.' Then she gratefully drifted off.

⌘ ⌘ ⌘

Doctors Maldonado, Schultz and Grafinetti saw new patients on Wednesday afternoons between noon and five. Chemotherapy patients entered through a door further down the hall and marked their time in a different waiting room. The teacher and those like her were spared sharing space from those patients ravaged by curative poisoning. In the less frightening space, Wendy filled out four new forms that seemed no different from the ones she completed at other offices. The last page was another

HIPA form she signed and dated without reading. Dr. Grafinetti wore a pink-ribboned Breast Cancer Awareness tie. He asked Wendy many more questions than the other physicians she saw. No, she didn't drink. No, she didn't smoke. No to drugs,

'Vicodin isn't a drug. It's a medication.'

None of Wendy's answers interested him. His silence while his pen scratched his folder papers seemed to chastise the teacher's boring family history. "Any other blood relatives living or dead diagnosed with cancer?" He looked down through his half circle glasses, waiting.

"Except for my grandmothers, everyone in my family dies of heart disease."

"Any Ashkenazi Jews in your family?"

"I'm from Queens. Everybody here is LBJ." The doctor looked over his tortoise shell frames. Clearly today's tack, her foray into humor was not amusing him.

"Little Bit Jewish. My maternal great grandmother was a German-American Jew."

His pen barely scratched the paper. 'Obviously my family tree is just garden variety.'

"HRT?"

'I can't say LBJ but you can ask HRT.'

"About four years ago when my periods became irregular my gynecologist told me to take hormone replacements. She said it would regulate me and help my heart."

"You're to stop taking them immediately."

"I stopped a few months ago. I think that's why I don't sleep. I read that stopping causes estrogen withdrawal."

More pen scratches. Wendy rubbed her side with the palm of her hand. As soon as he released her to an examining room, she'd take a Vicodin half.

"Do you have pain in your side?" It was the first time his eyes met hers.

'The jig is up. Just tell the man.'

The teacher described her symptoms. After her second groping of the week, he sent her directly to Community Radiological Associates and Affiliates for a pelvic MRI with contrast then offered her the name of a new gynecologist and a prescription for Tamoxifen.

Tim lightly kissed the top of his wife's head as he passed her on the way down to the den. "Jeez, I had to break up two fights today. At one point I got flung to the hallway wall. "Can you imagine how big that kid was that he could throw me? I can't see doing this another ten years.

Teaching SIE7 is a young man's game. I'm getting too old. Is the Vicodin in your top drawer? My back is killing me. I want to clean the rest of my wrenches with that stinky cleaner for a while. Don't worry; I'll shower downstairs to keep the house clean, OK Red?"

Wendy was stirring brown sugar into ketchup, adding cider vinegar, mustard, corn oil and lemon juice. She had already minced onion and garlic. The fresh made barbeque sauce would simmer on the stove till she used it to baste drumsticks and thighs for tonight's dinner.

"If your back hurts, go right into a hot shower. Why are you cleaning tools now?"

"You know me, I won't be able to think straight till it's finished" was the big man's off-handed reply.

Jane's mom took a quick look at the family schedule on the refrigerator door. Her daughter had chorus practice till 6 and it was Mrs. Dunbar's carpool turn. We're not eating till 6:30 tonight, Tim, Tim?" The Floral Oaks wife and mother started down the first two steps when a cough and garbled "No problem." answered her. She was happy to get back to her saucepan.

'He never asked me about my day. I don't blame him. I never ask Janie how she feels. I don't want to know. If she's sick, she'll tell me. I can trust her that way. I guess Tim feels if the doctors say something important, I'll tell him, besides what kind of man asks a woman questions about her breast cancer?' Wendy crept into her soul as she pictured tying up her own best friend, Wendy and taping her mouth closed so she couldn't whisper Jae Won Hyun's name to her heart.

⌘ ⌘ ⌘

Dr. Peter Grafinetti was the go-to guy to locate a malignant needle in a haystack. It was certainly a laudable ability in an oncologist but he had no bedside manner, something Wendy was about to learn. Pure 19 had ended signaling Wendy to create her fashion statement for the next morning. She deliberated between a wool tweed and velvet Ralph Lauren or a burnt orange Jones sweater set when the house phone rang. She recognized her newest doctor's voice and rushed to pick up before Jane could hear the message.

"Dr. Grafinetti?"

"Wendy, the results show a nodule on your kidney and one on your lung. They're both on your left side where you complained of pain."

"My lung?'

"The scan caught the bottom of your lungs. Have you had a chest x-ray recently? You should have one."

"The air in her bedroom was turning to gelatin. Wendy found it too thick to breathe. She tried clearing her throat. "Are you saying I have lung cancer and" she couldn't recall the term renal cancer, so blurted out "kidney cancer?"

"I'm sorry this isn't the result you hoped for. I'll send you a prescription for a chest scan. You should take a copy of your pictures to your urologist. I see you use Dr. Goodman. Call his office tomorrow."

Peter Grafinetti clicked off leaving Wendy drowning in his wake.

In near silence she tiptoed past Jane's bedroom door and scooted down to the middle of the den stairs. "Tim, Tim." she stage whispered. The talking heads on his favorite all news channel were solemnly pontificating to the sleeping Celtic son.

Wendy tapped lightly on Jane's door.

"Janie, mommy has a migraine. I'm going to lie down OK?"

Rather than wait for her daughter's reply, she downed two Ambien, lie on her side in bed and pulled her knees up like an unborn child.

Late Friday afternoon, before he left his office to spend the Sabbath with his family, Wendy's cardiologist called her cell phone to discuss her x-ray results.

"Abe, when did you get the report?"

"Probably when Dr. Grafinetti did. That's why I always tell you to send test results to me too. This is all normal.

Yesterday's lung scan came back normal too. Once you have a cancer diagnosis, everything is suspicious. He's just being cautious."

"Well, he nearly gave me a heart attack. Since I have your attention for free, the radiologist told me not to drink any alcohol ever. You told me to have a glass of wine with dinner. Who wins?"

"Good question. Hmm. Switch to grape juice. That's not a problem for you is it?"

"Not me, I prefer my calories in baked goods."

"That's probably why I have to keep you on Zocor. How's Jane?"

She chatted with her long time physician for a few moments more before their goodbyes.

'That damn oncologist had me whimpering like a beaten dog for nearly two days. All right, now I can concentrate on fun things like shopping with Jane and the contest. Where's Tim? Is he back down there cleaning? How many tools do we have in this house?

⌘ ⌘ ⌘

In the mid 1980's a shopping phenomenon took over the turn of the century model of apparel and home décor. Retailers realized customers no longer shopped solely to replace their worn out coats or broken serving dishes. This new breed of consumer shopped as a leisure activity but shopping weekly instead of seasonally required new skills. Finding designer labels hidden on clearance racks as well as selecting timeless fashions from last year's second go around bins were essential if the customer was now opening her wallet more often. Perfect timing for Wendy Dale since it coincided with her earning a living and dressing for work. Shopping was her bowling league, tennis match and bridge club. She was pleased to go with friends from work, delighted to accompany her daughter but happiest to go alone. She'd often stop in for a quick perusal after spending hours at Jane's hospital bedside. Going through rack after rack of skirts and slacks to match an Anne Klein plum and forest paisley blazer was her way of decompressing. When funds were low, she'd match up an outfit and leave it hung on an end cap for another woman to find.

Others shoppers could readily tag Wendy and Jane as mother and daughter. They had porcelain skin and enviable big eyes. Although only Jane was tall and thin, both walked like smug models on a runway. No one could guess their miserable memories or complicated present. A girl about Jane's age walked past them at the boot selection. She wore a silvery head-band to rule her wayward black curls, along with a miss-matched pink chenille top and embroidered jeans. Wendy looked from her to her daughter. A taupe and ecru scarf Jane wrapped twice around her neck dramatized her taupe baby doll shirt. Her maple hair hung loose under her knit beret.

'I may be prejudiced but she's a standout. She's always the prettiest girl in the room. So, why her, Lord? Why my little girl? Is she too pretty, too smart? Grandma Beatrice made me put a red ribbon under her crib mattress when she was born. It was supposed to ward off the evil eye. In Korea an invisible red ribbon attaches lovers forever. Maybe God's Korean and he misunderstood my prayer.'

Wendy shook her head to let go of her rambling daydreams. She reminded her daughter never to buy in season, never go without a coupon and always head for the clearance section in the back.

"Try on everything you like. Sometimes it's on clearance because the size information is wrong. Didn't I snare that $365.00 size 2 suit for 29.99 because it was really a size 8?" Janie stored the information for later use. Right now she had to have chestnut Uggs for the winter and no knockoffs or dregs of last season would do. She was patient while Wendy chose a Homemaker's brand 'make your own vanilla' kit and Christmas designed cheese knife. She even agreed to her mom's bargain Baby Phat puffy jacket and the cashmere skull-faced sweater reduced to 19.99 but her mom's passion for matching tops and skirts, scarves and shoes left her cold.

"I have to be home by three 'cause Courtney and Caitlin and I are going to buy jeans.

Bird and Fish

"Why aren't we buying jeans now?"

"Mom." Actually, Jane whined Wendy's title into two syllables till it came out Mah-ahm.

"Ooh, look at this Jillian Jones for grandma. What do you think?" Wendy pulled the winter white sweater under her chin.

"I think it's an old lady sweater." This was no different from toddler Janie squirming in her stroller from too much shopping. The girl slumped over the store's shopping cart filled with the day's booty including a pink pair of Uggs from last season as her extras.

"Grandma *is* an old lady. Did I tell you what she said to me yesterday? I told Gram that I finally disciplined myself enough to write a story for children that I thought was darn good. You won't believe what she said."

Jane cut in. She was restless and didn't wish to miss her time with her friends. "She told you not to waste your time."

Wendy cocked her head and looked at her daughter in disbelief. "Did Grandma tell you too?

"Mom, Gran always puts you down. She doesn't talk to me that way."

"You're right, she tells you you're perfect. Yesterday she told me I was stupid to take up time with a pipedream because I have a family to care for and it wasn't good for my marriage to have a hobby that didn't include Tim."

Jane started pushing their cart towards the check-out lines. Wendy acquiesced. She had to get home to clean anyway.

"Janie, do whatever you want with your life. Never be afraid to tell me if you're longing for clown shoes so you can join the circus. I'll back you."

"Maybe one day but I'm not like you. I'll probably work with kids who have chronic diseases. Maybe I'll be a social worker or psychologist." Suddenly there was a tremor in Jane's voice that echoed her responses when Wendy would turn to leave her hospital room.

"Do you want to join the circus, mom?"

"What if I wanted to change my life? What if I wanted to be a writer or make new friends? That would be OK with you, wouldn't it?" Ms. Dale had worked with eleven year olds for sixteen of her twenty teaching years. She could have scripted her daughter's reply even though she had hoped it would be different.

"Mom, I'm a kid. I don't like change. Can't you write when I graduate college or after I get married?"

"Sure, I'll just hang my life on one of these dress hooks till you and grandma say I can live." Wendy was already sorry for her stinging remark.

Bird and Fish

"Don't worry, baby. Mommy's not going anywhere. Oh, Janie, go get another sweater like this one. They're over there. Ours doesn't have a price tag."

⌘ ⌘ ⌘

By early evening her house was clean, her bills paid and dinner was roasting in the oven. The ache in her side was quieted with her usual half dosage. While Tim sidelined to his lounge chair, shouted epithets to several Jets players on TV, Wendy scouted through her closet. The suit she and Jane discussed was as pristine as when she bought it last spring. The calf length pencil straight skirt was black silk. The jacket was black silk and leather with a wide leather cinch belt.

'If tomorrow is as mild as today, I'll be warm enough.'

The oversized lapel called for an up-do with big bold earrings. 'Why not? I'll be on stage.' She dressed and pulled her hair up for a private dress rehearsal. Wendy hummed an original song she composed for last year's assembly program twirling around in front of her bedroom mirror like the sixth grader who sang it. The teacher's career had spanned two decades filled with original plays and lyrics she never considered important enough to save. So now she sang, "Something, something, dressed up for Cinderella's ba-ll." She smiled back at the redhead in the mirror then gave her one last look-over. The blue freckle grew to the size of a Lincoln penny before her mind's eye. She ran to her underwear drawer with the speed of a woman seeing her first gray hair and reaching for the

Clairol. She selected a valentine red lace camisole to hide her painful reminder then re-approved her image. As she raised her arm to undress, the growing stubble under her arms reminded her of tonight's task.

'They said no shaving, so I'm going to hot wax these hollows bald . That should see me through the next five weeks.' It was her first underarm waxing attempt. Wendy's nightly shower ritual was to shampoo her hair, rinse and apply her conditioner giving the product time to work its magic by shaving her arms and legs and then lathering herself with body wash. This was the death knell of her comforting habits. The doctors and nurses who spoke to her never mentioned the feeling of loss it would bring.

Mother Nature heralded Sunday morning by blasting the city with chilling winds. Wendy stepped outside to regret her ensemble choice. Her only black coat was strictly for show offering little warmth. She parked across from the Hyun-Kim home and ran across to Jae Won's heated car. The Korean word for 'wow' is *'whah'*. The pair used their languages' versions to describe one other. He tried out an easy-going, friendly voice to tell her she looked beautiful. She was more brazen.

"I've never seen a man so put together. Fishman, you've stepped out of GQ."

Up until now the only men she saw so dressed were on Korean television award shows. Black dress trousers, black silk button down shirt with pearlized studs in the middle of each collar-wing were topped with a knee length black velvet and wool morning coat. A sliver of a red handkerchief peeking out of his breast pocket added even more interest. She couldn't help but compare Jay's choices to her husband's 'only for special occasions' navy Brooks Brothers outfits.

"May I put the radio on? I'll keep it low."

"*Wheh?* Why are you asking?" He offered her a CD from his door compartment.

"It's rude to distract the driver." She pressed the rectangle and popped in the disc.

"Jay, will the stage music will be exactly like the soundtrack we rehearsed to?"

"*Neh.*"

She didn't recognize the first song on the CD but she knew "*Kah ji mah, Sah rang heh*" meant, 'Don't leave. I love you.'

"That's my only worry. It's like jumping rope. If I don't start right, I'll have to begin again."

"We should face each other at the beginning. Just look at my eyes."

Wendy allowed herself to recall the first time he said those words to her. The image reminded her she was starting radiation therapy tomorrow. A theme park roller coaster didn't yet exist that could raise and drop her as dramatically as her own fate.

Flushing Meadows Park was home to the World's Fair the year Wendy turned one. It was the must-see for sightseers who wished to glide on moving sidewalks to view Michelangelo's Pieta, gaze up at the helipad or circle the still standing Unisphere. Its glory and glitter was gone by the 1970's as the city left its New York State Pavilion to crumble. Perhaps the politicians thought the land would return itself to its former Corona Ash Dumps of the Roaring Twenties.

Still used for background shots in large and small screen productions, the park kept its heart beating by providing space to frequent ethnic and sports related events. The family photos of baby Wendy and her parents on pristine promenades reminded her these weren't always the weedy, slightly unkempt grounds she saw today. But nothing could dim the vibrancy of the day's festival. Korean businesses like Anycolor Paints had set up stalls for fellowship and sales. Mandoo and bean paste soup were sold next to K-pop and K-rock CD kiosks. Shoppers purchased silk scarves and jewelry, teapots and lamps after intensive un-westernlike bargaining. Anycolor sold brushes and other small items but was admittedly there to network and show camaraderie with its community.

Bird and Fish

The brightly colored banners and signs were in Korean. KoreanRadio who helped sponsor the event supplied the Korean music before the live coverage of the contest. Wendy had never considered that her voice would be broadcast into the homes of thousands of listeners.

They parked and were guided by members of the Guardian Angels to the contest area. The teacher wondered if the Angels had morphed into a private security company from its original benevolent vigilante organization. Yujin was dashing in his triple wrapped scarf and camel hair blazer while his wife looked elegant in her ruby and fuchsia silken hambok. She had slicked back her cropped hair to an ersatz bun heightening her glamour. Even Wendy had to admit the whispering sound of Yoon Yoo's silk in motion was magical. The teacher was sure Jay's cousin-in-law was startled by her affusive compliments but Wendy felt such pity for the woman she couldn't stop praising her appearance.

⌘ ⌘ ⌘

What's the first of our senses to signal danger? Do we see trouble heading our way? Can we smell it? Does it have a perilous sound? Maybe it invisibly blows the hairs on our skin. Wendy sensed something wrong with the way Yujin held his hand out for the next customer's money. The woman's hand moved awkwardly too. Were the bills slipping? Did a quarter drop? Wendy's gaz along the shopper's arm to her shoulder and f the New Seoul woman; same almost-pretty profile, same voice. Was she really laughing and playing handsies while her boyfriend's wife and children chatted happily at his side. A second look gave no evidence of the woman. She had gone as quickly as she appeared. The teacher closed her eyes hoping to erase the vision but instead pictured the television image of a former president and his young friend hugging in a crowd. 'What do the Chinese say? May you live in interesting times? What kind of world awaits my Janie? She turned her attention to the girls. Seromie and Ahromie asked if they could accompany *Kunapogee* and *Sunsengnim* to the stage but were instructed to stay till later. The teacher marveled at parents who didn't question their own authority and children who needed to be told only once.

The cousins culled their women from the herd of frenzied shoppers and directed them to their appointed places. Wendy and Jay sat on folding chairs in front of a massive metal and wood constructed stage. He asked if she was hungry but the pre-show jitters assured her that food would be tossed back if she dared eat. He brought her a Styrofoam cup of soup to hold in her frigid hands and offered his coat. She declined his offer, tightened her grip on the soup cup and convinced herself that she had imagined the woman she saw with Yujin.

"Would you mind if I used my hand cream? Wendy handed him her cup and opened her purse. She found a pink tube marked Insolence and held it waiting for his answer.

"American woman aren't usually so polite. Why do you ask for permission?"

"All day long at school my girls apply creams and cloyingly sweet lip glosses to themselves. The boys are worse. They spray something called Axe that makes me queasy. I won't use this if you don't like the scent. I don't think Americans are generally impolite. Other nationalities sometimes seem rude to Americans. At a Korean tee shirt shop, the male owner held up a tiny size and told me I would look very sexy in it. He thought he was making a sale. I thought he was acting lecherous um, dirty. Different cultures, different rules. One isn't more polite." She soon realized she was speaking as if he were a student.

"*Mi ahn hah dah*. I didn't mean to lecture you. May I put this on?"

"Is that what you always wear?" He pointed to the tube. "Insolence, I'm not sure what it means."

"It means bratty, a woman who does just as she pleases when she pleases."

Jae Won sucked the inside of his lips to his teeth making a 'pfft' sound, "That's a good way to describe you."

"I never do what I want. Really. Except when I'm with you. *Cham gahn mon*, wait. That didn't come out right."

Jay grinned, "I think that came out right." Then to punctuate his good mood, he took a deep breath of chilled Insolence that rode the blowing winds between them.

※ ※ ※

Episode 7: Pink Himalayan Salt

Wendy Dale compared herself to every woman she knew or even just happened to see but she only coveted the power of one, Injung Han. While Jae Won talked to the contest promoters, Wendy allowed herself to people watch. Heading for the roped VIP seating was Mrs. Han with Hae Sook Park the CEO of KoreanRadio. The forty-something woman was the Korean-American's community's mover and shaker. If she liked you, you would be featured in all the Korean-American newspapers, land an interview on KoreanRadio or be the subject of a talk show on the Hallyu TV network. If she didn't, fame in this community was unattainable. Luckily Ms. Dale had taught all three of the Han children helping to forge an appreciation of each other that had endured for six years. It was Mrs. Han who called Wendy asking for a DMZ article to coincide with Kim Jon Il's nuclear threat. More importantly, after being enthralled by the teacher's Land of the Morning Calm assembly program, Mrs. Han arranged Wendy's ambassadorship to Korea.

Wendy managed to catch Jay's eye by miming and signing till he nodded showing he understood that she saw a friend and would soon return. She was happy she had dressed up since Injung always looked polished. The woman's coffee-tinged hair was pulled tightly from her face into a perfect French twist. Her wide set mahogany brown eyes sparkled while her high cheekbones had people guessing she was a former actress. She smiled serenely as Wendy approached her. The women kissed the air near their cheeks European-style and held hands as they spoke. Their busy lives prevented them from meeting often but when they could, there was genuine warmth fueled by respect and friendship. Neither one would admit to a sprinkling of rivalry as well.

"Wendy, you remember Mrs. Park." The elder woman remained seated but smiled.

Wendy was playing with the big girls now and was careful to be extremely courteous. "*Yeh, yeh. Ahn young hah she mee kah.* You look so well. Thank you for the wonderful festival. It's so important for school children to experience activities like this."

Mrs. Park continued to smile like an empress but shifted her gaze for a moment for an important thought.

"Do you use the book, Weeping Trees with your students?"

"*Ahn neh nee dah.* Never. When I read it to give my approval, I found it was anti-Korean propaganda. I won't teach it at school. I hope you're fighting its use. Don't let the educrats tell you that schools practice freedom of speech because no book about mean slaves and their kindly masters or murderous Jews fighting humble Nazis would ever be in our school libraries."

The Korean women nodded to each other.

"Perhaps you'll do another broadcast with us next week. Injung will call you." The matriarch turned her attention to a family who brought their son to pay her obeisance. Injung Han took Wendy aside, "I heard you were singing today. How do you know the Anycolor owners, from school?"

'I'd better mind my answer. I need a favor and anyway, I *do* know Seromie from school'

"*Neh*." The teacher placed an innocent smile on her lips before continuing.

"I wanted to propose something to you. Between the shows on KBS and SBS, they have artwork behind the logos. HTV doesn't. Would Hallyu Television be interested in classical and contemporary Minhwah art, perhaps to animate?"

"Student art?"

"*Ahn nee.* Really stunning works by a Korean-American artist."

"You'll do the radio show?"

"Absolutely!"

"I'll stop by 347 on Wednesday with a sound crew. Bring three samples for me to take back to HTV."

'Bad idea. Teachers check their civil rights at the schoolhouse door. No principal would allow her to talk to the press in the building.' "I won't be able to meet you in school but we can meet up on Carthage off Marathon at 2:30, if that's convenient for you?"

Mrs. Han checked her blackberry and entered her new appointment.

"You're singing with Mr. Hyun?"

"*Neh*."

"I think you will like second prize."

They spoke of their children and parted while Wendy wondered what the first prizewinner had to promise.

She returned to her seat to watch Jay laugh and talk with two local businessmen. 'Suits' Tim would have called them. Jae Won's ebony outfit didn't seem to faze them. Wendy knew if a parent showed up at school so attired, there'd be laughter emanating from every classroom, including hers. But somehow Fishman pulled it off. She was not unaware of his silken sleeves tightly hugging his shoulders and biceps nor the narrowness of his waist.

'This is crazy.' her conscience scolded till a recalcitrant Wendy turned to view a shriveled grandmother on stage.

The old woman was tiny but her outlandish outfit gave her grandeur and even a bit of charisma. She sported a sensible woolen tam o'shanter and a totally irreverent hot pink jacket. Her long skirt was a prism cache of color. But it was her gooey red lipstick that particularly enchanted Wendy. 'Go for it, granny. Life is short.' The radio host and hostess who spoke to the old woman in Korean impressed Wendy with their quiet respectful demeanor. The woman began her song. The teacher assumed the melody, so different from any of her K-pop favorites, was old, perhaps a folksong. Her voice sanded down over her lifetime was raspy and sometimes faded. Wendy scanned the audience. No American Idol nastiness here. The adults clapped in time to the music and amazingly so did the teens who were waiting for their favorites. Wendy had to admit; America's youth would have come up short. They'd have taken their bathroom breaks or plugged in their ipods or worse heckled. 'What would Janie do? She wouldn't have cheered the old lady on. She'd probably pretend to listen but really zone out till her music came on. Western polite.'

Jae Won and the two men bowed and shook hands. He began clapping to the beat as soon as he headed back to her. The couple in black kept time and smiled wide for the ancient woman although she couldn't see their faces at that distance.

"Jay, were you going to pay me today?" They hadn't earnestly discussed her pay before.

"Yes, of course. I'll give you the money as soon as we get back to the house." 'What did she mean? Is this the last time she'll be with me? This festival must be too much to take in.' They would be called to the stage in a few minutes yet he wanted to take her by the hand and leave.

"I don't want money. I want three of your watercolors instead."

He immediately relaxed. "Wheh? Do you think they're worth more than your pay?" Because he trusted her, he didn't question her motives. More importantly, he was flattered by her request.

"I'm sure you know the women I just spoke to. Mrs. Han is a good friend. She's offered to show your work to her connection at HTV to use in their station identification logos. I know you've shied away from showing your paintings but this would bring you more satisfaction than ringing up a gallon of primer sale. Not that there's anything wrong with selling paint. It's certainly more lucrative than teaching. I just mean…"

"*Krum!* Do you want to help me choose?" Jae Won stifled the urge to rush the stage and tell the audience. The year wouldn't end for months yet he felt like it was his new beginning. "*Sun seng nim,* you are amazing."

Bird and Fish

"Are you serious? I thought you'd fight me. I almost lied about the paintings. I was going to say I'm borrowing them for school. Then why haven't you shown your work before?"

His eyes drew in her face in the same way he had breathed in her perfume earlier. The tip of her nose was blushed from the cold.

"Humphrey Bogart! I saw that movie in Korea. 'Of all the gin joints' Right?" He wanted to pull her up from the chair and hold her. As if she heard his desire, she moved back into her chair

"Why did you come to my store?"

"Oh, you mean fate, destiny. I was put on this earth to sell your paintings?"

"*Ahn nee. Uh-ri.*" I'm also here for you."

Yoon Yoo's brother and his young family finally arrived at the Anycolor stall to liberate the Kims in time to cheer on Jae Won and Wendy. Ahromie asked *Kunapogee* to lift her on to his lap but her real destination was curling her body under Wendy's arm. Wendy was happy to oblige and patted the little girl's arm in time to a teenage boy's rap rendition. Seromie took the seat to her teacher's right and folded her dancer's body till her head lay on Wendy's lap. The teacher placed her handbag between her ankles on the beaten grass below her to stroke the older sister's head. Yujin and Jae Won nodded slightly to each other. Wendy feared it was a signal of collusion since the men beamed like farmers with the prized heifer at the fair. Their redhead was an attraction. Yoon Yoo was disappointed to see Wendy's handbag placed on the hardened mud but soon forgave her cousin's friend as she watched the teacher's affection for her daughters.

The Performing Mothers Contest was over, the school groups had finished and the last of the solo acts was taking his bow. The Couples Contest hosted by the same solicitous young radio stars was beginning. Jay signaled the girls to get up. Wendy gave Seromie her purse and coat to mind. If he was nervous, he hid it well. Her lower lip began to quiver from the bracing winds as they followed a red-jacketed Guardian Angel to the side of the stage. Wendy saw the steep metal slatted steps leading to the stage apron and knew her spiked dress heels would slip through making her entrance head first and lateral. Jay looked at the same steps. "Uh-ri" he said as he put out his hand for hers. She couldn't hold his hand, not in public, not anywhere. She would turn 44 this summer, old enough to know if she took his hand, even openly on stage with a thousand eyes watching, it could change her path forever.

The bubbly announcer entertained the audience in English laughingly describing how much she hated her former English teacher in High School.

'Thanks for the great lead-in.' Wendy snidely noted and then led a deliriously happy Jae Won Hyun by the hand.

They beamed like the new millennium's racially mixed Sonny and Cher, this time Cher was shorter, Sonny taller. The singers were resplendent in jet black with two wisps of red silk and lace teasing the audience. Wendy put her arm around the female announcer as if they were sisters.

"You'd never hate me. We'd meet at lunchtime every day and talk about Korean dramas." Wendy faced the applauding audience and began as if all this was just another school assembly program.

"*Ahn yong hah seh yo, ahn yong hah shim me ka. Cho num*, Dale, Wendy *im ne dah.*" and bowed to the cheering crowd. "This is my friend, Hyun, Jae Won." The teacher let go of his hand and dramatically pointed to his face. "His Korean is not so good. Please applaud him too." The throng was eager to accommodate her. The announcers handed them microphones while a lone DJ hidden upstage pushed play. Wendy felt her heart thumping. The introductory music was different. She couldn't make out where to start. Jay's now familiar hand reached for hers and pressed his fingers into her palm signaling her to begin.

In the end, *Nam Heng Yul Cha* was only a familiar karaoke song sung by two people who could sing on key but like the lyrics in Gypsy's "Ya gotta have a gimmick." tell us, when you're different you're unforgettable. This was the first time the Korea Day festival featured a non-Asian on stage in their proud decade of yearly events. The audience cheered for their collective place in history.

Later, they waited with the other contestants for the results in a makeshift holding area. The senior citizen in the pink coat approached Wendy. She didn't speak English. Wendy bowed her head hoping it wasn't too low then inched down slightly in case it wasn't low enough. The woman took the teacher's hands in hers and began to sway and sing another unfamiliar song. Wendy swayed along and la-la-la'd as best she could. 'Only in America', thought the teacher. The women hugged and parted. From the other side of the paddock, Jae Won spied on the swaying women. He'd have to learn to be discreet, not easy for someone who never committed an indiscretion. The community, *his* community had seen them together. The first time would serve as a pleasant diversion. The second would be fodder for gossip. They wouldn't name him. They'd go after that red-haired woman over there pretending to sing Korean with a local *helmonnim*.

As promised they won second prize: two pink Himalayan salt lamps. Jae Won offered his to Yoon Yoo who gladly accepted. Wendy was as pleased as Mrs. Han predicted. The twenty pound hollowed translucent crystal sparkled in the last of the mid-October sunlight. It held a fifteen-watt bulb and sat on a polished agate base. The accompanying folder touted its ability to bring peace to one's home as well as increase energy and prevent illness. She'd convince Janie to put it in her room. Wendy lifted the heavy package and began tottering to the Santa Fe. Jae Won ran in front of her to take the cardboard box from her arms.

"I'm all right. It's not that heavy." The extra weight slammed her toes to the front of her three-inch pumps punishing her for lying.

"*Babbo ya.* I'm offering to take it. Don't make a show here."

'Did he just call me stupid?'

"I'm not making a show, a scene." She finally acquiesced.

"You don't need anybody?" He carried the carton as if it held feathers.

"Not really. I hate needy women."

Jae Won cleared his throat in response. Wendy knew the sound held meaning. She just wasn't sure what it was.

⌘ ⌘ ⌘

"Janie." Tim knocked on his stepdaughter's door. He never walked in without her permission. "What's the game plan today?" Jane opened the door and told the giggling voice on the cell phone to hold on.

"Could you drop my friends and me off at Mickey D's? Mrs. Dunbar said she'd take us home. We're just gonna hang out."

"All your homework finished?"

"Of course. I'm being raised by educators, remember?"

"I'd like to forget. I'll take everyone but don't eat hamburgers. Your mother will kill us. Have a yogurt. Drink regular soda, no diet stuff, OK?" The thought of rushing his step daughter to a hospital gave the big man neck shivers.

"Don't worry." The phone was back at her temple. "I've got us our ride." She closed the door quietly but in his face.

"Fido, wanna go for a ride to the cemetery today. First promise you won't bark at the annoying girls. When we get to Saint Anthony's, you'll have to sit in the car by yourself for a while. OK, pal?"

Fido rode shotgun while the four sixth-graders huddled together in the Camry's back seat. Two of the girls were afraid of the white-toothed hound. Tim pulled up at the fast food restaurant's back door. "All right ladies, what am I supposed to remind you of?"

"Don't talk to anybody we don't know."

"Stay together all the time."

"Even in the bathroom!"

"Call 911 or our parents if there's a problem."

Tim nodded his approval and added, "Remember, be marines. Nobody gets left behind. This is New York. Everybody else is crazy. My cell is on. Fido and I are going to the rock park.

"Where's the rock park?" asked Courtney

Jane laughed. "That's what Tim calls cemeteries."

Saint Anthony's Roman Catholic Cemetery was on a patch of northeastern Queens between Northern Boulevard and the Long Island Expressway. Consecrated in the mid 1800's, it was the last earthly home of New York assemblymen, veterans of foreign wars and Tim's uncle Timothy. The big man knelt easily as if he hadn't stopped attending mass over twenty years ago. He bought a red and white carnation cross and leaned it on the plain granite stone. Uncle Timothy's graveyard neighbors were Italian. Their markers were flowery monuments decorated with angels and other cherubim. He knew his uncle would have approved the sedate font and single shamrock chiseled over his name.

"Unc, I came alone today. Don't worry, Janie's still doing fine, beautiful like her mother. But my Red's got some kind of cancer I can't even pronounce. You didn't do so well with your cancer huh, Uncle Timothy. Driving over here I started thinking about Jane. I never adopted her. We never got around to it. If I mention it now it'll be like saying Red's gonna die soon. If anything happens, Lucille will take Janie. I'm too old to start over again. It's too bad 'cause I always thought having a step-daughter was my insurance policy that I wouldn't end up in a nursing home when I started crapping my pants."

Tim looked over at the Camry's half-opened windows. Fido was staring down a small brown bird sunning itself on a tombstone.

"I always thought I'd go first. I feel she dropped the ball, getting sick like this. She's so wrapped up in herself lately it's like the cancer became her secret boyfriend and you know me. I just retreat to the den. I gotta be honest. I even fell off the wagon. I'm stopping today. Pills and booze, the coward's way out. You would have beaten my ass if you caught me. You know the weirdest part? The more scared I am of losing her the more I hide from her. I'd like to move back to my old apartment after saying, 'Red, take care of this and let me know when it's over.'

Aah, what am I worried about? She's tough." The Irishman nodded yes as if assuring his long dead uncle. "I better go. There're some good college games on today, Texas and Oklahoma's kick-off is at one o'clock. I'll stop by Christmas week maybe sooner 'cause when Wendy finds out what I spent on these flowers, she's gonna kill me. *Ta deoch agat.* You have a drink for me.

Tim O'Hanlon stood, made the sign of the cross on himself and returned to his car and dog. He was glad he charged the flowers on their credit card. She couldn't scold him about the cost for another few weeks.

Bird and Fish

The city schools were closed Monday making this a three day weekend for the Jewish holiday, Yom Kippur.

'What is that one? The Day of Atonement? I'll go back on the wagon tomorrow.'

The three paint cans were still in the garage. He could charm her by starting the job. 'Wendy wouldn't mind finishing up during the week.' His frugal wife had already folded and packed away three old shower liners to be used for drop cloths. 'Where the Hell she put them?'

⌘ ⌘ ⌘

Seromie and Ahromie followed their cousin and Ms. Dale to the car. The girls had gotten permission to ride home with them. They coaxed Wendy to sit in the back seat between them leaving Jae Won in the chauffer's seat. The ride home began with them singing the second prize song as a quartet till the two grownups grew tired.

"Who's your favorite singer, Ms. Dale?" asked the older girl.

"Bi." the teacher teased.

"For real?"

"Well, I like him in the dramas." Each girl leaned her head on the teacher's shoulders. Ahromie eyelids grew heavy.

"Who's your favorite American singer?"

"Mmm. I have so many but I don't think you'd know them. I'm an old lady. I like slow songs, ballads"

"Then tell me a song. I want to tell my friends I know your favorite song, please." the girl whined.

'She's more like Janie than I thought.'

Jae Won told his cousin's daughter to stop asking the teacher questions. Wendy didn't need to speak Korean to translate what he was saying.

"*Quen shah nah*." she assured him. "I like a song by Joy Enriquez called How Can I Not Love You."

"Can you sing it?"

"I'm all sung out today."

"Can you just say the words?"

"*I goo*, you're wearing me out. I'll tell you what it's about but *bi mil*, it's a secret."

Jay shut off the whooshing hum of the car's heater to better hear Wendy.

"A girl loves a boy she's not free to marry. She knows they must part but she doesn't know how to stop loving him."

"That's an American song? It sounds Korean."

"You know Ballerina, you're right. It sounds American and Korean."

⌘ ⌘ ⌘

The butcher's son carefully seasoned the steak with pearly pink salt from the Far East then wrapped the T-bone in heavy brown paper and tied the package with thick white twine. "Father," asked the big strong boy, "Can we afford to bring 1000 cuts of beef to the princess?" "Be a smart lad," instructed the butcher in his pork pie hat. "We'll throw in some pig snouts and chickens' feet. If you listen to your father, someday you'll be Prince."

It was nearly two a.m. when Wendy stopped working on A Thousand Voices. She looked at her sleeping daughter. Janie's eyelids twitched in time to her dream. Wendy hoped it was pleasant. When Jane first suffered the ravages of Crohn's, she'd often complain of nightmares. It made sense. The horrors of her days were just voicing their opinions in her sleep. The teacher's own night terrors were often the same. They began with Wendy flying high above a calm blue sea. The wind would pick up darkening the waves and making them angry. Through the tightening clouds she'd see Janie drowning. She was never able to save her. Her racing heartbeat would wake her too soon.

She kissed her daughter's forehead and cheek. Jane managed a "Love you, mom." through her dreams.

"Mommy loves you even more, Janie." Wendy brushed a stray lock of golden hair stuck to the spittle on Jane's mouth.

'You don't look so grown-up now.' Wendy studied her daughter's face. 'Her color's getting better, rosier.' But when she turned she realized it was the glow of the salt lamp that bathed the girl in soft pink light. Wendy stretched and turned off the lamp. Her husband and daughter gushed over her prize all through dinner but quickly disappeared when Wendy began cleaning the dishes. Then there was that dicey moment at dinner when Janie said, "Maybe you'll be on YouTube." What excuse could she give for omitting that her solo was actually a duet with the Korean Johnny Cash? To avoid going to bed with that on her mind, the teacher walked to the dish drain in the kitchen to return the china and flatware to the cabinets and drawer. She wore an indelible grin while she relived her afternoon till she got to the ride back with the girls and Jay. 'Was I flirting? It wasn't meant for her ears so why did I tell Seromie the story of that song?'

Jae Won Hyun sat on his heels in front of a large carton he had carried up from the basement closet. It held years of silk screens and watercolors he had created then hid from his parents and wife. He wondered which would be Wendy's favorites. The one he studied now portrayed a woman and two little girls washing clothes in round plastic tubs. He tried to remember where he had seen the subjects but could only recall his cousins and Wendy singing to each other. 'What was the meaning of what she said? Why did she tell Seromie the story of that song?'

⌘ ⌘ ⌘

In place of the frightening brain tumor mask was an equally scary empty wheelchair. Wendy had certainly seen wheelchairs before but now they punctuated her days. They were in the radiologist's waiting room as well as the oncologist's. Were they there for those in the last stages of their murderous cancer or for the ones weakened by the poisonous chemotherapy? To end her daydream's query, she looked at the faces of those waiting for their treatments. A white woman as old as yesterday's singing Korean grandma sat opposite her reading a magazine. She wore a black and gold turban, which didn't disguise her obvious hair loss. 'At least I don't have to have chemo.' she assured herself while the door opened for two more survivors. The young woman looked no more than thirty. The red cotton bandana she wore to hide her baldhead couldn't mar her delicate European features. With her thin nose, pale lips and perfect semi-circle eyebrows over olive brown eyes, Wendy saw her as a classic beauty owning the kind of face one sees on a shard of Greek pottery. The teacher guessed the dark haired man who sat next to but never spoke to the woman was her husband. Tim was off the hook again today. If Janie asked her mom's whereabouts, he'd be available to cheerily answer, "Errands" while he watched the news. He said he had to finish cleaning the garden tools anyway. Wendy sucked on her second butterscotch candy.

They were both good excuses. Tim never asked if she needed him.

"Mrs. Dale." A young man who looked no older than Libby's sons stood at the counter waiting to escort her. 'A man? A man is going to do this? Did I blink while America lost its sense of decency?' Chris introduced himself by showing her where to change from the waist up, where to wait again and to inform her that today was just a run-through. Her actual treatments would begin tomorrow. Dr. Plotkin was out due to the holiday but Dr. Smithfield would see her. While Wendy pulled her turtleneck over her head, she entertained herself by musing that the only Smithfield she knew was a brand of smoked ham. Who better to work on the Jewish holiday? It would be her last laugh for a while. Another technician met them in the radiation room. Happily it was a woman about Wendy's age. They pushed her shoulders, slid her bottom down and moved her left arm like it was silly putty till they seemed satisfied with her position on the table. The woman kept measuring her blue dot's placement then drew another one nearby in black marker. In a lighthearted manner, she informed the teacher that the tattoo was incorrect. She assured the teacher that it wasn't a big deal. They would cover the new washable one with a special clear bandage that would make it semi-permanent for the next five weeks. It would work just as well.

Wendy Dale was a New Yorker through and through but she never followed the legendary Big Apple penchant for litigation. Another woman, a ballsier woman might have visited her lawyer directly from this doctor's office. The damn spot that marked her for life wasn't necessary and turned out to be in the wrong place. But as in the past, Wendy stored her anger in the part of her brain that crushed her authentic feelings like an industrial compacter in a scrap metal yard. The teacher took her Vicodin half for the emerging ache in her side and bit into her third butterscotch of the day.

She stopped at the greengrocer's two blocks east of Anycolor before meeting Jay. While her home in Floral Oaks was festooned with fall decorations or as Tim once remarked, "It looks like a gay Great Pumpkin came through here", the paint store hadn't even one little gourd. It would be good for business. The male customers wouldn't notice the holiday trimmings but the women would. They'd think of pumpkin pie and family perhaps leading them to spruce up the guest room before the Christmas holidays. Looking at the array of grapefruit sized pomegranates and smooth peach-skinned butternut squash refreshed her spirit enough to keep the painkiller's medicinal nausea at bay. From a side trip that was supposed to procure just two or three mini pumpkins, Wendy managed to spend nearly thirty dollars on produce and eggs. 'This was almost as much fun as buying sweaters.' She noted on her way back to her car.

Great Neck and Little Neck have large Jewish populations that had been observing their calendar's High Holy

Day since last evening. The halved commercial traffic produced a hush on the usually busy street. As she drove west on Northern, she noticed the boulevard less hectic than usual. 'Maybe the store would be quieter. After all, the kids were off school. Their mommies weren't about to drag them to purchase Do It Yourself projects supplies.' Although she knew that would probably be too much to hope for.

The parking meters lined up empty on Broward like metallic sunflowers. Even the free spots stayed vacant offering Wendy the best parking space for her dusty Nissan since she began frequenting the paint store. Earlier the sun won its wrestling match with the October winds leading most of the eight million New Yorkers to remind themselves that it's always nice weather on the Jewish holidays. The bright rays glistened on the last remaining pin oak leaves, the mica trapped in the concrete sidewalk and the copper strands of the teacher's auburn hair.

Her cousin Diane was Libby's age and like Wendy's colleague was a redhead. The three women had not yet shared the same space at the same time for if they did, heads would surely turn. The numbers of titian-haired Americans is only 2%. Diane was a carrot-top thanks to her father's Irish genes. He also lent her his peach complexion and chromium diopside eyes. Boys had been chatting up Diane since she was 13 and Diane liked it enough to flirt back. Wendy at five could easily recognize the differences in Diane's speech mannerisms when the caller was a boy. There was a playful coyness that taught the younger cousin the difference between talking and flirting. It's how Wendy recognized what the Asian woman in the store had in mind. Wendy guessed she was Filipino from her accent and almost Mayan features.

"How come you always in the store, Mr. Hyun? You should definitely go out sometime. You like movies?"

Jae Won looked sideways to catch Wendy's plaintive expression. Any remorse he felt for her worried look was beaten soundly by the cockiness her concern evoked in him. The new knowledge heated his cheeks, chest and loins. As soon as the storeowner smiled back at the woman he would readily dismiss, Wendy retreated to the back room toilet. Once out of earshot, Jae Won thanked the woman for her offer but explained he was married. He tilted his head towards the back door and whispered as if to a fellow conspirator that his wife was very old fashioned and unforgiving. The woman looked to the back of the store and placed a long cerise acrylic nail to her lips signaling her understanding of the charming Korean man's plight.

Wendy re-entered when she heard the closing front door. 'Sorry if you expected to flummox me Fishman, but I already have a date for the prom.'

She planned to talk only of work.

"What are we going over today?" she began. "I'd like to work on idiomatic expressions."

"Are you upset?"

"By what?"

They stood surrounded by quarts and gallons of primers and concealers and still couldn't cover the meaning of their terse words.

"*Ajummah.*" He pointed to the door with his thumb, "That woman who asked me for a date."

Wendy pushed her lower lip against her top one before answering. "Technically, she said you should go to the movies. She didn't say she'd take you."

He had only meant to tease her, to add a laugh that would allow him to bask in her reaction a few minutes longer. This was becoming ugly but he hadn't the skills to turn it around.

"Don't green eyes mean jealousy?" His jibe fell flat.

In a brassier voice than her usual, Wendy questioned, "Do they?"

"Should I raise my voice too?" It wasn't a question. They stood face to face like gunfighters in Fifties movies when her cheeks began to redden. Beads of perspiration dotted her brow and ran down the sides of her face. Wendy's hands flew up to her cheekbones and wiped the dew into her hair. She turned to the counter for the paper towel roll.

"What's the matter? I didn't mean to upset you. Do you want diet Pepsi?" Jay asked two more questions but the nausea and embarrassment she felt drowned them out.

"It's not you. It's not this. It's the medication. The doctor said this could happen. I'm so sorry."

Jae Won thought back to when his mother had first been diagnosed with breast cancer. She had undergone surgery, chemo and taken medications that affected her the same way. He now knew what kind of cancer she had. He led her to the modest bathroom where he put cold water on her wrists and patted her face.

She protested by taking the towel from his hands and drying her own with it. He stepped back in respect for her Yankee pride.

"That woman means nothing. Don't worry…"

She wouldn't allow him time to finish "I'm not worried. See," she placed her index finger on her cheek, "*ee poo dah*. I'm much prettier than she."

Jae Won let a burst of breath from his lips, "*Chee*. You're much bolder than she is too."

"*Ahn nee.* I could never ask you for a date. I'm not as bold as she." She wouldn't lift her face to meet his eyes as they brushed past each other leaving the little room.

"Don't you have paintings to give me, Fishman?"

By the time Yujin eased into the store at his new scheduled time, they had made three selections for HallyuTV; the laundry scene, a woman playing a *dahnso* and a lone bird on a snow covered tree branch.

"Huang, did you tell Wendy what a star she is? Wendy, customers in the Bayside store were asking about you this morning."

"Good because I don't want to teach anymore." The teacher startled the store's owners. Even a streaky blonde woman in tan Hush Puppies at the sample booklets noticed the sudden silence.

"*Sun seng nim*" Yujin thought of his daughters' love for their favorite teacher. "You're joking."

"Excuse me. Can someone make a quart of this for me?" The Hush Puppies lady was in their circle pointing to a Newborn Pink rectangle.

Wendy looked at the sample card like a De Beers agent inspecting an uncut diamond. "Have you looked at Pink Begonia or Deep Carnation? Don't spend ten dollars for a quart. You may not like it. Is this for a bedroom? If I was lucky enough to have your complexion, I'd surround myself in that one but this one is lovely too. Why don't you get a sample jar of each?" Wendy had no idea what colors she pointed to. She was flattering the woman as she flattered her students.

"That's a good idea. Let me have a jar of each." The happy customer didn't seem to mind that she had just spent twenty five percent more than the cost of the quart. Wendy was equally pleased. Without planning to, she showed Jay's cousin she was capable of doing other things well.

Thanks to Yujin's appearance Jae won was able to escort Wendy to her car. He began to take a white envelope from his pocket when she stopped him.

"I'm not taking money from you."

"*Wheh*? You won't teach me anymore?"

The teacher chuckled. "The whole time I'm teaching you, you're babysitting me. Let's call us even. Besides, when we spend an afternoon talking and you hand me money, it's a little ...like a *kisaeng*"

"Korean men say *kisaeng* are flowers that understand words."

"American women spell *kisaeng*; p-r-o-s-t-i-t-u-t-e."

Jae Won chose not to comment. Instead he laid the paintings lovingly on the back seat then removed a tan envelope from the twine ties. In it was a watercolor of children splashing and swimming in a mountain lake.

"This one is for your daughter. You said she was a swimmer." He appreciated her soft thank you. He disliked silly gushing or hollow platitudes.

"Will I see you tomorrow?"

"I start radiation therapy tomorrow. Don't get scared if I show up glowing like kryptonite."

If he were a native New Yorker, they would have kissed cheeks in front of the two teenage passersby without a second thought. But the Jamsil man stayed true to his roots by walking away after a shy, *"Chal ga."*

By the time she reached the Mc Mansion on Culligan, her body temperature was on the rise again. First her heart raced then nausea rolled across her belly stopping at her sensitive side to pummel her innards. Her cheeks flushed and a chilling sweat coated her. She pulled up in front of the red brick monstrosity and walked to the sewer grate at the sidewalk's edge. Wendy retched and vomited till the Guyanese home-owner in a bright green sari and matching flip-flops who watched from her kitchen window came out with a cup of water. In a melodic lilt she told Wendy to eat crackers throughout her pregnancy. It helped curb her indigestion with all three pregnancies. After thanking the woman, Wendy got back in her car with two thoughts vying for her attention. The first was she'd never survive the five year Tamoxifin dosage the doctors told her she needed. The other was more pleasant. At age forty-three, she was passing for a first time expectant mother.

The cobbler's twins were fighting over a pair of bright green open-toed wedgies, when their father threw a beaded flip-flop in their direction. "Billy, Libby, stop right this minute." He ordered. "The royal celebration is only seven days from now and I haven't started my sneakers yet." The six minute older twin grabbed the green shoe from his sister, "Father, we have lots of time. The fisherman and his daughter haven't started yet. "I'm not worried about the fisherman," he bellowed before he tapped another nail into a brown wing-tip's sole. "There aren't a thousand fish in the whole kingdom. The fisherman is a dreamer."

Jane was sleeping soundly with a curled Fido at her feet when Wendy stopped typing. As quietly as she could, the teacher scanned the four paintings and saved them on the hard drive. The hot flashes were coming every hour bringing knockout punches of nausea and cramping with each blow. 'What time is it in Seoul now? Three o'clock this afternoon? I'll need to be very complimentary but not effusive. I can't sound like I'm pressuring her.

Dearest Mi Young—Guess who can't sleep (again). I've just been thinking of the day you said you were the real power behind KimArt. (You were wearing those fabulous jute sandals.) I've always envied your talent and eye for beauty. You've really been an inspiration. I'm attaching four paintings from a Korean artist who caught my attention. Let me know what you think.

My love to your family. I promise to buy a phone card soon so we can really talk— Love W

Wendy took one last look at Jane. The girl's complexion seemed paler than usual even in the rosy lamplight. 'I'm just making myself crazy.' "Fido, go lie down near daddy." The teacher hoped the Dobie-mix would disturb Tim just long enough so she could scoot under the covers next to him and drop off before he began snoring again. The big man snorted twice and flayed his arms till one thwacked Wendy across her torso. She lay pinned under the blonde haired Bluto limb regretfully hearing then smelling passing wind. Neither the dog nor husband owned-up.

She stared up at the ceiling fan, 'What is grand passion plus a decade or so? Even the most exquisite lover who frequents your dreams would eventually litter your sleep with scraps of bodily functions. So why fall in love with a man like he's the only doll in the toy box?' She turned her attention to Tim's clothing already set out for his student's suspension hearing tomorrow. She had selected a cobalt and steel striped tie to go with his navy blazer and gray wool slacks. 'I guess so we can dress them.'

She closed her eyes as if calling on rapture to preclude sleep. 'Unless sometimes the passion lasts forever.'

The boys of 6A1 were more interested in the battle scenes than the Triumvirate dialogue between Lepidus, Antony and Octavius. The girls were clucking over

Brutus' luke-warm reaction to his beloved wife's death. Ms. Dale wasn't concerned with their preferences. She saw eleven year olds discussing Julius Caesar with all the excitement of an upcoming school dance. It's the stuff teachers' wet dreams are made of: children loving what they are learning. They were so engaged that the ringing classroom phone went un-noticed till the teacher heard it. "Ms. Dale." This time it was the frizzy-haired secretary. The office worker had little energy to answer private calls and let her displeasure be known through her voice. "It's another doctor's office." and quickly clicked off. The teacher was facing thirty-three children eating free breakfast muffins and arguing Shakespeare's merits when the gynecologist's secretary asked what kind of test she took last week. The answer was clear in Wendy's mind: transvaginal pelvic sonogram but her sense of propriety wouldn't let her voice it.

"Please let me call you back."

"Mrs. Dale, we need the results sent now. Julia has to go on break."

'Julia? Is she embarrassing me for the convenience of one of the doctor's secretaries?'

"I'm teaching right now."

"We're working too. Just tell us the test."

The teacher spelled it leaving gaps in patternless spaces so the children just steps away couldn't decipher her answer. The monster she thought she'd easily slay seemed to have sprouted humiliating tendrils.

⌘ ⌘ ⌘

Wendy in a fashionable Calvin Klein smoky gray straight skirt suit ran as fast as she was able to in her high-heeled sling-backs to get from school to Queens-Nassau Radiation on time. The pretty bandanad woman was already there with an older woman at her side. Wendy and the young cancer patient nodded to each other. The teacher was on her second butterscotch when Chris the technician called her in.

"How's that bandage, the one covering your new mark?" Yet again, Wendy didn't understand the question. 'It was an ordinary clear sticky square. How could it be a problem?' "Fine." She answered then closed her eyes to avoid staring into the machine's orb she dubbed The Death Ray. 'There's only one way to get through this. Zone out till it's done.'

In a half hour she was back in her car tossing a handful of Aquaphor samples into her purse. It hardly seemed necessary. The skin on her offending breast was still the same blood temperature as the other. She was soon back in Little Neck walking past the store's parking lot on Broward when she noticed the Lexus next to Jay's Santa Fe. It was a good thing she brought an ESL reader from school to quell any questions Yujin might have about her appearance so soon after the festival. She stopped at the local deli and bought three cold sodas and asked for paper cups. The men each with a customer smiled genuinely at her appearance. Jay's sale wrapped up first, leading Yujin to suggest they 'study' at the diner across the street. While they considered his suggestion, the phone in Wendy's handbag began to play its Korean drama theme song. Her chilling sweat returned. 'I'm not answering anatomical questions here.' But when she checked the caller, the news was worse. It read JANE'S SCHOOL. Jae Won abandoned his manners and looked over her shoulder.

"Don't worry. Just answer." He modulated the tone of his voice to appear calm.

"Mrs. Dale, This is Mr. Weinstein from The Queens School. We tried to call your husband since he's closer but his school said he couldn't be reached. Jane doubled over in pain a while ago. She said she's better now, but she looks a little washed out. I think you should come to take her home, unless you want us to call EMS. I'll let her talk to you."

"Mom," Wendy recognized the old hysterics in her daughter's voice. Jane was a gifted student with a healthy sense of who she was but Crohn's related reminders put the child in a tailspin. Wendy was determined not join in.

"The same pain came back. Mom, I've got it again. They didn't take it out right."

"Janie listen to me. I'm on my way. We'll go straight to Dr. Tapman's. I'm calling him as soon as I hang up. Is it still very bad? Would you rather go to the hospital?"

'Why do I have to be the mother who must ask these things?'

"No. It doesn't hurt now but could you come right away? I don't want to be at school."

Since cell phone usage became popular our personal lives are broadcast loudly for all and sundry. Wendy didn't care about the titillated shoppers or concerned Anycolor owners who stood eyes glued to her as she spoke.

"I have to go."

"I'll take you."

"That's all right, I've done this before."

Yujin acted swiftly, "Let Jay take you. You shouldn't drive now."

⌘ ⌘ ⌘

As the Santa Fe turned left on Northern, she gave Jay directions and thanked him. They didn't speak again till they were two blocks from Jane's school.

"Should I carry her to the car?" Jay reached to stop the softly playing CD. Wendy placed her hand on his, slightly and only momentarily.

"If she can't walk, we'll have to call an ambulance. *Co mah woi oh*"

The teacher looked out the window and into her former daydreams of being carried fireman style like a love scene in a Korean drama. The beautiful man beside her would do it, just for the asking, but she wouldn't be the one whose arms hugged his neck and it surely wouldn't end in a kiss. The scene would change to a hospital room. Again.

Barely waiting for the car to stop, Wendy jumped out and ran inside the soot stained red brick building. Jane lie on the school nurse's bench with her jacket over her and her book-bag as her pillow.

"Dr. Tapman is waiting for us. Did you eat anything too tough or too big?"

Wendy didn't wait for Jane's answer. If Janie's Crohn's was rearing its ugly head, it didn't need a reason. She signed her daughter out at the front desk before she remembered she hadn't driven herself.

"One of my friends from school brought me. My car's been hinky all week. His name is Mr. Hyun. Don't forget your manners."

In preparation, Jae Won Hyun had opened the back door for Wendy's daughter and then stood sentry at the school's entrance. Jane walked between her mother and the stranger and stepped into the Santa Fe's back seat. She closed the door leaving Wendy and Jay no need for excuses as they sat side by side in the front.

He was pleased the girl thanked him and called him by his surname. Even with her face the color of pages in his drawing tablet, he could see she was pretty. He looked at her in the back mirror as if she were a national icon. This was Wendy's love. How much room could there be left in her heart?

The girl met his gaze in the glass. "I'm sorry, I left my book-bag in the office."

"I'll be right back." Wendy bolted with the same intensity as when they arrived.

The pair was alone under the most uncomfortable circumstances. Jae Won never had a conversation with an American child but he comforted himself with his teaching experience.

"Did you get your homework for tonight?"

"You sound like my mom. Do you teach art at 347?"

"Neh?"

"My mom said you're from school. Are you the teacher who made my painting? Mom forgot to give it to me on Friday. I got it yesterday. Thanks so much Mr. Hyun. I like it very much. It's not like anything I have." The girl leaned her head on the seat rest."

"You're welcome." Jae Won quickly understood. He had given Wendy the paintings on a school holiday. She made an excuse why she brought something from school on a day it was closed. They'd had reduced themselves to sneaking about and lying to children.

Wendy returned.

"It's a good thing I went back. Mr. Weinstein gave me your homework assignments."

Jane and Jay shared a laugh.

As Jae Won's car turned east on Northern Boulevard, Wendy made what Tim called her 'mother noises' one more time. "Are you sure you didn't eat anything that could hurt you today?"

"No-o." whined an overly exasperated Jane.

Jay looked at Wendy. Her skin had the same ghostly pallor of her daughter's. Her fears kept her from thinking like a teacher. First rule, whether Baghdad or Mexico City, New York or Seoul; when scared, children will perjure themselves.

Jay turned his head towards the girl.

"On the holiday yesterday, Jane, what kind of snacks were your friends eating?" The former art teacher asked quietly without recriminations as when he taught at Kyung Gee Seoul High School.

"Peanuts. I ate a lot. I guess I forgot."

After his examination, Dr. Tapman concurred that it probably was a compacted lump of undigested peanuts that temporarily blocked her large intestine at the site of her surgery. He reminded the ashen-faced mother once again that Crohn's was a chronic not fatal illness and offered to draw Jane's blood to save them a trip on Saturday. Jane slept even as Jay parked in the Anycolor lot. Yujin stepped outside for a moment to help his cousin. Jay carried Jane to the Nissan and buckled her in. Yujin took her things from Wendy and placed them in her car. He immediately retreated back to the store.

"Janie should be fine but my schedule is crammed tomorrow. After my treatment, I'm meeting Mrs. Han then I have another appointment. Would you mind if I just called you to report what she says?"

They traded cell phones the way Korean lovers might have had they lived in a drama. She typed in Wendy. He, to protect her honor, pressed A n y c o l o r.

Jane never saw the parking lot. She didn't begin to stir till her mother pulled into their driveway. The girl's color seemed back to normal and her spirit returned. This was Jane, only two modes either scared stiff or hyper-happy.

"Mom, what was that teacher's name again?'

"Which teacher?"

"The one who drove us."

"Oh, Mr. Hyun. You have to send him a thank you for the painting."

"It's pretty but it doesn't go with my 5ive posters."

"It matches the breakfast room. The golden lake and mountains ringed in smoke will fit right in."

"But then it will be your painting. We just eat there but you're always in the breakfast room. You read the paper there in the morning and sometimes when I get up at night to use the bathroom I see you watching the sky from the breakfast room windows. Put the picture in your bedroom so you and Tim, you know, can both see it."

"No, no. If you don't want it, I'd like it in the breakfast room. You know me, matchy-matchy."

It was half past midnight when Yujin heard the neighbor's dog barking. He sat up next to his sleeping wife to listen again when a rimy presence told him someone had opened a door. He sat up fumbling for his balled up pajama bottoms at the foot-end of the bed. The frosted golden tips of his hair caught the moonlight as he looked through the blinds to his backyard below.

His cousin moved stealthily with a white porcelain bowl in his hands to a decorative outdoor kimchi jar. He placed the bowl on the jar's brown pottery lid. Jae Won's shadowy figure pressed hand to hand, knelt and bowed over and over in prayer. Earlier that evening his curiosity led him to a Crohn's disease website. The illness was no longer rare among Asians. The child could readily get treatment in Korea if they lived there. Soon his concern for Jane's mother took him to one of thousands of breast cancer sites. He managed to piece together that Wendy had stage 0 breast cancer that could easily return in the more hideous form that took his mother. Had he followed another faith he might have prayed for a miracle to save them but he was a Buddhist seeking only to clarify his confusion and turn suffering to joy. "May I be medicine for the sick nursing their affliction till they are cured."

Yujin blew stale sleeper's breath from his lips. *'Me che suh.* One sick wife wasn't enough misery. This time it's an American woman with a sick child and a husband. The joke is he would be faithful to her until death. Something I can't do.' As if awakened by her husband's thoughts, Yoon Yoo Son joined him at the window. "I think he really loves her."

"So what? It doesn't change anything."

⌘ ⌘ ⌘

Episode 8: A Quart of Milk

Libby nudged and repeated "Excuse me please." all the way down the three double flights of stairs to head off Wendy at period four's lunchtime. "When word spreads" the fifty-nine year old placed her hand on her Tahitian pearl necklace to catch her breath, "that you spoke ill of one of the region's book selections, you'll catch Hell from the administration."

Wendy's commented with a shrug and a wink.

"Ah, Libby, that's why tenure is a wonderful thing."

At the corner of Carthage and Marathon she braved the warnings of winter winds to tell KoreanRadio's audience why she would not use Weeping Trees in her classroom. She added that all students are free to read whatever their parents allow and stressed that she wouldn't and couldn't speak for the school librarian. She was careful to make clear that the opinions were hers alone. Ms. Dale spoke earnestly to the station's listeners while coveting Mrs. Han's Cavalli pants suit. The elegant woman studied the paintings during Wendy's speech. When it finally ended, the interviewer thanked Ms. Dale and joined the soundman in bowing and leaving. Injung Han walked up the side street with the teacher while regaling the health properties of Himalayan salt crystals.

"That's a good idea, putting the lamp in your daughter's room. How did you say you know Mr. Hyun?"

Wendy pretended preoccupation with searching for her keys in her foot wide Franco Sarto handbag. Casually and without looking up she said, "Well, I'm Seromie Kim's teacher and I guess the Kims' told their cousin about me. He needed translation work done so, I got the job."

"His wife suffered from clinical depression. I heard she drove off a mountain road and he didn't try to stop her but that may be just a story."

Wendy was careful not to defend Jay. "*Jin jah?* I had no idea. What do you think of the paintings?"

"I like them very much. They remind me of my childhood. I think also, HTV will like your animation idea. I will meet with them tomorrow and call Mr. Hyun. Do you have his phone number?"

"*Shil sim nee dah.* No. I just call the store if I'm running late. I'm sure you can reach him there."

Mrs. Han wasn't put off by the sham. If anything she wanted the game to last.

"How did you find out he was an artist?"

"Oh Seromie brought one of his paintings to school. I was so impressed with the playfulness and poignancy of his work."

The women walked to their cars like featherweight boxers after a round's bell.

⌘ ⌘ ⌘

Another in her stable of new physician's looked over his reading glasses at Wendy in her paper dress. She had been in two doctors' offices today yet nobody cured her aching knotted gut or profound icy sweats.

"The sonogram shows a thickening of the uterus. But I'm telling you that it's bullshit."

Wendy gave her new gynecologist her full attention. He certainly racked up points for shock value.

"See the problem with Tamoxifin is that it can bring on uterine cancer."

"Then why would anyone take it, to trade up from breast cancer?"

Dr. Scheinfeld took her remark to be rhetorical and continued.

"But you haven't been taking it long enough for that to be a factor. I'd like you to come in tomorrow for a hysteroscopy. I'll make time for you. Wendy, even if this is uterine cancer, I promise you I can make it go away."

The teacher redressed and returned to the waiting room barely remembering his name. 'Steinfield? Scheinfeld?' He was only a little handsomer than George Costanza but his accent, dotted with flat 'a' sounds said he wasn't from New York. Still he managed to present her future in a less threatening way than the others and she was grateful. When she handed his secretary a check for two hundred fifty five dollars she assured herself it was worth it even though he didn't accept her health plan.

There's an old joke that may have started in New York's Catskill Mountain resorts about a little boy who refused to speak. Finally one day he put his toast back on his plate turned to his mother and announced, "This is burnt." The mother danced around the table hearing her son's first words. She called in his father and sister to mark the happy moment. The beaming father looked at his son and asked, "You haven't said a word for your entire five years. What made you decide to speak?" The son looked down at the bread's blackened cinders and said, "Up till now everything was perfect."

It was why Tim and Wendy never fought. No raised voices attested everything was fine. After Jane's diagnosis they spoke only of her illness. They'd sit side by side in bed going over the child's hospitalizations, her new medications, her old treatments. Not once did they ask each other how it was affecting their marriage. They

Bird and Fish

were no longer husband and wife. They had become Jane's teammates. As poor a substitute that was for a loving relationship, this new scenario was worse. They laughed and chatted at meals in a royal performance for Jane. Wendy was nearly convinced Tim's basement hideout was a healthy outlet for him. After awhile she pretended herself into believing that Jay was Mr. Hyun the art teacher and friend. Tim and Wendy were keeping secrets from each other and playing nicely so when alone they could assure themselves everything was still perfect. But the burnt toast was about to hit the plate.

The hallway Rya rug was rolled up and lying on the dining room floor. In its place were flattened shower liners attached with silvery duct tape. The wallpapered light switch was removed along with the Gold toned mirror, shelf and pocket planters. The bronze and glass fixture's ceiling plate was loosened and dangling. Tim's Queens College tee shirt was already forming sweat triangles at his neck and underarms from this after-school activity. He returned from the garage with the three paint cans placing them on the shower liner tarmack. Why did the store stickers look familiar? Anycolor Paints II with each letter of Anycolor a different shade. He recognized the writing underneath to be Korean. He had seen enough on his wife's shows to tell the difference between Asian icons and her second language. The address was another clue to where she purchased the paints. It was near her school. Did they ever go there together? He saw that sticker somewhere else. 'Shit, there're no paint stirrers.'

His notation of missing supplies acted like a thumb in the leaky barrier of his memory

Wendy walked in debating the merits of take-out Chinese when she saw souvenirs of Jay's store among the debris on her foyer floor.

"What's all this?" she barked.

Fido had stolen an empty plastic margarine container from Tim's supplies and was busy making clacking sounds as his teeth and claws turned it to yellow and blue confetti. The steady clack pop clack pop served up even more jagged nerves.

"It's our pre-Halloween fixer-upper project." Tim announced expecting plaudits.

His wife's acknowledgement came in the form of four questions none designed to be answered.

"You're doing this now? We don't have enough on our plate? We have to take on a project while I'm going for radiation? What were you thinking?"

Tim wiped his hands with the dampened rag he had used to clean cobwebs from the walls. This clearly wasn't the reaction he expected. He was dirty, covered in perspiration and raging at the illnesses that were stealing his family.

The soft-spoken Irishman began a mulish bray, something he reserved for cursing at SUV's that cut him off on his way to work.

"I don't know, Red? Why don't you tell me what I'm thinking? You're the one who knows everything."

"What is that supposed to mean?" You're telling me this is a good time to paint? Her volume was meeting his.

"I'm telling you, *princess*, that a lot of women would be glad to walk in and see their husbands painting the God damn walls." He had finally surpassed the sounds of Lay All Your Lovin On Me traveling through Jane's headphones into her ears. The girl opened the door fearing a fire had broken out or the basement had flooded. She had never heard her parents shouting before.

"What happened?" the child removed one ear phone that now dangled and rapped to the boy band's "Now you know what I like and I like what you got" in the same beat as Fido's clacking. Neither Wendy nor Tim would give up their righteous indignation to address Jane.

Tim glared at his wife as his mother had glared at him before a Johnny Walker beating. Wendy shouted as she had never done before.

"Princess? You must mean the princess who cooks for you every night. You know the princess who bends over the bathroom sink to clean your stubble and shaving cream, the same princess who makes every dental, gardener and plumber appointment. I'm sick now. I'm tired. I don't need more work. I'll end up doing the scut work for this as usual. She picked up the Lemon Grass paint container ready to return it to a hidden corner of the garage.

"I don't know, Tim, we both work for the Board of Ed. but I come home to do a dark wash while you sit on two thrones, first the one in the john then the one in front of the TV. Maybe you're the princess."

"I could show you I'm not a princess but lately you're pretending to be asleep in front of your Korean shows."

Their bedroom hallway measured eight feet by three, hardly room for a man, woman, child and gnawing dog. Yet they all stood gulping the limited air supply decoding Tim's remark.

"Are you guys fighting?" Jane was witness to their unraveling and it frightened her.

"No, we're just discussing something." Wendy had no hiding place for her anger. It certainly wasn't in this cramped forum.

Tim joined the lie.

"I hate these colors, Janie. I don't know why mommy chose them. What do you think, too dull right?"

"Let's paint when we're sure these are what we want. Honey would you bring these things back to the garage?"

Perhaps if Jane had been a healthier apple-cheeked specimen they would have been more open but it wasn't likely. They each had secrets to keep from the other and Janie was their beard.

In a quarter hour, the paint cans and their accompanying paraphernalia were returned to the cool darkness of the garage. Wendy cleaned Fido's now abandoned plastic shards. Janie closed her door inviting back her boy band to supply music for her homework while Tim caught a sports update after his shower. The teacher took her cell phone and dog out to the yard. Everything was back to normal except now normal had a new definition.

During the first few years following World War II, Queens was a-buzz with new housing projects. America's fighting forces were back and their families needed homes. A Floral Oaks developer built hundreds of Cape Cod bungalows with the same two-bedroom one bath floor plan. The design was easy to convert. The attic stood ready to hold another two or three bedrooms and full bath. The oversized basement could easily shoulder a den, half-bath and a guest bedroom. They were built to last a lifetime and they kept their promise. Wendy often wondered which of her community's planners knew the special gift the houses gave each homeowner. Maybe none of them realized that building inexpensive middle-class Floral Oaks on Long Island's north-south gridlines meant the occupants could catch the sunrise each morning in their breakfast rooms and watch it set later in the day from their bedroom windows.

Ms. Dale stood alone on her patio squinting at the shrinking daylight. Jumbo clouds like ocean liners were gliding north breaking up smaller ones to froth. When one of the great ships dipped and lapped at the sun the entire airship exploded in auric glitter.

Fido brought Wendy downed branches till she understood him. The six-legged pair played Catch Me around the Leyland Cypress trees that bordered their back fence. The hound and mistress grew tired together and retreated to the driveway where Fido lay on the cold cement. His mistress slumped in the tattered canvas summer chair.

Wendy eyed the nearly barren vegetable garden. Just three months ago the center was filled with plump ruby raspberries that crowned blood red spiked stalks. Now the bush was reduced to dead brown nubs. The rosemary however was even taller and more pungent than her last visit. 'Let this be a lesson if I'm going to survive this winter, I should stop thinking like a redhead and start being a stinker.' With that mantra said, Wendy called a delivery order into Mr. Ling's Kitchen then tried to reach Libby. At the Spring's home, a maid informed Wendy that the family had gone out. Her friend's cell phone directed her to voice mail. "Lib, I hope you're the only one who retrieves your calls. I had this crazy argument with Tim. It was over nothing, really but I've got to get out for a bit. I'm telling them I'm going to TJ Maxx but I might end up..." the teacher's unexpected sigh followed her words to voice mail, "at a paint store. So if tomorrow the police find my body floating in Flushing Bay, tell them the truth. Not that I think anything like that will happen but my mother always says better safe... I'm babbling. I'll see you tomorrow."

Fido smelled the close of day and left the chill of his yard to bark at the side door. Wendy followed him in. "I called Mr. Ling's take-out", she announced. Jane flung open her door as if her mother had shouted, "Ashton Kutcher is here!"

"Did you get me spare ribs and brown rice?"

"Yes, but be careful. Only little bites, no gulps of rice. OK?"

Tim called from the den, "Egg Foo Young?"

Wendy winced. It was not one of her favorites. "Yes. I'm going shopping. Probably Maxx'. I'll be home before nine. Tim, please make sure Pure 19 tapes.

The teacher showered quickly not only because of her time constraints but because there was no joy in her unfeminine, many-ruled wash-up. No matter how easily she pretended she was as normal as everyone else at school, the new shower routine reminded her of the severity of her situation. Her pink tube of Insolence sparkling shower gel was replaced with a scent-free hospital sample for her top left half. She wasn't permitted to scrub or rub her breast during treatment leading her to lather her shoulder allowing the suds to run over and under her bosom. She had to give up the habit of underarm shaving nightly but happily the waxing had kept her underarms smooth for now. While Wendy applied her shampoo and conditioner with her head hung backwards so not to contaminate the radiation site, the sticky square began to prickle but in comparison to her throbbing side it was a minor annoyance.

Wendy shared a "good evening" with Mr. Ling as she passed him on her front walk. She drove to the Guyanese woman's turreted manse where she stopped. Rather than remind herself it was wrong to visit a male friend in the evening she applauded her good citizenship by pulling over before using her phone. Anycolor's number was between Annie the hairdresser and Barbara from P.T.A. She pressed the button with the same fervor as Janie when the child repeatedly tapped the Dilautin release button after her surgery. Now she understood her daughter's reckless twitching finger on the button. She needed the pain to stop.

The phone rang once.

"Oh dee ah?"

"Actually I'm in your neighborhood. I wanted to tell you what Mrs. Han said about your work."

"*Bally whah*. My cousins went out."

'Am I really the only woman left who cooks dinner every night? It took a day of work, radiation and a hint of uterine cancer to let me bow out tonight.' The teacher drove half way to school before turning so her approach wouldn't say she had driven from home. At the step above the entryway was a new pair of Korean-style slippers. She slipped into them without comment following Jay into the kitchen. They sat as they were meant to across from each other at the countertop with the gold and black fish watching them.

The teacher pushed up the sleeves on her burnt orange turtleneck and regaled the tale of her meeting with Mrs. Han. Wendy ended the story with a question.

"Are the paintings you gave me from Korea?"

"*Uh. Wheh?* Are they much different?"

"I'm not a critic, but I see the joy of life in them. It's as if you're inviting the viewer to share what you see. The new paintings show a kind of longing like 'This is what I miss most.'"

He made a gutteral sound to change the subject.

"Fishman, would you mind if I showed more of your work to Kim Dong Kook?"

Jae Won felt the same embarrassment that heated his cheeks as a teenager. 'If he never sees them, he'll never turn them down.'

"Those were all I took with me. My work is still at a friend's house in *Jongno-gu*. Did you eat dinner?"

'Why is he lying?' "Not yet."

"I have ramen. Would you like an egg in it?"

Wendy scowled in disapproval.

"Eggs are for breakfast, brunch or batter." She noticed his puzzled expression.

"Cake batter. Cakes are made with flour and eggs. I don't like coddled eggs floating in my soup but I like plain ramen. Can we cook it in a pot and eat it off the lid?"

"You watch too many dramas. I'll just add boiled water to the bowls. Do you want a drink?"

"I can't drink. Did you mean soda?"

"I have filtered water." He pointed to the Oasis counter top water dispenser next to the toaster.

"You don't need that here. This is New York. We have the softest, best tasting water in the country."

Bird and Fish

"Are you a commercial?"

"She allowed herself to look directly into his half moon eyes. "Fishman, I really envy you. You're just like Yakov Smirnoff."

"Is he a painter?"

"He did become an artist but that's not the connection. I watched him on television when I was a girl. He came from Russia and became a comedian here. Americans loved his jokes about how confusing it was in the U.S. He'd always end his routine with "What a country!"

"This reminds you of me?"

"No. He was comfortable with English and Americans. To embrace a culture so well that he could be funny in its language was something I wished I could do. That's why you remind me of him. So if anyone asks you how well you speak English, tell them 'I'm a regular Yakov Smirnoff!'"

Jae Won barely caught her meaning.

"*Kur ah suh*, he's an artist?"

The teacher knew the punch line was lost in translation.

"*Neh*, he's an artist too."

While sharing their Spartan meal, he asked if she had returned to Korea since her first visit.

"Janie became very ill two months after I came home. I could hardly think of making the journey then. One day I will do something extraordinary so I can return like a conquering hero at least that's my latest fantasy.

"What did you like most when you were there?"

"You read my piece in the Korea Times so you know the most inspiring place was the DMZ. The year before my father died, we took a trip to Saratoga. It was off season and I stood at the battle sight alone. But I didn't feel alone. The ghosts of America's first soldiers were all around. That's how I felt at the Demilitarized Zone... surrounded by the spirits of families torn apart."

The teacher took a sip of water.

"I liked the King's Palace and the shopping in Itaewan but my favorite time was walking with our teacher. We were hiking in the Kyeryong-San National Park and had become separated from the others. He used that time to talk about his country. Granted I still believe that anyone who comes to America would want to stay here. In my defense I always lived among immigrants so up until that very moment I assumed everyone in the world longed to leave his homeland to be an American. But Dr. Lee spoke with such passion and pride about his people, his government, his dream of unification, he taught me there were non-Americans who were just as patriotic as I. Our dreams may be different but we all have dreams.

Her gaze left his face to watch *Uri* snatch bits of food from the top of the bowl."

"Was there anything you didn't like?"

"Besides the coffee?" Her shoulders shuddered while she wrinkled up her nose. "I've always been a bit of a loner. It was difficult for me to spend my days with American and foreign educators from dawn till dusk. One group of Americans embarrassed me. They complained about the food, they demanded the guides follow their commands and they whined all the time. The term is 'Ugly Americans.' One day a principal from Colorado bad-mouthed teachers to me. She said we were lazy! A few days before we left they started a collection to buy the guides a gift. I didn't want to join them for any purpose so I was the sole dissenter. I had brought gifts from home anyway but it was a stupid way to make my point. I certainly had enough money. When I got home I sent a package for Dr. Lee's children. I put my leftover Korean currency in with the toys and candy in penance. I don't know, maybe those people weren't so bad. Maybe I'm just a hard ass."

"Hard ass?"

"Stubborn." Wendy knew she'd have to repeat, 'ass' if the conversation continued. "Ooh, it's getting late. She took the Styrofoam bowls from the countertop and tossed them into the trashcan and began clearing off the rest of the counter.

"Wendy," Jae stopped her from cleaning, "if you go now, you'll miss *Pure 19*."

She was eighty city blocks from her home yet she could almost hear the clicks and whirs of her aging VCR getting into gear. She wasn't missing anything, yet she raced barefoot to his living room.

"You're right. Are you going to watch it? I'll watch with you."

He would have eagerly watched dust settle if she sat at his side. They shared his living room couch; she watching the 60's flower power designs dancing to the show's theme song, he watching her. Within the show's first minutes, the farm girl had been ignored, berated and insulted by the Park clan but when they hurt her one true love, she broke down and so did Ms. Dale. Wendy placed her hand over her bottom lip to mask its tremors. Soon both her hands were wiping tears from the corners of her eyes. All this was done without a sound. If it weren't for the lava red highlights in her hair, she would have looked like a heroine weeping in a silent movie. The series would end in five months, making tonight's episode the expected time for the first big kiss scene. On a wintry rooftop in Seoul, Gukhwa and Yunhu shared a tender closed mouth kiss. The handsome young actor puckered his lips gourami-style and headed in to the tear-soaked cheek of the pure 19 year old. Neither

Wendy nor Jae Won moved their eyes from the screen. Their heads were aligned so stiffly with their shoulders, they looked like passengers on an amusement ride, each absorbed in his own embarrassment. Jae Won didn't feel confident enough to face her till the three-minute set of local Korean commercials had ended and the music break began. He turned to study her. She had abandoned her slippers in the kitchen and walked barefoot through his house, she was the only person he knew who had been born with red hair. She never respectfully lowered her voice to him and didn't even eat fish the staple of his cuisine. Everything that beguiled him set them apart. Wendy's host smoothed her obstinate auburn locks back behind her ear. She didn't protest. She didn't flinch. She was fast asleep. He watched her breathe till KBS news announced it was 8:35.

"Papa, will we have a thousand gifts for the princess on her birthday?" The fisherman's daughter looked so pale in their tiny cottage's candlelight. Her father leaned down, kissed her forehead and gently returned a wayward curl back behind her ear. "Why of course, think of how many voices there are."

"In the whole wide world?"

"In the whole wide world and maybe a few stars too." He teased.

The clock on the computer screen convinced Wendy it was midnight. Three hours ago when she returned home, she had awakened Tim from his lounge chair and walked him, her hand at his back and one step behind him to their bed. The den furniture seemed to have absorbed

Tim's new cleaner smell, perhaps because it was a basement. She made a note to air out the room over the weekend. Janie and she shared a small bag of Lay's Baked while going over the child's homework and discussing the school Halloween dance. The Queens School For Gifted Children held dances directly after school with strict adherence to school uniforms only. The students, including Janie protested but Wendy sided with the policy. Bringing kids back to school at night with the opportunity to show off skimpy tops and muffin-topped jeans is just asking for trouble.

Earlier, Jane watched her parents rise from the den stairway as if this afternoon's shouting match had never happened. The girl showered, stepped into her baby dolls and went to bed. David from seventh grade had already asked for the first slow dance. She squeezed her raggedy Pooh doll and settled down with her girl-dreams, while her mother looked at the silent street from the breakfast room windows.

The teacher wrote her schedule for the next day:

Tell kids no rehearsals on Hallo

Call mom and cuz

Call I.H. about HTV

Rad

Bird and Fish

Remind J can't be ther fri

Ask J for art again.

hystero

She scanned the seven items noting tidying house, grading shoe-box projects and preparing chicken croquettes were also her responsibilities. Tomorrow was thirty-four minutes old and she was already overwhelmed.

On the thirtieth of October, Ms. Dale matched black skinny slacks with a black marino knit shell and covered them with a bright orange silk and wool peplum jacket in homage to the Halloween season. Tomorrow, she'd wear her 'teacher' sweater, the one with the silvery spider dangling from a gray wool cord to entertain her six graders. 6A2 had just bounced, pushed and giggled their way out of her room when Libby, huffing and puffing from her three flight dash in her Blanick's dashed to Ms. Dale's room.

"Guess who's in trouble?" She gulped in puffs of air between each word.

"If it isn't you and it isn't I, who cares?"

"Thanks for your interest." Mrs. Spring mockingly rolled her eyes and continued. "I happened to be in the outer abattoir."

"Abattoir?"

"That's where they slaughter cows. Have you taken a good look at our secretaries? Moo! Anyway, Ira was blasting Nick because he's behind schedule, over budget and there's no educational component for Wildcat. I heard him ask, 'what exactly are the children learning from this play? Nick stammered. I don't think he even answered."

Wendy shook her head in disgust.

"Wildcat actually offers a big chunk of American history."

Libby loved when her friend went into what she called 'brainiac mode.'

"If I was going to take a Nash play" Wendy began,

"I'd pick 110 In The Shade. That's still popular. It's having a revival out west next year. But if I had to use Wildcat, I'd have the eighth graders compare the beginning of this century with the beginning of the twentieth because it opens in 1912, things like transportation, medicine, fashion. The ninth graders could explore the roles of woman at that time or America's dependency on oil. The Spanish classes could discuss Mexican legal and illegal immigrants in cities like the play's Centavo City. The sixth graders might do Nash's biography or even Lucille Ball's."

"What don't you know?" Libby fumbled through her Hogan Lizzy purse till she located a neon green post-it.

"I don't know how to keep my family healthy." The teacher lowered her voice, "I don't know what I'm going to do about Jay. But I do know I'm seeing you more than ever before. Lib, I know you don't have time to come here during our preps every day, Thanks."

"No whispering please. Nobody's at a funeral. Here," she handed Wendy the post-it. "Her name is Laura Weiner. She and I went to nursing school together. Ten years ago she was diagnosed with DCIS. She works for SHARE now. It's a breast and ovarian cancer support group like the Crohn's and Colitis Foundation you called for Janie. She's expecting your call *tonight*. Don't embarrass me."

Before Wendy could reach for her friend's hand, the door opened bringing in cloying lunchroom odors and Mr. Nick Shutter. True to his horrendous sense of style his tight black chinos crushed against his scrotum producing New York's first case of male camel-toe.

"Oh, you've got company." He was cheery but transparent while he leaned on the back of a student chair.

"My brain is buzzing with all the projects I'm doing in conjunction with Wildcat. I can't decide which to choose. I thought we could network for some ideas." His raptor eyes darted from Libby to Wendy trying to detect the weaker.

Libby jabbed first, "Wendy was just saying she doesn't know how you do your job. She couldn't even begin to come up with project ideas.'

Wendy cut in, "Nick go with what you have. I'm sure it will be great. Do you mind if I cut this short? Libby is helping me sew costumes for "Rubies."

With finely honed adaptation skills, the predator knew to end his visit. By the time the hallway door swung behind him, the woman were jumping in place and cheering.

"The best part? Anyone who takes even one look at me knows," Libby swept her recently manicured hand across her Tahari suit and proclaimed, "I'm no sew-er!"

Their laughter was interrupted when the classroom door opened for Claire Jackson who waved at Wendy.

"The boss want to see you." Her opinion of Ira Rubinstein came out through her sneer.

"Am I in trouble?" Wendy rubbed her side and walked to her locked closet to liberate a Vicodin half.

"That man can't give you no trouble. Is he the bank tak'n your house away?"

"She's right. Just go see what he wants. Claire stay and gossip with me till next period."

Bird and Fish

Claire moved two chairs to her usual hiding place while Wendy headed for the door. The teacher remembered the French class that would take over the room later and turned to her friends.

"Claire, stay where you can't be seen. Libby, do me a favor, take those sketches and supplies off my desk and hide them in my closet."

"I don't mind taking them to the prop room if you need them for the assembly."

"No, no." She protested a bit too quickly.

"Just hide them in my closet and lock it. They're not for 'Rubies'. They're just some illustrations I'm doing for a little story. They're nothing really."

Libby stood at the desk holding two pencil drawings, one a palace counting room the other a medieval peasant and child calling to a bird.

"Claire, look at what she calls nothing."

Wendy decided to return her A Thousand Voices drawings herself till Claire, taking a candy bar from her shirt pocket asked, "You talk to a radio reporter?"

The door had barely closed behind Ms. Dale when Claire turned to Libby shaking her head. "I gotta admit she still look good."

Libby looked towards the room's entranceway. "I think God sent her an angel."

"Yeah, she lucky in that department, havin' a good husband."

Libby couldn't repress her snicker. "Are you joking? Since when is Tim a good husband?"

"The guard was openly surprised. "Well, the first one," Claire lowered her voice as if the room was bugged. "I heard he beat her."

Libby placed her hand on Claire's trousered knee. "Wendy may be old school and a bit innocent but she'd never let a man hit her. Her first was a control freak, a blow-heart extension of Mrs. Dale. He'd go into his crazy tirades when he didn't get his way. They only separated. Wendy was afraid of upsetting her mother. If he hadn't died, she would have stayed chained to that head-case. She married Tim because he was quiet but I never trusted him. That woman is the smartest person I know and the charming Mr. O'Hanlon has still managed to keep her caged. I was hoping somebody would bring out the best in her."

"So who's the angel?"

"Eh, I just meant God must have sent an angel to… guide her."

"I never knew Jewish folk believed in angels."

Bird and Fish

"In the Book of Daniel, the angel Michael reaches his goal in one flight, the angel Elijah in four. Maybe Wendy's angel will be number three."

The security agent's walkie talkie was squawking about a marijuana smell on the second floor forcing her to stand and turn towards the door. "You sure know your old testament."

Libby stood to exit with her school friend, "It's not my *old* anything. It's our bible."

Claire smiled mockingly, "Well you said Wendy's angel will be number three. Number three, that's from *our* bible."

The woman shared the ecumenical joke before exiting the classroom together.

Ira Rubinstein wasn't having his best day. There was a rumor about a ninth grade student and her Earth Science teacher, both females, the latest math scores were in today's New York newspapers showing M.S.347 lagging behind M.S.343 by three tenths of a point. The school musical was floundering and a parent just informed him one of his teachers had given a press conference without his knowledge. The well-dressed principal opened his closet door to approve himself in the state prison made mirror. He adjusted his lime and navy striped tie and readied himself for Ms. Dale. Had she'd been a screw-up this would have been easy: A scolding, followed by her threat of union action followed by an argument and a letter for her file. But Wendy was one of the best he had and certainly the smartest. He'd have to finesse her.

"Yes, Mr. Rubinstein, you wanted to see me."

"Don't stand in the doorway, Wendy come sit down."

Wendy hated the whole process. 'Why couldn't he just come out with it? Well, if she was 'Wendy', he'd be Ira'. "Ira, I'm sorry if you took the heat for me talking about Weeping Trees but I wasn't on school grounds and I made it clear I was speaking for myself."

"You're a smart girl. You must have known the superintendent would get wind of this."

"Ira, I haven't been a girl since…in a long time. The superintendent, as omnipotent as he may think he is, has nothing to do with this. There are more important things to worry about."

"Ms. Dale, I don't know if I can protect you. I may have to put a letter in your file." His face began to flush clashing with his new silk tie.

"Sir, that would mean I'd be owed years worth of principal commendation letters right up to a few weeks ago when only the EMS thanked me for helping one of our seizure students. Where was my letter then?"

Even her codeine dosage had given up on her pulsating ache. Wendy arched her back while remaining seated.

"Let's stay calm. Here's my offer. I'll e-mail lesson plans and projects to you for each grade in several subject areas for Wildcat tonight but I will accidentally send them to the entire staff so unscrupulous persons can't claim them. You will tell the superintendent anything you like to make this go away so I am spared any undue aggravation."

Ira Rubinstein just got rid of two of the day's problems. To protest a deal would make him look like a schmuck, still he was taught to always use something to keep a teacher at bay. He put out his right hand to shake Wendy's.

"I won't even bring up the use of the N-word."

Wendy kept her hand by her side when she stood trying to recall any lunchroom brawls where the word was added to the scuffle.

"Who used the N-word?"

"You did. You said it to two special ed. students." Ira Rubinstein already knew he should have just taken the deal.

"No Ira, I wrote a script using the S-word for slave and now I'm going to use the R-word. I'm resigning. I'll be gone at midterm. I trust you will keep this under wraps until I've handed in my papers." Then she shook his hand like a pandering politician leaving Principal Rubinstein fumbling for a profound remark.

The Koreans have an expression; 'Women are weak. Mothers are strong.' Wendy made her way down to the sub-basement book room where she could rely on being alone this time of year. She wasn't Korean after all since her selfish woman-thoughts were what made her feel strong. 'I'll get Voices published then I'll write another book and then another.'

Yet the mother in her was falling apart. 'What about Janie's college money? What about her medical bills? What if she gets sick again? What on earth am I doing?'

Wendy looked up at the filled shelves. Books in every size and width shouldered her. There were scores of great works and rows of yellowing workbooks. Books don't grow like daisies. People who stop worrying about regular paychecks and pensions write them and now Ms. Wendy Dale was joining them.

Occasionally, teachers left grown-up books in the bookroom as offerings to other staff members. Wendy reached for a copy of McCourt's Teacher Man. She tilted her head approving her well- manicured hand. 'That will be the first to go. No more weekly nail salon visits. This is serious!' she mocked herself. Fatso Casta entered noisily munching popcorn from a 100 calorie snack bag.

"What are you doing here?" she asked as if Wendy had broken into her living room. A half hour ago Wendy would have lied about coming to retrieve a book and then exit rapidly giving the kernel-mouthed teacher the privacy she needed to steal books to use in her private tutoring business. But Wendy had just been unshackled from uncollegial colleagues.

"None of your business. Don't confuse yourself with one of my supervisors." She grabbed Frank McCourt's latest memoir discus style as if to throw it.

A popcorn hull dropped from the big woman's mouth as she exited faster than Wendy had ever seen her move before. Mild-mannered again Ms. Dale looked around one last time. 'Someone should write a story about forgotten books in a sub-basement room. When the door closes do they read each other their stories. Does Julius Caesar snub his nose up at Catherine Called Birdy. Do the workbooks instruct the easy readers?' The teacher closed the door behind her leaving the books to answer her questions in privacy.

⌘ ⌘ ⌘

Chris the technician leaned over Wendy's bared breasts and studied the square bandage in earnest. He had recently eaten a banana and the fruity smell was like fingernails on a chalkboard to her senses.

"Does the bandage bother you?"

"It doesn't hurt. If that's what you mean but it itches."

"We'll have to take it off." He said as he zipped it off her skin.

"Some people get a reaction to the bandage. You're one of 'em."

It left a perfect little red square in its wake.

"We'll just have to re-mark you every time. No problem."

Wendy made no reply, no angry diatribe. The technician would never know how revolted she was, thinking she'd wear that cadet blue mutilation forever when all along they could have re-marked her each treatment with 'No problem.'

⌘ ⌘ ⌘

"Diane, has my mother driven you crazy yet?" Ms. Dale sat in her car scratching the little red square through her wool top while talking to her cousin on her cell.

"*My* mother could drive me crazy. Aunt Lucille just gives me headaches." Diane Conroy put her hand over the mouthpiece and called for her aunt.

"Aunt Lucille, Wen's on the phone don't you want to talk to her? Wendy, don't let her get to you, you have your own troubles. She's in a bad mood because she has to go for her Dopler today."

Wendy Dale had enough guilt for leaving her mother's care to her obliging cousin. Hearing the senior Ms. Dale's medical test was scheduled without her made her even more ashamed.

"Diane, I'll be able to take over mom's care in February. Don't say anything yet. I haven't even told Tim but I resigned."

Her cousin cut her off, "Are you finally going to write the great American novel?"

"Well, I'm starting a bit smaller, just a children's book. Nothing, really."

"Of course it's something. If you take on Auntie, you'll never be a writer. Uh, uh she's mine till death. I'm sure she'll outlive me."

Diane's voice took a solemn tone, "Don't follow your dad. He was so talented but he died at a desk in a business he hated. Oh, here's your mom." Her last remark was in singsong to assure Wendy she'd be a good secret keeper.

"Hi mom. The test will be fine. Don't worry about anything."

"I'm taking three Xanax with me just in case. I need underwear. I don't want to ask Diane. Could you bring me ten pairs in cotton, not all whites. Get me some pastel ones too. You can drive 'em down here on Saturday."

Diane wrestled the phone from her aunt, "I'll get the panties. Aunt Lucille, Wendy can't drive four and a half hours to bring your undies."

The tourniquet around Wendy's intestines pulled tighter making numbing pinpricks all along her left leg.

"Diane, I'll pick them up this weekend and send them to her. I know the kind she likes."

In the background she heard her mother snarl, "Did she go to my house yet? I want someone up there to check before the snow starts and tell Janie grandma's waiting for her call this week."

"Aunt Lucille, Wendy has to get back to work, say goodbye."

"What the hell she call for? She only talks a minute anyway."

'I'm only one tragedy away from appearing on Oprah.'

Wendy thought over her phone conversation. 'To be invited on The Ellen Degeneres Show, I'd have to be in a movie. Not likely. To appear with Martha, I'd need to write a cookbook. Do-able. But Oprah, with my crazy family, she'd probably take me now. Maybe she'd send me to Dr. Phil. No, Oprah would just hug me before I sat on her couch and I'd be healed.'

Wendy stopped for pomegranates for Jay and Yujin before going to Anycolor. The Korean owner at the cash register was blotting up the spill from a leaking egg carton but managed a smile when the teacher said *Gom sah hah me dah* while taking her change. Wendy returned to her seat behind the wheel and tilted the rear-view mirror to a nearly vertical position checking if her sports bra made her look lumpy. She had pulled the straps too tightly in the radiologist's dressing room to cover the recent faint pink tinge sweeping across her left breast. She made a mental note that along with purchasing her mother's underwear this weekend, she'd buy more turtlenecks. With her left-sided sunburn, her misplaced blue bindi and the reddened square, the under wire medieval wench look was out of the question.

The massive Benjamin Moore trailer truck with the colorful paint cans under the logo was pulling away leaving Yujin on the sidewalk speaking Spanish to two workers Wendy had never seen before. The men jumped into the cab of an Anycolor Paints pick-up and drove away. Wendy guessed they worked at both stores. By the way they averted their eyes as she approached them said they were probably illegals. When Yujin opened the front door for her, Jay and Malik greeted her. The latter had been waiting for her while enjoying an orange juice offered by Jae Won. The day after their chance meeting, Wendy had looked over her former student's Blue Card to recall he lived with his grandmother and older, often in trouble, brother in Jackson Heights.

"Ms. Dale, heh heh," he turned to the Anycolor owners, "She always dressed up for the holidays. You still bake for the kids?"

"Not as often as when I taught you. How's grandma? Everyone well at home?" She was hoping he'd come to ask about colleges. New York is an expensive city. He'd never make ends meet with just a high school diploma.

"I got big news, Ms. D. I'm gonna be a daddy!"

"Oh, Malik, she hugged the former student while the cousins offered him congratulations in two languages.

"I didn't know you were married." All those hours soaking in the moral code of Korean dramas had somehow blocked America's new family order from Wendy's schema.

Yujin and Jae Won flashed their eyes in disbelief.

"Ha ha, Ms. D. Why I wanna get married?"

"Do you like this girl? Do you trust her?"

"I like her and yeah, I trust her. She's real nice. I'll bring her by but, Ms. Dale, come on you know what they say, 'why buy the cow when you can get the milk for free' heheh."

Ms. Dale was not amused. She put on her teacher face for the four men before her, the last an elderly white haired customer holding a twenty-eight inch bisque mini blind kit.

"Did you just call the mother of your baby a cow? Did I hear that Malik? Is your grandma an old cow, am I? Let me tell you why you're supposed to 'buy the cow'. It's a merciless world, full of sadness and trials. The best thing that can happen to you or any of us is to have someone who'll take your side. On the day your boss chews you out, or when your grandmother meets her final reward, it'll be your wife who'll rub your shoulders to comfort you. On the good days when you move into your first house or the baby says da-da, it's your wife who'll remind you to get the camera and laugh out loud with you. So please don't tell me when given the choice, you'll pass on a life support system for a quart of milk."

Malik Thorne might as well have been sitting in classroom B-4. His reaction was as it had been in sixth grade. He lowered his head, "I'm sorry Ms. Dale. They been asking me too, my Grams and Tanya."

Yujin went through the back to his car on a self-imposed errand. He was sure she was subliminally talking to him. Jae Won rang up the customer's purchase hoping this wasn't her way of saying goodbye. The old man thanked Jae Won, took a folded tissue from his coat pocket and blew his nose. His wife had been dead six years and he'd still pretend she was in the next room when he got home.

Wendy laughed. 'Talk about being a wet blanket! I've practically emptied the store.'

"Just think about what I said." She handed the bag of pomegranates to Malik. Give these to your girlfriend. They're very healthy." She shrugged at Jae Won trying to convey, "Yes, this was for you but what can I do?"

The outside of the plastic bag was sticky from the produce store's raw egg spillage. Wendy felt the tacky residue on her hands and excused herself to the back bathroom. She washed her hands then left the water running while she used the toilet. It wasn't till she rewashed her hands that the shouting in the store reached her ears.

"Chinky eyes, you let that nigger in here. Alls I want is fuck'n spray paint. You got it. Open the fuck'n cage."

Wendy had left her handbag and phone under the counter leaving her to dismiss any plans of dialing 911 and downing her emergency Xanax half. She stood at the sink afraid to turn off the tap. Jae spoke first, 'Get out! Get out now! No one's going to sell you paint." The teacher next heard Malik's "Come on, bro, there's three of you and three of us. It won't be pretty. Do like the man says. Get out."

"Nigger can't count. There two of you."

Bird and Fish

The voice was familiar to the trembling Wendy. 'I see a thousand kids a year. Who is that?"

The closed bathroom door prevented her from seeing Yujin come from the back wielding an aluminum bat. A cacophony of crashing, thumping and cursing ensued. After circling like modern dancers Jae Won and a bushy browed hulk threw wild punches at each other. The street boxing became wrestling when Jae's muscular arm came around the thug's throat. The boy contorted his massive frame till his offensive damp tee shirt rode up exposing his doughy A-cup breasts and a patch of brown hair that ran to his navel like train tracks. His free arm jabbed upper cuts to the storeowner's chin. Malik slipped and fell on his orange juice puddle as he tried to shield Yujin's back from a tall dirty-blond waving a box cutter. Luckily the metal sheath flew up and onto the floor revealing its true identity, a metallic comb case. Before Malik could rise, the third delinquent kicked his buttocks forcing him back to the tiles. Jae Won took an ear ringing blow to his temple but managed to subdue the mountainous hooligan soon after. Cans of paint thinner and wax remover fell to the tiled floor forcing all six males to hop-skip to dodge the rolling missiles.

The teacher in the bathroom was beginning her breathing exercises while she planned her escape through the parking lot and on to Broward's Deli for help when Malik's chilling, "Mr. Hyun, watch out!" crowded the little room. She opened the door and raced towards the melee. Jae Won looked up in disbelief.

"*Na ga, Na ga yo!*" He shouted 'get out' to her, jutting his chin towards the back door.

She scanned the flaying fists, swinging arms and air-born footwear to pick out Jay and the owner of the first shout.

"Ant'ny" the teacher called out while she reached for the counter mobile. In a voice she saved for assembly performances, Wendy spoke into the phone, "911, we've got a robbery in progress at Anycolor Paints II on Northern Boulevard."

Her words had the same effect as her signature three whistle blows at lunchtime. The store was immediately quieted except for the sounds of men and boys straightening their clothing and checking their wounds. Anthony Perez got to his feet with the grace of a tranquilizer darted elephant.

"No no, Ms. Dale please this ain't no robbery. I swear to God. We just wanted neon paint for tomorrow. These guys don't like white kids. They wouldn't sell us any."

"Officer," Ms. Dale spoke into the phone that had never been turned on, "never mind." Anthony and friends obviously were unaware that 911 calls are not dismissed with a 'never mind.'

"Whom do we have here, Ant'ny?" She didn't wait for his answer. "Oh, Greg from 9C2 and Luis. Luis, I never taught you. What class are you in?"

Luis Maldonado mumbled 9S.

"Ah. Well, the first thing and there are many things to deal with," The teacher reached for the Clorox wet towel container and handed it to Jay tilting it up for an instant to say pass this around.

"Mr. Hyun and Mr. Kim will say if they want to report your vandalism to the police. Mr. Thorne, do you wish to report their assault as a hate crime?

The cousins and Malik turned down her offer. Police presence would do the store no good and Malik would eventually have to take more time off from work if this grew bigger. Jae Won still seemed furious but Wendy hadn't the time to question his facial expressions.

"OK, then we'll go by Dale's law. You three, clean up those cans. Then empty your pockets on to the counter. Toss those chain wallets on there too"

Yujin went to wash his hands and face. Jae Won took the wet mop from the back room.

"Malik, take all the money that's on the counter and in those wallets and hand it to Mr. Hyun."

The teens groused but in low tones.

"You don't think this is fair? Should we call the cops?"

Their silence returned. Jae ran to the opening door and told the customer that there was a spillage and assured her he'd re-open in ten minutes.

"Tomorrow at lunchtime, you'll show me your apologies, three each. If you show them to anyone else at school, you'll make it a school matter. Then Mr. Rubinstein will call the police and your parents."

Yujin exited the bathroom wearing a crisp new white shirt. Jae brushed by him wishing they had installed a shower in the back.

"Mr. Kim, do you need these boys for chores? They'll come next week to pick up the trash from the parking lot if you want them."

Yujin Kim only wanted to see their heads smashed with the thicker end of his bat but he knew she was doing the right thing and agreed to a Monday, Wednesday and Friday after-school clean-up. As soon as Jay re-entered from the back room toilet, the teacher instructed the boys to get on their knees. The men looked on suppressing smirks as the teens apologized with their hands flat on their thighs, Korean style.

"Tell them you'll never do anything like this again, *Ah rhuh chee ?*"

"*Ah rhuh suh.*" they echoed as if seated in the cafeteria. Wendy handed each boy a dollar from her purse.

The men shook their heads at what they thought was a misjudgment.

"This is my money. Go buy a snack to remind you what you learned about mercy today. And for God's sake use shaving cream on the cheapskates' houses tomorrow. It washes off."

Yujin went back to his car while Jay helped the earlier customer return wallpaper samples. The store returned to its before business quiescence. Jay's eyes wouldn't meet Wendy's. Yujin returned with four green and gold bottles of Charm soju and a small bag of shrimp chips.

"First we fight, then we drink. Somebody get General *Lee Sung Gye* a chair."

Jae Won stood immoveable at the counter. His cousin placed a chair nearby for Wendy and went on to lock the front door.

"We'll toast to Wendy the general." Yujin placed four shot glasses on the counter. "I always thought American woman were scardy cats" he joked. In the movies, they're always screaming in the elevators.

"That's Hollywood. The rest of America's women are tough and Lunch Coordinators are the toughest."

Malik looked down at his hands as if they held a memory.

"Ms. Dale was always tough but she was nice too. My moms died the year Ms. Dale was my teacher. She drew me a portrait of my mom from an old pitcha I had before she got sick. Remember Ms. Dale, you told me to talk to the pitcha when I missed her. You said if I don't get an answer, I should call you. No teacher ever give me her phone number before or since."

Wendy couldn't remember the incident. Over her career, she taught five or six children whose parents died during the school year. Perhaps she drew pictures for all of them. Yujin tore open the bag of snacks and placed the bottles near the glasses.

"*Sun seng nim*, you draw?"

"I'm not an artist like Jay but I like to sketch." She looked over at Jay who busied himself by rubbing an emerging black and blue mark on his knuckles.

"Ooh, soju. Man, I had that once." Malik held out his glass unaware that tradition and his age required him to serve the others first.

"Wendy," Yujin asked while twisting off a cap, "you've had soju before, right?"

"No." She watched as Jay finally sat beside her.

"Not even in Korea?"

"I was with principals and educational supervisors not exactly the tent bar crowd."

Yujin mentally counted off ten seconds waiting for his cousin to offer Wendy a drink. When he realized Jae Won wouldn't, he poured and served a glass to each of them.

"I don't think I'm allowed to drink. The doctor told me I shouldn't have wine." She kept her voice so low the men thought she was mumbling to herself.

Her father taught her how to drink Glenlivet.

'Sip. Savor the moment, he'd say if he was here. But Daddy, a little while ago, the four of us had a pissing contest and I won. I'm not about to lose face now.'

The teacher downed the three-shot drink in one long gulp. After an audible breath she re-opened her mouth to let the heat escape. Soju is a master of disguise. It looked like tap water in the glass. Reminded her of sweet mountain springs on her tongue but once swallowed sent stinging lava down her gullet. In moments, she felt an invisible headband tightening around her skull.

Yujin and Malik pointed at her reddened cheeks and slapped their knees as if at a pagan loss of virginity rite. Wendy laughed along but worried over Jay's furrowed brow and her upcoming gynecologist's appointment. The teacher excused herself leaving the entrance door unlocked when she left. She heard Jay's footsteps come up behind her on Broward. He didn't stop her till they were well past the side widows of his store. His hand jerked her wrist from behind as he pulled her to face him.

"Why didn't you listen to me? *Wheh? Wheh?* Those thugs were dangerous. You could have been hurt. I told you to go out the back way. Why wouldn't you obey me?"

Since she began teaching at the mostly Korean-American M.S. 347, Wendy Dale had met countless parents and students who used pocket translators to better communicate with her. They were not always helpful. Type in *cha dahh* and 'niggardly' pops up. Not a word Americans would choose. She should have been sensitive to second language users who misspeak. Yet the hairs on the back of her neck stood at attention when Jay mistakenly selected obey to stand in for *duh-rhuh,* listen.

"Obey? Obey you like a dog?" Wendy shook her wrist free of his grasp. Jae Won angrily placed his hands on his hips, a traditional Korean male stance. Wendy saw an imitation of Superman who poked out his chin and snarled,

"Even a dog would understand if I tell him to get back."

"So now I'm stupider than a dog. This just gets better and better."

"Why do you have to have the last word? I'm supposed to protect you."

"From what, three middle schoolers with a pocket comb?"

Jae Won placed his hand on his belt buckle. "*Yah*, you want to be the man? Here, wear the pants."

"Keep your pants on Rambo. You were never getting into mine anyway."

She envisioned slapping and biting the powerful force that drove her to need him. He wanted to punch his uncontrollable ardor till it lay lifeless at his feet. Neither could beat down their ill-timed passion so they stood on a Queens street arguing over semantics and gender roles. They separated like *Kum Doh* opponents pledging never to stand in the other's shadow again.

⌘ ⌘ ⌘

"Remove all your clothing from the waist down. Put the gown on opening to the back and return to this room."

Wendy didn't bother looking at the face attached to the directions. Her palm drew circles into her side waiting for the aching to yield to her massage. As she lay on her back with her heels in metal stirrups, she realized all the body parts her mother gave cute little names and told her to hide, were lately shown only to strangers. 'This is a very bizarre sex life' she confided to no one. Just then Dr. Scheinfeld, whose head was under the paper blanket between her knees. Let out a joyful "Yes!"

"I told you that sonogram was bullshit. You don't have a thickening of the uterus. But you have a honking big polyp." Both he and his nameless colleague studied the computer screen displaying Wendy's reproductive organs.

"Get dressed and meet me in my office."

The oozing liquid used to expand her uterus was already running down her thighs by the time she reached the restroom. What she needed was a soapy hot towel. What she got was the opportunity to wet down her paper dress and clean up as best she could. Every time her argument with Jay prowled around her thoughts, she shook her head like a flea-tortured dog and returned to the moment.

"I already gave you the good news. It's just a polyp. The not so good news is it's not the source of your pain. I suggest you see a urologist."

"What about the polyp?"

"Oh, that has to come out."

Wendy wanted to howl like Fido on his way to the vet, 'Noooooo, noooooo.'

"Will you do that here?" Her voice lowered to just above a whisper. The physician assumed it was the usual patient fear of surgery

"Nah, we do those over at East End Hospital. Wendy, this is nothing, I swear. I'll remove it and be in the donut shop by the time you get home."

The teacher felt clamped to the chair. She couldn't remember the nice man's name. He had visited all her secret places yet he had no idea the tightness in her gut had just ventured to her chest and throat and shut down her brain.

"Doc," 'What else can I call him?' She finally looked up from the ski pictures of his wife and children to the crowded degrees and diplomas on his walls.

"Doctor Sheinfeld, I know you'll cut out my polyp with the grace and style of Zorro. And when I visit the urologist, he'll find another little something to slice out because after all I've already been diagnosed with cancer and we can't be too careful. Before long, I'll be in and out of Queens' Hebrew or East End three or four more times. I can only hope that my daughter who has Crohn's disease will have the good manners not to need hospitalizations at the same time because if Janie needs more surgery, you'll find me at Mt. Sinai keeping vigil over her. So my concern now is, if I scrub all the skin and viscera from my bones in the shower tonight will I get the stench of hospitals off me?"

Geoffrey Scheinfeld delivered babies for a living and while nine out of ten times the results were joyous, he still had occasions that were tragic. The few patients who were past child birthing years came because of his outrageous vocabulary and unwavering confidence. Wendy Dale was in another category. She was a stranger referred by Dr. Grafinetti. The gynecologist hadn't known the woman in his office had a child with Crohn's. He wouldn't be able to reach her with expletives and cockiness. He pretended to look through her expanding folder.

"Wendy, I see you've had a tough time. There's a drug called Effexor that really helps a lot of my patients. There're no contraindications with Tamoxifin. Let me see. What else are you taking?"

He scanned her list of medications.

"This will stop the pain?"

"Well, it works like Prozac. Just wait, I saw that look. Why do people think that..."

The teacher put up her hand.

"I'm sorry I vomited my concerns on you. I'll be fine, really. Can I have surgery while getting radiation? I've had a D and C before. I know I can still make my zapping appointment if I have an early procedure."

He scribbled a note to leave her depression discussion for another day.

"Ideally, you should stop for a day or two. The radiology will just end later than originally planned."

"No. My schedule is supposed to end right before the holiday. You don't know me but take my word that I'm a fabulous cook and for all cooks Thanksgiving is our Super Bowl. My insurance plan won't give me authorization for about two weeks anyway. Can't we make the surgery next month when my radiation is over, please?"

⌘ ⌘ ⌘

Just as Fido inhaled the last gasp of October air to detect the scent of marauders, Tim O'Hanlon went sniffing around the replaced paint cans trying to link his Irish sense of foreboding to a clear and present danger. 'What the Hell am I playing at?' The big man questioned himself as he copied the Anycolor II address and phone number off the lid sticker. He didn't bother with the web address. The house's computer had been taken over by Jane and her friends long ago. The Korean writing looked more like a scientific equation than words but that's what set him wondering. The circles, boxes and lines were familiar.

'These were definitely on the envelope stuffed with twenties and the manila envelope under that painting Jane showed me. She said Mommy's friend, Mr. Hyun the art teacher made it for her.' He wasn't much of a sleuth. Yoon Yoo Son had connected the dots of her husband's dalliances after his second night out. Had Yoon Yoo been Tim's P.I., she would have directed him to search through Wendy's school's yearbooks where Mr. Hyun's photo was prominently absent.

The teacher's steadfast Sentra turned into her driveway. 'Scheinfeld probably acquiesced because I was a pathetic neurotic but I don't care. My mind is set on when my radiation ends. It's the same day as the Greek girl's and I'm not going one day more.'

Fido raced to the fence yelping and woofing till he was content that Tim and everyone else in Floral Oaks knew the Alpha female had returned to the pack. Wendy faked three starts before she ran behind Fido to the yard. "You beat mommy! You're such a smart boy." She was kissing the downy black fur atop his head when Tim emerged from the garage with notepaper and pen in his hand.

"Taking inventory?" she asked as she massaged Fido's broad back. The big man quickly stuffed the paper into his chino's pocket and mumbled, "Yeah." Wendy moved one of the folding chairs off the patio and onto the driveway. He followed close behind in their secret ritual.

"What'd the doctor say?" He had no idea which physician she saw that day. There were too many to remember and besides she was much better at this kind of thing than he.

"The news isn't terrible but mostly I want to run something by you." He watched as she rubbed her side.

"I can't take off too many days, Red. There's gotta be doctors with evening hours."

"You're going to wish I just need a lift." While patting their dog, Wendy reiterated her hysteroscopy results and what she remembered of Dr. Scheinfeld's prognosis. She left out his urologist suggestion to avoid overburdening her husband. He seemed a bit scraggly lately; too weary-looking to learn he might become the sole breadwinner of their family. Just as she knew she'd never return to teaching after Christmas she also knew it would be too much for her Celtic Warrior to take in all at once. She cowardly renamed her permanent resignation.

"I'm taking an 'un-paid' leave in the spring. I really need some time off, Tim. I'm hoping you'll keep us afloat till I can earn…till I go back."

His head bobbed like a buoy on a ferocious sea but his icy blue eyes stared into a horizon he wouldn't share.

"You do the books, Red. Can we afford this?"

"It depends how much you like macaroni."

"I'm OK with macaroni as long as you're doing the cooking. Are you keeping your tutoring job?"

"Uh, no that's over. I'll try to get some of my essays published."

"So you're not tutoring anymore?'

"I don't think so."

"That's good. Forget the money. You don't need to be at some kid's beckon call." With that, he tore the palm sized paper into shreds and headed for the driveway trashcans.

"What are we going to tell Janie?"

"Change makes her nervous, we'll just say I'm on sabbatical." and the lie flew on eagle's wings straight towards Pluto.

Had Jae Won Hyun been there to paint the couple, he'd depict Wendy still seated, staring out towards the burnished western sky while her husband stood motionless in the driveway; she drawing warmth from the ardent sunset, he seeking solace from the burgeoning cool darkness in the east.

Janie's papa pursed his lips tightly and blew a trill that was soon answered by the robins overhead then the fisherman's daughter tilted her head and stretched her neck till she could also return their song. That morning she had called hundreds of birds with her just-learned sounds. At lunchtime, the father and daughter chatted in the voices of everyone in their village. The King's African dairy farmer and the Far-Eastern silk merchants were her favorites.

The teacher listened to her neck's creaks and clicks as she circled her head to keep awake. 'To hell with daylight savings, I need a thirty hour day just to keep up with all the crap in my life.' She replayed yesterday's events. 'I quit teaching. I e-mailed sixteen lessons and projects to everyone on staff to seal the deal. I'll have to explain to Libby tomorrow. I broke up a fight off school grounds. Somehow that cost me a friendship. 'Eeem' Wendy made the same tiny yelp her dog did when sleeping. She looked to see if she had awakened Jane. Her daughter's arm rested above her head on her pillow. Wendy could see her swimmer's muscle definition returning. The girl's body was healing. Maybe their family could exhale. A little.

At least the phone conversation after dinner with Laura from SHARE was helpful especially when she reminded Wendy that for the next ten years every test would lead to more tests. "It was why people got well from other diseases but *survived* cancer." The woman joked before their goodbyes.

Wendy rubbed her tired eyes.

'Tim is Tim.' She re-scripted their driveway talk. 'Everything's OK as long as his life stays the same.

'Dear Tim, I'm leaving my job.'

'OK.'

'We'll be living on pasta.'

'OK'

'There's a man I want to play 'Korean Drama' with.'

Adrienne Leslie

⌘ ⌘ ⌘

'O…'

Halloween even at 6:45 am is an educator's nightmare. The senior students had already hidden their raw eggs and squirt bottles of Nair in their classroom closets yesterday. The wilier ones figured out that if they stayed outside till after the late bell, they could enter the school via the late entrance without being searched. Leaving only the innocent students opening their schoolbags for the dean, guidance counselor and Ms. Dale as they pushed along to Exit A's stairway. The trio searched all 1188, leaving out the six who hid till the bell, the eleven who were home sick and the poor little sod in 6D1 whose hungover mother forgot to wake on time that morning.

Even the NYPD's rookie cops know to always directly ask suspects if there's anything in their pockets that can stick or jab the officers. Teachers aren't given gloves or any instructions on how best to run a search. Inevitably, one of the three rummaging through the gaping book bags will be gouged or scratched by a wayward compass or finely honed pencil. Ms. Dale hoped it wasn't her turn.

"Ms. Dale," Seromie's friend, Incha who had as much desire to smuggle Halloween contraband into the school as the principal, probably less, offered up her bag.

Bird and Fish

"Two things, can I be your monitor on open school night with Seromie and did you see them kissing on Pure 19?"

"Yes, you can be my monitor. Come see me at lunchtime for a pass and no I always close my eyes when the actors kiss." The teacher looked out to the nearly seven hundred children beyond the doorway unable to glimpse the three school aides who were given comp-time to bring up the rear.

"Ms. Dale, do you really?" Incha's ponytail hung from her glittering orange scrunchy like a perfect swath of wide black ribbon reminding the teacher she'd be going straight home after radiation that day without her Korean samurai elixer.

⌘ ⌘ ⌘

The light switch monitor chewing handfuls of candy corn turned out the lights. The two boys assigned to the window shades, pulled on the yellowed ropes till the drama classroom darkened. Holiday parties were forbidden at M.S.347. Directly following the nasally morning pledge, Principal Rubinstein got on to warn all revelers that if spotted, all candy would be thrown away and teachers would be disciplined. About a dozen of the children's' most beloved teachers mumbled 'Screw you' to themselves and handed out assortments of sugary delights.

Ms. Dale instructed her students to absolutely refute anyone who accused them of having a holiday party. The correct term was cultural symposium. This was their first of the year followed by symposiums for Thanksgiving, Chanukah/Christmas/Kwanzaa, and Easter/Passover. The last would be the new teacher's problem thought the teacher. Wendy's skull earring swayed from her lobes as she circled among the chip crunchers and lolly lickers. The teacher held a ghost-head flashlight under her chin while she spun the Irish folktale of the jack-o-lantern.

"Ach, dint cha know that Jack was a divilish lad."

The loud eaters were shushed by their neighbors as the lilted phrases of the teacher's dead in-laws circled each student table. By the end of the period, 6A1 learned about the hunger in Ireland, why pumpkins replaced turnip lanterns after the Irish Diaspora and a short botany lesson on Gregor Mendel to explain how Halloween pumpkins are different from pie pumpkins. In Ms. Dale's post 'slave incident' version Jack writes 'Truth' on the bark of the tree instead of making the sign of the cross. A small change so that the non-Christian children could enjoy the story without conflict.

The mayor, the chancellor and the principal; the tri-fecta of bad educational policies could forbid holiday parties. It didn't matter. Ms. Dale and her students were living their teachable moment.

⌘ ⌘ ⌘

Wendy returned from the driveway with Fido. A family's dog is their most cherished asset except on Halloween and any other celebrations that involve candles, stuffed toys or candy. After attempts at locking him in the bedroom to howl, keeping him in the driveway to bark incessantly at the costumed children along the street or simply putting all the treats in a big cauldron on the front steps, (the latter proving the most expensive since by early evening the candy and the cauldron were stolen) Wendy found that flat kid-approved Hershey bars could be handed through the storm door's mail slot safely providing that overzealous chocoholics kept their hands down till the bars dropped.

She left on her spider sweater and skull earrings but exchanged her black trousers for jeans. The teacher was about to fill an empty plastic jack-o-lantern with treats when the house phone rang. It was silly to hope it was Jay. He didn't have her home number. She let the answering machine discover the caller.

"This is Dr. Tapman calling."

Did her heart double up on its beats first or did she sprint for the phone creating its wayward thumpings?

"Yes, Dr. Tapman. What's wrong?"

"Well her numbers are lower but still above where we'd like them. Let's put her on half her dosage of Azasan. I'll send you a prescription for a liver scan, just as a precaution. I don't think it's anything. I think she probably has a fatty liver but let's make sure. I'll put Micheline on to get you an insurance authorization number."

He was gone, replaced by a pleasant voiced secretary who administered instructions the teacher couldn't decode.

Outside the sky blackened like a witch's heart. The stinging fall winds slapped the backs of toddler skeletons and teenaged zombies. Frankensteins and Freddy Krugers cackled and screeched to unsuspecting butterflies and princesses but nothing was scarier than the phone in Wendy Dale's hand.

⌘ ⌘ ⌘

Episode 9: Bird and Fish

The teacher wore black velvet. Battling the mid-November winds as she rushed across the street to enter her school, she held the A-line skirt down with her free hand. Her black winter jacket covered a velvet version of the turtleneck shells she now wore daily and a Calvin Klein wide sleeved cinched waist jacket accented with a wide leather belt. She could have passed for a mourner at the funeral parlor on Northern and indeed Wendy was marking her losses.

Her friend and colleague, Mrs. Spring waited in the cold, a transparent smile frozen on her face.

"Is that the Anne Klein T-neck you got last year? Lovely."

"Libby you don't have to check on me every day. I'm fine, really."

"You know, you always say 'really' when you mean the opposite. Am I the first one to tell you that. My mother would have taken one look at you and asked, 'What's with the black? It makes you look pale.'

"I'm just a little tired from the radiation. The funny thing is even though I'm tired, I still can't sleep at night."

"What's so funny about that? Since menopause, even though I'm losing the hair on my head I'm growing lots under my nose. Ah well, life's a bitch when you don't apologize to the one person who makes you happy."

"Hah ji mah."

They had reached the front door but stood outside in the chilly breezeway so not to be rumor fodder for the army of school gossipers.

"I'm not sure what that means, but I'm not finished."

"It means stop." Wendy opened her coat to release the Tamoxifin inspired hot flash.

"I'm exhausted and no one helps out at home. On Saturday, I was on my hands and knees cleaning the bathtub of everyone else's scummy remains when Tim walked by. I finally broke down and told him I might need him to help because my side hurt so much. Do you know what he said? 'Maybe we should look into cleaning services'."

Libby clucked and added, "What is he giving up to pay for them? Does he know they cost what we make a day?"
"I hope you answered him back."

"I tossed the bleached rag into the tub and asked, 'Is that Irish for fuck you?'"

The older woman burst into laughter.

"I love it. How's Janie? Is she finally eating right after the MRI scare?"

"I can't believe she fooled me. I watched her eat two bites of a roll each night for dinner never thinking she was downing fatty cheeseburgers at school. I thought the doctor was crazy when he said she had a fatty liver. My brilliant daughter thought she found the perfect diet, chronic diarrhea. Well, she's scared straight now, for the time being but with Crohn's, every test they give her takes ten years off my life.

Libby Spring inventoried her friend's waxened complexion,

"You look like Emily Dickenson. Why don't you call him?"

She re-buttoned Wendy's coat like a mother sending her child off to school.

"Dickenson wore white every day." Wendy corrected.

"I'm an English teacher remember, I wasn't referring to her wardrobe. The poet ended her days pining for a man."

Wendy looked back to the street. Two teachers and a carload of pre-teens were headed their way.

"What would I say, 'I regret you still live in the Koryo dynasty. I'm saddened I acted in a way no other man would have objected to?"

Libby opened the heavy tempered glass door to the lobby's outer room.

"How about I'm sorry you were upset. The last ten days have been Hell for me and if you miss me too, I'd like to be friends again."

"Nice stab at psychology, Lib." the teacher walked through the first door and held the next for Mrs. Spring. "Don't quit your day job."

It was Parent Conference Day. The school would host parent-teacher meetings till 9:30 pm. The friends wouldn't have time to speak again till tomorrow.

⌘ ⌘ ⌘

"We're going to take Ahromie with us to Parent Conferences. We'll leave right after dinner to bring Seromie to Ms. Dale's classroom. Do you want to come too?" Jae Won Hyun pretended he was too wrapped up in his Hallyu TV watercolors to hear Yujin's invitation. He was well aware that Seromie was Wendy's monitor since the eleven year old proclaimed it daily. Yujin returned to his wife waiting at the top of the stairway.

"I couldn't hear. Did he answer you?" Yoon Yoo whispered.

"No. It's the same as every day since the store fight. He works and paints."

"Why didn't you tell him she called you?"

"Because she called to talk about Malik. He told her I offered him a job. She made me promise not to hire him till he showed me a registrars' receipt from Queensborough College."

Yoon Yoo chortled. "One of the mothers at the Parent Association said the children would follow Ms. Dale through fire. I can see how she does it." Her smile stiffened. "*Yobo*, tonight, stay with me at school."

"Where would I go?"

"Let's just visit Seromie's teachers as a family, *Ah rhuh chee?*"

Yujin took a cigarette from the pack on the counter then used three or four seconds to pat his clothing for a nonexistent lighter. The cigarette was tossed back on the counter.

"Yeah. No problem." He left the kitchen. Years ago his father's philandering had finally cost his mother a stay in the hospital. One day the senior Mr. Kim pulled Yujin towards him and whispered, "Remember, nobody knows you like your wife." To free himself of that memory, Yoon Yoo's handsome husband grabbed a nine-iron and practiced his golf swing on the backyard deck till summoned for dinner.

⌘ ⌘ ⌘

Twice each school year Ms. Dale was grateful she taught a general subject and traded her English classes for lunch duty: Fall and Spring Conferences. When she was an academic teacher, the line of parents swelled at sixty-six grown-ups ready to do battle for their children. They'd come armed with sheaths of tests and projects summed and averaged to two or three points more than their child's report card grade. She'd have to humble them by pointing to lower grades that never reached home or roll book marks designating missing homework assignments. Then the teacher would point out the five extra points she gave to remind little Mindy or Min-Ki to do better next quarter.

Tonight, less than a dozen parents would 'show'. Instead of negotiating higher grades for their children, this group would beg for lead roles. Ms. Dale often wondered why the sports coaches weren't approached as often as she. The parents swallowed hard when their offspring failed the baseball cuts but fought like mountain cats for a half page of lines. So, on this night, Ms. Dale awarded more non-speaking parts to soften the blow of not being the stars. The sparse turnout allowed her monitors to giggle and gossip for service credit and Ms. Dale to ease her churning side with her 'usual' while grading papers.

"Ms. Dale." Seromie used her best grown-up voice to announce her parents. Yujin and Yoon Yoo raised with Asian inscrutability shook hands and smiled as if the drawn look on her pale cheeks wasn't there. Since her radiation therapy remained her secret the couple collectively thought she was languishing for their cousin.

"Ms. Dale," Yoon Yoo spoke first.

"Mr. Hyun would have come with us but he's so busy working with the television…" She asked her daughter how to say animators in English.

Wendy was overjoyed but kept her school pose.

"I'm glad that worked out." she answered as if she'd already known. Wendy lavishly praised Seromie's dance number then handed the girls tootsie pops.

"Ballerina, give one to 'Itchy' outside and one to your sister."

Ahromie tugged at the teacher's jacket hem.

"Teacher, Can I have a name like you gave my sister and Yu Incha."

Wendy leaned down to curl the cherub's pig tails with her fingers. "You, you are my 'Cutie-Patootie.'" She looked up at the girls' parents.

"Would you like them to stay with me? Ahromie can color or read in here. Then you two can split Seromie's subjects to insure you see all of her teachers tonight."

Yoon Yoo nearly jumped from her seat to answer.

"We're going to stay together for the whole conference time. We'll pick up Seromie at 9:30."

Incha, called Itchy, rapped on the front door three times signaling the five-minute conference time had ended. Ms. Dale and Jae Won's cousins exited with softened smiles and softer goodbyes. The teacher eyed the hallway. Mrs. Breslin's math room had over twenty parents pacing outside its front entryway. Last year two mothers had a shouting match over who was next. Wendy's doors stood quiet while her monitors slurped and chomped their way towards their pops' tootsie centers.

"Girls, hold the fort. I'm off to the ladies' room." Wendy checked her watch for the dozenth time that evening 'tsking' over its turtle's pace. Once in the stall, she pulled at her cotton sports bra hoping for a bit more comfort, refreshed her make-up and creamed the backs of her hands neck and ears with Insolence. She longed to go home and rest although even exhaustion couldn't vanquish her insomnia, which was now empowered by her Tamoxifin dosage.

The teacher stepped out of the lounge jostling a parent couple looking for the math room. *Shil sim nee dah.*" Wendy tilted her head down then up with her apology. The handsome couple charmed by her Korean began to speak in their first language. Ms. Dale's jaw swung open after a closer look at the woman in the exquisitely tailored ivory suit. It was that flirty slag who tickled Yujin Kim's hand at the festival. Wendy turned in her leather pumps to make her escape from the bewildered couple. The less than beautiful woman tugged at her arm.

"You are Mr. Hyun's friend?" The saccharine-like inquiry suggested a warning, 'You tell on me. I'll tell on you.'

Ms. Dale managed a warm countenance for the sake of the cuckold husband who stood beside them.

"I do translation work for Anycolor Paints and Yoon Yoo Son's daughter is my student. Perhaps that's why you thought we were friends."

'*Ahjummah*, don't even think of comparing me to you. Outside of my family and a busload of doctors, nurses and technicians, nobody else has seen me naked.

No wonder Yoon Yoo wouldn't give Yujin free rein. Oh my God, what if I teach this woman's child?'

She arrived back in time to find Patrick Flanagan's mom signing the monitor's guest log. 'Saint' as Wendy called him was a ninth grader now and no longer her student. Maybe he needed an after-school job recommendation. The teacher gushed over how tall he'd gotten since sixth grade while guiding the harried mother into B-4.

Claire Jackson entertained herself with daydreams as she kept guard at the lobby desk. She recalled laughing on a parent conference night the first time Wendy Dale clocked out and said, "I'm going home to The Big Irishman."

'That must have been seven-eight years ago. I tol' her I was going home to my Big Black Man to rest my head on his big black arm. They was the fun days before I caught that ham hock arm around the manicurist from Nubian Princess.'

From her post at the front entrance she could peruse the crowd of dads for potential husband number two candidates.

'Ooh ooh, who's that tall light and sweet walking towards exit B? Damn, that heifer behind him must be his wife. Who she think she impressing with that fur coat?'

"Yes sir, can I help you?"

The Asian man stood politely at her desk waiting for her woolgathering to end before speaking.

"I'm looking por Missus Dale."

'Mmmm, mmm. Whose daddy are you with them big sweet lips?'

"Take that stairway to the basement then make a right and a left. She's in room 4."

Claire gave him a ten for his tight rear end and narrow waist as he turned towards the Exit sign. He lost points for hairstyle. 'Somebody tell that fool, the hippie days are over. Why he wearing a pony tail?'

A wrong turn saved him from walking directly into his cousin's daughter. Instead Jae Won found himself entering through B-4's exit door. Hidden by the jutting coat closet wall, he silently bided for Wendy's parent to leave. The room was a trove of painted backdrops and cardboard scenery. A Roman column leaned next to a fisherman's cabin complete with Oriental paper fish kites hung from its corrugated eaves. Above the pretend doorway was a hand painted Korean sign. The word made no sense till he realized it spelled out the English word HERMIT in Korean.

The woman sitting at a table with Wendy cried into a shredded tissue. Her dull gray hair needed a wash and cut. Her tatty mom-jeans were more appropriate for a stable clean out than a school visit while the tee shirt under her stained jacket advertised a bar the teacher would never frequent. Yet Wendy patted the woman's arm and handed her a clean tissue as if she were an honored guest.

"You can't keep waiting for him to make the first move. You're the grown-up." The teacher's voice was strong but Jay was alarmed by her noticeable weight loss.

"I'm going to tell you a story. It might be from the bible so don't quote me to the principal. At the Department of

Education, quoting the bible has the same punishment as smacking a student."

The parent chuckled and dabbed her eyes with the new Kleenex.

"A rabbi and his son never saw eye to eye and one day after a terrible blow-up the son left home. The rabbi waited till the days turned to weeks and months but his son did not return. One day the rabbi learned where his son had gone. It was very far away so the rabbi travelled for days and sent word for his son to meet him halfway. The son did not meet him. Then the rabbi traveled closer to his son's hiding place and asked a messenger to tell the boy he'd need only come a quarter of the distance. His son didn't come. Finally the rabbi traveled the rest of the way. When the son saw his father, he turned his back on him. The rabbi placed his hand on his son's shoulder and said I've come all this way so you need only turn around." The teacher stopped there. Jae Won lurking near the doorway had the same question as Mrs. Flanagan.

"Did the boy turn around?" the woman asked.

"Why don't you talk to Patrick tonight and find out."

The second set of three door raps sent Wendy and 'Saint's' mother to the classroom's front door where they hugged goodbye.

"Call me tomorrow." The teacher instructed. "I'll track him down at lunchtime and have a little talk."

Five days after her father's funeral, Wendy Barrie Dale sat alone in her parents' kitchen crying. She couldn't remember her parents' house that silent or gloomy before. Upstairs, her aunt placed cool compresses on her mother's pasty forehead while at her feet sickly Fido II lay sleeping. At first her father's voice hovered like a hummingbird near her temple. She lifted her head from the table hoping to learn she had just awakened from a horrible dream. She heard it again, clearer this time, "Don't cry." She never heard his voice or any of its fantastic variations again. The teacher wondered why she conjured up that memory now.

Behind her Jae Won cleared his throat.

"Are you sure it wasn't a Buddhist monk who said I've come all this way so you need only turn around?"

She twirled with the grace of a Dervish till she faced him then stiffly repeated Libby's script.

"I'm sorry you were upset. The last ten days have been Hell for me and if you miss me too, I'd like to be friends again."

"Did you practice that?"

"Just two times. It needs work."

"*Jhal hess suh*. It's fine."

Upstairs Claire Jackson straightened her back to prevent her numbing bottom from cramping. She had been stuck in the lobby chair for over two hours. The only parts of her to stretch during that time were her lips delivering the greeting her principal insisted upon, "Yes sir/ma'am, can I help you?" She was bored and tired. A quick Hershey bar would brighten her till she said goodnight to the nearly thousand visitors. 'None of these bitches on the first floor would share any of their classroom candy with me. Mrs. Spring would have expensive chocolates in her room but she's up on the third floor.'

The security agent would have to settle on the bagged candy offered by Ms. Dale. Claire took a tentative peek into Mr. Rubinstein's office catching him nodding affirmatives to the PTA's co-presidents. She knew he'd be placating them till well after the conference. She opted for the back stairway that led from the auditorium to the drama room's back door.

The Korean girls who moved from their make-shift sign-in desk to the tiled floor in front of the exit door let go of their *kongki* cubes (Korean jacks) and snapped to attention. They stood shoulder to shoulder and bowed their heads at the formidable Ms. Jackson in front of them.

"Ms. Dale got a parent in there?"

"We're not sure." Seromie offered hoping the scolding would be short.

"You not sure? What you keep them log papers for? Is somebody still in there or not?"

"Well," Seromie pointed to Mrs. Flanagan's sign out initials. "The lady who signed in left, but then I went to the bathroom and Itchy said she heard Ms. Dale talking to another parent."

"Sit back down over there and pay attention before I tell Ms. Dale not to let you do service anymore."

Claire quietly opened the back door to avoid disturbing a possible conference. Wendy Dale and the Korean man with the inviting lips were looking into each other's eyes. The agent's mocha hand slapped over her mouth when the man took Wendy's hand in his. She backed out in two long steps.

"Don't let anybody bother them." She growled to the innocents before her. "That's a parent with a whole lotta important business. You hear me?"

Claire charged up the back steps and ran to her desk phone. It took four rings before her party answered.

"Ms. Dale, It's getting late but all these people are still walking the halls so I just thought that maybe that parent you with would want to leave about now."

⌘ ⌘ ⌘

The King and Princess Jenny-Purr giggled and shouted the names of hundreds of the kingdom's voices. "How did the fisherman copy the Hindu Alchemists lilting sounds?" wondered His Royal Majesty. "Isn't he amazing?" echoed his daughter. Even the Queen who had been in a terrible funk lately gleefully called out, 'It's the cooper's wife!' when she recognized the nagging spouse of the town's barrel maker. When the laughter and guessing quieted down, the fisherman had duplicated the voices of five hundred and two of the kingdom's five hundred and five royals and subjects. He wisely omitted the royal family since he liked his head where it had been since he was born.

Tim O'Hanlon's snoring grunted into a snorting gasp that awakened him. He was prepared to hear the tapping on the computer's keyboard but the additional sound of his wife's singing prevented him from easing back to his slumber. This was no Ethel Merman recreation. Wendy Dale sang as the rest of us do in elevators or long waits on train platforms, in a voice barely above a murmur but the melodies were new to their recent silent nights.

'I forgot Red used to sing to herself all the time, in the kitchen, in the shower. She even sang to the dog. I guess she stopped around the time Jane got sick. She didn't even practice at home for that Korean thing.' Fido lifted his head from the nest-like blanket folds he created earlier. Tim and his dog traded glances. "Sorry to disturb you Fi, I gotta take a leak."

In deference to his step-daughter, the local and national laws as well as common sense, the big man slept in gym shorts since he and Wendy married. He yawned and scratched his arms and rear end till he reached the bathroom. Fido returned to his favorite squirrel catching dream that made his eyelids twitch and his paws jiggle. After a shake and a flush, Tim stood in his sleeping stepdaughter's doorway unheard and unnoticed by his wife. She sang as if an invisible Ipod gave her the tune.

"Red, Red." He took a step into the room.

She turned towards her name and whispered back.

"Sorry, did I wake you?"

The salt lamp bathed the room in an early sunrise radiance. But the fist in his chest told him she glowed from the inside as well.

"How'd it go tonight?"

"The usual. God, I wish my region would have conferences from four thirty to seven like yours. I'm wired from talking so much. Did you eat the lasagna? Was it dry? I put it in before conferences when I came home to feed Fido."

"It was good. I heard you singing."

Wendy wouldn't change subjects or let go of her obvious contentment.

"What time did Janie get home from practice?"

"Eight. We came home the same time. What song was that?"

"Oh, that was the one I sang at the festival."

Her light auburn hair nuzzled her shoulders as she pulled off the rubber band that held back the claret waves.

"I'll have to do something to keep busy while on leave." She offered while shaking her hair free. "I'll probably tutor again."

Tim wasn't sure if what he felt was raging anger or loathing self pity but he knew coupled with each of them was the shame of hating his wife for the one moment she stole from the last three years to be happy.

⌘ ⌘ ⌘

Everyone cries in middle school. Teachers and other staff members cry in lounges or toilet cubicles alone or among friends. Their tears are usually shed for grown-up problems; a death of a parent sometimes a spouse, a recent divorce or a pending one, a cheating lover or the stress of being a cheat. Preteens have lower standards. They'll cry over a low test grade as easily as their parents' broken marriage. Getting stared at or being snubbed causes the same volume of waterworks. This morning shed its tears early.

Ms. Dale had just herded 1191 students into the building when she turned to the wails and sobs of Chanel Isadore.

The tall slender eighth grader was on her way to her former teacher's room and took the opportunity to fall into her nurturing arms.

"Oh, Izzy, what's the matter? Who hurt you? I'll kill them!"

"The girl looked two inches down to meet Ms. Dale's eyes.

"My brother beat up Eric." She managed through her gasps and gulps.

"Because he's your boyfriend?" Wendy easily put together the puzzle. While there were representatives of hundreds of ethnic and racial groups, M.S. 347 population was a pie chart of Asians, Whites and Blacks. They got along New York style, which meant in lieu of crosses burning on lawns, slurring each other mercilessly appeased them. Occasionally a member of one group would beat up a member of another who dared to cross over. In middle school where hormone levels reign supreme desiring a mate in chocolate, vanilla or butter pecan was common but consequential.

"Where's Eric now? Where's your brother?" The teacher only had fifteen minutes till period one to resolve this.

"Eric's waiting in your room. Mrs. Jackson let him in with her key." Wendy pictured Claire slamming the black-eyed Eric Park into a chair while sprinkling her reprimand with 'boy' and 'fool'.

"My brother's probably showing off to his friends in the sub-basement."

Wendy didn't acknowledge Eric till she called Claire at her lobby post demanding 'Joel and his hoodlum friends immediately.' She held Eric's chin in her hand.

"Let me see that face. You've got a shiner all right. I don't know if I can make this go away."

Claire led in Joel Isadore with two black boys Wendy knew only from ninth grade lunch duty.

"White boy!" Ms. Dale shocked the group to silence. "You hang'n with your homies now? What are you going to do when this one wants to be your sister's next boyfriend?" She pointed to the black teen whose dew rag stems hung from his neck. Are you going to call Eric to help you beat him up? Let me get this straight. You don't want this Asian to be with Chanel because he's not American?" Her voice was more strident than the toughest female basketball coach at halftime. Claire stood silent at the door hoping no paper work would ensue. She had heard Ms. Dale's 'Ute' speech before.

"I din't say that, Ms. Dale." The boy whined

"Your fist said that for you Mr. Isadore. Close that pie-hole. Which one of you is a Ute?"

She mockingly walked among them as if looking for a raised hand.

Bird and Fish

"Who's Cherokee? Anyone a Navaho? No? Everyone one of us comes from someplace else. Isn't that right Ms. Jackson?"

"Yes Ma'am." Claire looked forward to the next part.

"So since we're not Native Americans, none of us belong here. You want to chase Mr. Park back to Korea? Then you better book your flight to wherever the Hell you belong too. The teacher quieted her voice. Claire hoped it signaled an in-house solution.

"You can all go to the dean right now or" Wendy stopped to heighten the tension, "or you can each get a copy of Romeo and Juliet from Mrs. Spring in 301. Meet me with your books Monday 7:00 in the play yard. Together we will discover what happens when prejudiced people tell others whom to love. Is that OK with you Mr. Park?"

The boy nodded his affirmation.

The teacher patted her palm on her side in anticipation of the familiar pain but the pain must have been sleeping in that morning and Wendy lowered her hand.

"As for you Mr. Isadore, you and your friends will allow Eric and Chanel their friendship. I'm sure it's just friendship since everyone here is much too young to date. *Ah rhuh chee?*"

"*Ah rhuh suh*" came the group reply.

The children exited with three minutes to spare. Claire turned to Wendy.

"Jeeze, I hope none of them goes home to tell their mama's."

"Then we're screwed. They're only acting out what the world still believes. Separate is better. Keep your people away from my people. Let's face it even in Queens if you walk down the street holding hands with a racially different man, you turn heads."

"Something to think about, huh, Ms. Dale." Claire closed the door quietly leaving Wendy to recall her own words and wait for the end of Friday.

⌘ ⌘ ⌘

Yujin took the call in the store's back room. Even with two customers in the store it was quiet enough for Jae Won to hear his cousin's apologies.

"Mi ahn ah dah, egg-ee."

Jay knew it was unlikely his cousin was calling Yoon Yoo 'baby'. The older cousin guessed this latest affair started a week or two before Choesuk which meant, if Yujin's pattern remained, it was halfway to its demise.

"Tsee." He let the air in his mouth escape through his slightly parted lips in disdain for Yujin's capriciousness. There might have been a bit of jealousy in that Korean hiss as well. Jae Won wished to have a bit more of Yujin's charm, just enough to convince his cousin to leave that afternoon allowing him a private moment with Wendy. As if rehearsed, Yujin snapped his phone shut just as the entrance door opened for his wife.

Yoon Yoo Kim was visibly frazzled. Both her husband and cousin held their collective breath anticipating an accusation.

"Misses Ha could only remember my phone number." She panted as if returning from a run.

"*Moi yah*? What are you talking about?"

Our realtor was mugged on Bayside Avenue in Flushing. The *gom pei* took her attaché and laptop as well as her phone and Blackberry. She was going to drop off the papers for the new store but now she's resting at home. She asked me to pick them up."

Yujin didn't bother hiding his annoyance. "Why didn't you?"

His wife stood in front of him. Without glaring or rolling her eyes she managed to convey the folly of acting on her own. Aside from his constant philandering, he was a wonderful provider and a patient father best of all he made love to her as if they remained moonstruck college students but he was still a man. Had she gone to fetch the papers on her own and the slightest detail in the contract was amiss, she'd never hear the end of it.

"*Kunapogee* is here. We can go together now."

Jae Won was elated.

Yujin was not. In the last few minutes both his mistress and wife needed his attention in distinctly non-lusty ways. Still, he knew how to get his wife in the mood.

"Yobo, stay here with me" he enticed. "*Kunapogee* knows what to do."

Jae didn't know how his afternoon had changed so quickly. "I'm meeting *Sun seng nim* here in a little while.

"Even better." assured Yujin. When you get back, Misses Dale and you can mind the store and *Seromie umah* and I can go home for lunch.

Jae Won took the address from his cousin-in-law and headed for the parking lot. He placated his ill feelings by assuring himself the faster he went on the errand the faster he could return to a waiting Wendy.

Wendy Dale had expected a medical mugging. After her radiation therapy, she dressed, hugged the head-scarved woman she now knew as Eleni in the waiting room and rushed off to her urologist's appointment. Dr. Goodman's secretary requested she bring copies of her x rays taken three years ago. In a time of super-fast computers, Wendy had to drive low tech style to her former radiologists' office, pay seventy five uninsured dollars for pictures she thought were rightfully hers and hand deliver them to her urologist.

The waiting room was crowded with graying, balding or silver-haired men. None of them looked younger than sixty. All were grateful for the red headed diversion whose teal and gray tweed skirt rose as she crossed her legs.

"If nothing else I'm pretty sure I don't have prostate problems like this crew."

Throughout the day she warned herself that the doctor would call for more tests, scare her with words like renal adenocarcinoma, and threaten more surgery. By the time Sean Goodman put her scans on his lightbox, Wendy's knotted intestines had her bent like an old crone in his patient chair.

"Looks good. This is the same nodule you had three years ago. See, here it is same size as then."

He didn't use the C word. During a desultory exam he asked where she taught and offered tales of his eleven-year-old son.

"You can check this again next year" he offered as he helped her to a sitting position.

Wendy wanted to kick up her heels and kiss him on his mouth. When she wrote out her check, the jeri-curled secretary asked if she needed to make another appointment.

"No. No no no, pretty lady but thanks for asking."

"Glad to hear it." the jovial woman shot back.

Ms. Dale stopped at the restroom with her Nordstrom's shopping bag. She unpacked a dampened and soaped washcloth, the most form fitting sports bra she owned, a sheer black thong and a fresh pair of pantyhose. She undressed and scoured herself as best as she could in a doctor's office toilet stall, rubbed her arms with Insolence Shimmering Body Milk and spritzed a shot of the same fragrance behind each ear. Who'd ever think her next stop was a paint store?

The front entrance door of Anycolor Paints II was held open by a large plastic spackle jug. Two local house painters and Yujin Kim took turns loading the Devine Décor panel truck with assorted wares from his store. Wendy waited for the men to finish and entered as Yujin shared his cigarettes with the blue-collar entrepreneurs outside. She hid her surprise and forced her delight to see Yoon Yoo counting the money in the register.

"Oh, *Sun seng nim*, Jae Won will be right back. Are you here to talk about his Hallyu work?"

"*Yeh.*" Wendy answered in Korean hoping to seem more believable. She looked closer at the young woman's face; pretty enough to demand fidelity. It's strange that Yujin strays and stays but it's stranger still that his elegant wife lets him. The wayward husband returned smelling of Marlboro and as always dripping with charm.

Meeting with this pair last night gave her a new idea. Seeing them together this afternoon was a sign her plan would work. She spoke before Yujin had the opportunity to remark on his good fortune to be surrounded by such lovely ladies.

"Actually, I'm glad you're both here without Jay. There's something I want to ask you."

The teacher retold her story of her friend, Kim Dong Kook. She had sent copies of Jay's work to the art impresario who called her days later to ask for actual pieces to be sent ASAP. Since Jay seemed reticent, would they have a few good pieces like the birds in Seromie's room she could dispatch to Seoul.

"We only have Seromie's Sparrows in Spring." Yujin hastily offered.

"He did bring his paintings and other things like sketches and some enamels to the U.S. but I don't know where they are." Yoon Yoo began, "Maybe they're in our house. *Yobo*, we could look in the attic and garage." The dark-haired woman was overjoyed to have a secret project she could share with her husband.

Wendy's green eyes traveled from Yujin to Yoon Yoo and back again foreseeing the venture's doom.

Their conversation ended abruptly when Jay and a weather-beaten faced contractor walked in together. The Anycolor co-owner attempted a cough to cover his elation after seeing Wendy with his family. His cousins could go or stay. The customers could fill the store. Like the wedding band on her finger, none of those things mattered. She was back. Yujin rushed his wife out the back door to the parking lot promising her sweet *duk* from Korydong's bakery on the way home. He wanted to get laid before the girls were due home which meant not decreeing *Kunapogee's* paintings off-limits till later.

"You seem brighter today." Jae Won walked back to the counter after guiding the contractor and his packages through the front door.

"Smarter or shinier?" she pushed the hair behind her neck up with her hands and let it fall red ribbon after red ribbon back to her shoulders.

"Wendy, Malik said you did a portrait of his mother. Did you also paint all the artwork in your classroom?"

"I wouldn't be much of an educator if I did all the artwork. Some of the scenery I have to sketch out for my students some they do on their own. Did you see the hermit's cabin? That's for The Tiger's Whisker. I rewrote the Korean folktale. Do you know it?"

Jae Won worried his inexperience prevented him from reading her signals. 'She's a nine-tailed fox changing from seductress to teacher all in a minute.'

"*Ah nee. Mal sum hah seh yo.*"

"It's too long to tell but I'll share the moral with you." Through kindness and patience you can tame the tiger."

Her gaze met his. 'His eyes are like a tiger's, coppery brown with provocative lids that shear off the tops of his irises.'

Jae Won brazenly stared back.

"Then I guess I can't tame the tiger. I may be very patient but I'm not always kind."

Wendy let out a 'hmm' sound and added "I think I'm kind but I know I'm not patient. I guess that means I can't tame the tiger either."

"*Ah nee* it means we'd have to tame it together."

"Fishman, are you really patient?"

"*Krum yo.* I would wait till death for something I… wanted. *Ah nee* I'd wait in my next life as well." He felt a blush heat his cheeks.

"I have something for you. I thought I'd give it to you at Christmas but I'd like you to have it now."

Sadly, Wendy's panicked thoughts were only concerned with where she'd hide the present, whatever it was. Jae Won took a manilla envelope from the counter drawer and handed it to her. Inside was a postcard sized watercolor portrait of her. Wendy outlined the delicate mirror image with her fingers.

"She's beautiful"

"She's you."

"Her eyes are closed. Is she sleeping?"

"She was dreaming."

"*Co mah woi oh*, Fishman. Do you know what I wish?"

"*Moi yah?*"

"That she learns to live her dream."

⌘ ⌘ ⌘

Wendy Dale couldn't believe the sound of her high heels tapping on the concrete sidewalk since as far as she could tell she was floating back to her car.

'Finally, a good day. First, dispensation from a doctor. That hasn't happened in awhile. Then, hopefully, I've secured a team to spirit those Minhwah pieces to Seoul. I

Bird and Fish

think that will be good for Jay. It's an appropriate thanks for my beautiful painting.'

As valid as those reasons were, Wendy knew her soul felt airborne from something far more uplifting.

The teacher got out of her car and waved to Fido. The hound's claws clicked on the cement driveway as he pranced in place yowling to her.

"Did they forget to let you back in? You have a bad sister and a bad daddy. Come, mommy will bring you in." She swung open the side door making the pilgrim and turkey wreath flap against the glass. Dog and mistress were greeted with empty cereal bowls, smudged, stained glasses and spoons in the sink, a half filled container of Silk left out on the counter and the wrappers and wax-covers from Baby Bell mini cheese wheels forgotten on the breakfast room table. The sticky kitchen floor gripped the soles of her shoes as she began her kitchen clean-up by putting down her purse and picking up the Swiffer. Her daughter remained on line with friends never to observe her radiated mother loading the dishwasher while still in her coat. Her husband stayed in the basement backroom while the now familiar odor of tool cleaner emanated from his space. Like the wedding band on her finger, none of those things mattered. The former Wendy, the one before Crohn's and cancer surgeries, medications and terrifying phone calls was back and in gratitude for resurrecting her soul she'd return her savior to his calling.

Lately, Tim had begun showering before dinner. He approached the kitchen smelling of Irish Spring and Scope walking in time to his wife's tune.

'She's singing again.'

The song stopped. Wendy poured a full bowl of Life and doused it with soy milk. She ate like it was Mardi Gras, even humming between spoonfuls. Tim forced a smile.

"If I knew there'd be singing in the kitchen, I would have come upstairs earlier. After all, I'm the one family member who hails from the land of sad songs and happy wars. What's the name of it?"

Wendy put her bowl in the sink and held the spoon as she did Jay's wooden paint stirrer. "No no they can't take that away from me" she sang. Then she lifted Fido's front paws till he stood almost as tall as she and began a waltz.

"The way you sip your tea hmm hmm. The way you haunt my dreams."

"I guess you had a good day." Tim O'Hanlon ached for the happy wife, who danced just steps away, to assure him she was still his Red.

Bird and Fish

"When are we eating?" Jane walked in on her mother's dancing dog show and reached into the cereal box. "Why is mom dancing?"

"I was just asking her that. Why so happy?"

"Because the urologist told me I'm fine and never to darken his door again." Wendy let Fido go.

Jane's voice wavered spotlighting her alarm. "Why wouldn't you be fine? Why did you go to a urologist?"

Tim and Wendy avoided eye contact.

"Both of us go once a year." he said.

"It's because we're past forty." she said.

Right to Pluto.

After singing, chirping and warbling like all the birds in the kingdom, the fisherman reproduced the howls, barks and growls of every pedigree, mixed-breed and lonely cur. He meowed like the cats and even croaked like the frogs in the king's pond. When he was done he had given the princess one thousand and eleven voices. He and his daughter bowed to the royal family who applauded till their hands were red. Princess Jenny-purr even put her two blue-blood fingers in her mouth and blew the fisherman a whistle of approval.

Wendy hit the save icon before rising and going to bed. 'I feel so happy, if I knew how, I'd whistle just like Jenny-purr.'

⌘ ⌘ ⌘

It was a dryer than usual New York November. The leaves crunched and crackled under the heels of the teacher's burnished leather boots like twigs popping in a cozy fireplace. Wendy waved to Libby already at the breezeway. Her friend was draped in glossy black fur right down to her ankles.

"The science teachers will throw things at you if they see that coat." Wendy warned.

"I've already presented their lesson on my wardrobe. This is a dyed French rabbit garment. In France, they eat bunnies. *Mange les lapin.* Hence no rabbits were killed specifically for my pleasure. If any of those PC phonies continue, I'll point out that their shoes are their luncheon cheeseburger's relatives."

The women linked arms and headed for the glass door. Libby stopped mid-way.

"Are you all right?" Wendy asked.

"In my tax bracket, if I'm not all right, I call my lawyer not my doctor. Just let me look at you. Hmm, one and half days with your Mr. Sweet Lips and you look better already."

Bird and Fish

The teacher blushed. "Sweet Lips, that's something Claire would say. Do you really think he has nice lips?"

"Eh, sure. Didn't I tell you before?" The older woman blew a puff of lung air from her mouth.

"I hate this walkway in cold weather. It takes the breath from me."

"Lib, You never let me thank you for…."

Libby put her hand up. She wouldn't tolerate gushy emoting.

"You have a short memory, Ms. Dale. Whenever I'm absent, you check on the sub and my kids so I don't come back to ripped notebooks and missing crayons. When I had oral surgery, you made me two kinds of chicken soup packed in little microwaveable bowls. But most of all when my youngest discovered the wonderful world of marijuana and Adam and I threw up our hands in defeat, you went after him like a she-lion till he walked the straight and narrow. Even now when a senior partner compliments him at the firm, he tells me to tell you. I'm no do-gooder. I just believe in pay back."

The friends lingered at the glass doors. Wendy studied her friend's face. She hadn't noticed the loose skin under Libby's jaw before or the marionette lines from her mouth corners to the sides of her chin. She only now observed the feathery lines above Libby's mulberry lined and glossed lips. Wendy had nearly forgotten Libby was approaching sixty. There was an aura of fatigue about her that filled the younger teacher with guilt.

"Stop meeting me out here at dawn every morning. I'm all right, really."

Libby began to smirk.

"I mean really, *really*." Wendy insisted. "I'm on the other side of this."

⌘ ⌘ ⌘

The teacher used the late afternoon lull to display her storybook sketches for Jay to critique.

"Bring the castle portico in closer like this." Her personal artist took a pencil from the counter to recreate a more child friendly entryway.

"And if you use more cross-hatching over here," Jay began.

"I see it." She gently took Jay's pencil and followed his instructions. "This is much better. Now it pops."

"Wendy, I finished the Hallyu TV work last night. I have the time. Do you need me to illustrate the book?"

"I have to make this my project. I've never done anything just to please me. I've only told a few people that I'm resigning from work. Except for two, everyone's reaction was the same, 'At last you're going to write the great American novel.' But that's the kind of empty platitude bestowed on a little girl who say's I'm going to be president some day. Not you. You asked to go over the illustrations as if I was an author all this time but just changed venues. *Co mah woi oh.*"

The couple appraised the sketch as if neither one was speaking. "The only other person to encourage my choice…"

Jae Won didn't want to hear the big blonde haired man's name. "You don't have to tell me." He immersed himself in her depiction of the royal counting room to avoid her words.

"was the oncologist."

He looked up into her heather green eyes. In their ten-day hiatus, he had tried to paint them from memory but the shape was never right and the color seemed off. He imagined pulling her face towards him till he had time to study everything about them. They were double lidded. The eyelids across the top of her pupils rolled back to hidden creases that led to the bisque skin under her brows. Two little snips of her green irises were hidden between her top and bottom lashes. There were starbursts of teal hugging her lenses that he hadn't noticed till then. Perhaps it was just the reflection of her blue-green turtleneck that she covered with a maple cream jacket. He covered his smile with his palm. 'Her eyes match her sweater and lapel pin. How long does it take her to dress in the morning?'

"What did the oncologist say?"

"He's usually standoffish but he told me to go for it. He said lots of his patients change careers after cancer. The saddest times are when they regret what they haven't done. When I left that day he kissed me after shaking my hand."

"He kissed you?"

"Not a creepy kiss. A wish-you-well kiss. Maybe he lost a patient that day." She post-scripted her words with a sigh.

Jae Won Hyun didn't know any American jokes so he offered to be her illustrator again.

"Would I have to pay you?" she asked playfully.

"*Krum yo!* I'm a big shot now. I work for HTV.

"You could be a bigger shot, Fishman if you'd let me show your work to Kim Dong Kook."

"Ahh, Wendy, you burdened Yujin with your request."

"Yujin told you? Of course he did. I doubt Yoon Yoo would. I can't believe he told you. Does he know where your paintings are?"

'Bingo, you flinched, Mr. Hyun. Maybe his wife can find out.'

"*Ah nee.* They're not here. Anyway men don't get involved like that. Don't ask him again, please. *Ah rhah chee?*"

Wendy bristled at being ordered. Her first husband delivered edicts. It was why she traded up for solitude after five miserable years.

"*Ah rhah suh.* What bothers me, Jay, is that your cousin has a plethora, you can look that up later, of secrets to keep but I asked him for one *bi mil* and he rats me out. Ugh."

The music on the Bose changed and with it Wendy's mood.

"Oh could we make this louder, just till a customer comes in? This song sweeps me up. It's probably from a drama that hasn't been shown in the US yet. I've only translated the first lines, What should I do? What can I do?" She tilted her head and hummed along with the gravelly voiced Im Jae Bum.

"Mmmm. Jay, tell me what he's singing."

Jae Won reached over the counter to raise the volume.

"He's saying, 'What happens now? Even I don't know'."

He looked over the counter between them. Wendy had taken her pretend microphone paint stirrer and held it to her chin. She closed her eyes while she swayed and sang. Jay's strong arms lifted his torso up and across the space in one swift move. The subtle touch of his lips felt like draped silk as they brushed over then held her bottom lip. It seemed that she would return his caress as he secretly counted, '*hannal... dul*'. But the teacher jumped back as if she hadn't joined him for two seconds.

"Are you crazy?"

"*Ah nee.*"

"Too much soju?"

"Did you taste any?"

"Ahhh!" She whined. "Don't you get it? I have nothing to give you. There's nothing left of me to take."

Jae Won lowered his voice. "I didn't think I was taking from you. I wanted to give you something."

Wendy began speaking as if correcting an ill behaved child.

"That's the kind of thing you give when you're free to love someone."

He refused to quit his confrontation.

Bird and Fish

"I'm free to love you. Is it so crazy? What would you say if I told you I loved you?"

The teacher put down the paint stirrer realizing she was using it like a chalkboard pointer.

"I'd say, a bird and a fish can fall in love but where would they live?"

She was not to know his answer since the front door opened loudly with a harried mom, hushing her infant in its stroller while her twin boys took punches at each other in her wake. Wendy scooped up her sketches and looped her arm through her handbag exiting the store as if escaping licks of flames in a burning building. Behind her Jay called, "Our schedules changed. I'm off tomorrow. Come to the house. I'll teach you how to add color to the sketches." To which she answered, "I can't come. It's Saturday, Janie has swim practice."

One of the twins pushed his brother hard enough to jostle the new Benjamin Moore Aura display which diverted Jae Won's attention long enough to let Wendy sidestep further conversation.

⌘ ⌘ ⌘

Wendy Dale finally had a reason to appreciate weekends; no radiation therapy. Although the two days off were filled with constant reminders; the unfragrant soap, the contortions in her shower, the new circles drawn by technicians and the radiologist, which turned wavy under the congealed Aquaphor she daubed on twice a day to ease the stinging radiation burn that began two weeks ago. They all joined forces with the inconvenient onset of exhaustion while in the midst of her Saturday chores.

Her husband poured a third cup of coffee into his 'Turkey Day' mug. The googly-eyed orbs on the ceramic turkey handle were more sinister than cute. Soon they'd be replaced with the Christmas snowmen cups more to his liking. While luxuriating in the mellow warmth of his last two coffees he considered telling Wendy to rest but in truth, he didn't want to clean the house. It was Saturday, his day off. A couple of weeks of dust till she felt better weren't going to kill anyone. There were husbands who didn't do any at-home chores. He was chauffer and backyard turd cleaner. His self assurances didn't deflect his guilt but were enough to keep him from assisting her.

"Janie," Tim stood at the top stair leading to the den. His blue eyes pointedly avoided his wife in jeans and Eddy Bauer turtleneck attacking the rim under the toilet seat with a scrub brush and bleach. His stepdaughter opened her door.

"What's up?" This morning Jane had pulled up hair up like her mother. On Jane it looked angelic with tiny golden wisps surrounding her face. On Wendy, decrying her commode cleaning, the wayward loose curls said, sexy. Tim took a gulp from his mug to swallow down his remorse for letting them down today.

"I'm gonna take a buy on practice today if that's all right with you? There's a Michigan State-Notre Dame game at one and I've got to cheer the Fighting Irish on, right?"

Jane curled the left side of her lips up slightly. 'Grown-ups are so weird.' She turned back to her room dismissing the stupid request. Over her shoulder she offered, "The only men who come to practice are the divorced dads anyway. You don't have to be there."

Without further consultation with his wife, he patted his thigh twice for his dog to follow him downstairs.

"Janie, what time do we have to be there?" Wendy called over the rinsing double flush. It was futile. Her daughter's headphones plugged her into other worlds far from home. Wendy walked barefoot to the refrigerator calendar. Her own handwriting confirmed 'swim prac. 1pm' in the Saturday square. No mention of car pooling. Which meant every family would fend for itself today.

'Makes sense. The holidays are fast approaching. People want to get their kids in and out of practice so they can shop or whatever families do when they aren't plagued by illness.' Wendy was ashamed of her disgruntled thoughts. She grabbed the Lysol spray bottle and plied chemical warfare tactics on the bathroom sink.

She creamed her hands with enough Insolence to extinguish the bleach smells she was sure followed her to the Y. Her daughter was out of the car and in the middle of a girl gaggle before Wendy parked in the adjoining lot. The teacher would soon be welcomed by another chlorine scent, the one that reminds us of summer and youth; the smell of a pool. The Floral Oaks YMCA offered activities in anything from macramé to body building, a nursery for toddlers and a pilates class for seniors. The jewel in its crown was its swim team. Jane was only in one of its divisions but they were having their best year and after a year of hospitalizations her daughter would finally have 'a sound mind in a sound body.' Once inside the massive blue tiled pool chamber, Wendy waved to the few mothers she knew. Every adult greeted another by commenting on the unseasonably warm November. Last evening's news promised another record breaking 70's weekend. Since she wore a pair of Jane's cast-away jeans, high-heeled boots because they were the closest to the closet door and no makeup, save a bit of lip gloss, she was sure she'd run in to a present or former student. Instead, one of the oiliest divorced dads left the parent pews to approach her.

"Nice to see your daughter back." He glided into a conversation.

"Mmm."

"I usually see you with your old man, the big guy. He's not here today."

Wendy sighed like she was teaching a drama lesson on emoting. "He'll be here any minute. So we'd better move away from each other. If he sees me with an ugly guy he doesn't care but somebody good looking like you…He goes crazy."

The teacher was alone again to cheer on her daughter. Jane swam under the ropes to pool side after their warm-up.

"Can I go home with Colleen today. She just got new furniture in her room and wants me to see it. Mrs. Maher said she'd bring me home at 5." Wendy nodded to the blonde woman sitting with her youngest, Conor on her lap.

"Is it OK?" she mimed.

The woman with the squirming two year old waved her hand down from her wrist in a New York hand signal for 'No problem.' Wendy knew that by 5:08 that evening there'd be a serious plea for a new bedroom suite.

⌘ ⌘ ⌘

The Loveholic theme sang from its choking surroundings in her jeans' pocket. The word Anycolor came up. Wendy looked up at the swimmers, coaches and parents as if caught naked at her bedroom window. 'I told him I wasn't coming in today. If I say hello in Korean, people will notice, especially those three Korean mommies I know from the neighborhood. I have to make sure I don't say his name, maybe I…Just answer the damn phone.'

"Yes."

"*Yuh bho seh yo.*"

With two floors of concrete and steel above her, it sounded like Jay was talking through thunder claps.

"J...yes?"

"I need you to meet me." Kkhhtch crackled through his sentences "...very important meeting."

"Are you all right?"

"I need you to pick me up."

"Are you joking? Where's Yujin? Why don't you call a cab?"

"I forgot my wallet."

The swim meet was ending. Jane would soon wave goodbye without so much as a 'Love ya, mom' as she drove off with the Maher's.

"Where are you?"

"Hanyang Plaza on Northern. *Ohl leh?*"

The teacher didn't know why she asked him for reasons. She knew she'd fetch him from the moment he asked, even if Jane wasn't going to the Maher's. She would have hastily dropped her off at home. The thought of how easily she was allowing someone else to take precedent over Jane unnerved her but not enough to change her plan.

"I'm leaving now."

Wendy found her daughter amid the shrieking pre-pubescents in the locker room.

"My tutoring job just called." She held up her phone for proof. "I'm going as soon as I thank Colleen's mom." She leaned in to kiss her daughter's forehead but quickly moved to a five fingered 'toodles' when Jane's embarrassed glare cut her off.

Wendy was already on Commonwealth heading north when Colleen, still at the Y, asked Jane if she could borrow her Happy Feet video. Mrs. Maher obliged the girls by stopping at Jane's house.

Tim heard the side door's wreath banging on the glass and one set of sneakers racing above his den ceiling.

"Where's mom?" he called from the sidelines.

"She had to go to her tutoring job." Jane made a quick stop in the freshly cleaned upstairs' toilet. The big man lifted himself from his lounger.

"Was she dressed up?"

"No, why would she dress up?" Inside the pristine bathroom, Jane pulled up her underwear and jeans.

"I just thought she'd come home first to change. You know how mom is about her clothes."

Jane ran her fingertips under the tap to appease the mother who wasn't there and ran out leaving her stepfather alone on the top step of the stairway.

"Come on Fi. Let's go to the garage." He called to the hound sleeping on the den sofa.

Wendy whisked her cheekbones with blusher and drew a mascara wand through her lashes at every stoplight. She pulled the Nissan over to spray her glove compartment sample of Insolence on the back of her neck. She hadn't bothered to put on the relic of a car radio. She was playing her warning of never doing this again over and over.

After crossing the Expressway, she took the service road to Springfield Boulevard then turned left on to Northern. Every third store's awning advertized in Korean. In a few lights they'd all be written in the neat circles and lines Wendy had come to know. Wendy plucked at her black silk scrunchy then pulled down on her sweater in an attempt to look more kempt. The cotton knit swished over her skin to trumpet an urgent reminder, no bra. Midway through her radiation treatments the stinging flush grew to a gnawing burn, which eased when braless.

Often on the drive home from work she'd unhook the back band at the first stop sign, unhinge the right shoulder strap at the next and zip the bra through her left sleeve when she deemed viable. The weekends began and ended brassiere free. At the traffic stoplight on 160th Street, she flipped down the visor vanity mirror. The teacher grimaced.

'I'm forty-three. Too old to wave free like this. Oh my God, is it bumpy over my scar?

If I keep my arms sort of criss-crossed like this at Hanyang Plaza and then hold the wheel like this while I drive him home, he won't see anything lumpy.'

From that light to the Flushing Bridge after Main Street, the former salt meadow would cease looking like its original Dutch town, Vlissingen and more like a post card from Itaewan. Groceries and hardware stores, restaurants and physician's offices all sported Han gul awnings and signs. The remaining European heirs to the neighborhood mumbled under their breaths about the loss of America. They fought through their Congressional leaders to enact English-only advertising. They settled for English-too laws. Perhaps they had forgotten the salumerias, kosher butchers and bodegas of their childhoods. To Wendy the changing face of Flushing was America - at least New York style.

The road congestion rivaled Manhattan's. Hanyang Plaza was on the south side of the boulevard. Like all big city denizens, she knew the long way 'round was usually the fastest. She drove north on the first side street without a one way sign pointing back at her and came around to the building's parking lot.

Tim hated valet parking and would often pass a fiver to an innocent car park attendant while 'confiding' he was 'on the job' and had to park the creaking Toyota himself. No one ever discouraged the big Irishman at the wheel from doing as he asked. Wendy had no parking idiosyncrasies. She was glad not to drive aimlessly through the narrow streets looking for the illusive NYC parking spot. A quick check of the back seat before relinquishing her keys to a teenage driver showed one of Jane's little denim jackets in the back seat.

"Oh," Wendy shook it in the sunlight fearing Fido fur residue.

"I have an outfit."

With her big black handbag in her fist, she woman-walked to the massive brass and glass entryway, gleefully aware of the approval rating from the parking staff.

Hanyang Plaza, advertised nightly on Hallyu TV, was the first office building/catering facility/upscale mall to grace Northeastern Queens. Wendy wasn't privy to the business offices on the top floors and was disappointed with the ballrooms whose decor was indistinguishable from the older non-Asian wedding mills that dotted the borough but the lower level stone and glass atrium for shoppers and diners was lovely. Small stone tables and Lucite chairs meandered through the wide walkways encircling the high-end shops and restaurants. She would be the only non-Asian there. It didn't concern her. Growing up in the Melting Pot meant you were often the only white at a black wedding, the only non-Greek at an Orthodox christening, or the only shicksa at a Bar Mitzvah. Maybe not the last one. The last former student's Jewish coming of age celebration she attended had more Kim children than Goldsteins.

The little butterfly flutter in her chest told her the black silken hair tied back into a loop at the neck belonged to Jay. He had placed himself at a window table facing Manhattan although the city couldn't be seen from this part of the boulevard. He wore jeans, a black turtleneck and denim jacket making them fraternal twins once again. The table was cluttered with a short stack of paper napkins, two *Ahn Dong* soju bottles, a pack of Winston's and a clear slender drinking glass.

The open bottles led Wendy to wonder if Yujin came for him as well as she walked to his chair.

Wendy often wondered if Korean drama actors sprayed their eyes with glycerin to give them that rainwater coating for 'unrequited love' scenes. Now she knew they didn't. Jae Won looked up revealing brimming watery eyes. The teacher pretended not to notice.

He waved his arm toward the other filled tables, "Welcome to my America." then finished his drink.

She sat down trying to quell the interest of the families and business men cutting short their activities to further observe hers.

"Fishman, you're just stopping, remember? I've got a birth certificate at home that says this is *my* America." She lifted the cigarette pack an inch off the table. "Since there's no smoking allowed in New York, not to mention you don't smoke, is this a prop?"

"I was in the mood. But I forgot America doesn't want its citizens to smoke. They just like to push it on other countries."

"OK." The teacher stood not caring whose attention she caught. "You just won a free pass for pissing off the Yankee. *Kah jah*"

"*Ahn jeh seo*" Jae Won pointed at the clear plastic chair next to his.

Although the lounge remained subdued she felt as she had on her first day in Seoul when everyone in the city's giant Technomart looked back at the only red-head shopping with them.

"*Ahn jeh*." His palm came down on the backrest of the empty chair too hard for Wendy's liking.

"*Shiro!*"

"Wen-dy." A female voice with a distinct Korean accent called her name.

If she any doubts about being the opening act at Hanyang Plaza that day, they were dispelled when she heard her name called twice more. She stared down at Jay as if she was his mother signaling; 'Now you've done it!'

Annie Kang left a party of friends to greet her only red headed hair salon customer. Wendy turned smiling while Jae Won offered a polite greeting to the younger woman.

"Wen-dy, oh see," Annie gently tapped the auburn ponytail. "...hair too long. Come in soon. *Hep-un gotchee muh rhee heh du rlil gay oh.*"

"Uh, *yeh yeh*. You're right I need a cut. I'll call you. *Gom sah hah mee dah, neh*"

Annie's quick exit took Wendy's ire. She sat down grateful her brush-up with Jay was over.

"That's why I need to learn more Korean. I said "Yes" but I don't know what a hep-un is."

Jae Won held back a snort. He had no desire to bring back the squabbling.

"She said she'd give you a haircut like Audrey Hepburn's."

Wendy's hand flew to cover her laughter.

"I was worried about my Korean. I've got to learn more English! Ooh, Hepburn's hair would be too short. Come on, I'll take you home."

The sun drenched room dimmed causing the other patrons to look up towards the incandescent lighting suspended from the ceiling. Jay's artist's eyes turned towards the windows. The innocent scattered white clouds salting the sky darkened into fists to bring a surprise punch downpour over the scattering passersby.

"All right Fishman, no more Mrs. Niceguy, my too long hair's going to frizz. Haul yourself out of that chair and let's make our run for it. *Hanna, dul, set.*"

They pulled their jean jackets tightly around their chests as if denim could deflect rain and raced to the parking lot. Attendant Kim Bong Chol took Wendy's ticket and Jay's crumpled dollars and returned the forgettable car to them.

No one knows why the immediate aftermath of running in the rain is laughter. Perhaps it's that one small grab at childhood exuberance before we remember life still sucks and now we're stuck in the rain. They filled the air in the sedan with teenage laughter till the windshield became sandwiched by foggy steam on one side and watery iridescent sheets on the other. The downpour grew torrential leading Wendy to prudently pull up to a fire plug till it passed.

"Oh, I needed that laugh. I bet that sobered you."

Jay allowed himself another chuckle then took his handkerchief from his pocket and pressed her dampened burgeoning curls above her brows.

"Wendy, aren't you going to ask me why I'm not at the store, why I called you? Why I stink from soju?"

She gently took the cloth from him and blotted the crystal beads from the top of his slicked back hair. She joined his gaze through the windshield at the drenched cityscape before them.

"I don't know why the impressionists make rain look so beautiful on dirty city streets. See the way the drops pop up off the gutter. They may seem like water sprites to artists but to me they look like bubbling brew in a witch's cauldron."

"There's a rainbow in water. Do you know 'Umbrellas in the Rain' it's American."

"Prendergast right? The rainy day in Venice?

"*Whah.* You're very smart at some things. One day you should look at it again, the vibrant reds, the mellow ochers, all his blues and greens brightening up the world below the rain. I don't know what the artist thought, maybe that it rains on everyone. We should provide our own rainbows against the inevitable storms.

Wendy pulled at her jacket to insure it shielded her nipples before she turned to Jay.

"I don't feel like it rains on everyone. Your paintings are beautiful. Perhaps when you look at them you see some flaws, things you might have changed, maybe you even tweak some you once considered finished. What if you couldn't paint again and one day you came home to see all your work washed away in a deluge. Would you find beauty in the water? Or would you cease to find beauty anywhere. I've created only one beautiful thing in my life, my daughter. I was supposed to give her a wonderful life but she'll never live the dreams of her friends. She's stuck in a world of prescriptions and examinations, missing school and missed opportunities. You think I'm afraid of my cancer for me. I'm scared I won't be around for Jane. So I can't ask you why you're sad. You're already nuzzling your way into my heart. I can't...I just don't need this right now."

They drove in silence to the two-family house with the swip-swapping of the wipers keeping time with their thoughts.

The soot gray clouds had moved east but Jay feigned sleep during the drive securing Wendy's decision to see the groggy man into his house. She opened his door with his key and kept her shoes on while he changed into slippers on the mudroom top step. She held out his key ring but Jae Won kept his back to her as he removed his dampened jacket.

"*Kah*." He turned to face her. "You said you don't need this." His right hand made a loose fist as he tapped his chest. "So go, you're right, you don't need anything." He turned back without his keys.

Wendy looked down at the wooden Buddhist open-eyed fish symbol on the ring. She cleared her throat.

"Don't turn around but I need to tell you something."

"Then give me your hand. I won't turn around. Just give me your hand."

She kept her hands at her sides.

"You were going to hand me the keys anyway." He coaxed.

Wendy took two steps towards his back and breathed his pheromones off his sweater. She gingerly placed her hand and key ring beyond the side of his waist. Daily exercises had given Jae Won a surprising furtiveness. He pulled her hand to the front of his flat abdomen leading her other hand to grab on to his. He held her arms around his middle.

"*Mal sum hah seh yo*"

His directive for her to speak was so soft, it calmed her as the day he massaged her palm in the store.

"You would have been right about me up until August." She hadn't stood with a man this way before. She never wrapped her arms around such a slender waist before either. She wanted to record everything; Uri playing in the fish bowl on the counter, the silence, the clean smell of him.

"I didn't dare need anything because everybody else was so needy. Kids at school needed me, their parents needed me, my mother was widowed and sickly, my husband still doesn't know where the washer's start button is." Her voice lowered. "…and Jane. When Jane got sick I finally had a need. I needed to be with Janie…always. Sometimes she was hospitalized for weeks at a time, Christmas Day in a hospital, her birthday in a hospital. I'd sleep at the hospital, sneak a shower and rush off to work. On the days I thought she looked too sick to leave, I'd stay with her to brush her hair and wash her face."

Jay rubbed his thumb over the back of her hand not sure where her ramblings were headed.

"If you have a devastatingly ill child, the doctors are very obliging when you ask for tranquilizers. I asked the gastroenterologist, the surgeon, the pediatrician even my cardiologist till I had five bottles of Xanax, each with 90 little pink ovals. That was all I needed then, an overdose. You see, my Janie is so beautiful, so lovely I knew if the angels took her, they'd be good to her but I'm the only one who knows how to untangle her hair and the way she likes her socks rolled, so if she died, I'd have to go with her. She's my little girl. I'm her mommy."

He guessed no one else had known this about her. Western culture disallowed discussions of suicide even in retrospect. He stayed holding the backs of her hands while her elbows nestled into the sides of his waist.

"I'm sorry. I shouldn't have said this. I forgot about your wife."

"That was different. You *know* that was very different, *ah rhah?*"

"*Neh.*"

Wendy pressed her temple into his back. "Hmmm" she whimpered.

"Even with everything that happened to me, I go to school because after, I can be with you. I write because I can read my work to you. I draw because it will be looked at by you. God forgive me, I need you. I can't be your wife or your lover. I have nothing to offer you so I know it's shameless to say it."

In one smooth move, he released her arms and turned to face her. He expected tears but her smile greeted him.

"I feel much better. Not that I've ever exercised, but this is probably like a runner's high."

Wendy had formally ended the moment. Jae Won would have to savor the words that he memorized later. For now, he wasn't sure how to let her leave.

"Are you sure you don't want to try to be my wife or lover?" he teased.

"*Neh*."

"Then you shouldn't hold me like that. I'm not one of your drama characters. I'm a man."

"*Ah rha yo*."

Wendy closed the door behind her and stood on the brick steps long enough to exhale deeply.

'Fishman, you may be a *man* but I've got a spreading rosy blotch across my chest, short and curlies growing out of my armpits and a cheap pair of Costco cotton briefs on my butt. Today was not the day I was gonna' be your woman!'

⌘ ⌘ ⌘

Episode 10: On behalf of the President of the United States

America's home cooks know that Thanksgiving dinner starts the Sunday before the holiday when the 'Free with $200 purchase twenty pound turkey' comes out of the freezer and into the fridge. There it will remain till the start of the Macy's parade when Wendy would clean it with scalding water, blot its gut and neck cavities with paper towels and stuff them with country sausage, an assortment of dried fruits and fresh apples as well as cubed toasted bread from leftover loaves stored alongside the big bird himself. To Jay's chagrin and Tim's delight she spent all of last weekend preparing corn pudding and honey pear muffins, sweet potato pecan casserole and fresh cranberry-raspberry compote. This year the desserts included crunchy sweet pecan and caramel apple pies, creamy smooth coconut layer cake and individual pumpkin cakes in pumpkin shapes thanks to mini bundt pan molds that produced perfect little harvest gourds when attached top to top and frosted orange. She was reminded of her rainy childhood days with Playdoh as she created stems and vines from marzipan nubs and ropes dusted with cocoa powder then flattened dyed green marzipan discs before cutting them into leaf shapes.

The dining room table was set for eight. Jane enjoyed helping her mother spread the autumn leaf patterned tablecloth and swiping each napkin half way through the brass turkey rings. The Mikasa glassware, a wedding gift from Lucille sparkled under the colonial style chandelier. Grandma Dale's red and gold Homer Laughlin's dishes rested on golden chargers and tag-sale turkey candlesticks marched down the table's center. Mother and daughter covered the photo-shoot table with a clean cotton bed sheet that wouldn't be lifted till minutes before their guests arrived.

Tim and Fido stayed in the den clear of the bustling upstairs. Down here the big man was safe among the holiday paper goods, sodas, bar offerings and appetizers. The last placed strategically atop the entertainment center away from Fido's tongue. His mood was celebratory as he once again tossed away the most recent note paper in his wallet. He no longer had to locate the source of his wife's unprecedented gaiety. Obviously, it was simply her immersion in the bustle of the season.

Tim stopped mixing his pain killer-plus-vodka cocktails a week ago. The combination numbed his lips making him fear detection. Instead, he fell into an easier pattern of a swig in his orange juice before work, Dewar's at the Jew's Harp on Astoria Avenue at lunchtime and two icy Grey Gooses while watching The News Hour after dinner. Wendy's radiation treatments had finally ended. 'As soon as she has that polyp removed we'll be home free and I can make my Christmas pilgrimage to Uncle Timothy's clean and sober.

Bird and Fish

The guest list hadn't changed since their first Thanksgiving in Floral Oaks. Lucille entered first racing directly to the bathroom muttering, "Damn Lasix." to all who'd listen. Diane followed with two Pathmark grocery bags containing the green bean casserole no one would eat, creamed pearl onions which they would, a bottle of Cold Duck and box of Russell Stover's dark chocolates. Diane's widowed uncle Martin shook hands with the couple whose table he graced each year. In payment, he'd open his Queens Village home to his dead brother's granddaughters, daughter and her aunt saving them from the arduous drive back to Pennsylvania till tomorrow. Soon he'd eat platefuls of Swedish meatballs and sliced kielbasa appetizers only to complain he was stuffed when the bird made its debut at the table.

Diane's daughters appeared named after their parents' DNA. Heidi, 20 was Aryan blonde with iolite blue eyes while Deirdre, 25 was a Celtic two-punch of red hair and green eyes. The young women kissed the cheeks of their host and hostess while still holding their cell phones to their ears. They happily fussed and coddled their baby cousin, Jane but usually skipped out before the after dessert clean-up. It was as it had always been even the year Jane was bedridden but with two slight differences, hardly noticeable to the unsuspecting. Tim paled when his mother-in-law asked for a vodka and cranberry juice to welcome the holiday season.

"Lucille, Janie hates cranberry juice. Wendy stopped buying it." he offered knowing he'd finished off the last bottle of vodka earlier. "Let me pour you a glass of Cold Duck. You'll be my cheap date, huh beautiful?" And later, after she served fragrant steaming bowls of butternut squash soup, Wendy slapped her hand over her vibrating pocket and disappeared downstairs to the guest bathroom off the den. She returned to clear the emptied bowls singing "Here Comes Santa Claus" and kissing her mother's cheek.

"Wendy gets everyone in the holiday spirit. That's just what Dad used to do. Right Wen? You remember, girls?"

"Of course we remember." assured Deirdre. "He'd start reading A Christmas Carol to us on Thanksgiving. He could do all those funny English accents."

Lucille took a sip of her bubbly wine, looked into her daughter's eyes and spoke as if no one else sat at their holiday table. "He could do anything. You know Wen, sometimes I could kill Daddy for dying."

On Saturday before dawn, Wendy would strike the Thanksgiving set to begin two days of Christmas decorating. Monday morning she'd be back at school gently correcting Maria Kissel's Act 5 performance, "Room ho! Tell Antony Brutus is ta'en." wondering why women called all this work 'the holidays.'

Janie had begged to sleep at 'Uncle' Martin's so she too could hit the seven a.m. sale with her 'cool' older cousins Black Friday morning. The young women readily agreed but with the caveat that they wouldn't be home till very late tonight leaving Jane at their uncle's with 'old people' for company. Jane was an only child. The company of grownups for a few hours before bedtime was easily bearable.

The princess circled the baker's tables one last time. She drooled over the soft white cupcakes robed in pink fondant and decorated with miniature almond paste fruits. She licked her lips when greeted by the sugary scent of flaky bear claws but just as she stepped towards the lone misplaced chocolate chip on the cookie tray she heard the whisper-like sounds of the tops of her thighs rubbing together. She raised her highborn head fearing others in the state room may have heard the swish-swashes too. "Bring me the royal looking glass." She commanded and when it arrived, she perused her plump cheeks and double chin. "I don't want a thousand baked goods. Daddy, make them take these away."

Wendy kneaded the back of her neck after typing and watched Fido sleep and dream of all the hand held bits of turkey and trimmings that stuffed his belly.

"Another great meal, Red." Tim called from the kitchen then punctuated his compliment with a loud belch. Fido leapt off the child's bed, stretched front paws and back legs and trotted till he was nose to nose with the leftover turkey carcass being further man-handled by Tim. He surprised his wife earlier by offering to load the dishwasher with the china and glass remnants of their feast. Wendy jumped at the chance to sit in the ergonomic task chair at the computer never to guess that her husband like a homeless man at a dumpster was downing the leftover wine, scotch and beer before placing their containers on the wire racks.

"I'm going to take a quick shower." noted Tim. "Turkey smells great but not before sleep. What's your schedule tomorrow, that early morning Christmas sale debacle?" He returned the turkey to the refrigerator guarding the pan with his strong legs between his dog and the shelf.

"I've set the alarm for six so I can pick up Libby at seven thirty. I've finished all our shopping. I'm just going to keep Lib company. I promised to take her out for Korean food lunchtime so I'll be back two-three. The girls are dropping off Janie at noon. Will you be finished with the tree lights by then?" Only half of her itinerary was true but at least she wasn't lying to Jane as well.

"Well," he called from the bathroom after flushing, if Janie is coming home at noon, I'll wait for her. Maybe she'll help me."

The sound of the shower head spewing covered the husband and wife's identical comment, 'Fat chance.'

⌘ ⌘ ⌘

Belmont Park, home of the final jewel in America's Triple Crown of horse racing, is in Nassau County, New York but still within walking distance of southeastern Queens. Some locals from the two counties take their children to Breakfast at Belmont festivities while others enjoy the thirty-three day Fall Championship season. Residents

Bird and Fish

from the adjoining neighborhoods know in the quiet of the off season they can park near the Floral Park Memorial High School running track for an up-close view of some of the finest racing horses in the world. After Ahromie asked her cousin to paint a horse picture for her room, Wendy decided to surprise Jay with an early morning visit to the semi-hidden gated area across from the school.

The teacher wasn't dressed for standing around horse muck. She was meeting Libby at Dal Ja's restaurant in a few hours. Each woman would try to out-dress the other in Golden Ghetto chic; metallic leather blazers, buckled and chained high heeled boots and yards of costume circle necklaces. They weren't going for 'pretty'. Lunch with the girls meant looking rich, outer borough style.

Wendy was grateful Jay had become Yujin's silent partner. She didn't comprehend all the ins and outs he explained about his new work model but she grasped that he'd take less money out, invest more in and paint full time at home.

Of late their afternoons at the store made her fearful of being exposed at school. Even if the rumor mill only spewed out her needing another job she knew that before the end of the term there'd be speculation about a gambling or drug problem at home and a need for extra income. Too many former colleagues left among whispers and accusations. She wanted her exit free from scandal.

Sid Shyman, Holocaust survivor, American citizen, retired court reporter and widower walked his curliqued terrier mix outside Jae Won's home. The dog matched his owner's plodding steps as they both sniffed the early morning pre-winter air while Wendy exited the Nissan.

"Now that's a gorgeous woman, right Tattalah?" He patted the scruffy pooch's head. "She must be friends with the lady with the two girls. Uh, look who's coming out for her. The boarder."

Perhaps it was his tragic beginnings that enabled Sid to see into souls that weren't bared. Perhaps it was only because he was old and finally had the time to see rather than just look but the eighty four year old took note of the crackling current between the Asian and the redhead as they neared one another.

"You don't see too much of det combination, and they're not teenagers." The elderly man lightly tugged the leash attached to his best friend's collar. "Remember the 'tzimis' over Bessie's daughter marrying the 'Talaina' and they vere both vite. I guess it's a different vorld now. Come, Papa vill put a little cream in your cereal."

Wendy greeted the venerable man with a "Good morning" and smiled down at his wheezing dog. Jay reflexively bowed his head with an equally cheery response. He handed his drawing pad to her and opened the Sana Fe's passenger's door beaming at her respectfulness towards his aged neighbor. He often marveled at her ability to hold spoon and chopsticks Korean style and the way she covered her mouth while laughing but he also knew that it was her Western features and Yankee cockiness that enticed him.

"*Uh ri oh dee gah?*" he asked again.

"*Bi mil.* Just drive where I tell you. Make a left on Culligan and a right on Little Neck Parkway. We'll take that all the way down to the county line."

The drive took less than ten minutes. Jae Won took his pad and pencils as instructed and quietly crossed the roadway with Wendy. Thanks to their post-holiday tryptophan high, most Long Islanders were sleeping in that morning giving the artist a personal viewing of the approaching magnificent thoroughbred and rider just on the other side of the chain link fence. Shatan's Blade, roan with a white blaze won his last three races. The 'all out' stallion was famous for extending himself to the utmost. Steam rose from his nostrils forming an inverted teardrop vapor in the frosty November air. The rider was gingered-haired and pale cheeked with almost delicate features.

"Morning to you." Wendy boldly greeted the rider. "He's a beautiful beast, he is. Too bad I'm afraid to ride. My hat's off to ye. 'May the angels protect you.'"

The rider, safe in his gated paddock looked through the links at the pretty woman just outside and completed the Irish rhyme, "And heaven accept you."

Jae Won looked at his companion in amazement. She had planned this right down to assuming an Irish accent for the impressed young man.

"I'm Wendy Eachen. My friend, Jay's an artist. Would it be all right if we stayed here long enough for him to sketch you and your horse for his niece?"

The young man touched the rim of his skull cap black helmet and introduced himself as James Tolan originally from Cork and then obliged them by circling slowly near the stables. Before he and the roan left, young James pointed out the best area to view the steed's paces. Wendy stood mesmerized at the fenced viewing area while Jay sketched. She envied Shatan's Blade for his speed and passion but when her eyes moved from his glowing coat and flexing muscles, she was forced to view his bridal and saddle. "He's no freer from worldly woes than we are." she voiced.

Jae Won looked up from the artist's pad.

"It depends on him. If he thinks only of how good it feels to race in the early morning, or to eat all he wants and sleep protected from the rain and cold, he is free. And if that is true, we are also free from as you say 'woe'."

He quickly returned to his Minhwah version of the Irish horse.

"How do you say horse in Korean?"

"*Mahl*, Missus Ee Chin. How did you know he was Irish?"

"It wasn't much of a gamble. I often see the track people at the neighborhood stores. The blondes and red-heads have Irish accents, the darker ones, Hispanic or Cajun. Eachen means horse in Gaelic. I would have said you were Jay McGough if I thought it would get you more face time with the horse."

She watched him finger the plug of gum spirit he used for erasing.

"Perhaps I just wanted to be Ms. Eachen for a little while. She's carefree, has a handsome friend and has never been sick a day in her life."

⌘ ⌘ ⌘

"I told you no one would stare at us." Wendy assured Libby.

"They're too polite I guess, but we're still the only white people in here."

"If this was a Chinese restaurant, you'd say that means the food's good."

The two friends laughed at the tired New York urban legend. Wendy covered her mouth reflexively and Libby quickly imitated her as if in a Korean Culture class. Libby placed her Gucci magnifying glasses on the bridge of her nose and scanned the English side of the menu. Wendy, like a personal tour guide, looked for samples her friend would find similar to Chinese restaurant fare. They chose scallion pancakes and kim bap for their appetizers with a main course of gujeolpan to share. Libby looked forward to wrapping chiffonades of vegetables into wheat pancakes since her favorite Chinese dish was anything prepared moo shoo style. Wendy was careful to sprinkle her requests to the young waitress with Korean words she could easily pronounce. It won platitudes from the woman and even a few silent thumbs up from the next table's diners.

Libby held up her eyeglass case before returning her readers to her handbag.

"I hate these things. If I wasn't so afraid of doctors, I'd have that CK procedure and say goodbye to glasses forever. Then again if I wasn't so afraid, I'd get a lift."

She put her fingertips on her cheekbones and pushed up towards her eyes and then to her temples while digging her thumbs into her jaw line erasing her wattle.

"Doesn't that look better?"

Wendy squirmed. "Put your hands down before they ask us to leave. You'll cause a breakdown in Korean-American relations."

"Make fun now. Your day will come. You'll strut down a street in your three inch heels and the only eyes to follow you will belong to other women admiring your shoes."

"So get the surgery if you're that self conscience."

"I wasn't kidding about doctors. I'm petrified. It's probably because I was a nurse. I saw too much. The only reason I had my bunion removed was because the pain was so intense, I was starting to hobble."

A waiter set down an array of side dishes for patrons at another table.

"We're getting those too, aren't we?" Libby was eager to change subjects.

Wendy dared a glance at the tiny crispy fish, kimchi and marinated soy sprouts among the other four offerings.

"I don't know if they come with what we ordered. Probably, I'm not completely sure but we'll certainly get kimchi."

With that remark, eight petite side dishes and the scallion pancake arrived at the table. The glistening golden triangles were specked with pungent spring onions and hot from their oil bath in the kitchen's frying pan.

"Isn't this better than leftover turkey drowning in dollops of mayo and cranberry sauce on rye?" Libby teased as her chopsticks whisked a crunchy serving into her watering mouth.

"Sometimes." came Wendy's quick reply.

Their chopsticks continued to clatter when the kim bap arrived. The tightly wrapped-in-seaweed slices of filling and rice are a treat most New Yorkers call Korean sushi even though their centers were filled with succulent bits of steak instead of raw fish. The friends continued their conversation but changed their subject to tales of the preceding night's feasts.

"I'm not kidding, Wen." Libby said of her oldest son's latest girlfriend. "From the time she arrived till the last of the liquors and petifours were gone, she sat like a mannequin. That girl never moved."

"She didn't help you clean up?"

"I have people for that." She whispered.

Sometimes Wendy forgot they came from very different homes. To cover her faux pas, she told how Tim had poured a foamy glass of Lowenbrau for their 'Uncle' Martin and the old man growled, "Whad 'ya pour me here, a Coney Island head?"

Libby nearly choked on her nori-wrapped tidbit. "I'm an old Brooklyn girl but I haven't heard that expression since my father died. It meant the cheap barkeep was giving you mostly suds. Tim should have poured better...unless he had one too many himself. He's still on the wagon, isn't he?"

"I know you're not Tim's fan but trust me, he hasn't had a drink in years."

"I don't dislike him. I just wish you would have married someone who treasured you." Wendy placed her chopsticks down flat next to her plate. She pressed her lips together deciding whether to share her secret.

"Jay called in the middle of dinner." She began.

Her friend surprised her with a serious expression and a sage like tone in her voice.

"I know in the beginning, I encouraged you but don't you think it's time to let this go? When you took him home that day and he said he was a man, you thought he just wanted to get laid but what if he meant I'm human. I'm entitled to a full life too?

How long do dogs live, ten, twelve years?" Libby put her hand up signaling no response was needed. She was about to teach a lesson and like all good teachers was creating a memorable lead-in.

"Dogs are perfect. They love you rich or poor, young or old, fat or skinny. They look at you like you're the messiah and take whatever kind of love you return. Who else but a dog would kiss you or do tricks for your attention and then, if you weren't in the mood, just go in a circle and sleep with no recriminations or grudges. Still, dogs have the final 'Fuck you.' They don't last very long. The dog you thought would be your lifetime soul mate up and dies. It always ends with weeping and the gnashing of teeth."

Wendy raised and waved her hand like an over-zealous schoolgirl.

"Ooh, ooh, Mrs. Spring." Wendy said sarcastically. "I know why we're talking about dogs. They're really symbols for lovers, extramarital ones."

The younger teacher wasn't comfortable with the warning and added.

"I told you, Lib. Nothing's going on."

"I'm not talking about sex. You're a smart woman. Would you prefer Tim had a drunken one night stand after a Christmas party or spent the last year falling in love with a colleague?"

The gujeolpan was placed between the women at the table. But although they lauded the delicate pancakes and fresh vegetable morsels to placate their waitress, neither friend began eating.

"You *do* remember where I did my nursing?" Libby pushed on.

"Of course, Vietnam."

"I was a healthy twenty two year old surrounded by beefcake in uniforms. Everyone was getting high and love was free. Did you think Adam was my first boyfriend?"

Wendy eyed her friends stunning Escada suit and glittering Swarovski crystal pin at her lapel.

"Lib, I'm having trouble picturing you as a hippy. Where is all this leading?"

"My parents would have been upset if I wrote home about some Christian country boy so there was no way I could tell them about Ham. His name was Ham Tran. The people on the base called him 'Porkchop'. That was the first thing I noticed about you when you came to teach at 347. You gave the kids nicknames like soldiers do."

Wendy tried to bring a smile to her friend's saddened face.

"And all this time I thought it was because we were the best dressed girls at school."

Libby poked at her food as if somewhere on her plate she'd find the 1960's.

"He worked as one of our bus drivers. I was crazy in love, the kind that prevents you from asking questions, like where could this possibly go." Anyway, there are just so many places for a redhead and a local to make-out unnoticed. One day my commanding officer, Colonel Bethany 'Betty' Bell summoned me. We called her 'Three B' for Baptist, belle and bull dyke. Actually, she was pretty nice about it. She reminded me, that my parents would say Kaddish for me. Obviously, she didn't choose that exact term. More importantly she said there were rumblings from the men's side. If Ham ended up beaten to death, who'd report it? I was a dopey kid but I recognized impossible when I heard it. Besides, I couldn't let anyone hurt him. Eventually my tour was up. I went back to college to become a teacher and met Adam. And before you think I settled, I love my guy. It wasn't the same but it's still love. I guess it was the right decision because life's been good. We've got the boys, we're healthy. We even got rich."

Wendy reached across the table and took her friend's manicured hand.

"Lib, I appreciate what you're saying but my…Jay and I…it's just not the same."

"You're twice the age I was, Wen. How come you can't recognize impossible? Eventually you'll have to leave him unless you leave *with* him. OK, class is over besides I didn't cross over into Queens this afternoon to eat cold food. Let's eat this goofoo. How was the horse expedition this morning?"

The younger teacher giggled and grinned as she told of her outing with Jay. Libby viewed her happiness and regretted her earlier reproof."

"He's so incredibly talented." Wendy gushed as she wrapped up fried egg yolk slivers and shredded Nappa cabbage. "Somehow I've got to get his work to Kim Dong Kook."

"Isn't he the dirty old man from Korea?" Libby cut in.

"Dirty or not, he's the one who can make Jay famous."

"You're not going to contact that perve are you? You told me he grabbed you in his fancy smancy gallery while his wife and kids were in another room."

Wendy shrugged away Libby's inconvenient comment.

"If I had some more of Jay's paintings, I could send them. I'd never have to be alone with Touchy-Feely." She rose from her chair. "I'm off to the ladies room. Think about dessert."

The restaurant was filled with its usual Korean clientele; businessmen schmoozing clients, workmen from a nearby gas station, families enjoying a day off. Wendy could pick out snippets of the Korean conversations but not enough to listen in on any. Just steps before the stairway to the restroom she heard a familiar voice.

'Cheesy' in any language translates very easily. Wendy recognized the slippery charms of Yujin Kim convinced he wasn't flirting with his wife. She used her time seated in the stall to review the situation. After deciding her plan of action, she wiped, pulled up her underwear and high kicked the flush handle with the side of her boot, a trick to avoid restroom germs taught by Lucille. After tossing her wet-nap, Wendy Dale stopped at Yujin's table fully intent on a payback for his earlier snitching on her.

"Imagine running into the two of you like this!" Wendy made sure her tone was both obnoxious and foreboding. Yujin and the infamous seventh grade mother he dallied with were visibly jolted. Wendy recognized the parent she saw at school the evening Jay had come to her. The woman, still stylish in a black wool suit, showed little remorse after her initial surprise.

Wendy was prepared. "See that woman, the other red-haired lady at the front table. She's scheduled to be your child's English teacher next year. Worse than that, she's got the biggest mouth at school. Your family is doomed. Take yourself to the washroom, *Ah ruh suh*? Mr. Kim and I have business."

The woman stood, took her purse and chose to exit via the front door rather than hide in the ladies room never to realize that New York City teachers aren't given next year's rosters till August.

"Have a seat Wendy before we're noticed." Yujin even stood and pushed out the former occupant's chair.

"I'm not staying. Here's the deal. Tell your beautiful wife, the mother of your children, that she was right. It would be a good idea to find Jay's paintings and show them to me."

In a treacly voice she added, "Wouldn't it be wonderful to have a famous cousin? I'll give you one week to make this happen."

Yujin was inscrutable except for a tiny facial tick above his left eye.

"I could say, I'll tell your husband about you."

"Then maybe I'll become your cousin in law, but one thing's for sure, I'll get custody of my daughter. This is America, Mr. Kim and Yoon Yoo's a woman scorned. How often do you think you'll see your girls? The drama teacher took a step towards her table and turned back to Jay's cousin. "Remember, one week. Tell Yoon Yoo to call me at school when you have the paintings."

By the time Wendy returned to her lunch, she was shaking. Libby looked up from her own image as she reapplied her lipstick.

"What happened? Are you all right? You're white as a sheet."

"I just realized the importance of what you said. Right now I feel I could do anything to make Jay happy. If it weren't impossible, I'd run away with him and never look back. I'd live a different life in a different place."

"Did I say that? Are you sure you're all right? Let's get the check."

⌘ ⌘ ⌘

From the time their house was rebuilt, Yujin had never entered his cousin's apartment through Jae Won's outside door. They were family members who lived together. If one of the cousins needed the other, he would use the connecting stairway. So Jae, absorbed with his depiction of a russet brown race horse was startled by the sight of Yujin stepping out of his shoes after entering through the outer door.

"Wheh?" The artist rested his brush on a cloth and removed his reading glasses.

"Hyung, I don't interefere with your life do I? You don't want to work in the stores anymore? *Teh soh.* It's OK. But, I don't know why you have to keep seeing that woman. It's bad for the girls to see you with Seromie's teacher. She's married."

The younger cousin opened the refrigerator to scout out a beer or soju bottle. The cold shelves offered neither.

Jae Won rinsed his *nak juk bud* and carefully set them out to dry.

"What's going on?"

Yujin sat at the counter in the seat Jae had come to think of as Wendy's.

"Your girlfriend is some piece of work."

"*Yah*, watch what you say."

Yujin apologized but added his defense by retelling the incident with Wendy at Dal Ja's.

Jae Won covered his mouth with the thumb side of his fist. He hoped the stance would make him look concerned as he tried not to smirk at Yujin's comeuppance. That crazy redhead, the one who pretended to be Irish in the morning and ate *bab* in the afternoon was fighting for him.

"I'll put a carton in my bedroom. Just say you found it and let her come and select whatever she wants. Tell her I won't be home. You can say I had to go to the new store. Don't plan this for Wednesday. She has a doctor's appointment after school."

Yujin ran his hands through his blonde highlights.

"Will you listen to yourself? There are women everywhere. Find one without complications. Let Yoon Yoo find a wife for you."

"So I can dishonor her like you do yours? Do you have any idea how much you've hurt your wife? I'd understand it better if you hated her but I think in your crazy way you still love Yoon Yoo. You know, for the first time I don't envy you."

Yujin felt the sting.

"I'm just saying, *Hyung*, why did you pick her? Why love her?"

Jae Won gently tapped on the fishbowl. The black and gold playmates raced to the top for their snack.

"I didn't pick her. I wouldn't have. She belongs to another man and loves her child to the exclusion of all others. Half the time I'm not sure what she's talking about. No one has ever made me as angry or confused me so much. She'll walk in here ignoring the slippers on the step like a barbarian and yet…"

Jae Won shook his head as if snowflakes flew onto his slicked-back hair.

"I want her to like what I paint. I want her to taste real Korean food. At night I fantasize what it would be like to have her next to me asleep on my arm. Whenever I'm with her, I try to touch her face or her hair just so when we part, I can put my hand to my nose and breathe her into me. Why love her? I don't ask myself. I'm afraid if I could put it into words, I would diminish it."

He sprinkled the top of the bowl with papery flakes.

"I want to stand with her looking out on the Han River. I want to buy matching t-shirts and walk along the beach at Jeju. I guess what I really want is to take her home to Jamsil. You and your wife are free to live out those dreams but you're content to sleep with any other woman who'll have you. For Wendy's sake, I may have to let her go. Think about leaving Yoon Yoo. She'd have to be happier with a man who'd be faithful to her."

⌘ ⌘ ⌘

The weeks between Thanksgiving and Christmas vacation are heralded at school with half-eaten candy canes stuffed into desks and sign-up sheets for holiday parties posted in the teachers' lounges. Ms. Dale and her students were creating one-act plays with holiday time settings. The teacher, in her red cashmere sweater set and black and red burnt velvet skirt looked like an animated department store tableau. She flitted from table to table listening to scripts about Christmas and Chanukah, Kwanzaa, Eid and the lunar New Year. The titles delighted her sense of whimsy. Table one produced, "The Festival Of Fried Foods while table five worked on The Last Noel. She didn't notice the assistant principal standing at the classroom door till Amaz'n Grace pointed to the woman.

Ms. Sakai was a jowly dog-faced woman in her early fifties. Her five foot frame seemed even more diminutive since she wore Easy Spirit Anti-gravity flats under ankle length skirts to school to ease her plantar fasciitis heel pain. She rapped on the door window's art work and asked the teacher to speak with her. Wendy rose from her crouching position between two burgeoning playwrights and approached her supervisor.

"Ms. Dale, you're not a new teacher." was her opening salvo.

Wendy had been looking forward to sneaking into Jay's painting trove at the invitation of his cousins later that afternoon. Even the tiresome unhappiness of Ms. Sakai couldn't curtail her joyful eagerness.

"No I'm not, Harriet. What's up?"

"Only secular displays are allowed by the Department of Education. The children may create pictures of Christmas trees and dreidels but no menorahs are allowed. You certainly wouldn't put up a picture of the nativity would you?"

Wendy refusing to merit the woman with her attention focused her gaze solely on her students while answering.

"Da Vinci's Adoration of the Magi or Poussin's The Nativity? No, I'd never let the children see those awful things. These pictures were made by my students and for what it's worth I explained the rules about secular and religious."

The assistant principal's cheeks reddened. She was out of her intellectual depth. If she didn't end this discussion soon it would be all over school that she didn't know who Da Vinci was, although she had to admit she never heard of Poussin.

"Just take down the giant menorah."

"Where is it?" Wendy asked innocently.

Bird and Fish

In answer, Ms. Sakai knuckle-tapped on the offending Crayola'd picture on B-4's door.

Wendy looked at the red, black and green still life, Kinara Surrounded by Crops, Corn and Cup lovingly committed by Jeffrey Kirk as his tribute to a holiday he had only seen celebrated on television.

"Preacher, come here." She called to the boy. Ms. Sakai wants to put your Kwanzaa picture in her office. Is that all right with you?"

⌘ ⌘ ⌘

That afternoon the teacher sat cross-legged on Jae Won's bedroom floor like a child opening up early morning Christmas presents. She removed one after another from the crate and studied the works of a man she lovingly called Fishman. There were colorful flowers and birds, comical magpies and mountains that soared to the heavens and tickled the clouds. Her fingers traced giant peonies and delicate lotus flowers while her eyes tried to decode the symbolism in his turtles, pine trees and cranes. A faded brown folder protected a dozen vibrant hunting scenes all in the simple yet very alluring Minhwa style.

Tissue paper swaddled a package of handmade lacquered boxes decorated with kissing carp.

"Excuse me" she called to Jay's cousins in the next room. Do either of you know what carp symbolize in Asian art?"

Yoon Yoo answered, "My mother has a little round box with carp kissing each other. It's supposed to be married love, forever love."

'Oh, Mr. Hyun,' she chided herself, 'all the time I thought you had a crush on me I had a rival named, *Chosun*.'

In the same way she hummed to express her pleasure when opening childhood gifts, Wendy purred the calliope theme song from the Korean drama, Yellow Handkerchief oblivious to Jay's cousins seated at the kitchen counter awaiting her departure.

"Is this how people love each other when they get older?" Yoon Yoo asked her husband. They spoke in Korean not to exclude Wendy in the other room but out of their secret habit of protecting their daughters from unpleasantness.

"*Moi-uh?*" Yujin stopped staring at the playful goldfish.

"Did you notice they're satisfied just being good to one another."

"Unless she's a lot sicker than she looks, that wouldn't make sense. Why wouldn't they, you know, want sex?"

"Not everyone's like you."

Yujin Kim turned to the frozen glare of his wife.

"You know everything about me don't you." His voice was just barely above a whisper.

"Do I? Then why can't I stop you." Yoon Yoo's voice was even softer. "I was hoping *Kunapogee* and *Sun seng nim* would inspire us. That's silly, I suppose."

Yujin began to take his wife's hand but returned it to his lap instead.

"You want me to be inspired by her adultery?"

"I've heard things at KAPA meetings. She's had a terrible life. I don't know anything about her marriage but I doubt she's a cheat." Her last word brought her fingers to her lips to stifle her sobs. Her husband left his chair and circled the kitchen island to massage her shoulders.

"*Bah bo yah*, he nuzzled her ear. "You should have left me long ago. I can't promise I'll try. What if I try to try?"

"I'll stay," She sniffed in the drips from her nose and patted his hands with hers. "if you do two things. You will try and succeed." She felt his hold easing. "Uh, uh that's only the first thing. You will cut those blonde streaks out of your hair."

"*Yobo!*"

⌘ ⌘ ⌘

The blue light of Jane's computer screen was soothing. Wendy considered pulling an all-nighter. She had stopped taking sleep aids two weeks ago hoping her body would soon find its inner clock. It seemed to be coming around but tonight was special. The vision of all that beauty in her hands and the delight of sending off several key samples covertly to MiYoung kept her too jubilant to sleep even in her Floral Oaks peaceable kingdom.

In her bed next to the desk, Jane's mouth twitched as she dreamed of a conversation invented by slumber. Tim's thunderous snores and wheezes traveled through both bedrooms defying the silence of the early hour calm while Fido stretched out alongside the big man ready to defend the spot should his mistress come to roust him. The writer wiggled her stiffening fingers and clasped her right hand with her left stretching her slender arms in front of her. This was the thinnest she had been in her adult life. While she didn't grumble about having her clothing fit better or the ability to squeeze into Jane's caste-off's. It was hard to be proud of a form not earned by diet and exercise but rather exhaustion and loss of appetite.

The year after Jane was born Wendy noticed the premadonna pounds put on during pregnancy were fast becoming permanent fat deposits around her hips and thighs. She signed up with a local diet shop called B-Slim and made weekly pilgrimages till the weight came off. It was an easy diet to maintain: breakfast, light snack, lunch, light snack, dinner, light snack. The coach reminded the mostly female audience that unless they

Bird and Fish

stuck to the plan, they'd never reach their goals. Wendy embraced the B-Slim model like a new religion. One day she was asked to relate her success to the other members.

"Well" she began, "I had just had my last snack of the day when a former student stopped by to visit. She brought *duk*, Korean rice cakes for me to serve with coffee. It would have been so easy to enjoy a piece with her. But I remembered what we learned. To 'B-Slim', we must stay on course. And the course has no place for rice cake." The dieters nodded and clapped their chubby hands together till it was time for sharing a new skinless chicken breast recipe.

Jay was her sweet rice cake, mouthwatering delicious but there was no place for him in the course of her life. Even now with her medical treatment appointments ebbing, her days were full enough with home, work, outside errands, inside chores and motherhood. Her wanderings took on speed as she pushed their unwelcomed analogy from her mind.

"*Cham gon mon,*" She noticed the Korean word for wait sneaking into her vocabulary. Before my cancer, I didn't know I could push an hour's worth of radiation therapy into each of my days and I did it. Why couldn't I find time for Jay and me?"

A snort and a cough escaping the master bedroom landed on her ears in answer. Wendy returned to her writing.

Princess Jenny-purr easily sent away the milliner. She didn't want or need a thousand hats. They hid her tiara and ruined her hair. She dismissed the butcher by tossing a lamp chop at his sheepish son. And though she loved shoes, she still only had two feet so she turned down the cobbler's gifts. Besides by the time she'd wear the 365th pair, the rest would be unfashionably out of season. It was the same for the seamstress, the carriage maker, the cooper and chocolatier, the last being the easiest to send away when the princess checked the royal looking glass a second time.

She tapped her royal cheek with her delicate be-jeweled index finger. 'That man didn't just copy sounds, he captured them.' Jenny-purr concurred that the only gift that was portable, low fat and always in fashion was the fisherman's 1000 voices.

Wendy yawned. Maybe she'd go to sleep after all. Tomorrow was the last day of reading Julius Caesar and after school, her first breast MRI. 'I bet Libby never had one of those. It'll make good conversation for our morning breezeway talks on Thursday.'

Faithful to her plan, Thursday morning before crossing the street to her school, Ms. Dale outlined how she would share all the details of her ordeal with her friend.

'I'll open with the nurse taping vitamin E capsules to my nipples. That'll get her attention. I wonder if she knows they inject you with dye that makes your arm veins turn cold and your vagina get hot.' Wendy shuddered as she walked past the die-hard basketball players in the frigid

Bird and Fish

play yard. But her buoyancy sank when she eyed the empty entranceway. 'Of all days to heed my advice to meet inside, she takes today. I'm not telling this story in the lobby. She'll have to wait till period three.'

In November of 1963, Lucille Dale, wife and mother of a baby girl was given a free day spa pass complements of a neighbor. Her mother and sister eager to play with the family's new baby offered their services. On Friday, the twenty second, they babysat so Lucille could enjoy a morning of pampering at Elizabeth Arden's in the city. The beautified mom was glowing as she climbed up the subway's Flushing line steps leading back to her apartment and family but something unseen stirred in the shadows along Roosevelt Avenue. She stopped in front of Gertz' department store pretending to admire the array of winter coats while eavesdropping. Shoppers were emptying the big store's entryway like clowns from a Volkswagen making it impossible to overhear. An old lady wiping her teary eyes with a crumpled tissue bumped the young mother's shoulder as she headed for the sidewalk. Something was very wrong but in those days before cell phones, Blackberries and instant messaging, Lucille would have had to ask a stranger. Instead she rushed home to her Forty First Avenue apartment building. Her older sister opened the apartment door never to comment on Lucy's blushing cheeks and lovely coiffure.

"They killed the president!" their mother announced as she carried baby Wendy to the doorway.

Wendy had heard the story nearly every anniversary of Kennedy's assassination. Perhaps it was because Lucille had retold the story recently that she thought of it now but more likely it was the whisperings in the lobby and the way the custodial crew refused to lift their eyes to greet her that reminded her of her mother's yearly phrase, 'something unseen stirred in the shadows....'

Ira Rubinstein stood ashen-faced at the main office swinging doors.

"Wendy, come into my office, dear."

'Dear? It can't be about Janie. My cell is still on and they'd definitely try my number first.'

Wendy followed him inside. There around the conference table still covered with sample textbooks and stacks of blank report cards, sat a sobbing Claire Jackson next to the stoic school psychologist.

'Oh my God, what happened to Claire?' Wendy asked herself just as the principal took tissues from his desk box and said, "Libby Spring passed away last night."

'It was ridiculous. Libby was going to walk through the loggia doors and cluck her tongue at everyone seated there.' But even as she thought it, she knew it wasn't so. The principal went on to say that Libby had gone for a thallium stress test after school. Right as the test ended she stepped off the treadmill and fell to the floor. Her last words were, "Where's my handbag?"

Her husband reading a Sports Illustrated in the waiting room was summoned into the doctor's office while EMT workers were called to resuscitate her. She was taken to Queens Hebrew Hospital where she died at 6:00pm. Wendy committed to memory every word Ira spoke even as Claire's sobs became wails.

Ira Rubinstein put his hand on Wendy's back, "The burial is tomorrow so she can be in the ground before Sabbath. Her son said to invite only you and Claire. Here's a copy of the chapel's address.

The teacher took a step forward to put space between Ira's palm and her spine. "I'm going home, Ira. Use my substitute folder. I won't be back till Monday. Claire, could you walk out with me?" Mr. Rubinstein straightened his silk tie. After the phone call last night, he envisioned her leaving like this. He mulled over tens of phrases to convince her to stay in school but she was on short time now and nothing could stop her. The women left together, rubbing each other's shoulders. As they passed the time clock, the fattest of the bovine secretaries was putting a freshly typed sign over its face. Wendy noticed the bold faced last sentence, "Private ceremony."

'That's my Lib, screw 'em.'

At the breezeway doors, she asked Claire if she needed a ride to the service.

"Ms. Dale, you mind if I don't go. I gotta take off if anything happens to my kids. I can't afford no extra absences."

"You know what Libby would say, 'Stop being crazy. Your kids come first! And she'd be right."

"I ain't been to no Jewish funeral. Let me know how it goes tomorrow."

Wendy smoothed down her gray wool suit skirt and called her husband from her car. Tim had never met Libby and confined his comments to Ahs and Ohs and What a damn shame. He reminded his wife that he had already taken a day off this month when he woke one morning sickened with a headache, leaving her to excuse him with a reassuring "I'll be fine." She drove to Jae Won's house and sat at the wheel blinking in disbelief as a buzz-cut Yujin bustled his daughters into his Lexus and drove them to school. Minutes later, Yoon Yoo holding a gym bag was picked up by two Asian women in a white SUV. She found her cell phone at the bottom of her handbag and located a number she had only called once before.

Dr. Abraham Bogoff's direct line was given to his staff, family, several friends and a small number of patients. Sometimes it was offered to those in his care with serious needs and even those he simply worried about when he should have been sharing quality time at home. He had given Wendy Dale the number three years ago. She had only called him once last spring when Jane's surgery took longer than the expected two hours. He was on rounds at East End Hospital when his cell phone buzzed.

"What's up?" was his light-hearted opening. It took a moment or two before he could follow her ramblings but soon everything became clear including her last plaintive question, "How can that happen, Abe? She was in a doctor's office." Before he answered he heard the guilty self chastisement he had heard too often, "I didn't know she was sick."

Without filling her already crowded thoughts with too much information, Dr. Bogoff assured her that what happened was very rare. Her friend's death could have easily occurred while dashing across a busy street as well. Wendy thanked her cardiologist while grimly noting he was unable to heal her aching heart.

It took Wendy a full minute to shake the image of Libby charging across Northern Boulevard to get her first glimpse of Jae Won Hyun.

She tapped the send button one more time.

"*Yuh bho seh yo, uh Wendy*, What's wrong?"

"I'm in front of your house. Is it too early to…."

"It's cold outside, *Bally whah*"

Jae Won brushed his teeth, stepped into sweat pants and grabbed a tee shirt from his bureau's top drawer. He opened the door for Wendy who forgot the reason for her visit long enough to gawk at his loose hair and dragon's face tattoo cupping his left shoulder. Jae Won spun around pulling his shirt over his head and arms but not before Wendy caught the dragon's green and gold scales and tail descending his muscular back. He led her to the kitchen while tying his hair in his usual fashion.

"Do you want coffee?"

"Just cold water. Did I wake you? I'm sorry. *Mee ahn hah dah.*"

He let her tell all the details of her horrible news without comment while he busied himself by placing washed and soaked rice into a blender. When her words wound down, he expressed his genuine sorrow for the loss of such a vibrant woman and added that since her death was sudden it was fortunate that she didn't suffer.

Wendy kept her eyes on the back of his cotton shirt.

"My father died like that. Not on a treadmill but fast. He had a heart attack and died. I can't even do that for my daughter. If this cancer comes back, I could be sick for years. My hair will fall out and I'll stink the house with my vomiting."

"*Ha jih mah!* Stop writing a drama."

She took a sip of water, fed Uri a pinch of food and attempted nonchalance when asking about his slithery tattoo.

"University students do foolish things. Some carry reminders" he answered.

"I thought perhaps, it had a story."

"Sorry, no story. *Wheh?* Do you have a tattoo with a story?"

"No!" Wendy softened her protest, "not really…no."

Jae Won wondered how much sleep he'd get tonight pondering the design and location of her secret inking.

But for now he concentrated on cutting a dried jujube and measuring out pine nuts into a cup. Wendy stopped talking, leaned her elbow on the countertop and rested her chin in her palm. She had never watched a man cook before. In fact since she left her mother's home, no one had ever cooked expressly for her. The kitchen welcomed the whirring sounds of the blender followed by the gurgling bubbles from the pot on the stove.

"What's this?" Wendy asked when the bowl of rice and pine nut porridge was placed in front of her.

"*Jat Juk*. Eat something healthy."

"It's gruel."

"It's good for you."

His spoon made a circle in the steaming bowl before he lifted and blew on it. Then as if she were a toddler, he put the filled spoon to her lips.

Ms. Dale had a considerable and eclectic vocabulary yet this was the first time she could use pampered to describe herself. His indulgence un-nerved her and soon after the first affectionate feeding, she took the spoon from Jae to feed herself. When the porridge was half gone, her cell phone rang.

Adam Spring was using the auto-pilot ghost inside him to function. It guided him through his nightmare from last evening till now. It helped him take and make phone calls, contact a funeral parlor and meet with his rabbi. He had only retrieved his former self once since his wife's death when his sons came home and the three men held each other crying in the front hall.

"Wendy, I just wanted to invite you personally. Your principal can't come because there's a state test tomorrow. I know Libby would want you there."

Bird and Fish

"Of course I'll be there. Is there anything else I can do? Shall I bake or order cold cuts?" 'She winced at her cold cuts suggestion to the newly widowed man.

"No thanks, we've got it all under control. We'll see you tomorrow."

'Libby would have called him on that last remark. What's under control, ya big lug? I'm dead!'

"Fishman, would you like to be my escort at a funeral tomorrow."

"Would that be…what's the word?"

"Kosher."

Jae Won convinced her to rest on the couch and turned on a Korean channel to keep her attention. After cleaning their breakfast dishes, he joined her to watch As The River Flows. Wendy's green and teal eyes watered when Youngseon's baby was stillborn. Then the enormity of the morning crashed through the drama's world bringing gulps and sobs so violent that Jae Won held and rocked her till the show ended.

⌘ ⌘ ⌘

End Of Day Funeral Home's parking lot was filled to capacity by 8:30 that morning. Those who came later were directed to the parking garage across the boulevard.

The sandstone and stained glass building held nearly 200 mourners. Someone whispered, "That's Donald Trump." and was instantly informed "The governor is here too." The largest chapel room filled early leaving most of the well-heeled guests to watch the proceedings on closed circuit televisions. A brass easel with a blow-up photo of Libby in uniform in front of an army jeep served as a silent queen's guard in the lobby. Tacked to the picture's edge was a scrolled notice reminding friends and family to use this occasion to support the following charities:

The National Alliance of Vietnamese American Service Agencies

SHARE for breast and ovarian cancer patients and survivors

Jewish War Veterans of the United States

The Crohn's and Colitis Foundation of America and "In honor of Shadow who lost his mom, North Shore Animal League."

Two Hispanic women in black pants' suits and holding wicker baskets flanked the easel offering traditional Jewish head coverings. Jae Won placed a skull cap on his head as Wendy bobby-pinned her black lace circle into her hair. She was impressed with the speed in which Adam had arranged the event but soon realized that Libby had probably left detailed instructions long ago. The only flowers were a spray of red roses over her country's flag on top of the plain pine casket. All flower arrangements delivered that morning were dispatched, at the family's request, to the Sunset Nursing Home two doors down.

Most of the guests in the first room wept aloud throughout the service. So different from the inconsolable silence at Wendy's father's staid Protestant funeral where the only wailing came from the lone piper dressed in the Dale family tartan. In a voice worthy of a Broadway opening, Rabbi Jacob Blassman officiated. He introduced the eulogists with enthusiastic praise and reminded the mourners that a life is not only measured by how much we love but the love we earn from others. The sobbing would ebb for each eulogy and start again between speakers. Finally two female soldiers in white gloves gently lifted the rose spray and folded the flag into a triangle while the rabbi's resonant voice silenced the weeping with his closing comments.

"The armed services of our country are now filled with brave young men and women who have volunteered. This was not always so."

A soldier took the folded flag and handed it to the speaker. Wendy wondered why the protocol was changed till the rabbi continued.

"For a long time our nation used a lottery system called the draft. But one arm of our country's fighting forces was always an all volunteer unit. That is the chaplaincy. I'm an old man, older than our dear Libby who served in Vietnam. I served as a chaplain in Korea and it is because of this I have the honor to present this flag to the Spring family."

Rabbi Blassman stepped away from the podium and walked to Libby's husband and sons.

"On behalf of the President of the United States and a grateful nation, I present this flag to you."

Wendy drove Jay's Santa Fe back to his home. The dignity of the service and the somberness of the burial were usurped by the abundance and joviality of the late luncheon at the Spring's sprawling Long Island home. The afternoon was filled with Libby's relatives and friends embracing Wendy to remind her how much she was loved by her colleague and friend. Libby's Uncle Jack took an immediate liking to Jay and plied him to smile with shots of single malt scotch.

After pulling into his driveway, Wendy and Jae Won walked to her car across the street. As they stood under a dampening streetlamp, he admitted a fondness for all the exotic fare they consumed earlier. He especially liked the thin delicate pink slices of fish called lox.

"It's sold in any local supermarket. I'll bring some next time." She promised.

Sid Shyman, out walking his wire-haired pooch, was still in earshot when Jae Won asked Wendy to repeat the name of the toast they said before drinking.

"It means 'to life.' L'chaim." She held out her arm in a pretend toast. Jay tapped her fist with his. "L'chaim, to life!"

The old man stood still for a moment and then restarted his evening ritual. "See, Tattalah," he told his dog. "It's a different vorld."

⌘ ⌘ ⌘

Episode 11: Like The Main Character In Episode 100

Whenever the teenage Wendy Dale would write her stories of knights and maidens, her mother would yank her back to the twentieth century with the warning, "Take your head out of the clouds." Holding her steaming snowman coffee mug and standing at her breakfast room windows, she realized how profound a remark that really was. The clouds outside in their massive entourages of whites and grays were indistinguishable from those in spring. It was only when she looked at the bare trees below or stepped outside to be whipped by an icy winter belt that she was aware of her time and place. The reminders of her situation included the lies to her daughter about her day's activities, her plans with her cousin Diane to keep Lucille in Pennsylvania for another week in case Wendy was slow to heal from today's surgery and the easy out she gave Tim when he voiced his concern over too many absences. Mrs. Dunbar had already generously offered her chauffeuring services.

'God bless stay-at-home moms.' she murmured to the silk and flock poinsettia wreaths hung from each sash. At this moment, Wendy aspired to see only the clouds, she welcomed this morning for Jay's meeting with KimArt's president and CEO at the company's Manhattan suite on East 70th and Lexington Avenue.

Jae Won Hyun flipped open and then shut his cell phone three times that morning before driving to the parking lot on Prince Street in Flushing. He wanted to wish Wendy well just one more time but he knew she would worry about his interview right down to approving his wardrobe selection and he wanted her to concentrate on getting through her surgery, the last hurdle of her return to wellness. He navigated through the crowded narrow streets, first by car and then on foot till he stepped down on the same Flushing line stairs as Lucille Dale ascended the day Kennedy was shot. He was counted among the over five million strap-hangers glad he rarely had to join them on their foray to the city. Three train rides later, he was spilled out onto Lexington Avenue making his way uptown with the world's most exquisite and detailed holiday displays beckoning him from the stores at his right.

In a foyer more art gallery than entryway, Jae Won was asked his tea or juice preference. After sipping a strawberry-kiwi concoction he tried Wendy's breathing technique to prevent any unseemly fawning over his life-long idol's entrance. Oak and stained glass pocket doors opened to fanfare the arrival of a silk-robed Kim Dong Kook and a still sleepy eyed Nordic blonde beauty. Even if Jay hadn't seen the happy family photos in Wendy's little album, he would have been just as certain that the woman next to Mr. Kim was not his wife. In one gliding movement Jae Won placed his glass on an antique table, stood and bowed.

"You speak English, right?" The man twenty years his senior was moving towards Jay with his hand extended for a handshake. The artist extended his greeting Korean-style by grazing his right elbow with his left hand while bowing and shaking his childhood idol's hand. The art dealer shook hands long enough to be polite, asked Jae Won to be seated and patted the blonde woman's rear end instructing her to have coffee with someone named Juri. She reclosed her robe at her thighs more for her comfort than modesty as she exited with a stony smile that softened after Mr. Kim's additional comment, "We'll go shopping when I'm finished here."

Two young Korean women in business suits entered through a side door laden with portfolios and folders as well as a lap top. For the next ninety minutes, Kim Dong Kook was all business as he and the women explained how Jae Won would be showcased.

The coming true of dreams is heady stuff. When the details of gallery shows and television appearances became too much to take in, the artist took long suctioned sips of his juice for respite. Jae Won had enough business acumen to know he was being promoted. There'd be a website, talk show circuit, lectures and a documentary all to champion the latest rebirth of Korea's folk art with him leading the charge.

The nameless women packed their paraphernalia and left through the same doorway that brought them. Art mogul Kim snake-eyed their exit.

"So you're the man who got her to lay on her back! Of course, she's a few years older now. Maybe she's not so choosy any more or maybe you're not. Is her red hair real...you know *both* collar and cuffs?"

Jae Won's high had sunk into nausea. He was in New York but Korean manners prevented him from walking out. He was trapped with the sleazy Mr. Kim till the older man dismissed him.

"I only know Missus Dale professionally." He listened to his weak defense and felt his cheeks flush.

"You think I got to be where I am without being able to read people, Mr. Hyun? She's either giving you Western head or you're wishing it. I saw your fist tighten when I mentioned her. Don't get so testy. I could have had her. I just met her at a bad time...never could get her alone."

Jae Won fixed his gaze on the Aubusson rug under his satin slippers. Before he met Wendy, he was a master of concealing his feelings. Now he was ashamed at the speed in which his former technique returned.

"More importantly," Mr. Kim pontificated, "I don't think with my *cha-chi*. Your work is the finest I've seen in a lifetime of investing in winners. You should have come to me when you were still a young man back home. Your life would have been very different. We'll see you in three weeks in Itaewon. Come with the redhead or send her alone a few days earlier." Dong Kook laughed alone at his hollow joke, cleared his throat and called out.

"Suk-jin!"

A young man in the same navy business suit as the presenters walked Jae Won back to his shoes.

⌘ ⌘ ⌘

Dr. Sheinfeld was holding Wendy's hand as she blinked at his wavy post-surgery image.

"Hubby not here today?" It was more than polite conversation.

"He had to take off so often for our daughter and then my cancer. I gave him a reprieve."

Her answer seemed to be the right one as the doctor quickly went on to say the laparoscopic myomectomy went as planned, nothing seemed suspicious, he'd see her for a post-op in two weeks.

"Go home put your feet up, take Tylenol if you have cramping. You'll need to wear a pad for the next few days. Remember, no intercourse this week." He patted her hand one last time.

"Whatever happened with your side pain? Did the urologist help you?"

"He gave me a clean bill of health, besides the pain went away on its own."

A half hour later, Wendy treated Mrs. Dunbar to a thank you pancake breakfast at a local diner. The woman tried to protest but Wendy hated to feel beholden. During their drive home, Wendy called Tim assuring him all was well and asking if he'd like turkey tetrazzini for dinner. She hadn't noticed the tsking sounds made by her driver at her closing question.

After letting Fido out and back in, Ms. Dale opted to forego resting for a nearly scalding shower. There under the adjustable head turned to pulsate, she covered her body in Insolence Body Wash to scrub all hospital remnants away. Wendy waited for her skin to lose its heated blush before dressing in her favorite cashmere trapeze neck sweater and gray wool trousers. She wondered if Jay would be home by lunchtime and entertained herself by imagining his immanent international success.

"Fisherman," the princess began, "You win the king's prize for best 1000 gifts."

The fisherman and his daughter high-fived each other and pumped their knees in a joyous end-zone dance till they noticed the startled expressions worn by the royal family. The embarrassed winners of the King's prize respectfully bowed their heads in thanks.

Since this was her birthday present, the princess was allowed to make a proclamation. "As of this day, The Fisherman and his daughter, Jane will live tax-free in the kingdom, wear expensive clothes and..." The princess had never proclaimed anything before. It was harder than she thought. "Eat all the treats they want, sleep in really comfy beds and get some cool royal parting gifts as well."

Soon she'd be done with her little kingdom and characters. What subject would she choose next? Her daughter's room offered no inspiration. The rock band posters and bold colors forecasting Jane's countdown to teenage weren't whimsical enough for a Wendy Dale story. She opened the desk's side drawer, the one Jane begrudgingly deemed, 'mom's'. The Sleeping Wendy portrait lay waiting for her daily perusal.

'I guess I talk so much, he chose the one time I was quiet to paint me. If Libby was here she'd say I have been asleep for so long that maybe Jay thought he could awaken me or something brilliant like that.'

Wendy was startled by the jingling sounds of a key ring just outside her kitchen door. She rested her portrait on the computer's mouse pad and dashed towards the side entrance. Fido was already wagging his whip-like tail at his neighbor-friend who walked him on weekdays.

"Oh, Lou, I'm sorry. I forgot to tell you I'd be home today."

⌘ ⌘ ⌘

Mr. O'Hanlon stood outside his classroom door as his three special education students were escorted by a safety officer to the school psychologist's office for their weekly counseling. The big man was about make a toilet stop when Joe Michaels his colleague across the hall greeted him.

"I thought your wife was having surgery today. I didn't expect to see you. Wha'd they cancel it?"

"Nah, the wife told me it's a simple procedure. They used to do them in the doctor's office years ago. No big deal." One of her friends took her. She's home already, cooking up leftover turkey."

Tim hoped this wasn't going to be a long conversation. He had already promised his bladder that relief was a few steps away.

"You are a lucky Mick, O'Hanlon. My wife doesn't go to the dentist without me in tow. Must be that Kraut DNA that makes her so tough."

"Yeah."

At the men's room urinal, Tim used his time to think.

'Why did I let her go by herself? Ah, Red, I screwed up. I'll make it up to you.'

Tim O'Hanlon rinsed his hands and walked down the corridor to his principal's office where he concocted a story of his wife's post-op bleeding as an explanation invoking his contractual three and a third hours leave for emergencies. In less than an hour, the SIE 7 teacher approached his parked Toyota. He'd make a very quick stop at the Jew's Harp for fortification and then surprise Wendy.

Hyun Jae Won walked downtown on Lexington Avenue for several blocks before his fists unclenched. It was only then he realized he had passed his 68th street subway station. The avenue was as crowded as when he arrived but the short term goals of the people rushing past him had changed from getting to work on time to scooping up Christmas bargains. His anger had dissipated only enough for him to sort out whom he blamed the most for trampling his teenage dreams. The puffy-eyed Kim Dong Kook's vile allusions to Wendy sickened him. Jay couldn't end the image of his swollen hand patting the blonde woman's bottom. The image became a day terror as the blonde morphed into a red head forcing Jay to squeeze his eyes shut only to be startled into opening them when an annoyed mink-swathed diva's ratty dog barked at the artist for nearing his mistress. Even as he followed the city's masses into a child's Christmas heaven at Bloomingdale's flagship store on 59th, his thoughts would not turn to good will to all men.

He had intended to congratulate her on getting through her surgery but when she answered her cell, he raised his voice. Luckily he was in the frenzied fragrance section of the store where no one noticed another noisy cell user.

"Did you forget to tell me something?" It was his first stab at American sarcasm.

"What? That Mr. Kim's a creep."

It un-nerved him that she was prepared for his harangue.

"I could never work for a man like that. How could you think I would?"

He was a grown man who sounded like one of Wendy's sixth graders. At least once a school year, a student would whine to Ms. Dale about a hated teacher as an excuse for not succeeding in a particular subject. Wendy offered little solace when instructing the child to tolerate the ogre or sacrifice his own future. She'd point her finger and say, "I'd never let that old bat bring my grades down, but if you want to…."

It was with that tone, she answered him.

"Jay, listen to me. Every woman and I mean every single one of us has been a victim of sexual harassment. Sometimes it's only a co-worker or friend who makes slimy suggestive remarks; sometimes it's a hand where it shouldn't be. Sadly sometimes it's worse. If I told you what kind of man he was, you might not have met with him but if you'd rather spend your days ringing up drop cloth purchases…."

Bird and Fish

The static and crackling of their cells phones couldn't mask the unmistakable sounds easily discerned by the daughter of the 1000 voice man.

"Where are you now? Are you in Bloomingdale's?"

"Shiro!"

"He liked your work didn't he?" she cooed.

Unfortunately unlike Mr. Kim, Jae Won was thinking with his *cha chi* as he rounded the Prada Tendre display.

"He never touched you, did he?"

"Fishman, you know me. If he had touched me, I'd still be in *Yeosu* Detention Center for assault on a national icon. When will you be home?"

"In an hour."

"Call me when you get to Flushing. I'll meet you at your house. You can tell me about your meeting."

His voice took on a youthful shyness. "There're too many pink ones. What's the name of your perfume?"

"Look for the counter that says Guerlain. G-u-e-r-l-a-i-n then ask for Insolence."

⌘ ⌘ ⌘

Tim O'Hanlon fingers wrapped around a filled rocks glass as he sat with his shoulders hunched staring at the black TV screen. Just moments ago he pulled out all Wendy's bureau drawers and checked her chock-a-block closet for indications she had deserted him. Had it not been for the Glenlivet they saved for special occasions, his hands would still be shaking. The big Irishman had come home to what he believed would be a hero's welcome, only to find a silent empty house with just Jane's blue-lit computer screen to greet him. It was a casual movement, nothing that required thought. He entered his step-daughter's bedroom to turn the damn thing off. How could soulless squares of techno-plastic components harbinger the devastating blow he was about to receive? The postcard sized painting of his sleeping wife lay displayed on Jane's mouse pad, soaking up blue-screen light and forcing him to recognize the wisdom of his recent apprehension.

'Why should I be surprised? For years she's been glued to those Korean soaps. She's even told me the guys were cute. Oh God, did she meet him in Korea? It was so crazy after she got back with Janie getting sick…maybe she told the guy to wait for her. Maybe he got impatient and came here to take her back.'

He downed the first glass and poured another. Fido's dog senses led him to safer ground on his master's bed upstairs.

'It's the paint guy, the one giving her packets of twenties. She's been singing in our kitchen for no reason. Is she dancing on his bed for money? What does that make her? What the fuck does that make me, their *bull-calf pimp*?'

The third double shot, as any bartender will verify, turned the anger to guilt.

'I let her shoulder all our burdens. It's just that she was so good at that kind of stuff. Red, I should have helped out more, should have gone with you to the hospital. Jeez, I never bought you flowers.'

He submerged an ice cube with his finger then licked off the fine scotch drippings.

'Pretty, pretty wife, never bought you flowers…'

The gold labeled bottle fell to its side as Tim lifted himself from his chair. The big man's frame assured him he was at least capable of fighting for her. He had the Korean's guy's address and after years of TV images of his wife's favorite actors, he knew he was easily the size of two or three of them. But first he had to straighten up the bedroom in case Janie came home early from practice.

⌘ ⌘ ⌘

Hyun Jae Won had a wife for several Christmases and anniversaries yet he couldn't recall enjoying gift buying before. He pulled into the empty driveway then exited his Santa Fe tenderly looping his hand through the handles of the miniature Bloomingdale's shopping bag before giving his usual once over glance to his property. A single sheet of Newsday had gotten caught under the lone snowman decoration at the steps of Yujin's front door. He scooped up the offending litter and walked to the backyard's trash can shelter. He turned back in time to view Wendy's slower than usual pace as she made her way up his walkway. He chided himself for fearing her abandoning him when here she was, just hours after leaving the hospital, ready to scold him till he bettered his life. He hid his purchase inside his coat and picked up his pace to be at her side.

"You're so pale." Jae led her to his couch. "Sit here, I'll go upstairs to Yoon Yoo's and get some soup. It will give you energy."

Wendy whined like a child.

"No soup. Don't you have any candy? Dark chocolate will give me energy."

The couple looked at each other as if a cartoon balloon above them showed each thinking the other's opinion absurd.

"Just sit beside me." She patted the leather cushion. "Tell me what he said."

The artist sat as commanded with the addition of leaning down and pulling her legs by her ankles till her calves rested on his lap.

"I'll massage you. Don't worry," he tugged on her gray wool cuffs. "You can keep these on."

"What if the girls come home early?" She was a teacher. She knew that was unlikely.

"This is not just for lovers. At home, family members massage one another. We could be brother and sister." His palms covered her shin bones as his fingertips pressed deep into the backs of her legs then released slowly easing not only those muscles but the tension in her recently offended uterus as well.

"Just look at the resemblance! We could be twins." She laughed.

"Would you prefer resting in my room? When you were in Korea, did you sleep on a floor mat?"

"You don't sleep on a mat. You have a bed." She flinched as soon as the words left her tongue. She'd have to admit she, not his cousins took his precious art work from that room.

Jae Won was tickled by her first show of innocence. Had she really not figured it out?

"How do you know what I sleep on?" he teased.

"I walked past your bedroom on my way to the bathroom one day." She lied, "I peeked."

"*Moh?* Oh, that's why I know everything about you too." He enjoyed his closed mouth grin.

"What do you mean?"

"When you went to the bathroom, I peeked!"

The peals of laughter that ensued nearly filled the apartment. When Wendy held back her last chuckle to say, "You really are a funny Fishman." he answered, "I know, I'm a regular…Ivan the Terrible." bringing on even more waves of wind chime giggles.

For her entertainment, he described the KimArt sitting room's furnishings, elaborating on the oriental and European rugs and lamps. He told of the young interns and their portfolios. He shared selections of his conversation with Kim Dong Kook before presenting his foreigner's take on the vivacity and sparkle of New York's avenues at Christmas time. Wendy's Oohs and Aahs quieted into hmm's as the effects of her post-surgery wind-down tired her. Jae Won's cell rang as he rose to retrieve a blanket from his bed.

Yujin Kim ran his hand over his bristle-topped head. Clearly this would take getting used to. Malik had re-entered the store after loading the J&D Decorators' van with the owner's purchases.

"I'll be off then, Mr. Kim," the new manager in training called to Yujin, "unless you need me for something else."

Bird and Fish

"Aren't you and your girlfriend picking out wedding invitations today?"

"Yeah but, if you need me…"

"If you stay here long enough, my wife'll stop by and then you'll have to take her with you. You know how women like that stuff."

"I hear ya, Mr. Kim. See you tomorrow."

The door opened tentatively. It happens occasionally. Customers change their minds, realize they left their measurements in their cars or homes, neither man took notice till it opened wider bringing a chilled December bluster and the distinctive reek of alcohol. The blonde man filled the entryway. Yujin debated whether to ask Malik to stay but feared Wendy's wrath if her former student was harmed again. So when Malik raised his neatly trimmed black eyebrows to signal a willingness to assist should the huge man cause trouble, Yujin sent him off with a hand wave.

The man was clean and dressed casually well in a navy golf shirt and khakis. Only the steady staring of those ice-blue eyes and scowl on his face unnerved the Anycolor owner.

"Can I help you, sir?" Yujin thickened his Korean accent in case he had to beg ignorance of any real or imagined problems.

"You the owner?" The man's mountainous frame had Yujin wondering how much liquor it would take to get someone that size drunk.

"Just manager. You need help?"

"Does a white lady work here? With red hair?" Tim took Jae's portrait from his pocket. "This lady?"

For all his philandering, Yujin didn't have a poker face. That was probably why Yoon Yoo caught on so early in their marriage and why Tim O'Hanlon knew he was in the right place.

"I only work here sometimes. The owner's not here."

"The big Irishman raised his voice. "Call him. Tell him to come to the store." A meaty hand flopped down on the counter. Yujin thought it was a show of the man's rage but Tim squeezed the Formica edging to hold down his bile. He sincerely regretted this confrontation and hoped his next move wouldn't include vomiting on the cash register.

Jae Won's cousin was eager to call him. He wanted to make sure Wendy and *Kunapogee* stayed far away till what surely must be her husband slept off his rage.

"*Yuh bho seh yo.*" Yujin was betting the big man couldn't speak Korean.

"Wheh?" Jae Won stood still holding his folded blanket listening to his cousin speaking a kind of English gibberish. "Oh-I just get voice-e mail. I leeb-a messagee." Followed by the finest Korean Yujin had ever spoken.

"*Hyung, Sun seng nim's* husband is here looking for you. Is she with you now?"

"Neh." Jae sat on the edge of his bed. Magical thoughts of carrying her to the Taebaek mountains where they could grow old together to Hollywood screenplays of Americans with guns swept through his brain.

"Send her home and stay at the house. I can take care of this. *Ah rhuh suh?*"

Hyun Jae Won sent Wendy off with a tale of assisting Yujin with a broken toilet at Anycolor II, took an eight inch metal pipe from his car's trunk and tossed it onto the passenger seat. Whatever the amount of testosterone that pumped through his veins during his race to Northern and Broward, it had all evaporated by the time he walked empty-handed through the backroom and into the store. Both Yujin and Tim turned towards him in a kind of fat and skinny ballet, but Wendy's men eyed only each other. Yujin pitied both of them knowing they shared the same thought, 'It's already too late. I've lost her.'

"Did you paint this?" The Dreaming Wendy on the deckle edged moleskin trembled in the big man's hand.

Jae nodded his head for Tim to follow him to the back storeroom leaving Yujin in charge of the young Korean mother and baby who just come through the front door.

Jae Won had already sold his soul for a career this morning. Lying now would be prudent as well. He rationalized his deception easily; the blonde man could go into a rage and kill everyone, even the infant in the store. Such things happen in America. Or worse, he could go home to hurt Wendy and that was something he couldn't let happen.

"Yes. Of course, that's our tutor."

"She tutors you?" Tim was grateful the bang softened to a whimper.

"Missus Dale tutors our whole family."

"Why are her eyes closed?"

"I made a joke and said I only paint Asian faces and couldn't paint green eyes. She took the painting for payment. That's not OK?" An hour ago Jae Won was planning to ask Wendy to return to Korea with him. Now his choice of words made him ashamed to see her again.

Tim's runny eyes took in all of the Asian man before him. 'Is this guy her type? I always thought I was. What the hell did her first husband look like? Oh, Jeez, now I remember he didn't look like either one of us.'

Yujin held the door for the exiting mother and child happy to hear the door to the parking lot quietly opening as well. He headed towards the storeroom.

Tim was eager to accept the explanations the Korean man fed him but 2600 years of Celtic tenacity stuck in his craw. With one foot already on the parking lot's asphalt, Tim O'Hanlon turned to his dueling partner.

"You ever have sex with her?"

"No." He had finally told him the truth.

Yujin stood at the doorway that connected the storage room and store watching the big man leave. Not once in all the years of sharing other men's wives had their husbands ever confronted him. Maybe what he offered wasn't worth the fight.

"Not one word!" Jae's anger at himself was re-directed to his newly shorn cousin.

"I was only going to suggest you call Wendy to get your stories straight."

"It doesn't matter what she tells him. She'll repeat the last thing I said. That's all he'll care about."

Fido showed no interest in going out to the yard when Wendy arrived home leaving her ample time to wash up and prepare dinner. She covered the tiny counter space with button mushrooms and grated Swiss as well as nine other ingredients. The recipe called for vermouth but she felt too tired for the trip to the den's bar. An additional quarter cup of chicken stock would be an acceptable stand-in. She placed a large stainless steel pot of salted water on the stove and opened the cabinet where noodles and pastas were stored. Stocked full with macaroni, rotelle and angel hair pasta the cabinet offered no wide noodles for her dish. Instead she found the Homemaker's vanilla extract kit hidden between two boxes of Ronzoni. The soju sized bottle held three dried vanilla beans and an instruction pamphlet promising to turn two cupsful of vodka into the finest Madagascar vanilla infusion.

'I wondered where this got to. Aw, it needs four weeks to steep before it's ready. It'll never be ready for Christmas. But if I make it today, I can use it for Valentine's Day sugar cookies. I wonder if Jay eats cookies, probably fish and seaweed flavored ones.' She joked to herself.

Now two recipes required a trip to the house liquor supply. Wendy gave into fate, wiped her hands on a paper towel and headed for the bar. The Glenlivet still on the floor stayed un-noticed but the unmistakable 'barroom in the morning' odor soured the air. The last ingenuous thought she had before opening the bar's cabinet door was that a bottle had probably spilled out during the Thanksgiving clean-up.

Bird and Fish

There was no spillage in the cabinet. The only bottle on its side was an empty airline sized taster of Sauza Blanco Tequila. Nearby was a drained liter of Stolichnaya, a bare jug of Zhenka she used for punches and cooking as well as two empty Grey Goose bottles all waiting to rat out their master. Wendy went from a crouch to a full sitting position on the carpet. One by one she removed bottles from the teak and ebony cupboard and circled them around her. The Dewar's White Label held only a half cup, the pretty blue Bombay Sapphire was two thirds spent, the missing Glenlivet showed up as Wendy shook her head in disbelief. Her eyes locked in on the near-empty bottle at the side of Tim's lounger.

Last week, just three minutes before the loudspeakers would broadcast Chopin to begin the schoolday, a fight broke out in the seventh grade yard. Two Asian boys rolled as one while flailing their arms and fists hoping for direct hits. Wendy ran to them despite her fashion choice of three inch chocolate suede boots that morning.

"Boys!" she shouted pulling the top boy to his feet first. "Get up, now!"

The twelve year olds, one with a bleeding lip the other rubbing a crooked scratch under his right eye immediately began blaming the other. The teacher forced herself to feign interest since pubescent explanations for violence rarely held any validity.

"OK. OK, I got it. You did this and he did that. You each have a battle scar, so shake and stay away from each other in the future. You're *same-same.*"

That's how she felt sitting amid the heralders of Tim's fall from his wagon. Her hurt and anger shook hands with her guilt for burdening a good man with a sick family and her shame for passionately loving another man even if only in her heart. 'Times got rough. You did this and I did that. Now we're *same-same.*'

Wendy took a black trash bag from the basement laundry room shelf filling it with every opened bottle in the bar.

'But I'm still going to chew you out like a red-neck drill sergeant for going back on the sauce.'

She raced to clean up quickly since her mushrooms were still waiting to be sliced and sautéed upstairs but when she heard Fido's 'family-member at door' whimpers, she called Tim to meet her in the den.

Wendy's husband stood silent as she ranted about setting a good example for Jane, maintaining his good health and making good on his promise. When she seemed to tire of her own voice, he took the portrait from his pocket and held it between them.

"Tell me, Red what's the 'good' of this?"

Bird and Fish

If he was waiting for a tearful admission, he was watching the wrong drama. Years of Lucille's mothering techniques taught Wendy to keep authentic feelings to herself in times of danger. It was her personal version of fight or flight. Telling the truth would crush Tim and eventually devastate Jane.

"It's from the people I tutor. Are you going to use that as your defense?" She jutted out her chin defiantly.

"But Jane said the new painting in the breakfast room was from an art teacher in your school. I'm an educated man, Red. I can tell it's the same artist. Are you going to tell me the paint store guy is also a teacher?"

Clearly Tim had time to review, time Wendy lacked right now. Good thing she taught improv.

"Keep Janie out of you machinations. I don't know why she thinks the artist is a teacher. What's your point?"

"Why are your eyes closed? Did he paint you sleeping?" Tim's voice was developing an adolescent squeek that annoyed rather than softened her.

"No. I don't know why her eyes are closed. Ask the artist."

"I did."

Wendy felt the carpeted floor turn to vapor that couldn't hold her, dropping her like a torpedo straight to the waiting jaws of Hell. But her mouth kept speaking as her ombudsman.

"Then Mr. Hyun must have told you."

"You don't think I was at the store, Red? You doubt I was talking to both the 'Euns'; the one with the pony tail and his baby brother with the crew cut?"

Wendy patted Fido's head to erase the vision of the three men together at Anycolor Paints.

"You do realize I had surgery today. I'm tired and more importantly, you've been drinking. We'll talk about this later." She handed the bloated trash bag to her husband.

"They're your bottles. Throw them out."

Tim took the bag without letting go of his anger.

"Did you have sex with him?"

"No."

"That's what he said too."

When Jane arrived home after Chorus practice, she found her mom pulling a bubbling creamy casserole from the oven and her step dad feeding just-baked garlic knots to their dog. It was an idyllic scene of comfort and joy till Jane's proclamation. "Hey you guys, our house looks so dark. You forgot to turn on the Christmas lights."

⌘ ⌘ ⌘

Jane called her mother away from her drama.

"You left the computer on your story."

"I'm sorry. Did you make sure to save it?" The day's cocktail of hospitalized surgery and the cutting open of her marriage gave Wendy's speech pattern a kind of android cadence.

"Mom, I taught you how to save stuff, remember?" Wendy hadn't the strength to scold her daughter's insolence.

"Anyway, I read it. It's a little babyish, but I liked it. Jane's kinda boring but the princess is funny and the illustrations are really cool"

"I guess I geared it for the under-ten audience. My father taught me to imitate voices when I was younger than you."

Mother and daughter sat side by side on the twin bed. Wendy ran her hand through Jane's hair and smiled at her real-life masterpiece.

"How are you going to end it?" Jane asked. "Will the fisherman and his daughter live happily ever after in the palace?"

"I'm not sure. The fisherman has a responsibility to fish and his daughter should stay to help him. I suppose they'll turn down the princess."

Fido yawned and got off the big bed to follow the voices into Jane's room.

Jane slapped her thigh to command the sleepy hound into her bed as well. He obliged and was soon asleep resting at the backs of his pack-mates.

"I don't like that ending. Shouldn't they like break-out and I don't know… go on stage with their talent. That's what you keep saying I should do."

"Hey, you're the one who thinks change is bad. I was going to end the story the way I thought you'd like it."

Mom, you're a teacher. You know kids change their minds all the time. What if when I was really sick last year, I couldn't change? Then I'd be sick forever."

"How'd you get so smart?"

"I don't know. Maybe I have a brilliant mother."

⌘ ⌘ ⌘

Bird and Fish

The king-sized bed gave them room to lie without touching.

"I'd like to put poinsettias on Uncle Timothy's grave this weekend. Come with me. I promise I'll get on my knees and swear I'll never drink again. That's something you wouldn't want to miss, Red."

The joke lay flat between them.

"I'd like to visit Libby. She doesn't have a stone yet. I think I'll take off Friday, drive up to her cemetery and then sleep at my mother's."

"It's dead up there this time of year. Take Fido."

"With the geese, burglar alarm and my dad's shotgun, I'll be fine. I'll call the sheriff and my mother's neighbors to say I'm coming. So you can keep Fido, the house and Jane for two days. I just want peace and time to think."

Tim took his hand from its resting place over his navel and timidly patted her hand at her side. He had the Irish gift of blarney. He could be the center of attention at a cocktail party or the world's funniest step-dad but heartfelt words were beyond his reach.

"We'll both have to make some changes." he attempted reconciliation.

"Not me." Wendy rebuffed. I'm already changed. I've got hot flashes, a new scar, a blue tattoo and yesterday I noticed the left cup on my bra doesn't fit the same. It's getting looser. I've made all the changes I've had too. Any future changes will be put on hold for awhile."

Just a year ago, Tim was her team mate, the man who refused to let his family sink in the drowning pool of Jane's disease. How could she possibly have changed idols as fast as her Korean students changed drama star favorites. Wendy closed her eyes forbidding her dreams to star a pony-tailed fish-man.

⌘ ⌘ ⌘

The teacher sat at her desk adjusting the sleeves on her red cashmere sweater, awaiting her first meeting with her replacement. The young woman sent a copy of a Plays for Teens workbook she intended to use as her text for Wendy to peruse.

Wendy was so appalled, she griped out loud.

"To introduce my children to William Shakespeare only to have them end the year with this crap. I should be ashamed."

"What you got to be ashamed of?" Claire Jackson had entered through the back door to sneak a quick respite on a student chair.

Bird and Fish

"The crap my replacement is going to teach when I'm gone."

"Ms. Dale, you think your kids won't survive without you? Presidents been shot and we still a country. Popes die every few years, we still got plenty of Catholics. Them kids'll be fine. I just came from my rounds up on the third floor. Everytime I go by Mrs. Spring's room it just breaks my heart but them kids…they was all doing their work with the new teacher. You can't keep mop'n around cause you just lost your best friend."

"I lost three of my best friends, Claire."

The classroom phone rang. Wendy and Claire assumed it was to announce the new drama teacher's entrance.

"I'll let you have your meeting. See y'all lunchtime."

"Claire, I'm taking Friday off. I'm going to pay my respects to Libby and spend the night at my mom's."

"Ain't your mom with your cousin?"

"Exactly, that's why I'm going there. I've got to clear my head."

"Wendy, I'm so proud of you. Last couple of years you been too afraid to leave your child. Better get that phone before them heifers in that office get mad cow!" Claire's laughter followed her to the stairway exit.

"Ms. Dale's room."

"Ms. Dale, Mr. Spring is on the phone. Will you take it?" The secretary barely hid her annoyance over the number of rings it took the teacher to answer. Her curtness was lost on Wendy who thought she said, 'Mrs. Spring' and was ready to dismiss the recent past as a wormhole in time.

"Mrs. Spring?"

"Mr! Are you going to take this call?"

There was a double click and then the quiet voice of Libby's second love. After thanking her for packing and sending Libby's personal belongings from school, Adam Spring delivered the message he called for.

"Wendy, you're going to get a letter from our family lawyer but I wanted to tell you first hand. Libby left you an annuity. For the next five years, you'll receive $20,000 per year from her estate. There's a letter explaining why."

"I don't want any money, Adam. Keep it for you and your sons."

"I knew about this since she changed her will last month. Wendy, I'm not trying to be smug but we don't need this money and Libby wanted you to have it. The letter was added right after Thanksgiving. Maybe she had a premonition. I have the copy of the letter if you want to hear it now?"

Wendy tightened her lips together. She wasn't sure she could handle Libby's message from beyond the grave but at this moment she couldn't refuse the grieving widower anything.

"Yes, Adam. Thanks."

"My darling friend, if you're still teaching, you're the only red-head on staff now but this is to make sure you keep your word and bring the count to zero. I always believed you were supposed to be a writer. For the next five years I'm putting my money where my mouth is or should I say was."

Adam Spring stopped reading. When he began again, his voice had changed to a higher pitch as if he was being choked.

"It's not much but it will float you till you're published. If that takes less than five years, give the rest to charity. If it takes longer, you're not the girl I thought you were. There are no criteria for what you write even though I'd appreciate a novel about lovers from two different worlds. Don't pine for me Wen, I'm probably busy getting alterations on my wings as you read this."

The drama department's newest staff member entered the room twenty minutes after her appointment time.

"Ms. Dale, I'm Lindsy Kauntz. I'm replacing you."

'Hardly.'

"Come in. I'll go over as much as I can before lunch duty. Don't worry, you won't be taking that position, Mr. Shutter, the senior drama teacher requested it. Would you like to meet some of your seventh graders?"

Wendy looked at the twenty three year old with a discerning eye. In a school half filled with teenage boys, the jeans and low-cut black leotard top could make the pretty new teacher an instant star. If she didn't back it up with good classroom management skills, the students would bully and embarrass her for entertainment.

"I don't have time today. I'll meet them when I teach. I pretty much know what to do."

Wendy smiled benevolently. She was painfully aware of their age difference. Twenty years ago, before Wendy's first teaching assignment, she shadowed the outgoing teacher's every move. She cleaned out filthy cabinets and scrubbed marked desks while impressing her first supervisor with sensible wool suits and irreverent high heels.

"I'm sure you'll be wonderful. I have to meet with a student anyway. It'll get too mushy if I say goodbye to all of them, so I picked just one."

"He must be your favorite."

Bird and Fish

⌘ ⌘ ⌘

The entire drama room stank of body odor and drugstore cologne. Anthony Perez slumped in a chair one leg out the other bent at his bulbous knee cap. He folded his arms around his middle in preparation to close off any authorities' accusations.

"You and I, An'tny, we're not exactly a dream match are we?"

"Huh"

The teacher already regretted this last ditch attempt to turn the boy around.

"Who's the kid I think about most at school?"

"I don't know."

"You. I think you're smart and show strong leadership skills. That's why I worry about you."

Ms. Dale, I don't know what you heard but I ain't done nothin since, you know, that time in the store." The massive legs switched positions.

"I know."

'His family took fourteen years to produce this semi-literate violent young man sitting in front of me. A three minute speech would waste both my time and his but still...'

"I'm not going to be a teacher anymore. I've decided to become a writer. No one else knows and I'm trusting you to keep it that way." She handed him a post-it with her home phone number and e-mail address.

"This is if you need anything, just school related advice, I'm not a life coach."

The boy put the folded paper in the wallet chained to his belt loop.

"Ms. Dale, I wasn't foolin when I said I ain't been in trouble since then. Not just cause of you. That black guy met me outside school one day."

"Malik?"

"Yeah, but he made me call him Mr. Thorne. He told me you all be watchin me."

⌘ ⌘ ⌘

Like a heavenly wash day, the clouds shook out a dusting of snow that morning. In other places the quiet white crystals gather to blanket hillsides and country lanes. In Queens, the snow squalls powder the oily tarred streets wreaking havoc during the morning rush hour. Jae Won looked out his kitchen window comparing the pristine flakes before him to the sterile furnishings at his back.

Uri and their glass home had been unceremoniously relocated to Seromie's bedroom along with a pink packaged gift set. Jae's kitchen had returned to its original stark whiteness.

By Friday, Yoon Yoo's information demands on her husband were fever-pitched. "Find out what's going on." was her direct order. With a final sigh at the top of the stairs, he mustered his resolve and visited *Kunapogee*.

"You know what I would do?" Yujin decided on a lighthearted opening.

"Neh. And that's why I didn't ask for your advice"

The artist was hoping his cousin would abandon his snooping and allow him to return to his former colorless life in peace.

"At least hear me out. I was the one who brought you here. I talked you into pursuing money over art. I'm not apologizing. It was a good idea at the time. But no matter what you think of me. I know more about women than you. She's waiting for you, *Hyung*. She's as embarrassed as you are. Don't look at me like I'm crazy. You think when that yellow haired giant went home, she fell into his arms?"

Jae Won dismissed his cousin's opinion and envisioned sending him back upstairs but in the short time since Wendy entered his life he'd come to enjoy sharing its details. Kim Yu Jin was his reprobate cousin but at least he was willing to listen. Jae was eager to share his feelings again.

"She never spoke ill of him, so I didn't, not for a minute, thought I was rescuing her from an evil husband. I drove past her house last night. The evergreen near the front door sparkled with hundreds of tiny lights. There's a huge red-lit wreath in the center window and smaller copies on the others. There are red bows on the fence posts and three wire deer wrapped in white lights. She's decorated her home and her home is here. I'm not saying she didn't love me. I know how she feels because it mirrors my heart. But karma is karma.

Yujin walked to the connecting stairway. "You've been in the States three years. Start thinking like a Yankee, 'Me want woman. Me take her.' Unless you're scared she *didn't mirror* your feelings."

"Was that your mantra when you chased all those women? Is that your advice?"

"*Ah nee*, When I saw what you and Wendy had, I knew the only place I could find that kind of love was with Yoon Yoo." The younger man patted the top of his half-inch hair strands.

"So I took her Sioux style by giving her my scalp."

⌘ ⌘ ⌘

Claire Jackson ignored the static sputtering on her walkie-talkie as she left the senior grades' lunch room. This day had been trouble right from the beginning. The

Bird and Fish

dean failed to quash a fist fight during early morning line-up then the coverage teacher forgot she was filling in for Ms. Dale's lunch duties. In an effort to help, Ms. Jackson's regional supervisor sent a rookie security agent from a nearby elementary school. One look at the size and attitude of Einstein's teenagers had the young man begging for desk duty. Now he was calling her to the lobby. 'That boy's just hopeless.' she moaned. Her plan was to cop a squat with Big Mary even if it meant breathing in all that tar and nicotine. The static crackled again. This time she managed to hear, "Man…looking for Mrs. Dale….Absent?" Claire's agile limbs took the Exit B steps two at a time racing to intercede the visitor.

Except for the rookie returning to his Daily News Jumble, the lobby was empty. Claire bolted through the heavy glass doors to the frigid breezeway.

"Sir" she called to the slender man with the pony-tail. Jae Won turned and smiled at the woman in uniform.

'Them lips must be som'thin.' "You're Ms. Dale's friend, right?"

The man made no move to answer.

"It's all right, I'm her friend too."

Jae flashed back to several tales from school that included a guard named Claire.

"*Yeh.*"

She took the day off. She went to Mrs. Spring's grave and then to her mother's house upstate. You know where that is?"

"No, no that's all right. I'll come back."

Claire Jackson took one more admiring look at those full sandstone lips. 'Someday somebody like this may come look'n for me and I hope he gets help find'n me.'

"There's nobody at the house. Ms. Dale goes alone sometimes. Nobody bothers her there. I can get the directions if you want to wait?"

"No. Thank you so much. I'll come back another time."

⌘ ⌘ ⌘

It was safe for Wendy to roll her eyes at her mother's whining. Lucille was two hundred miles west of Floral Oaks still safe at Diane's.

"Since you're going, pick up groceries like macaroni, canned tomatoes. Buy some apples. They'll keep. Don't forget bread, just the dough in the tube. If we don't come next week, that won't go bad." Wendy sprinkled the conversation with 'yeses' and 'sures' till Diane plucked the phone from her aunt's hand.

Bird and Fish

"Wen, we can pick that stuff up ourselves. We'll probably go Wednesday, so she can pack a few things to bring at Christmas."

Wendy was Diane's precious baby cousin since Lucille let her hold the new arrival forty three years ago. After her mother's death, Diane thought of her as a sister who up until Jane's illness, could be counted on to take the three and a half hour drive to York for any request at any time. Serving as her aunt's guardian was small payment for all Wendy's kindnesses but today there was more. The younger woman sounded uneasy. Diane immediately worried it was another medical crises.

"Wen, something you need to discuss?" She feared asking more with Lucille just steps away. Wendy exhaled for three full minutes to unfold the soap opera story that had become her life. Luckily by the time she needed to take in air, Lucille's Laxis kicked in as well forcing the cranky pensioner to head for the bathroom.

"First, throw the drunk out. That's what I did. It was good for me, good for the girls, even the cat was happier. Then, well, you gotta sleep with *him*. It could be a disaster. What if he likes things we don't even do in this country?" Promise to tell me everything. I've only been with American men, you know, I've never seen one that still had its headdress."

'No wonder I miss Libby so much.'

Haven, New York was incorporated in 1837 and soon became a thriving village all thanks to the Lois Sewing and Needlecrafts Company. Less than twenty years later, immigrants fresh from Ellis Island made their way north to start lives as soldiers for America's second Industrial Revolution. Haven boasted a higher standard of living than its neighboring communities and became a bastion for religious tolerance as Italian Catholics, German Lutherans and Eastern European Jews worked and raised well-fed families in their little corner of America. A hundred years later Haven was a near ghost town, its downfall traced to Black Tuesday 1929 and a Lois heir who preferred wine and women to heirloom crochet patterns. Its heyday reminders were in walking distance from each other, Saint Dominic of the Holy Rosary, Zion Lutheran and Star of David cemeteries.

Wendy decided to luxuriate in her hooky-from-school day. She and Fido made steam clouds as they ran and panted in the backyard. The biting December cold re-awakened her appetite till she succumbed by downing teaspoons of peanut butter and her home-made raspberry preserves out of the jars. She had just poured her second cup of high octane black coffee when she allowed herself the memories of choking down sweetened, Cremora laden instant Maxim in Korea. She wanted no images of that country or its countrymen till she reached Libby's new digs in Haven. It was well into the afternoon before she stopped working on her illustrations for the newly titled, The Fisherman's One Thousand Voices. She rushed to Waldbaum's Supermarket as her mother had instructed deciding to treat herself with a home cooked favorite meal this evening as well.

On the day of Libby's funeral, Jay drove from the chapel to Star of David and back to the Spring's home. Wendy had to admit she left the details in his hands. Today, after two wrong turns on Westchester Avenue she finally pulled up to the massive wrought iron front gates gently swinging closed by a white-haired man in a worn black suit and skull cap.

"Excuse me, sir" Wendy left the Sentra running as she dashed from the car. "Are you closing? "I just wanted to pay my respects. I won't be that long."

The gentleman smiled at Wendy and turned the key into the lock simultaneously.

"Missus, any other day, I vould vait for you, but its Friday. Ve all go home by four o'clock. Shabos starts at 5:13 tonight. I'm sorry. Is it family?" He knew the answer before he asked.

"No, but I just miss her so much. What time are do you open tomorrow?" Wendy hadn't enjoyed the melodic cadence of Yiddish since she and her father played with it in their voice game.

"Ve don't open till Sunday. Everyting stops for Sha...dah Sabbath. Did you come from far avay. You got a place to eat tonight?"

'He looks so harmless. Is he asking me out to dinner?'

The man put his hand on his heart. "Don't tink I'm a crazy. On Shabos we can't allow a stranger to go hungry. He pointed across the street to a dilapidated Dutch colonial. "Dat's mine house and dat's mine vife on the porch vatching us." His pointing softened to a wave at the scowling matron.

"Thank you. I have a place to eat. I just wanted to talk to her." Wendy knew he was waiting for her to turn back to her car but her feet stayed on the same frozen grass patch at the gate.

"Perhaps you know where's she buried? She died suddenly and I'm afraid I didn't notice much the day of her funeral. There's no stone yet. Maybe there's a temporary marker…Elizabeth Spring: wife and mother."

"And friend?" The same hand that he waved to his impatient wife now made a stop signal in her direction.

"Your friend is buried at deh corner of dis fence. If you drive to the end, you'll see deh spot. Nobody vill bother you. Deh outside still belongs to Star of David. It'll be dark soon. Don't stay too long. A real crazy could come. Misses, I'll pray at the grave on Sunday. Meanwhile, tonight I vish for you what I vish for mine family."

Bird and Fish

Wendy drove along the cemetery's chain link fence till she recognized the site. She longed to hug the bars like an orphan in a Victorian workhouse but her New York sensibilities prevailed. Wendy stopped the car, faced her friend's final resting place and spoke as if Libby was in the passenger seat coming along for the ride.

"Some friend you turned out to be, Lib. You deserted me. Don't think that money's going make up for lost tete-a-tetes in the drama room or the end of gossipy manipedis at Stylish Nails. I appreciate the funding, Lib but I really need to talk to you. I tried confiding in my cousin Diane. Did you look down on that, Lib? She reduced my life to a page from People Magazine. Anyway, this is where I stand now. I'll keep writing. I've grown to like the people in my little kingdom. I want to tell each one's story. So, thanks for the money, Libby."

Wendy turned the heater's lever one bar to the right to warm her chilled feet.

"I'm going to forgive Tim. Don't argue, I'll tell you why. In a way we both just self-medicated to get through our family crises. I found Jay Hyun and he found Jim Beam, just kidding but the important thing is if I can't forgive him it could mean I didn't love him after all. I don't want to believe that. So, don't you think he deserves one free pass? Just one. Lib, you can't ask me all these questions. I keep changing my mind.

Adrienne Leslie

She adjusted the little toothed wheel in the dashboard vent to stop the hot blast from joining forces with her post-Tamoxifen sweats. In a few days she would have to admit to her oncologist that she had stopped taking the medication.

"Most of all, It's over with Jay. I haven't heard from him since the day of my surgery. No, no, don't tell me I should have called him. It may be the twenty-first century but, he's the man. He should have called by now."

Wendy tapped her fingernails on the steering wheel.

"Lib, it's getting dark and I've got over a hundred miles between you and my mom's place. So before I go, I just need to tell you, I fell in love with the paint store man. I regret not getting close enough to him to feel the heat rising off his cocoa butter skin. I wish I could have cooked him a meal, waltzed in his arms and kissed the dragon on his back. Maybe I can't sleep at night because in another life that's when we'd make love." Wendy put the car in reverse and rode backwards to the cemetery's front entrance.

"It's a good thing you're dead, Lib. I'd never say those things to another living soul."

⌘ ⌘ ⌘

"No, I didn't notice my phone was off. I'm in Grandma's house right now. No, there's no snow. It hasn't snowed all week. I just ran in to use the bathroom. The Christmas lights on the timer worked out well. I've got to bring in the groceries and I still haven't gone to the toilet. Janie, you're starting to sound like Gran. I love you the best. Bye."

Wendy couldn't resist the laminated cardboard King and I LP on the top of her parents' original hi-fi. She watched the record drop then picked up the needle's arm and placed it on her favorite childhood selection.

'My mother must have loved this musical. She saw it when she was 19 and saved it for me to play as a girl. So why didn't she save any of my Barbies?'

The needle engaged the plastic disk. Chict-chict-chict… "I have dreamed that your arms are lovely." Wendy hummed along in the pink tiled bathroom and as she removed a pair of mittens from her bedroom dresser. It would be a good night for star gazing; clear and bright from the three quarter moon. Lucille's penned geese, fat from the neighbor's over-feeding began a second round of squawks as Wendy stepped out onto the porch to see her favorite face in the light of a smiling Santa wreath.

There was no time for questions as he barked out remonstrations and warnings to her puzzled expression.

"*Mee chu suh*? Do you know how long I'm here? Three hours. I thought you were in a car crash. I thought you drowned in the lake. I was just there searching in the darkness. Why would you do this? *Wheh? Wheh?* Jae Won ceased shouting in Korean as he placed his gloved hands on her cheeks and moved his face within inches of hers.

"Don't make me say it in English. I'll be too embarrassed. *Sah rang heh. Wend-dish ay, Sah rang heh.*

Wendy drew in the breath from his mouth as she awaited his kiss but Jae Won's hands dropped to her shoulders as he pulled her close to whisper, "*Mi ah nay* I didn't mean to scare you."

The damp on her panti-liner belied her reaction was fear.

"Three hours? You must need the bathroom. Come inside." Wendy forced the mood to change.

"I'm all right. I went at the lake."

"You're lucky the sheriff didn't see you. You would have been his most wanted. Are you hungry or did you also catch a fish at the lake?"

Jay pointed to the chimney flue on the A-frame's roof.

"If I make the fire in the fireplace, would you feed me?"

The finely minced fresh white garlic simmered golden in the hot olive oil while its fragrance, meshed with the burning pine logs, warmed the first floor of the rustic vacation home. Soon they were dining on wilted spinach and bacon salad and steaming bowls of spaghetti in marinara sauce. She used dinnertime to unleash her heart.

Bird and Fish

"When Janie was little, she went through a jig-saw puzzle phase. She had a favorite one she'd pull apart and re-create over and over till one day a piece was missing. We searched the house all week but we never found it. She put the rest of the cardboard pieces back into the box and never enjoyed it again. That was my life till you. I kept trying to make a beautiful picture but it couldn't happen till you filled in the puzzle. Don't ever doubt that I love you. Believe you'll live a million Buddhist lives but in none of them will someone adore you more than I do.

My mother will survive if I leave my husband and soon my daughter will outgrow her need for me. I can write anywhere there's a pencil and pad but this is my America. Most of my countrymen don't think New Yorkers are patriotic but we're the ones who got our two front teeth knocked out and we still get on the subway, buses and choked highways making our way to work every morning as if we're asking the terrorists, 'What the fuck you looking at?'

I like coming home to Christmas lights after spending the afternoon at a Jewish cemetery. I like looking out on the school play yard at blondes, corn-rowed brunettes and curly-topped red-heads. I like the thousand voices I hear along Northern Boulevard. My family and my country are here and you've got your own path south of the thirty-eighth parallel.

Wendy began to clear their dinner dishes off the oak table. Jay took her hand and led her to the couch. When she was seated, he paced in front of her, his black sweater sleeves rolled up for labor and his brow dotted with flop sweats.

"There is a place in China called Hainan. It's very beautiful. On the beach is a giant boulder with carved out Chinese characters that say, Hai Pan Nan Tian: the sea and the sky joined together. Will you meet me there?"

"In Hainan?"

"It's where a bird and fish could live."

Wendy had seen the pristine beaches of China's Hawaii on a drama. She hadn't made the connection before. She let Jay continue his thought.

"I'd never ask you to stop being American but the world offers more of the things you like. We could travel for a while. I don't know where we'll end up. It could be right back here.

Wendy was long past her teen years. She knew men made many fervent promises before sex. She raised her hand to get his attention.

"Wendy, let me finish. No country has a cure for Janie's illness. Why shouldn't she see the world and experience art and music to give her vitality? If she gets sick again, she's a plane ride away from her doctor."

He pushed up on his left sleeve. "And so are you."

Bird and Fish

Angus Dale's sealed copper urn guarded his last mortal home from the mantel over the burning fire. Wendy's father had been dead so long, she couldn't guess his opinion of what was playing out in front of his ashes. She walked from the couch to place her hand on the warm metal jar.

"Fishman, I'm still married. You're leaving for Korea soon. I know you're not expecting perfection but I still don't feel comfortable with the recent changes in my body, Mostly, I don't want to reduce our memories of each other to one night, so if I told you I was absolutely not going to make love to you tonight, what would you say?"

Jae Won Hyun placed his hands at his hips and blew a puff of air in a preamble to a speech but soon put his hand over hers and answered sheepishly, "Could you please change your mind?" Their laughter rippled down their arms till the urn toppled unscathed to the wooden tongue and groove flooring sending a reverberating board to jar the table next to the record player. The needle arm lowered again to Lucille Dale's teenage crush, Yul Brynner talk-singing 'Shall We Dance to the red-haired Deborah Kerr. Wendy placed her fingertips over what she knew was Jay's dragon's spine and breathed in the virile scent of his sweater's wool fibers as he held her at her waist and waltzed her in her mother's parlor. 'Puh pum pum.'

Downstate the Big Dipper is barely visible yet the same Ursa Major constellation twinkling down on Pine Tree

Grove is above New York City as well. There it's hidden by the Big Apple's own brand of sparkle. Wendy pointed to one of the sequins on the black velvet sky. "That one's called Alkaid." Her teeth began chattering. Jay raced into the house and brought back a flame stitched throw. He placed one side around her shoulder while holding the other over his as they stood as if sharing an umbrella.

"*Ee pooh dah*. Did you mother make this?"

"My mother? Hardly. She never seemed interested in creating anything. My father adored her though. I envy her that. They had an enduring marriage."

Wendy allowed herself to tilt her head onto Jae Won's shoulder.

"Jay, I'm sticking to what I said but would you stay here tonight anyway?"

He looked straight ahead into the darkness of the pine grove.

"I'd like to stay. I worry you're not safe here alone. Where's your big dog?"

"He's home with the rest of my responsibilities. Where're your fish?" She meant to make a joke.

"I gave them to Yujin's daughters."

"Uh." She moved her head from his shoulder.

"I want you to go with me. Janie will be on Christmas holiday soon. If you need me to, I'll wait till we can all go. But, Wendy, if you're not…don't come to the airport. Don't make a show."

Wendy reflexively put her hand on her cheek thinking how odd it was that Jay's 'Don't come to the airport.' smacked with the same sting as the doctor who first called her calcifications cancer. Two decades of teaching spoke for her.

"Scene, don't make a scene. Where do you want to sleep and don't be funny."

Jae Won surprised her with a petulant answer.

"I don't want you to sleep in his bed. Sleep in your mother's room or Janie's. I'll sleep on the couch."

"Would you mind if I put a blanket on the floor and watched TV in front of the couch."

"I'll sleep on the blanket. You watch TV from the couch."

By midnight her sleep was so deep, her arm dropped from the couch onto his forehead. Jae Won reached up and held her hand till Saturday's fourth hour.

⌘ ⌘ ⌘

The teacher crossed the drama room after her monitor picked up the classroom phone. She couldn't bring herself to teach from a workbook so she offered to show 6A1 Mulan if they promised to say it was to learn about musicals. "Who is it?" she shouted above the laughter. The boy shrugged and relinquished the receiver.

"Ms. Dale. Who's calling?"

The nasty secretary fumed at the length of time this took from her chat with her daughter on another line.

"A parent, obviously."

"What's the parent's name?"

'Just one more week of listening to the secretary's attitude.'

"Mr. Kim."

'Very helpful.'

"Put him through." She plugged her other ear with her index finger and repeated her name.

"*Sun seng nim,* It's Yujin."

Wendy pulled an empty chair away from its table and sat to stop shaking. Yujin asked then pleaded with her to meet Jae Won at the airport later that afternoon. He offered to drive. He told her Yoon Yoo would drive if she preferred. He said Malik would work overtime so the whole family could take her. He even offered up Korean guilt with a depiction of Jae leaving with no one waving goodbye.

"Jheh sung ham nee dah. I have to hang up." The end-of-class music had drowned out Mulan's song and the children's 'Aw's'. Wendy was alone. For the rest of the school day and after school rehearsal, although bounded by staff and students, she couldn't shake the feeling.

The aging Nissan took its usual ten December minutes to warm up for the drive to her errands. Dinner would be courtesy of Mr. Ling again tonight. Wendy was mailing more copies of The Fisherman's One Thousand Voices to another list of publishers. She turned right onto Marathon Parkway heading north to the Little Neck Post Office. When the light on Northern and Marathon changed she made a second right to look for parking only to swerve and make a hairpin turn to face west amid blaring horns and irate shouts while just missing the driver's side door of a Cadillac exiting the corner's McDonald's. As if she hadn't brought traffic to a screeching halt, she placidly turned left heading south to JFK International Airport knowing she'd be on time.

Only a red-haired drama teacher could coax, cajole and flirt her way through the parking and pedestrian madness of a post 9/11 airport terminal. She planted her three inch heels firmly on the concrete waiting for the one Korean face she hadn't yet seen in the crowd. Two little boys each holding a green balloon on a red string ran by. The littlest boy's balloon popped bringing tears and the tossing of his red tether to the ground. One end rested at Wendy's shoes. Her eyes followed the trail to the curb where a taxi had just pulled over. Jae Won Hyun's first step was atop the red string. His first inhaled breath exiting the cab was laced with Insolence.

"Why are you here?" He took his luggage from the driver then set it down.

"To make a show. Why are you here?"

"I will stay. Tell me to stay."

"Absolutely not. You're going to paint what inspires you."

Wendy thought it was starting to rain when she felt the drops on her cheeks and chin as she watched Jay follow the string towards her. His fingertips soothed her throbbing temples while he wiped her tears with his thumbs.

"*Eur ji mah.*" He spoke softly.

"I'm not crying. I only cry during dramas." She sniffed in like a child.

"*Uh-ri ga drama ya.*"

Across from the taxi drop-off area is a parking lot marked by five white washed two-story pillars. This afternoon the middle column has a clear view of Ms. Wendy Dale crying and kissing her leading man like the main character in Episode 100 of a Korean melodrama.

⌘ ⌘ ⌘

Epilogue: Final Episode:

The fourth grader held the book tightly in her arms while her mother prodded her to move towards the woman sharing a chicken and apple salad nearby. The girl's father tried to stop his wife knowing his attempt was in vain. The woman went so far as to ask the waiter to accompany her daughter to the corner table.

"She'll just say hello to Ms. Dale."

Her husband cringed. "Hon, the woman's talking to other people."

"That's not just people. I saw them on that morning show we watched at the hotel. That's her daughter and that's her husband" she pointed, alerting the threesome having lunch.

"Well, that's not his daughter. That's for sure. Hey, she's waving Emily over."

The author put down her water glass and asked the pig-tailed princess if she liked the book.

Emily Hong said she read all the books in the SpringThyme Kingdom series and hoped there'd never be a final episode but this one, her well-scrubbed fingers pointed to the cover's burnished sunset, The Milk Maid's Malady was her favorite.

"Oh, then you should speak to my husband because he did all the illustrations for that one."

Jae Won turned to shake Emily's hand but the girl's attention was on Jane.

"You're pretty and you look just like the Fisherman's daughter."

The teenager smiled, "Well, in some ways I am."

Made in the USA